The City and the Dream

By the same author

A Georgian Love Story
Gentle Greaves
The Mountain Farm
The Old June Weather

The City and the Dream

BY ERNEST RAYMOND

There the dreams are multitudes:
  Some whose buoyance waits not sleep . . .
  Some that hum while rest may steep
  Weary labour laid a-heap;
    Interludes,
  Some, of grievous moods that weep.
                                    ROSSETTI

Saturday Review Press/E. P. Dutton & Co., Inc./New York

ISBN: 0-8415-0384-2

Library of Congress Cataloging in Publication Data

Raymond, Ernest, 1888–
    The city and the dream.

    I. Title.
PZ3.R2153Cm8   [pr6035.a9]   823'.9'12   75–6810

For Bryen and Kathlene Gentry

The City
and
the Dream

1

Clerkenwell to begin with. Clerkenwell, standing beneath the sun on a May morning, a tall congregation of factories, warehouses, printing works, foundries, distilleries, and tanneries, interspersed with huge high hideous tenement dwellings to house the workers in these and other trades—Clerkenwell with its clockmakers and watchmakers (once famous the world over), its jewelers, hairworkers, lapidaries, silversmiths, and glass-benders, all at their fine and delicate labors under the sun-straddled roofs—Clerkenwell, with all its old and famous residential streets pressed out of it by the urgency of London's industry, and with the sun looping around the single spire of St. James's Church, is the creation, more surely perhaps than any other square mile in this vast conglomerate London, of God and the devil together.

For Clerkenwell came about in this fashion. When it was nothing but fields under a clean sweet air, with many a springing well of wholesome water among its green and gentle slopes, men with God in their hearts came and built here for the Knights Hospitallers of St. John of Jerusalem their Grand Priory in the English Realm. And to the north of their priory their brothers in God built also, for some good Benedictine nuns, the Ecclesia Sanctae Mariae de Fonte Clericorum—which is to say, the Church of St. Mary by the Well of the Clerks. Meanwhile, down on the fenland, in the smooth field of Smithfield, Rahere, the jester and juggler of Henry I, converted by a vision of St. Bartholomew to a sense of his sin and to great sanctity, had raised his church and priory to the honor of that saint. Then, many years later, on the east side of St. John's Grand Priory, the good Sir Walter de Manny founded and placed his Carthusian convent; and now almost all the land hereabout was occupied in the name of God and His saints.

The men of God came first, and in these early days the people living on the slopes and plains, apart from the knights and monks and nuns, were chiefly their masons, joiners, smiths, gardeners, grooms, and cooks; but with St. Bartholomew's festival came Bartholomew Fair and the entrance of Folly and Misrule, splendidly attended by charlatans, mountebanks, swindlers, and pickpockets. Then, with the horse market, established at Smithfield, came jousting and racing and wrestling and all their attendant rogues; and soon to the same place, under the church's wall, a yet finer entertainment, in the form of executions at gibbet or stake.

Now taverns sprang up by the old sweet wells to dispense a livelier water; and when, London growing larger and larger, it became plain that much dirty work could be done on the margins of the Fleet River, more of the devil's handymen came crowding in. Many of them settled in Turnmill Street alongside the Fleet, or in dark courts and lanes behind it, and here they turned their master's mills with vigor and taught his ways to their children. In the old books the Turnmill Street area is coupled with Ratcliff Highway as a sink for all the vices of London; in the old plays its name is used as a metonym for wickedness, or it is dubbed Jack Ketch's Warren since so many birds for the hangman's table were bred here, like game in a squire's preserve.

It is perhaps a parable of Clerkenwell that almost the sole relic of its godly days is now beneath the traffic-beaten ground in the shape of a lovely vaulted crypt. This is the crypt of the Church of the Knights of St. John. No grasping monarch, no venomous enemy bomb, has ever reached it. Its columns and groined arches, the work of old dead Normans and old dead English, still spring from their capitals, underground, with the dust of centuries rising like a slow tide below them; and the

traffic of the Clerkenwell Road thunders past this old subter-
ranean loveliness with no knowledge that it is there.

Of course, the gatehouse of the knights' priory is still there
for all to see, and a noble structure it is, with its ragstone face
and flanking towers; but, alas, its groined archway, spanning
St. John's Lane, leads to no cloister out of the world, but only
northward to the muck and hurry of the Clerkenwell Road and
southward to the raucous hucksterings of Smithfield. Today it
leads only from trade to trade, from business to business, and
all too often, as one suspects, from sin to sin.

Now, Red Lion Street, running precisely between, and paral-
lel to, St. John's Lane and Turnmill Street, has manifestly the
pious memories on one side of it and the impious on the other;
and it was this exceedingly symbolic situation, together with his
love of the past, and one other far more secret reason, that
brought Mr. John Kenrick Betterkin to live in the attics of a
house in Red Lion Street some score of years ago.

2

No. 55a is one of the few Georgian houses among the shop awnings and small factory fronts in the Red Lion Street of today, and outwardly it unites the grace of its date with the charm of its age. Its finely proportioned windows are flush with the mellowed red brick and, for the rest, its tall and narrow facade wears, like a lady of taste, only a single ornament: the shapely doorway with its elegant fanlight and carved white pediment.

It is a dignified presence in the street; but after two hundred years the dignity is but skin-deep. Pass the jambs of the shapely door and you exchange the year 1719 for the Clerkenwell of today, no longer a place for the wealthy and leisured but straitened and struggling and given over to labor. On the morning when Mr. Betterkin came to Clerkenwell, Mrs. Hitchin, who let the rooms and lived in the basement, stood in the front attic with a broom. She rested the broom in a corner, came out onto the small landing, and, leaning over the spindly balusters, called, *"El*-fred."

No answer.

She bent her body lower and pitched her voice higher. "El-
FRED."

Again no answer.

A fine head of white hair emerged from a door on the landing below and passed on the cry in full male tones that would
have echoed all over the Albert Hall: "Al-*fred!* Mr. Hitchin! Ho,
there!" A lodger, no doubt, or tenant, ever ready to act as a
go-between and bellow Alfred's name. "AL . . . FRED," he
roared; and "AL . . . FRED" again. Then went back into his
room.

From the foot of the basement stairs rose a grudging
" 'Ello?"

"Gimme a lift with this 'ere," called Mrs. Hitchin, turning to
look at a large wooden crate, as if this would enable Alfred to
see it.

"Hell," said Mr. Hitchin.

"Come on! I can't move it by meself."

"Oh, all *right.* Damn the woman. I'm coming, aren't I?"

"So's the year after next. So're *they,* at any moment."

Mrs. Hitchin, hearing a lazy and heavy tread on the basement
stairs, stood waiting with fists at rest on her wide hips. Once
she threaded her fingers into her gray hair, left them there, and
sighed. And Mr. Alfred Hitchin came creaking up. In the fullness of time he turned the last bend in the narrow staircase and
was in full view for her disapproving contemplation. He was
hardly a sight for a wife to love. A large, heavy man with moist,
untidy gray hair and sloth-dulled eyes, he still wore, at nine
o'clock on a May morning, a collarless gray shirt and his trousers with the top buttons undone and the suspenders fes-
tooned over his hips. He bent himself wearily to the last few
stairs.

Arrived in front of her, he said simply, "Blast 'em both."

"Eh?" inquired his wife.

"What's he up to? That's what I want to know."

"He's up to living in these rooms, stupid. What else?"

"Yes, but . . ." Mr. Hitchin, wanting to look dubious, contrived it with an upward pressure of his lips. "Yes, but . . ."

"Yes, but a fine sight you look, I must say. Why didn't you
come when I call?"

"I had dropped off, I don't mind telling you. I was asleep."

"Asleep. There's none so fast asleep as you when there's a
bit o' work to be done."

"You say I wasn't asleep?"

"About as much asleep as I am."

Mr. Hitchin lifted a palm and spoke solemnly, deliberately—on oath, in fact. "As Gawd's me judge—"

"Never mind Gawd. I been married to you long enough to know what all that's worth."

"You still say I wasn't asleep?" He stared at her as if bewildered, defeated, by the contumacy of people and their readiness to believe the worst.

"I know you wasn't. You was reading."

Mr. Hitchin raised the palm again but only a little way this time, in his despair. "Gawd forgive you," he said.

"Well, He will, I fancy. Now come on and help."

"What you wan' me do?"

"Gimme a lift with this 'ere."

"This 'ere?" Thumbs in trouser pockets, he looked down at the large unlidded crate. "Lord 'elp us! What are they?"

"Books. What do they look like? Potatoes?"

"What's he want with all them books? This is about the twentieth bloody box. And I'm not sure that I care for 'im mucking about with these attics, carpentering and knocking in nails, like the house was his own."

"I reckon he's made 'em look very nice. And as he said very civilly, the shelves be landlord's fixtures if he leaves."

"Landlord's firewood, more likely." He bent down to the crate. "Aw well, I'm a kindhearted man. Come along. Nah then, boys!" Together they lifted the crate. "Hell and law' awmighty! Oh, my Gawd!" After some panting and grimacing he said, "Who's she, anyway? 'Ave you see 'er yet?"

"No . . . steady now. . . ."

"She never once come to put anything to rights?"

"Not yet."

"What? Left the man to do all the work? It don't seem natural."

"She's been ill, he says. Jest put it down 'ere."

"Thank Gawd." Since they had now got the case against the wall of the back attic, Mr. Hitchin came erect to give his strained arms a rest. He rested them on his hips. "I suppose they *are* brother and sister. Yeah, I hope so. I'm a shade enxious, I don't mind telling you."

"Why, for heaven's sake?"

"Because I like things nice and proper in my house. I don't want any fiddle-de-dee under *my* roof."

"*Your* house? Since when was it your house? And a nice fine moral type you are."

"Well, what are they living together for, brother and sister?"

"Some brothers and sisters do."

"Don't seem natural to me."

"Well, I can't help that. I thought him a thoroughly nice little man. I liked him the first moment I see him. He couldn't 'a spoken pleasanter, I'm sure."

"Mebbe, but that don't make her a sister." For a diversion during this interval of rest, he picked up a book from the case. "*Med'eeval London*. Gawd lumme." And another and another. "*The Knights of Malta . . . Archives of the Order of St. John of Jerusalem*. Chrimes! I don't mind telling you that I shall know very soon if it's all straight and above board. I can always tell if they really are brother and sister. Uncle and niece, they sometimes call themselves. Bless my soul, I've known them call themselves father and daughter."

"Well, he can't do that because he's not above thirty hisself," said Mrs. Hitchin, sweeping up sawdust from around the crate. "And she's older than he is."

"Is she, and all? How much?"

"Ten years older."

"Oh, then she probably *is* his sister."

"*Course* she's his sister!"

"Well, I feel happier about that, I must say. But look 'ere: why're they arriving so early? Yes. . . ." He was pleased to have a new reason for suspicion. "Why come at ha' pas' nine in the morning?"

"They can come when it suits 'em, I suppose."

"You don't think they're flitting without paying their rent? Because what I mean to say," he added sententiously, walking about the room and offering no help, "is this: if they do that once, they can do it twice."

"He's not the sort that flits. He's obviously a gen'l'man."

"A gen'l'man in a garret like this?"

"You can be a gen'l'man and poor. He says he wants to be nearer his work in Fleet Street."

"First time I've heard they're gen'l'men that work in Fleet Street. Thought they were pretty doubtful stuff, there."

"Did yer now?" Mrs. Hitchin left him and his thoughts where they stood. She hurried with her broom into the front room. Mr. Hitchin, since he was up aloft like this, and it was less effort to remain than to return down four flights of stairs, followed her with his hands in his pockets. They pushed the unbuttoned trousers farther beneath his paunch.

"This is to be their living room, is it?"

"Thet's right. And he's made it nice, hasn't he?"

"Wurl. . . ." Mr. Hitchin cast his eyes around the walls. "He thinks he knows how to paint, but he don't. Lawd, more books, and more shelves mucking up the walls." He began to fill an indignant pipe.

"Aw, don't smoke in here. It'll make the room smell common." Mrs. Hitchin straightened the cover on a divan in the corner. "Come, help us a little. Give a look to that table, do."

Mr. Hitchin gave a look to it, and nothing more. "She's going to sleep in here, is she, and him in the back?"

"Thet's right."

"Gaw' lumme! Well, I don't understand it, meself." He went to the window. "There's those in the street that have said to me they thought 'im an odd-looking customer."

"I'm sure they have. There's fools in every street—and in most rooms, as fur as I can see. Without looking too hard."

"Meaning by that? Eh?"

"Meaning what I mean."

"I'm the fool in this room, em I?"

"P'raps yes; p'raps no. When there's a woman married to a man like you, it's more often the woman that's the fool."

"Lawd forgive yer." Mr. Hitchin sighed and pulled out his most sarcastic stop. "I see. Now I know where I stand." And he turned back to the window.

"Thet's right. Well, shift along a little, while I tidy up this 'ere."

"You won't have no time to do it, because"—Mr. Hitchin had a sense of drama and knew that an exciting announcement was best spoken calmly—" 'ere they are."

"Really? No, never?"

"Yep. 'Ere they are. Wait while I button up my trousers."

Mrs. Hitchin had rushed to the other window. "Law, yes, that's them. But don't let them see you watching. It don't look decent."

Mr. Hitchin continued to stare. "Gaw', they aren't half interesting Mrs. Jeans and Sam Grover."

"Oh, people oughtn't to stare like that. Some people ain't got no shame."

"And 'ere's old Mother Aarons," said Mr. Hitchin, with great appreciation of the swelling scene. "Come aht to see 'em, she has."

"I don't see what's so funny in two people coming along a street, I don't really. Come away, Elfred; do."

But Mr. Hitchin seldom gave much heed to his wife's words. "He's no bew'y, is he?" he commented. When he dropped into the clipped staccato of a Cockney, Mr. Hitchin lost most of his mid-verbal *t*'s. "Nah, one couldn't call him a bew'y."

"But it's a nice face. Kind."

"And she—Gawd save us—she's not so pru'y either. Blimey, what a pair!"

"You can see she's been ill, poor lamb. Pale as a pound o' lard."

"And skinny too. Well, that's one comfort: she must be his sister."

"Oh, come off it, Elfred! You're not as funny as you think. Anyone can see she's his sister. They favor each other."

"If you're as small as that," continued Mr. Hitchin, studying the man again, "you didn't ought to wear a bowler 'at." Mr. Hitchin was a big, thick man. And on state occasions he wore a bowler hat—wore it with pride, in the house as well as in the street. "Especially if your head's too big for your body. It makes you look like a comedy turn."

"She don't look happy, do she? And, come to that, nor does he today. And that's funny, because yesterday he seemed on top of hisself. Making his little jokes to me, one after the other. It's not like him to look like that. Usually he's the merriest of the merry. The most comical little gentleman. Can something have happened?"

"Probably he's picked up sixpence but lost a shilling," suggested Mr. Hitchin.

"Looks to me more like he's seen a ghost," said Mrs. Hitchin.

Watched from a high window, the two approaching figures certainly looked a sad and rather comic little pair. The man was short and slight, with sloping shoulders, and, as Mr. Hitchin had said, his head was too large for his body. In the bowler hat and on the top of the small, weedy frame it suggested a large oval tulip on an oddly undergrown stalk. A very keen eye might have guessed that the brain beneath the hat was ashamed of being so near to the ground. Those round rubber heels screwed under his leather heels, were they not there, perhaps, not only to save shoe leather but to add a little height?

It was true, too, what Mrs. Hitchin had said: the large eyes under the hat, as they glanced up at the garret of No. 55a, had lost all gaiety, and seemed full of, and stilled by, doubt and wonder and perhaps apprehension. Under his arm he carried a very large brown-paper parcel.

The woman with him was taller than he but, even so, remained small. And from head to foot she had no feminine beauty. Though she was no more than forty, her hair was already an oxidized silver. Her features were large and masculine, and in her eyes today, large like his, there dwelled looks of strain, bewilderment, and fear. Her skirt, a graceless compromise between ankle-length and calf-length, showed her thin legs and outturning feet. This outturning of the feet seemed to throw her body a little forward as she walked, so that her back appeared rounded.

Neither was speaking. They came with hurried steps and silently toward the house door as to some passage in their lives that had best be got through quickly. Often he walked a step ahead of her as if he were in control and she his led charge.

By the time they stood together before the door, Mrs. Hitchin stood on her side of it. But in her decency she waited for them to press the bell.

On the doorstep, beyond the door's thickness, Mr. Betterkin threw away all sadness and began to joke. With a finger touching but not pressing the bell he said, "This, my dear Pearl, is a moment of great drama."

"Drama?"

"Certainly. This exceedingly handsome door is a gateway to the Lord-knows-what. I press the bell and ring for the future. So." The bell sounded within. "There you are! The bell rings. That means we've hit the bull slap in the eye. Now, if Mrs. Hitchin opens the door, that'll mean everything's going to be fine; if Mr. Hitchin, well . . ."

Mrs. Hitchin allowed a few seconds to pass after the bell had stopped so that they would not know she had been standing within inches of them, then opened the door. "Ah, you've come," she said, as if she had not seen them from the window. "You're very welcome, I'm sure."

Nothing preoccupied and wistful about Mr. Betterkin now

that he stood opposite his landlady. Rather, he was deliberately smiling and jocular. He raised his bowler hat, brought it down to the level of his waist, and made her a bow. "Yes, here we are indeed. Pearl, this is my dear Mrs. Hitchin, who's so kindly taking us in. Mrs. Hitchin, my sister Pearl."

"Pleased to meet you, miss, I'm sure. I hope you'll like it here."

Pearl put her head to one side in an archness that matched ill with her forty years, her large features, and her lack of feminine charm. "Oh, I'm sure we shall, Mrs. Hitchin. Yes, I'm sure of it. And what a lovely old house this is. My brother told me all about it. He—"

Instantly her brother stopped the gush of words. It was as if he thought her deliberate use, so early, of Mrs. Hitchin's name, and something overacted in her assumption of ease, could prompt suspicion. "Can we go straight up?" he asked and hung out a nervous smile for Mrs. Hitchin.

Strangely, the sister consented to this quick interruption, only casting a curious and perhaps frightened glance at him.

"Haven't you brought nothing with you, sir? Only that parcel?"

His eyes shot away. They were shy eyes, seldom looking long at anyone's face; not, you felt, because he was sly but because, behind his shows of jollity, there lived a creature small, self-conscious, afraid of social clumsiness, and eager to be liked. "No, everything's already upstairs. I brought all my sister's things in gradually, you see."

"And are you better now, my dear?" Mrs. Hitchin asked of the sister.

"Better?"

"Yes, your brother said you'd been ill."

"Ill?" Now it was her eyes that looked frightened, as if she feared she was out of her depth and floundering. "Oh, yes . . . I see . . . yes, but it wasn't anything really serious."

"No, that's all over now, thank goodness," her brother interrupted quickly and cheerfully. "Yes, this parcel is something I seldom let out of my sight."

"Is it something valuable?"

"Ah, that remains to be seen." He looked knowingly at his sister. "It's valuable to me. To anyone else at present, it's worth exactly nothing at all. But . . . things may happen to it. Who knows?"

Mrs. Hitchin looked at it again, a rectangular square-cornered parcel, but it told her nothing, so she turned and led the way upstairs. Politely Mr. Betterkin ushered his sister in front of him and followed her. Unlike Mr. Hitchin he did not wear his bowler hat in the house but held it before his waist as he climbed.

Now, since Mr. Hitchin came downstairs much more slowly than his wife, he was only at the top of the first flight as Mrs. Hitchin started up it, so, coming thus face to face with his wife, and being agog to appraise these new tenants, he was obliged to effect an about-turn and take over from her the leadership of the procession.

This he did in silence. He led it into the front attic and even here he did not speak. Thumbs in his suspenders (which he'd slung over his shoulders on his way downstairs), he turned to face his followers, smiled an ingratiating smile at the lady, and waited to hear what his wife would say to her.

"I think everything's nice and in place," his wife said. "I give it a tidy-up this morning."

"I'm sure it's ever so nice, I'm sure it's most kind of you," Miss Betterkin hurried to say. Evident again was that pressing, nervous need to talk fluently, to talk brightly, to talk people down; and again her brother threw a sudden anxious glance at her. "My brother said it would make a delightful home—"

"Yes," said Mrs. Hitchin, having hardly listened. "Yes, this is Mr. Hitchin."

"I guessed that!" Miss Betterkin was attempting an arch humor. She proffered a hand. "Good morning, Mr. Hitchin."

Mr. Hitchin, not expecting the hand, took it and said, "Ah, yes. Hah d'ye do? Yus."

Mrs. Hitchin, with contemptuous nostrils, changed the subject. "There's no reason why this shouldn't make quite a nice little room for receiving your friends."

"Oh, but I don't expect many people'll be coming to see us," corrected Miss Betterkin, still driven to talk—and again her brother looked at her anxiously as if she'd spoken an unwise word.

Mrs. Hitchin apparently saw nothing odd in this answer. Perhaps she hadn't heard it. "And now," she said, "I expect you'd like a nice cup o' tea."

"Yus," Mr. Hitchin agreed, not to be behindhand in hospitality. "O' course."

"Oh, don't trouble, Mrs. Hitchin. We had our breakfast only half an hour ago. And it was a large one too."

Mr. Betterkin tut-tutted behind his teeth, and beat with his heel on the floor.

"Still, a cup o' tea never comes amiss. And you'd like a nice piece of cake, I dare say?"

"Yurse, give 'em some cake. Yurse," said Mr. Hitchin, the hospitable.

"Oh, you really mustn't go to all this trouble."

"No trouble at all. Elfred, nip down and see if the kettle's on."

"Me?"

"Yes. 'Urry up."

"Well . . ." Mr. Hitchin took a moment to get used to this idea. "Well, I'll do that for you. Yus. Certainly. I'll see about that." He thought of it further. "Yus, you leave that to me. Good morning, sir, and lady. Nance, you look ah'ter the lady and gen'l'man."

He went out, and down the stairs heavily.

"Seems a nice man, your husband," said Miss Betterkin, still striving to be affable.

"*What?*" asked Mrs. Hitchin, amazed.

"He's kind, isn't he?"

"Mr. Hitchin? Elfred?" she asked, as if not yet sure of whom she spoke.

"Yes, I thought . . . I thought him ever so nice."

"Elfred? Oh, I dunno. Sometimes I feel I'd like to hit him."

"No! Whatever for?"

"Oh, nothing. Just for being like what he is."

This left Miss Betterkin's affability defeated and without words, so Mrs. Hitchin pursued: "I dare say he's all right sometimes. But never mind him. I'll nip down and get you that tea. I expect there's things you'd like to be doing alone."

What Mr. Betterkin liked to do when they were alone might have astonished her. The door was hardly shut before he seized his sister's hands and danced her around in a kind of ring-a-ring o' roses. "Well, here we are," he sang. "Nicely lost in London. Nobody'll find us here in a hurry. Clerkenwell's the other side of the world from Bayswater. Maybe only three miles away but it's in another hemisphere. An ocean of about six million people rolls between."

"Let me go, Kerry." She laughed, pulling at her hands. "Let me *go.*"

"Not a bit of it. Good old Clerkenwell. We'll have fun here. Yippee! And, furthermore, highty-tiddly-ighty! But what in hell were you up to, saying no one'd come to see us? And that we'd only just had a huge breakfast. Pearl dear, really! Pull yourself together."

"You don't think"—she turned white and snatched away her hands—"you don't think they—"

"No, of course not. I was only joking. But you'd better let me do the talking at first."

"I shall get used to things all right."

"You're doing fine." He strolled to the window and looked over the roofs toward the western sky. "We're not far from brother Godfrey here. Just down into the old Fleet Valley and up into the Clerkenwell Road, and there's brother Godfrey sitting in his garden among his lawyers. Do we go and call on him?"

"No, *no.*" Her white face had fired, her frightened eyes hardened. "I'm never going to speak to him again. Never, never. Brother or no brother."

"Now, now!" he chided, proud to be more magnanimous than she. "Oh yes you are. Poor old Godfrey can't help being Godfrey, and a pompous, selfish, hypocritical ass. Do you like this little aerie? Like the curtains? Took me hours to choose them. I went to shop after shop."

"Oh, they're nice, I think."

"Going to be happy here?"

"Yes, of course, oh yes, rather!—but . . ."

"But what?" He was disappointed by that "but."

"But it's all factories and workshops and warehouses, and there are some rather terrible streets. Seems a funny place to live in."

Instantly his frivolity disappeared. It went out like a shooting star. It died like a firework spray in the sky, and darkness possessed the world. He had chosen to be hurt. He was indeed hurt, but not as much as he chose to pretend—or not at first as much as he managed to make himself with bitter, corroding words. "Well, I'm sorry. I thought you'd like it. It was exactly what I needed and what, I imagined, you needed. It wasn't easy to find. I walked my feet off, hunting for something that'd suit you and that I could afford. Damn it, I can't afford a palace. Well, anyway, I like it. I love it."

"I only meant it was hardly a place for people of our class."

"*Our* class!" He looked suddenly at her as if he could think of a shattering answer to *that,* but in pity must not speak it. Instead he grumbled, "Is our class so exalted? It's one above the lowest; that's all."

"Oh, you know what I mean. This isn't exactly a residential district. You do take offense so easily. I think you've done wonders—the only one who's done anything—and I'm awfully grateful to you. You know I am."

But he did not want to be too soon appeased. Having climbed at such speed to the summit of a high grievance, he didn't want to descend at once. That would suggest that the climb had been unnecessary. Or that it was the wrong hill that he had climbed. So he continued to address her from the crest of the hill.

"They're not dreadful streets; they're haunted streets, for those who have eyes to see. But most people are blind to that kind of thing; and women especially, yes, women especially. It may be hideous—it *is* hideous—but, my God, what is Bayswater? *Bays*water! Give me Clerkenwell every time. Every step we take here we tread on a compost heap of history." In the midst of his wrath he was delighted with this phrase. Heavens, but I have my creative moments! Shakespearian. "Clerkenwell's a bit raddled but—" Humor was returning because he'd been pleased with his metaphor. It settled back upon his shoulders as quickly as the wrath had come. And he was able to grimace at the recollection of the wrath and to smile at Pearl.

The smile, like a magnet, snatched her arms onto his shoulders. "Don't let us quarrel, Kerry darling. Please not. You've been so wonderful. I'm sorry if I hurt you."

"And I'm sorry if I was rude. I'm a beast." Now he intended to exceed her in penitence. "I haven't a doubt about it: a hog. One of the lowest of God's creatures. But try to be happy here. We're going to have heaps of fun together; I've made up my mind to that. And remember: if you find you don't like it, it may not be forever. Only give me time." He glanced at the brown-paper parcel on the table.

"I know," she said, her eyes having followed his. "And, oh, if only it—"

But at that minute, as he was about to put a reconciling kiss upon her brow, the door opened. They sprang apart.

Mr. Hitchin. "The missus is bringing up the you-and-me," he said.

"The what?" asked Kerry. "Kerry" was everyone's contraction of Kenrick. No one called him John.

"The tea," Pearl explained.

"Thet's right, miss; but come to think of it, how did you come to know that? Tea. Yes. Tea. Mrs. Hitchin is bringing it up."

It being woman's work to carry a tray, he had come up empty-handed. He had come because he liked a chat at all times and because he was in a mind to learn more about these new tenants. "I thought I'd come and see if I could help you in any way—see? Now what can I do for you—eh?"

He stood there behind a grin that was patently designed to recommend himself to them as a character most friendly and helpful.

"Nothing much, Mr. Hitchin," said Pearl with her immediate and hurried utterance that feigned ease. "My brother seems to have done everything before we arrived. But do sit and have some tea with us."

"Well, I don't mind if I have a bit of a crack with you. No." He sat down on a chair by the wall, putting his thick palms on his knees, their fingers apart like a spider's legs. "The missus was saying you was interested in this neighborhood, Mr. . . . Mr. . . . blow me tight . . . Mr. Betterkin. Yes. Betterkin."

"I am indeed. Tell me all about it. Have a cigarette."

"Don't mind if I do. Thenk you. Lotta books you got 'ere. Got any novels abaht the splits?"

"Splits?"

"Detectives," Pearl translated again. For a moment she seemed proud of this knowledge.

"Yep, detectives. Thet's right. Yup. She knows everything, don't she, sir? I like detective novels. I always think I'd 'ave made a pretty good-class detective meself. Funny you should choose a part like this to live in. But p'raps it's no business of mine. There now: I admit that: it's no business of mine. 'Ad your reasons, no daht."

"I did." No further answer.

"May I arst what they were?"

"My brother wants—" began Pearl; but her brother interrupted with an impatient and warning frown. "I came because it's a most interesting part."

"Interesting? Well, it may 'a bin once."

"You mean when the Knights Hospitallers were here?"

"Knights 'Oss-what'll-ers? Never 'eard of 'em. No, I mean when Turnmill Street was really going."

"Ah yes! Tell me about that." Abruptly, as if this was one of the things he'd come to learn, Kerry sat down.

"Shocking neighborhood it use to be. Shocking." Mr. Hitchin shook his head in disapproval. "Something chronic."

"So?"

"Yep. One of the worst in London. In the old days the cops never went dahn it except in a crahd. It was full of pogue-hunters and tea leaves." And Mr. Hitchin glanced at Pearl to see if she could translate *that.*

This time, however, made nervous by that warning look from her brother, she did not. So Mr. Hitchin did. "Thieves. Almost every house was a den a' thieves, if it wasn't a you-know-what."

"A brothel," Kerry supplied cheerfully.

"Pardon?" It was not that he didn't hear, or that he didn't understand, but that he was shaken by the use of such a word in front of a lady. So firmly did he believe in correct behavior to a lady that, whenever he spoke to Pearl, he lowered his voice a couple of notes and smiled.

"A dish of tarts?" Kerry expounded mischievously, since Mr. Hitchin was not yet recovered.

"Tarts?"

"Yes. Prostitutes." He made it simpler.

"Oh, prostitutes. Yup," Mr. Hitchin accepted this word, after a shocked glance at the lady. "Janes we call 'em in this part. Actually. Yes. Jane Shores. You probably call yours different. But that's all a long time ago. There's nothing like that in Turnmill Street now. Just business hahses, most of 'em. Dull. Just decent and dull," he grumbled.

"And this street? Red Lion Street?"

"Ah. Just respectable." He shook his head as if bored by its respectability. "Never bin anything but respectable. A very high class of gentry used to live here once. Carriage folk."

"I know. This house was built for a Sir John Monmouth in 1719."

"Gaw' now! Was it? How jer know that? And there are other houses in the road quite as old, but I don't mind telling you they're not as nice and clean as this one. I like things nice and clean, I always have. I mean"—he waved a palm around Mrs. Hitchin's handiwork—"look rahnd this room. Spotless, eh?"

"It's all so nice," Pearl asserted gushingly. "It'll make such a pleasant room, I'm sure."

"And have you looked aht'a that window, miss?"

"No. Not yet, Mr. Hitchin."

"Well, you should ought to. There's a view there what only

that window's got. Lean aht and you'll see all the domes and spires and whatnot of Ludgate Hill. You'll see St. Paul's and, jest below it, the O' Bailey."

Mr. Hitchin thought himself a shrewd fellow, with eyes wide open, but he would have needed an eagle's vision to perceive a sudden stiffening and stillness in his two hearers and a brief mantling on Pearl's cheek. Kerry's eyes did not move; Pearl's swung toward her brother's.

Perceiving none of this, he only repeated with a laugh, "Yah, S' Paul's and the O' Bailey. I always say you can choose between the two. Though, personally, I've managed to keep aht'a both. Not but what I nearly took to churchgoing once. I did, straight! The parson who owns this house—"

"Parson?" Kerry interrupted in surprise.

"Oh, yes, it's a parson that owns it, and we rent it from 'im. A very holy parson, and he's very particular as to what we do here. Reckon it's my dew'y to tell you that; I shouldn't be doing my dew'y, if I didn't tip you that. He was the curate here for years and years and very famous in these parts because he was that saintly and good. He got hold o' Nance and made her like what she is; he did and all! Law' love you, he had a go at me, and I almost decided to be God-fearing too—yes, and I really did feel God-fearing for a little, though nobody believed it; but how was they to know what goes on inside me? I gave it a lot a' thought, I did, but I decided against it. So now I got to keep aht'a the O' Bailey, ha, ha—" He suddenly stopped the laugh and turned his head toward some fidgetings and bangings on the other side of the door. Evidently Mrs. Hitchin, encumbered with the tea tray, had difficulty in turning the door handle. And since Mr. Hitchin only stared at this area of noise, remaining in his seat with his hands on his knees, it was Kerry who jumped up and opened the door with a small unconscious bow. Mr. Hitchin watched the tea tray coming in. "Ah, yurse," he said, still seated. "Give 'em their tea. Yurse."

The Hitchins gone and the tea drunk, Kerry picked up the brown-paper parcel and took it into the back room. He laid it on the little table in the center of this slope-roofed attic. This was no more than a kitchen table, but its deal top was covered with a cloth of green baize. Standing on the baize, in the midmost place of honor, was the ancient portable typewriter that he had bought some while since for four pounds. Flanking it on the right was a small brass tray for pens; and on the left its twin for pencils—pencils of all colors: blue, red, yellow, and green.

All this he had arrayed here yesterday, taking care that the typewriter was properly centered and the trays flanked it at the right angles. He had dressed the table almost as if it had been an altar that would be put to ceremonial use tomorrow.

He put his hands in his pockets and his head to one side while he drank pleasure from this array. The table was small, and he was small, and as he stood beside it, looking down, you could imagine that the one had been made to the measure of the other.

The hands in the pockets had thrust his jacket open and uncurtained an assembly of pens and pencils in his left waist-coat pocket. The fountain pens were of many colors, and so were the pencils. They might have been sisters of those in the trays, looking down upon them from a balcony.

Pulling the string off the parcel, he opened it and laid the contents on the table. They were several thick foolscap writing books. He stared down at them while he tried to unknot the string. But the knots proved recalcitrant and he had to turn his eyes on them, picking and pulling at them with teeth set. It was long before he loosed the knots and possessed a fine stretch of string for later use. His first motive for disentangling any piece of string was economy, but since it often cost him a shilling's worth of time to give back virtue to a farthing's worth of string, an accompanying but less obvious motive must have been a powerful fellow. To unravel a tangled string was always the blessed solving of a problem, and it was so much easier to do than to untie some of the larger entanglements of life. The string untied and put in a tin box, like saved capital in a bank, he felt a glow that was both a sense of conquest and a small ministration to his feelings of insecurity.

Now his eyes could return to the foolscap books. Idly he turned the pages of one, glancing down them. He sat down slowly on the tall-backed Windsor chair before the table and put on large spectacles to read more. He felt in a vest pocket for his single black lead pencil. It was not there. Instantly, as in alarm, he stood up and felt in all his pockets. Distrusting his fingertips, he patted jacket pockets, vest pockets, trouser pockets. Not satisfied with the negative answer given to his flat palms, he shook himself, hoping the pencil would drop from the folds of his clothes. It did not, and misery seized him. Time stood still while he felt in all his pockets again. Life was now weighted with pain. The loss of a penny pencil could always lay waste for him a shilling's worth, five shillings' worth, of time. He sighed and stood thinking of all the places he had visited since yesterday and where the pencil might lie. He felt an urge to hurry back to the lodging in Earls Court which he had vacated that morning. But now an idea! It was sweet with hope. Could the point of the pencil (which he liked to keep as slim as a needle) have pierced a hole in the vest pocket and dived down to the bottom of the lining? Oh, good: a glow of triumph; this was what it had done—yes, yes—it lay there like a sand eel buried from sight.

With the pencil like a prize in his hand, he sat again on the Windsor chair and penciled an alteration in the book. This amendment he read, altered again, altered a third time, and a fourth—then shut the book.

Rising, he stood and looked at all the books that yesterday he had arrayed on his shelves in an order of military smartness. "Tallest on the right, shortest on the left." But now he felt the parade could be improved. Was it not possible to get more red spines together, more blue spines with blue? And to get the book tops more level. Half an hour he gave to this difficult business of rearranging books when one had to arbitrate between the claims of color, size, and subject. But at length he had them in as beautiful a parade as possible and felt a glow like that when he'd found the pencil. He had solved for the present a problem of order and beauty.

Hello! Look! Was there an astonishing light in the room? He went quickly to the attic window. Yes, there had come a change in the midmorning light, giving strangeness to the hour. Heavy leaden clouds were playing for position with soft and rosy ones on a great blue tiltyard of sky. Extraordinarily brilliant looked the roofs and gutters and chimneys in this thundery light; they had an excessive precision like that in a colored photograph; a world of London roofs was suddenly unaccountable beneath an unfamiliar sky.

Staring at the strange light, he now saw something that gladdened him: a flag tearing after the wind that had come racing into the cool beneath the storm clouds. It was the flag of the Knights of St. John, white cross on red field. Just broken from its mast on the western tower of St. John's Gate, it flew and rattled and drummed amid the chimneys and the smoke.

For reasons that shall be disclosed, the sudden vision of this flag flying so bravely there, in a romantic, almost theatrical light, seemed to him a favorable omen and stirred the secret hope like a tide.

3

On the morning of the next day two people stood at the window below the front attic, watching him walk away to his work: a diminutive figure in a dark suit and bowler hat.

One was a man, the other a woman; and the man had a fine head of white hair. It was the head which had emerged from that room yesterday to give full and rich voice to the cry, "Alfred! Mr. Hitchin! Ho, there!"

Both of them were in dressing gowns, and both gowns were lively affairs. The woman's was of a pink taffeta glacé, somewhat soiled, but frothing at breast and elbows with exuberant lace. This general pinkness and frothiness suited her abundant figure, for hers was one of those ample and overflowing bodies that should raise only a worshipful thanksgiving for nature's prodigal munificence. It had the glory of an apple tree heavy with autumnal fruit or of a silken-flanked, soft-eyed Shire mare. The man's gown was a Chinese robe, embroidered with dragons and storks and mandarins; but, somewhat freckled with soap after shaving, and much faded and stained after long wear, it looked as if it had come out of a theater's property basket, as, in fact, it had, long ago.

Both watchers were elderly: the woman's gold-brown hair was streaked with gray; the man's white hair outshone the whiteness of bleached wool.

"Isn't he," said the lady, watching the diminutive figure in the bowler hat, "a honey?"

"What did you say, my dear?"

"I said I think he's a perfect daisy. Wouldn't you say so too?"

"Oh, yes, he's off to his day's work all right."

The lady knew that a man hates to believe he is getting deaf, so she accepted his interpretation of her words. "Yes, he's off to his darling little job."

"I conceive it's a gentlemanly job, since he wears a collar as high as that."

"Yes, isn't his collar affecting?"

"Do you know what the job is?"

"Nance Hitchin says he's something in Fleet Street."

"Not the editor of a national journal?"

"No, just a little clerk. A dear little clerk."

"And the sister, what does she do? Evie, my dear, surely you've found that out by this time? They've been here twenty-four hours."

"She's going to keep house for him."

"Not much house to keep up there. Two cocklofts and a stove in the passage. Where do they sleep?"

"She in the front, he in the back, dear little man."

"My God, over our heads! He'll creak about in the middle of the night. Couldn't we get 'em to change over? Men get up at night more than women. She might lie still."

"Now don't be a buffoon, Georgy. I'm sure he sleeps like an angel."

"And she'll be over this room all day. Creaking around and dropping things. My dear, our peace is at an end. You say he *writes?*"

"That's what Nance Hitchin thinks."

"Then he'll walk up and down all night. He'll never go to bed." Still studying Kerry's figure, not yet out of Red Lion Street, he declaimed sadly in his old actor's voice, "Methought I heard a voice cry, 'Sleep no more. The gentleman upstairs does murder sleep' "; and as Kerry turned the corner and out of sight, he quoted further to himself, "Macbeth shall sleep no more. . . . Not poppy, nor mandragora, nor all the drowsy syrups of the world—"

"He's gone now. Come away, Georgy. Don't let everyone see you watching out of the window."

He came away. "The sister's still up there, I conceive. If we keep quite quiet we shall probably hear her breathing. These ghastly floorboards, hundreds of years old. Listen." He stood still, an ear turned to the ceiling. "What had Nance to say about the sister?"

"Only that she's been ill. And I'm sure she looks it. Worn to the bone and pale as death. But she's a lady. Nance says that she talks like a duchess. And so does he. They're very much the little lady and gentleman."

"Well, why do they come to live here?"

"Because they're poor, my dear man, and because Hoss Comfort told them about those two rooms." Mr. Horace Comfort, generally nicknamed Hoss, lived on the first floor, with Evie and George above and the Hitchins below. "Hoss knows him in Fleet Street."

"Oh, him! That fat homo-boy. Aha; perhaps that's why your little clerk isn't married." He nodded. "Aye, aye; that might account for a lot. He's one of them like Hoss. One of Hoss's mistresses."

"Now then, Georgy, don't be an unpleasant old man. I think Hoss is a pet. I love my Hoss. He comes up sometimes and amuses me."

"I think he's an overblown pansy. And I expect any moment to hear he's got his five years. Heavens, we don't want one of them below us and one above. Clearly we must know about *them.*" He pointed to the ceiling. "You must get busy."

"Oh, but I've a wonderful idea. We'll have them down for drinks, as a little welcome. To make them feel they're loved, poor little souls. A little party, you and me and them."

He thought over this. "Well, yes, and I could tell them about the floorboards. I could beg them, whenever possible, to creep on tiptoe. Yes, have 'em down."

"Oh, this *will* be fun," said Evie.

Kerry turned out of Red Lion Street into Benjamin Street, and his daily dream went with him. Benjamin Street, a narrow canyon between high, grimed houses, led straight into the once-vile Turnmill Street, its cobbles tilting downward, because here was the fall of the land toward the old Fleet Ditch, which once upon a time ran open to the air, fouled and noisome and stinking. Turnmill Street would conduct him into Cowcross Street, and so to the Farringdon Road and Fleet Street and his work. That now he could walk each day to his work and save a fare was giving him the same small glow as when he succeeded in untying the string.

It was part of his dream that, as he went down the cobbles of Benjamin Street, he should be seeing it as it was in the days of the old books and plays. Then it was one of the evil alleys that lay behind Turnmill Street. It was one of the hangers-on, as you might say, of that master criminal. It supported its master by housing the cutpurses and the footpads, the highwaymen and the strumpets, the fugitives from Hatton Garden over the Fleet, and sometimes, perhaps, an escaped debtor from the neighboring Fleet Prison. It was almost the only hanger-on left. Its sister courts and alleys had almost all disappeared since industry instead of villainy set up in business here.

One dark alley there was at the foot of Benjamin Street, and Kerry always stopped to stare down it. Others might never have noticed it, so narrow its arched entry, so secluded and shadowed its long slit between the houses. Faulkner's Alley. Because the sun never reached it, its walls were blackened with soot and its paving flags oily with damp or pooled after rain. At the far end of it you could see the clean daylight again. Had some of its low, crippled houses once been haunts of infamy? Had petty or sinister crimes been hatched behind those dirty, ill-favored windows? Did footpads at dusk come slipping out of this archway into Benjamin Street?

To step out of Benjamin Street into Turnmill Street was to come out of shadows into sunlight. It was the sunlight that had undone Turnmill Street. When they pulled down its western side, where now the railway runs in its smoke-black cutting, they let the wide clean sunlight, a whole skyful of it, flood down upon Turnmill Street and fling light into the courts and yards behind. And the wide boys went. That was the end of Jack Ketch's Warren, for his clients loved the darkness rather than the light. Today printing works, foundries, binderies, and a great distillery faced the western sun unashamed.

Now he was walking down the Farringdon Road, one of the thousands streaming to their work along the course of the old Fleet Valley. He was thinking of his schooldays as he walked, because he had been at the City of London School on the embankment ahead of him and he would wander after school hours in these streets. He felt glad those days were over when he remembered the shy, timid boy he had been, ever shrinking from the rough games of his fellows. He had been afraid of most of them because they made fun of his appearance, so small and bony his body, so oval and large his head. He would escape from their banter to walk alone in those thronged and jarring streets or to read his childhood away in some empty and tight-shut room. Sometimes his abstraction in a street was like a stupor, and kindly strangers might touch his elbow and say, "Come on, sonny. You're holding up the traffic. You can't stand there gawping for ever."

And yet even then, behind all the timidities and shames, was the tremendous ambition, the dream. He might be smaller than his fellows, but his dream was larger than they could imagine; it was as large as the world that the eye could see. "A man can do anything if he only wants to enough," he would tell himself in classroom, playground, or street. "Enough." His fist would clench on the word to possess it for ever. "Enough." And the same dream traveled with him now, like an encompassing aura, along the Farringdon Road: a rooted obsessional certainty that he was destined to create something that would endure. There were moments, one beneath the Viaduct and one near Ludgate Circus, when he was thinking, with the usual warm glow, that none of these mere ordinary people in the street knew that, walking behind them, came one whose name would be immortal.

There was not always a glow around him as he walked the Farringdon Road. If he was thinking of the past rather than the future he might be remembering some foolish word he'd said before many hearers in an effort to impress them and be admired, or some social gaffe he'd committed at a supper table, and then his heart would so sicken unto death that his voice, slipping all control, would say aloud in the street, "I wish I were dead," and people ahead of him would turn around in amaze. Then his second state would be worse than his first because now he had made a fool of himself before the people in the street. And he would wish they were dead.

This disastrous tendency of his voice to become an autonomous agent and speak aloud whenever he remembered a humiliation happened this morning as he approached Ludgate Circus. His memory threw up a horrid occasion, fully eight years ago, when addressing a literary club, he had tried to impress them by appearing to speak without notes, though really he'd learned his speech by heart, and at one point he totally forgot how the speech continued—and, indeed, what it was about. His brain stood still; it stood empty as a void in a half-created world; the sweat leaped to his brows and the nape of his neck; there was a silence like a death of time; and, worst of all, the people murmured their sympathy, some fools even trying to encourage him by clapping. As he recalled this, eight years after, and six paces from Ludgate Circus, his voice said aloud, "I'm for dying," and the hurrying City workers before and behind him turned to look into his face, just as his wretched voice spoke again: "Oh, why not die?" A horrible boy ran up from behind to stare at him and see if he was mad.

Out of Ludgate Circus into Fleet Street and there ahead of him was his office building and his clerk's desk and chair.

A wearisome occupation, working as a clerk from nine until five-thirty, but there had been this need for a money-earning job ever since his father died when he was only sixteen, and more so than ever now after the astonishing collapse of his sister. He must go on and on at it with only one chance of escape: the fulfillment of the dream. Oh, if only fulfillment would come like Peter's angel and throw wide his prison doors. But until that miracle (which was coming) he could take no risks—less than ever now, with Pearl a burden on his back. A burden, of course, and yet, of all moments in life warmed by a glow of satisfaction, none had been quite so good, quite so self-pleasing, as that first time when he stood in the witness box and promised to look after her if the magistrate would only put her on probation, or that second time when he pleaded for her in the box at the Old Bailey, or that moment, only twenty-four hours ago, when he met her at the gates of Holloway jail and led her to a new home where he could hide her and watch over her and help her to be happy again.

4

"Ah! Come *in. In!*" The fine white head, having heard a soft and unsure knock, had risen. To his wife, seated as a waiting hostess, its owner said in a lowered and dramatized voice, one finger uplifted, "Here they are, my love." Then he spread the door wide, with a trained actor's bow. "Come in, dear lady. And you too, sir."

No Chinese dressing gown hung today about his graceful figure; he had honored these guests with his best black jacket, a fawn waistcoat, a wide-winged collar, and a buxom black cravat with a dark pearl in its midst—which at once suggested to Kerry a gray gull alighted on a dark heaving sea.

His wife echoed his welcome. "Yes, come in, my dears. How *very* nice to see you."

Kerry and Pearl entered. They, too, were in their best for this occasion. It was a Tuesday evening, but Kerry had worn last week's shirt two days longer than usual so as to be able to wear for these hosts a newly laundered shirt in its state of shriven purity. His hair lay parted and glossy, after strong strokes with a brush dipped in water. And Pearl, so far as she could do anything with her meager figure, rounded back, features too large, and hair prematurely gray, had done it all. In a dark-green velvet dress she was groomed for a party.

"It's so nice of you, Mrs. Windsor," she began, urged as always to show by rapid words her complete social ease. "We are truly strangers in a strange land. We know no one at all in these—" but Mrs. Windsor had her own drives toward the full social gush, and her rapids quickly overflowed her visitor's stream. "We thought that the least we could do would be to get to know each other, since we're all inmates of the same little asylum, ha, ha, ha, with only the floorboards between us."

"Ah, yes . . . the floorboards," began Mr. Windsor, but decided that perhaps it was not the moment to speak of them as yet. So he just smiled at the visitors, as if this would help them to forget what he had just said; and he pushed forward an eighteenth-century ladderback chair for the lady. "Sit down, my dear." Only when she was seated did he make her a small bow, probably unconsciously, and go himself to an extremely baroque ribbonback chair.

Pearl sat uneasily on the brink of her chair, quite unaware of its value, and opened her floodgates again. "What a nice room you have here, Mrs. Windsor. Kerry, we must try to make ours something like this, though of course it's not so big and lofty; and I understand, Mrs. Windsor, that you've got four rooms— this floor and the one below—and so have plenty of space, whereas we've had to crowd everything into two little attics."

"But I always think," said Mrs. Windsor, when she could speak, "that you can make attics so attractive with their low ceilings and odd corners and—"

"But we have no such lovely furniture as yours," Pearl inter-rupted with her nervous, anxious, forced garrulity; and Kerry, who had not managed to get a word in yet, saw how she was thinking that one way to appear at ease would be to speak with modesty of one's income. "What a beautiful sideboard, isn't it, Kerry?"

"Oh, but this furniture . . ." began Mr. Windsor, who had more than once parted his lips to speak but been obliged to shut them again, since there had been no break in the women's chatter. Now, however, both chatterers turned, as one woman, toward him. "These few bits and pieces are only the relics of the nice home we once had, where we used to entertain a lot —didn't we, dear?—before we . . . before we retired. But now they're just dead props." He said this sadly. "Dead props, which the plot no longer wants. We were both on the stage, you know: my Evie and I."

"Yes, we knew that," began Pearl. "Mrs. Hitchin—"

But Mr. Windsor, having got started, did not desire to be stopped. "Yes, the stage, but that's all over and done with now. You behold two outcasts, my dear. Two on the waste heap. Forgotten. And do you know what my ambition was when I began? To be the head of the profession. Yes: nothing less. To assume the mantle of Irving and Tree. Instead"—he offered a sweeping gesture with an upturned and empty palm—"this. Up the spout. Down the drain."

"Now then, Georgy!" his wife rebuked him. "Never mind that"; and she turned to Pearl. "Unlike Georgy, I never expected anything else. Not for me, at any rate, not for a woman, so I wasn't disappointed. For Georgy it ought to have been different, but there—I've always known that injustice is far more likely than justice in this world. Georgy can't accept it like that. Men are always surprised and disappointed if things don't go as they want them, while we women are only surprised if they do. I don't expect pleasant things in life, but he thinks he ought to be happy. Georgy, instead of talking about yourself, get up and give the poor dears some sherry. They've come for a drink."

As Mr. Windsor went to the sideboard for the sherry, his wife said softly to Pearl, "You can understand them not wanting me anymore. I mean, like Jack Falstaff, 'one is fat and grows old.' You must give in when you get fat and shapeless; but you'd think that Georgy . . . so beautiful . . ." The sentence was never finished because Georgy had come near with the decanter. She changed it abruptly to "Georgy takes it to heart terribly."

"Certainly he does," said George, with the decanter poised near Pearl's glass. "He had dreams of conquering the world when he was young, and there were times when it looked as though he would do it. Remember my Petruchio, Evie, love? And my John of Gaunt? I thought the world was won then. But it was not. That was twenty-seven years ago, and it's all forgotten now. George Windsor is forgotten and so is Evie MacNeil, that very lovely actress. But she is able to accept it philosophically. Not so George. Never George. George's bread is sorrow and his milk is tears." At which point he bowed over Pearl's glass. "Sherry, dear lady?"

"Oh . . . thank you, yes . . . but only a little. I—er—not

much. . . ." All her social striving failed to conceal that she was not used to being offered sherry. "What a lovely decanter! Cut-glass. You do have lovely things, Mr. Windsor."

"The bits and pieces, dear heart—"

But Mrs. Windsor had leaned forward and touched her arm affectionately. "Don't let's talk about the silly old Windsors. Let's talk about you. You have some profession, have you, sweetie?"

Silence from Pearl. And Kerry to her rescue, quickly. "My sister was a teacher till she very kindly consented to keep house for me."

"And you, Mr. Betterkin? You are a—"

"By force of necessity a clerk in Fleet Street. By desire—and indeed intention—something rather different."

"Such as?"

"Ah!" Kerry smiled mysteriously. "Perhaps I'll tell you one day. Not yet."

"My brother likes to keep it a secret for the present," said Pearl. Words of supererogation, since Kerry had just made this clear; but at least it was something to say on a social occasion.

"Well now, Mr. Betterkin, do tell us all about your work in a silly old office. Tell us all that goes on. I love the inside information about anything. And Fleet Street! Wonderful!"

Kerry told them all he could about an advertisement clerk's work in the London office of a big provincial newspaper. His material was dull enough, and he told it stumblingly. Kerry had a reputation among his friends as a gay and often brilliant patterer, but somehow he could only get this lively talk going, he could only scintillate, if he was among those whom he loved and who loved him, or among those whom he knew to be his inferiors in brain or rank—Pearl, for example, and Mrs. Hitchin. In the company of all these, the lovers and the lesser people, some buried power seemed to surge up in him and pour out in jets of sparkling jocularity; a demon came to life in him and laid witticisms on his lips that surprised him to hear and moved him to secret admiration. None of this issued today in the presence of the Windsors' furniture.

He did the best he could. He described the two other clerks in the front office and tried to make fun of the office manager, "a real old Fleet Street character"; but all the time Mr. Windsor only looked on benignly and smiled inattentively, being always less anxious, it would appear, to hear of other people's careers than to talk of his own. If by chance some fact did for the moment interest him, the smile left his face and he turned his better ear to hear. His wife, on the other hand, a gifted listener to any gossip, was interested in everything, from first to last. Kerry concluded, "I was living in a dismal boardinghouse in Earls Court, and I suddenly decided that I'd like to be nearer my work and have some sort of home of my own, so I asked Pearl to come and look after me, which she very kindly did."

"And I'm sure you both did right. Georgy, fill up their glasses. And now, my dears, is there anything we can do to help you settle in?"

"Yes," said Kerry promptly. "Tell us more about Mr. Hitchin."

"Ah! About our Elfred?" Clearly there was nothing Mrs. Windsor would better like to do. She compressed her lips in a grimace that was the very hieroglyphic of disapproval. She nodded some nods that were heavy with meaning. Clearly a revelation was coming. It opened with a terse sentence. "Our Elfred's a wrong 'un."

"That was rather my impression," said Pearl, still holding on to the talk so as to keep afloat in this social sea.

"And, my dear lady," Mr. Windsor commented from his distant chair, "you were quite extremely right. Come in, Mrs. Windsor. Tell 'em more."

"Well, quite simply, dears, old Hitchin is a bad old bounder. But Nance Hitchin is a darling. Extraordinary how often you find a thoroughly nice woman tied up to a horrible old twister."

"As Mrs. Windsor to George," suggested George.

"Now, Georgy, be quiet. Nance is the breadwinner in this house. It must be ages since old Hitchin did a proper job of work. If it hadn't been for Father Aylwin—"

"Oh, yes," put in Pearl, "do tell us about this Father Aylwin. Old Hitchin rents the house from him, doesn't he, Mrs. Windsor?"

"Nothing of the sort. If anyone rents it, it's Nance. But don't call me Mrs. Windsor, call me Evie. And Georgy George. We're all in the same old boat with only floorboards between us."

"Yes, those floorboards," began George. "They—"

But it was not his cue line yet. Evie hurried on. "Father Aylwin worked here for about forty years, merely as a curate, refusing every kind of preferment because he so loved the people and they loved him. Obviously he was one of the world's poppets. He had bags of money, and about twenty years ago he bought this house for his home. Nance had adored him from her childhood, and he made her his cook, giving the basement to her and Alfred, who then guarded the delivery trucks at the distillery there." She threw a hand vaguely toward the west. "But after a time Alfred lost the job. He always says he was laid off with others in the slump, but I wonder. Do people drink less when they're in despair? I should have thought a slump was excellent for the gin business. Anyhow the distillery never took him back, which enables him to grouse about being 'too old at forty-five'; and it was Father Aylwin who found him odd jobs about the parish."

"Where's Father Aylwin now?" asked Pearl.

"I'll tell you. When he was about seventy his old bishop insisted that he must take things more quietly, and he tucked him away in a country living in Essex. But Nance didn't want to leave Clerkenwell, where she'd lived all her life, and I don't think the good Father wanted to take old Alfred along with the rest of the furniture, so it ended by his letting her have the house so that she could make some money by letting the rooms in addition to what she could earn with her cleaning at Sadler's Wells Theatre. That was where I first met her—she asked if I could send her any theatricals as lodgers. Nance is really only his caretaker here. He lets her pay a small rent if business is good, as it generally is, but I'm pretty sure it's not enough to pay his taxes. Or keep the place in repair. This is an old house, you see, and—"

"And you can hear everything through the floors," said George.

"Georgy is very sensitive to noise," Evie explained.

"What sort of noise?" asked Kerry, suspecting at once that he was included in this explanation.

"Practically every noise by now," said George. "At first it was only the raucous noises: children in the street, motor horns in the Clerkenwell Road, a dog in a backyard. Now it's anything on earth: the wireless next door, Nance Hitchin singing downstairs, old Hitchin clearing his throat with fervor and resource and a praiseworthy refusal to be beaten. I wait, I wait, while the heroic business advances to its climax. Yes . . . Hitchin . . . and, if you don't mind my mentioning them . . . the few noises overhead."

"Do *we* make a noise? Oh, Pearl!"

"Not, dear boy—not more than can be helped, I'm sure.

Sometimes, perhaps, a little walking to and fro, like Satan in the Book of Job—a little walking up and down in the world, and going to and fro in it."

"Oh, that's Kerry composing a sentence," Pearl said, laughing, but George's face suggested that, for him, it was nothing to laugh about; while Kerry tossed a small frown at her, as if, forgetfully, she'd given a secret away.

"I expect I'm writing letters," he said. "In future I'll just creep about."

"That's extremely kind. I admit that my dislike of all noise is now somewhat excessive. Even natural noises irritate me now. There's a thrush in the garden makes a filthy row."

"The extraordinary thing," said Evie in a lowered voice to Pearl, "is that poor darling Georgy's getting as deaf as a post and yet he can always hear the smallest creak that he doesn't want to hear. But of course"—she held up a warning finger—"he doesn't like people to think he's getting deaf."

George heard none of this. "I realize," he said, "that I shall never now enjoy that perfection of quiet which one learns to desire. Not even in my grave. The worms will make slippery noises on the lid of my coffin. Creeping about. Why, my dear boy, when like you I am walking around, trying to compose an admirable sentence, the tassels of my dressing gown *will* swing this way and that and hit things, and make maddening noises. They turn me sick till I know it's only me—and then I'm pleased. My own footsteps too: I've known them to annoy me a little."

"But have you never," asked Kerry, "tried earplugs?"

"Earplugs? You mean cotton wool?"

"Gracious, no. Wax. You can buy them at any chemist's. Fit them into your ears and you go into a paradisal peace."

"My dear lad, lead me to them tomorrow."

"I can give you some now."

"You can?" Mr. Windsor rose as Kerry rose. "Evie, my love, this is a great moment. I feel like someone on whom a divine miracle is about to be performed. Say the man possessed with devils. Or Lazarus before he was raised from the dead. Dear boy, lead me to my peace."

5

Kerry paused at the foot of the garret stairs. It was evening and one of those moments when he was feeling the pressure of an intolerable gaiety. One could only relieve it by bellowing out nonsense. "Where's our Pearl? Now then, woman, come out. Emerge. Show yourself."

Pearl emerged from the front room. She came with a smile, ready to respond to his nonsense. "Here is Pearl," she said.

"Good evening. How are you?" He climbed to her side and placed a kiss on her brow. Then, picking up her hand, he led her back into the front room, and she showed by her smile that she was content to be thus led, like a child.

"The Commodore was at his bridge-house window again," said Kerry, as he flung his briefcase on to the table. "He saw me safely into port."

"The Commodore" was his nickname for George Windsor below. He gave it to him, he declared, because George's finely sculptured features looked as if they had been chiseled by the North Sea gales, and his paled blue eyes looked as if they had gazed through sunlight and storm at the farthest horizons. To be sure, they seemed to be always gazing out now from his living-room window.

"The Commodore's lady has been up here for a gossip most of the afternoon," said Pearl. "And oh, my dear, can she rabbit!"

"Can she *what?*"

"Rabbit. Talk."

"Oh, 'rabbit' means 'talk,' does it? Well, who'd have thought that? What did she rabbit about?"

"She sat and told me about every play she'd ever played in. And she gave me a brief summary of George's career too."

"It's a remarkable fact, Miss Betterkin," said Kerry, flinging himself onto a chair and letting his arms slump wearily to his sides, "that whereas the journey from this house to my office is precisely three-quarters of a mile, the journey from the office to this house is three miles and a half. How do you make that out?"

"It's your poor old plates of meat. Take off your shoes and put on your sneaks. I'll get them for you." She went to the closet by the small fireplace and drew forth his slippers.

Plates of meat. Sneaks. The old prison words for feet and for slippers. Deliberately, at times, she would fly this old prison patois before him like a flag. She did it in a kind of defiant gaiety, or with a kind of spinsterish archness. There was something heroic about it, but he could seldom respond by uttering the stuff himself. The words would burn his lips as they passed.

"Thank you, dear," he said and took the slippers.

"You're not going to work this evening, Kerry?"

"I certainly am."

"What? Tired as you are? So you'd like me to bring you your supper on a tray."

"Of your charity. And you? Did you eat at all properly this afternoon?"

"Of course I did. There's a little teashop in Jerusalem Passage. I had a tightener there."

Tightener. A meal. Again the lively grasping of a hated nettle. She wanted the prison slang to be a joke between them.

But you overdo it, my dear, and it rather breaks my heart. Still, I mustn't show any pity, I know. Perhaps I had best join in the game. Yes; what's the word for a thick slice of bread and butter? "And I'll tell you, young woman, what you consider a good meal. You had a cup o' char and a doorstep."

"Not at all. I had two doorsteps. And a piece of cake."

"Pfooh! Have you bought yourself something substantial for supper?"

"I bought some pressed beef and lettuce."

"Enough for you as well as me?"

"Yes."

"If there isn't, I shall take you out and forcibly feed you."

"I bought as much as we could afford. We've got to be careful."

"Damn the woman; I know what that means. It means I shall have to take you out and feed you just when I want to work."

He was in the midst of this affectionate teasing when his eyes, straying to the empty fireplace as weary eyes will, saw the base of the basket chair which was accepted as *her* chair, and in which she always sat with her sewing, her paper, or her book. All around its base lay that which irritated him to the point of pain. All around it were little spatters of cigarette ash, little gray broken asterisks where the ash had been knocked by the touch of a little finger from cigarette to floor. This was a habit of hers that could hurt him like the prick of a knife. It was one symptom of her blindness to order and beauty. Quickly his eyes, seeking more pain, found other symptoms: the day's newspaper lay on the sofa in a wild dismemberment; the curtains were not pulled across the corner where her clothes hung, and he could see that all her jackets were hanging, not by the tabs provided, but by the inside of their necks, carelessly; even from his chair he could see the accumulated dust behind the pictures on the mantelpiece.

The pain caused by these irritants, like an abscess aching to be lanced, could be relieved only by a spoken protest. But he must not speak. Hold up. Hold up. Try not to speak. *Don't.* Hold out. It's not really her fault after all she's been through. Accept. You told yourself you'd accept everything, no matter how much it irritated you. God help me to accept. Other women do just the same with their cigarette ash. You see them doing it in pubs. But this isn't a pub. It's a room I labored on for days to—but give her time. A cigarette must be wonderful to her after all those months of longing for it. Didn't she say that the longing for one whiff in her cell was sometimes an agony? And she must have a nervous need to smoke and knock away the ash after all she's endured. Have some mercy. God help me to be merciful.

But if one was not to speak, one must act; one must *do* something. One must clean up the mess and so show that it was

[45]

wrong to care nothing where you shed your ash. He rose and tried to do this gently: he just picked up hearth brush and dustpan and swept around, saying, "Oh, look at all this ash."

But even this was a word too much. Pearl's bruised heart was still so sore that a touch could hurt it. "Oh, don't find something wrong directly you come in. Don't start getting at me for untidiness just because I dropped a speck or two of ash. It's not kind."

To be rebuked when he'd nobly held himself in check was like a blow on the abscess so that it burst—to his great relief. Purulent words gushed from the burst. "I can't live in the midst of mess. I'm sorry, but that's me. And I'm not ashamed of being hurt by slovenliness. It's not that I'm a tidiness maniac like some people. I like a room to look lived in and—"

"Oh, God, surely a room's meant to be happy in."

"If you'd allow me to finish, that's what I was going to say. I like a room to have nice homely things lying about, but that's not the same as dust and dirt and muck. Look at that paper."

"What's the matter with the paper?"

"Well, if you can't see, you can't. I'm not at all ashamed of liking things as perfect as possible. I spent hours and hours trying to make this room beautiful for you, but I felt all along that it'd soon be turned into a junk shop. Or a refuse pit." Oh, it was good to speak one's mind, to hurt her; it was a glow within one like the gift of a fiery drink.

"Oh, I do think you are brutal to say things like that. You don't mind how you hurt when you're in the mood to."

"It's no good starting to cry. Crying cuts no ice with me. It only puts my back up." He drew his finger through the dust on the mantelshelf. "Looks as though we'll have to invite the dustmen up next time they're around."

"Oh, you're cruel. Utterly cruel. How can you be so pitiless sometimes?"

Cruel? *Pitiless?* After he'd—but no, not a word about that. That at least was something he'd never say. He tidied up the paper instead.

"Cruel you are. After all, perhaps I'd better go and live by myself. If I only make you miserable—if we are so different—"

He longed to say, "You don't make me miserable. We're not so different," but he couldn't. To soften now would imply that his anger had been excessive. He kept silent, lips tight.

"I was going to get some sort of job in any case so as to help you with the expenses, and I've no doubt I can get enough to keep myself somewhere—"

His heart, but his heart only, cried, "Oh, don't, *don't;* stop it; I can't stand it." Aloud he said, "I haven't asked you to do that," and, putting the paper aside and drawing the curtains across her ill-hung clothes, he hurried from the room lest he said something too cruel or too kind.

In his own attic room, its door shut on his penitence, he stood looking down upon the manuscript books, the pens and pencils and eraser. He'd set them all in good tactical array this morning with a view to a considerable advance this evening. But now he felt like crying as he looked down upon them. "I meant to work. I wanted to work. But that row's churned me all up. One has only so much creative ability and now most of it's gone into a filthy row, or it's all dispersed. One should be left in peace so that the cream can rise and settle. But I *will* work; I *will.* I never give in. I'm never beaten." He was accustomed to stiffen his will and his faith in himself by repeating fifty, a hundred times these statements that he was not beatable. "I never give in. Nothing ever gets me down. Or if I get down, I get up. I've never been known to give in."

And so, with his heart on these crutches, as it were, he sat down at the table. He put on his large spectacles; he drew from a side pocket a snuffbox which, however, contained not snuff but the earplugs; he pushed two of these into his ears, and gradually the far-spread murmurs of London grew mute and died. He picked up a pencil; he beat its point on the blotting paper; he twisted it in his fingers—and he did nothing else with it, because he was floating in a sea of misery as he contemplated his selfishness, his temper, and his cruelty. In the great silence behind the earplugs he was imprisoned with his sin.

"I'm a loathsome type. Selfish and cruel. Can't stay kind or even decent for ten minutes. If there's anything I don't like, or if she utters a word of criticism, I go off like a bomb. And I can't stop myself. Nobody must criticize Kerry. Oh, no! And nobody must do anything Kerry doesn't like. Not on your life. Call that even decent civilized behavior? I don't. I call it plain filthiness."

In some despair at this verdict he dropped the pencil and joined his hands over the blotting paper while he gave himself to meditation.

Was there really much credit in what he'd tried to do for

Pearl? That first time when he resolved to make himself, at whatever cost, responsible for her, had he not been pleased with his magnanimity and with his superiority to his brother, Godfrey, who refused to do anything? Had he not felt a warm satisfaction in his sense of duty, and so got pleasure out of Pearl's anguish? Up till that hour what had he been but atrociously self-centered? Thinking only of himself and his dreams. After that moment of vision he'd tried hard to be loyal to it, but always, sooner or later, the old self-centered Adam leaped onto his back like Sinbad's Old Man of the Sea. He sighed over the table. "I can never finally unhorse the old brute. Always the old bounder comes jumping back into place again. I may do a few kind things now and again, but fundamentally, as I say, I'm filthy."

Pearl was right: he'd been grossly cruel. "Invite the dustmen up." The memory of those whiplash words was now a whiplash on his own back, so that he leaped out of his chair and walked miserably to the window. Poor Pearl. Probably she was now being unbearably miserable in the next room. Probably she was staring out of her window as he out of his. She westward over London, he eastward. Pity cried out that the only right thing to do was to go in and say he was sorry and comfort her with a kiss. But he couldn't force himself to do this as yet. "Not yet," he said to the roofs and chimneys before him. "Not at once. I'll do it later. A little later, when I've built up some decency and strength. It takes time after a total collapse like this. Damn it, Rome wasn't built in a day."

Relieved by the thought that he would behave properly in due course, he felt free to work. And there across the roofs, to encourage him in his work, flew the red and white flag of St. John: it danced and laughed amid the drifting chimney smoke, bravely against a dull sky.

And his head became an arena filled with Knights of St. John marching in their red sopravests and white crosses. It became Clerkenwell, but Clerkenwell in a splendor of medieval color, Old Clerkenwell risen again from under the debris of ages. Just now the knights were in procession along a narrow road; and the road was St. John's Lane yonder, in a chasm below the roofs. The brilliant procession went through the groined archway of St. John's Gate, passing under its molded ribs and carved bosses and halting in the priory's great courtyard. Procession followed procession, and in one of them rode the Princess Mary with fifty gentlemen in velvet and gold chains before her and eighty of her Catholic lords and ladies behind. As she passed under the archway he saw the Tudor chamber over the gate, and there a fat monarch in doublet and hose was presenting a gold basin set with jewels to the grand master, after that old warrior had fought Suleiman the Magnificent and all his shaven infidels for the possession of Rhodes, the knights' island home.

But larger and more real than any monarch or grand master on the stage of Kerry's mind, as he gazed from his attic window, was the figure of one hospitaller, one who had never existed but who was thus terribly real, achingly real, to Kerry, because he was his own creation. At first he had called this noblest of knights Sir Godfrey Mayce, partly in mischievous fun at the expense of his brother, Godfrey, because in every way, in magnanimity, generosity, and unselfishness, the knight seemed the opposite of brother Godfrey. But soon Kerry made a remarkable discovery about the strange potency of names in this business of fictitious creation. As long as he gave his hero the name Godfrey, he couldn't make do with him because he couldn't love him. But directly he sloughed off this strait waistcoat of a name and called him instead Sir Nicholas Shelley, he was able to create him with fire and love. In fact, Sir Nicholas was now almost the opposite of himself, a dream portrait of what he would wish to be, but knew he was not. Sir Nicholas, like all the Knights Hospitallers, was a gentleman of ancient family, able to prove his nobility for four generations; he was tall and broad and well shaped; he was highly educated and widely traveled; he was strong in character and indifferent to praise or blame; he was bountiful to the point of prodigality, whereas Kerry was timid with money and afraid to spend; he was chivalrous and magnanimous and forgiving—and here at least Kerry hoped he was like him, if only sometimes. . . .

When the bloat king, his greasy palms itching for gold, suppressed the priory and sold its church to the lord high admiral of England for a thousand pounds, most of the knights withdrew to Malta, which the emperor had ceded to them after the loss of Rhodes; but one or two proud souls remained, among them Sir Nicholas. "I neither submit nor run," he said. "When I was created a Knight of St. John I was given a sword with a cross hilt to show that I must always fight bravely in defense of the true faith. I was rapped thrice on the shoulder with the sword to show that I must suffer for Christ. I was given a taper to hold to show that I must be a candle to others if darkness fell. Did they not adjure me when I was admitted, 'We place this cross on your breast that you may love it with all your heart; and may your right hand ever fight in its defense. Should it ever happen that, in combating the enemies of the faith, you should desert the standard of the cross and take flight, you will be stripped of this holy sign according to the customs and statutes of our order.' Such, as I seem to recollect, was my ordering, and I cannot therefore submit to, or fly from, any heretic, whatever his crown. I cannot bow my head before him save it be in honor upon his block."

For such words the dues were death. Sir Nicholas with two companions no less haughty was marched to Tower Hill for execution. Standing before the block, he raised a hand toward heaven and said, "I thank my God that He has allowed me this, that I am able to stand as a victor on this little hill. If vengeance for this deed is right in His eyes, He will repay it. If not, I am but His knight to do as He commands. Sir Executioner, I have no rebuke for you. You are but the servant of your master as I of mine. Do your task, and God be with you thereafter." Wherewith he knelt down, made the sign of that cross which he had never deserted, and laid his head upon the block.

One who stood watching and heard these words was Edward Seymour, the king's brother-in-law, Earl of Hertford and soon to be Duke of Somerset.

Years later a noise of great explosions rent the Clerkenwell air. The great bell tower of the priory church and the walls of its nave crashed down; choir and sanctuary cracked and in part collapsed. And the Lord Protector Somerset, whose order had placed the gunpowder under the nave, took away the sacred stones for the building of his house on the Strand. The building began, but he never saw it finished. One night in a dream he saw the figure of Sir Nicholas Shelley, gaunt in death, standing by his bed and looking down upon him, even as he had looked down upon the block. After this silent watch the horrid phantom raised a hand toward heaven and said, "Sacrilege. Sacrilege. I asked no vengeance for myself but I ask it now for my Master's house. He will repay; and even as the great tower stooped its head to the ground, so shall the great lord protector. Beware the Lords in London." This said, he kneeled by the bed and, having made the sign of the cross, laid his head against the protector's side.

One casts out a nightmare like bitter bread upon the waters, but it may return after many days. This dream, its details strangely clear, was with the lord protector when, attired in all his best, as for a king's occasion, he stood before the block on Tower Hill, charged with treason by the Lords in London. It was the block on which Sir Nicholas had died; and the lord protector was seeing the gaunt knight at his bedside, as he put his own head down upon the block, after first making the sign of the cross. Sir Nicholas's cross.

What a story! What pageantry, what drama, what a grand tragic close. Sixteenth-century London, and Clerkenwell at the greatest turn of England's history. "Green and Pleasant Clerkenwell"—what a title. "By John Kenrick Betterkin." Kerry watching it all happen, much of it at his own command, was now alone with his great secret. And his great hope. He loved to be alone with them. He would write such a romance as would excel those of Scott, Dumas, and Victor Hugo. We have said that he was a "brilliant patterer," and could scintillate, only if he was in the presence of those who loved him, or those whom he knew to be his inferiors. Among these, the lovers and the lesser people, must be accounted the vast imaginary audience, worldwide, that sprang up like an army of lovers from the fields of the future, when his manuscript books were open before him. Then, as he schemed and dreamed, the surge of creative power rose in him, charging his throat with excitement, inflating his breast with hope, and shaking his heart with fear. The words and the wit and the new ideas poured forth in spate; and it was this strange, shaking fact which gave him hope that his dream was not illusion and folly.

Down in the world he might be a small nervous creature, not wholly at ease among the big and tough and successful, but in his attic he knew that he was going to surpass them all one day. His dream, soaring to its highest, even into the stratosphere, saw the book's publication as a young man's triumph that had not been equaled since they flung the copies of Byron's *Childe Harold* from the publisher's windows to the clamoring buyers below. Like Byron he would wake to find himself famous. Along with fame would come her desirable sister wealth; and Kerry from his height of fame and wealth would do handsome —and picturesque—things for Pearl and for Godfrey. Upon Godfrey he would smile down in friendly fashion and, disdaining all malice, be generous to him with gifts and help and coals of fire.

Back at his table, spectacles pushed home, brow cupped in a hand, he wrote. He halted the pen, wrote again, stopped again, and wrote on. The scene that he was trying to create tonight showed Sir Nicholas fighting under the grand master, in the famous defense of Rhodes. A most colorful scene. A far more picturesque scene than that in which he himself was playing a part, which was no more than that of an underpaid clerk fighting with fate in an attic, while the unheeding tides of London's traffic roared about him, beyond his window and beneath his care.

6

Because the earplugs muted all sounds, it was only at the third time that he heard a dubious and apologetic knocking on his door.

"Damn!" he muttered. "It's the Comer-up and Dropper-in."

This was what he now called the Commodore in merry chatter with Pearl (when they were on chatting terms), because Mr. Windsor, frequently attacked by ennui in his room below, and fully charged by this time with affection for "the little Betterkins," was likely to come up at any moment and drop in for a little talk. Having possessed himself, after a few such visitations, of Kerry's great secret, he would usually declare his determination not to interrupt "the great work," and stay in his chair nonetheless.

Oh, well . . . let him come, thought Kerry. Never could he discourage an interrupter (unless it was Pearl); never protest "Oh, God in heaven, can't you see that I'm working?" lest he hurt them, and lest they ceased to like him. So he flung up his fingers to remove the earplugs, but then decided to leave them in place, hoping this incursion might be brief. And he bellowed gaily, *"Come* in, sir."

The low attic door opened and the undulant white hair and pale, sculptured features of Mr. George Windsor came around its rim. "Ah," he said. "Don't let me disturb the divine afflatus."

"She's in the next room," said Kerry. With the plugs in position he had heard only the shrouded ghosts of his visitor's words; and it was his guess that George, in his extravagant style, had said something about "Miss Pearl, the divine lady." "She's dealing with the food, I think. Cold meat and bread."

"I'm sorry to hear that." Mr. Windsor spoke sympathetically; and it would seem, from later words of his, that he had understood Kerry to be saying that Pearl had got a cold and gone to bed—or something in that fashion. He pursued, "We thought she wasn't looking well. So pale."

"What?" demanded Kerry, who'd caught some of this and couldn't conceive to what it referred.

"I said we both think she looks dreadfully pale. But she's recently been ill, as you told us."

"Recently believed as I what?"

"What?" begged Mr. Windsor, at a loss in his turn.

"Oh, death and the devil!" Kerry laughed, whipping out the earplugs and dragging off his spectacles, as if their removal also would help his hearing. "Now I can hear. What did you say?"

"I said, 'Don't let me disturb the divine afflatus,' " Mr. Windsor repeated, but he came into the room just the same.

"Oh, that doesn't matter." Kerry smiled encouragement. "I saw you at your window just now, as I came up the street."

"Me?" The lifting of his eyebrows, the lights of surprise and doubt in his eyes, the incipient shake of a fine head were all the best of an actor's art. They implied that Kerry must surely be mistaken, since it was no habit of his visitor to stand at a window and look down the street. If there is a point where an unspoken lie is no longer a lie but an excellent piece of acting and therefore praiseworthy rather than blameworthy, Mr. Windsor had just stood nicely upon it. He now sat himself in a chair by the wall.

"I will not stay, dear boy. Evie is out, and I heard you moving overhead, so I thought that perhaps you might be free for a little converse, but I see you are nobly at work, at work. Did you say that your sister was ill and had gone to bed?"

"I? I said nothing of the kind."

"Nothing of the what?"

"The kind."

"Oh yes, she certainly is."

Kerry left it where it had arrived. With a nod he agreed that Pearl was kind.

And George admitted, "I suppose I didn't quite hear you aright. I must confess to being a tiny bit deaf sometimes. A bad thing for an actor. Either you don't hear your cue or you hear it long before it's spoken and say your piece, and then the sequence of ideas can be rather a problem for the audience. It never mattered in the plays of Sir James Barrie, of course, because the audience supposed it was just Barrie being whimsical and they pretended to understand, even laughing extra loud, to hide their bewilderment. I must have got Sir James quite a few laughs that he hadn't earned himself. Ah, I may joke about it, but it was one of the things that put an end to my career. Who wants a deaf old actor? But I could have managed. Beethoven managed. . . ."

Kerry, perceiving that there was no hope of work, leaned back in his chair. He tilted the chair onto its hind legs and stretched his feet under the table.

Mr. Windsor, sitting against the wall, continued. "Another thing that helped to finish me off, my dear boy, was my name."

"How do you mean?"

"Don't you notice anything remarkable about my name?"

"I do not."

"George Windsor. It's my real name—no stage name—and I thought it suited a romantic actor rather well."

"So it does."

"In my best days, when I still dreamed my dreams, I had ridiculous hopes of turning it into Sir George Windsor."

Sir John Betterkin, thought his listener. Sir Kenrick Betterkin.

"And it is possible I was on the way to doing it. I was near enough to the top when I was playing with dear Tree and dear Hare and my beloved Martin Harvey. But then, as you will remember, in the year 1917 our good and patriotic King George, rather than be thought a German, assumed my name by royal proclamation. My dear lad, he became George Windsor—and it wasn't his name at all. His name was Guelph. It was my name, inherited from a dear and honored father. And, lo, it suddenly became slightly ridiculous on a program. They wanted me to change it in case it was lese majesty of some sort, but I said I'd see the government and the Privy Council and the prison commission in hell before I changed it. I'd spent thirty years trying to assemble a little fame around it, and was I to cast it from me now? Between ourselves, my dear boy, I did for a moment consider changing it to George Guelph—as would have been only fair—but the few I suggested this to were discouraging: they felt it might be some sort of offense against our Sovereign Lord the King, His Crown and Dignity. I had another suggestion: that His Majesty might, of his grace and dignity and since he surely owed me some small reparation, change Mr. George into Sir George Windsor, which would at once avoid any confusion between us. But I can't feel that anyone conveyed this most equitable idea to him. In this world one's disappointments mean precious little to anyone but oneself. Prepare, my boy, to suffer alone."

"Do you really think the name mattered all that?" Kerry swung his chair to and fro on its back legs.

Mr. Windsor shrugged. "Perhaps not. Perhaps I exaggerate. Maybe a new generation had arisen that had little use for the old faces and the old styles." He looked at Kerry's manuscript books and at the pen that was still in his hand. "You can thank your stars that the fame you seek is not on the stage. An author never knows for certain that he is cast out and done with, and that soon no one will know his name or how good his work was. An author can hope that his books are being read and loved somewhere—they probably are not, but he can keep his hope —and that one day they will be crowned as classics—they won't, of course, but he can die thinking it. Your actor knows that all his finest efforts perished on the air as he created them. They are gone—gone for nothing—into the everlasting silence."

Listening, Kerry felt a compulsive and swelling certainty that no such death would attend his efforts.

And Mr. Windsor, as if he'd caught the edges of this thought, sighed and said, "I'm not so sour that, having missed the luck myself, I want no one else to have it. I wish you all you wish yourself, and I expect that's a fine lot. Confess that you want nothing less than immortality."

"Nothing less." It was curious, but, this friendly neighbor having trapped his secret, Kerry enjoyed pouring out to him the whole of his ideas and hopes. He spoke of them at length now, with many a joke and much loud laughter at his own jokes, tilting back in his chair.

But always, when Kerry wanted to talk and joke, Mr. Windsor

would sit by the wall with a kind of stately patience, occasionally smiling but rather in politeness than in enjoyment of someone else's joke. Indeed, it was likely that he had not grasped the joke because he was thinking of what he would say next about himself. If there is such a thing as an impatient patience adorned with intermittent smiles, this was it.

"Yes," he said when Kerry paused and the answer should have been no. "Yes. Of course. Certainly. I used to think sometimes, as I walked along to the theater, that none of these commonplace pedestrians knew that a man with a name that would become immortal was walking just behind them or just in front or—"

"Oh, but I do that! I think that often," said, Kerry laughing.

"Yes . . . yes . . . and sometimes I used to—do you indeed? Really? You too?—sometimes I used to think, if some woman asked me the way, 'You will never know, my dear, that it was George Windsor who gave you that information.' And if some fool, speaking about someone else, said to me, 'You've got to make excuses, you know, for people with genius,' I used to think, 'Good God, man, don't you realize you're talking to one—' "

"I know!" cried Kerry, as one who was delighted to meet a similar sufferer. "And when they say, 'Ordinary people like you and me,' don't you want to retort, 'Ordinary yourself!'? I always do."

"I did once—once upon a time—but that's all over now. Can you imagine what it's like to walk past the windows of theaters where they wanted you once? I am very silent if I walk down Shaftesbury Avenue now. Very silent, my dear boy. Just thinking, The long fight is done, and the answer is defeat. . . . But, mind you, I sometimes tell myself that to know when to give up the battle, to recall one's forces and to send them home with thanks, is a kind of victory. You agree? A very sorrowful victory, though. 'Tread light o'er the dead in the valley.' But once your campaign is declared at an end"—and here he shrugged sadly —"what, I ask you, is really left but to die? Nowadays I often find myself envying everyone I think of who is safely dead. Even those who were hanged. Their troubles are over. Were it not for my dear comrade, Evie, my very gallant comrade, I'm not at all sure I wouldn't claim every man's right to close down his business in this world and retire with dignity. But Evie's been my loyal comrade through everything and it wouldn't be fair to hurt her so cruelly and leave her all alone."

[57]

"No, you mustn't do that." Kerry laughed. "No, no."

A lifting of the white eyebrows, and of the shoulders, suggested that Mr. Windsor wasn't so sure he mustn't. "Any man has the right to stop playing a game if he's weary of it."

"Oh, no, George, he hasn't. Not till the whistle goes."

"Oh . . . ah . . . well. . . ." Liking a picturesque metaphor, George was momentarily cornered by this one. But he managed to elude it. "One may retire hurt," he said.

"Well, please don't, for all our sakes. Stay on the field."

"Of course, if Evie came too, it would be all right. But she would not, I think, do that. She does not grieve as I do. Not but what she has every cause to weep: a very lovely actress, forgotten. But she has the gift of acceptance, which I so conspicuously lack. Women are wonderful. No, I don't feel she'd consent to come along too."

"Glad to hear that. We certainly can't spare *her*."

"Talking about death, I sometimes look at those extremely narrow stairs and wonder how they'd ever get Evie's coffin down them. Me they could get down quite easily. There's ample space for my shrunk shank. But Evie? Still . . . in a couple of hundred years I suppose many a fine handsome lady has gone down those stairs, feet first, and with her troubles all over. Do you ever think of these things on the stairs?"

"Often and often. On any stairs that are centuries old."

"Good. Then you are an artist, my boy, and may do great things. Go on working and hoping that you will achieve all your ambitions. Some do. One in ten thousand does. I will pray daily for your success. And now I must go from you—"

"No, no, don't go," Kerry begged, unwilling to let anyone think his presence wasn't wanted.

"Yes, I will go. I have enjoyed hearing all your hopes and ideas. But now—"

"No," Kerry persisted, though pleased at the prospect of working again.

"Yes, yes." Mr. Windsor rose like a man of understanding and self-command. He swept an elegant hand toward Kerry's books and pen. "*Au revoir*, dear lad. I leave you with every good wish, and not a little confidence, to the divine afflatus."

With two affectionate smiles, one following three seconds after the other, he went through the door, closing it very gently on such good work and fine hopes.

The next dubious knock on the door was Pearl's. It was more than dubious, it was timid; if a knock can sob and snuffle, this one did. And Kerry's heart rushed toward it even faster than his body. "Rome was not built in a day," he had said when contemplating, without hope of early action, an apology to Pearl and a reconciling kiss. But by now he had built in his heart this City of Penitence; indeed, it was towering there, and when he saw her before him, bearing on a tray a little pressed beef and a little lettuce, it flung its gates wide to her, as to a conqueror. He took the tray, placed it on the table, and then, with his hands on her shoulders, kissed her. She smiled gratefully through eyes lately wet and asked if he was going to work much longer.

"Yes," he said, happy to be able to joke with her again. "The Comer-up and Dropper-in came up and laid waste an hour of my time. But I'm not going to lose that hour. I shall work till midnight."

"Well, then, I'll say good night now," she replied with the same smile. "I'm rather tired, so I think I'll kip down cosily."

Kip down cosily. In an attempt to be jolly too, she had once again made her desperate joking play with an old prison word. He answered nothing but gave her another kiss. It was a salute which, to her mind, was a silent good night but, to his, an award for courage.

7

One morning, in his high garret, hidden from all eyes unless the angels who rejoice to see a sinner repenting were looking down in suspense, Kerry walked about the room engaged in a violent effort to throw the old sinning self off his back. But the more he struggled, the harder gripped that Old Man of the Sea, "the Old 'Un," as he called him when in joking mood with Pearl.

It was June now, and he had two weeks' vacation, which he and Pearl must spend at home because they could afford nothing else. And this morning his better self had most undesirably put a suggestion before him—had thrust it up like a golden crocus above some hard wintry ground. One should not bear malice, said the crocus; one should forgive; one should deal kindly with those that despitefully use one; in short, one should throw overboard one's indignation against brother Godfrey and, trying to understand him, go and tell him that his sister and brother were now living only half a mile from where he sat in such pride and neatness at his desk.

It was a crocus all too golden.

But there had been something fine, one must admit, in the

way Godfrey had raised himself to his present position. By heroic studies, while serving as an articled clerk in the offices of Messrs. Padgett, Liddiard and Co., Solicitors, he had passed his law examinations and taken first-class honors in the finals. He was now a qualified solicitor, with hopes of becoming one day a partner in his famous firm.

But, struggling thus alone against the world, he had refused from the first to do anything to help Pearl. On the occasion of her first arrest for shoplifting, he had refused to come to court and offer to help her, and Kerry had found a somewhat suspect pride in going into the witness box and showing him exactly what he ought to have done. By promising to look after her, Kerry had secured that she should be saved from prison and put on probation. And when she had fallen a second time, during the period of probation, and been sent to prison, it was the same thing: Godfrey had maintained that as a clerk in a lawyer's office and so a servant of the law, it would ill become him to seem lenient to larceny: the real meaning of which was that he wanted none of the mud splashing onto him.

On that first occasion, Pearl being an unimportant school-teacher, the story had not reached the papers, and Kerry, going with her to the headmistress, had persuaded her to take Pearl back. But the second time, after a term in prison, this was no longer possible, and so Kerry had taken her to live with him in his Bayswater lodging, she earning a little now and then with her sewing. Would Godfrey contribute a little to her upkeep? Not a penny. He hadn't, he regretted, a penny to spare.

Pearl had gone many months without succumbing to the horrid compulsion within her, but one day in a Gatts and Welby store, feeling safe in the jostling crowd, she had felt and gratified again this lust to take something without paying for it. She had slipped a cheap but brilliant dress ornament into her bag. And the store detective had been watching her. Prison for a year this time, after stern words from the judge that had found a small place in the evening papers. Once again Kerry had pleaded with Godfrey to join him in helping her on discharge; but Godfrey, strutting up and down his office, dressed in morality, had declared that Kerry was "just being soft and sentimental"; if Pearl would persist in behaving like this, she must take the consequences of her deeds. A sentimental and dangerous fallacy he called Kerry's argument that Pearl's offense was the outcome of a mental aberration that produced an irresistible compulsion. Irresistible compulsions, he said,

pacing the floor in his robes of solemn probity, must be resisted, or the body politic would founder in chaos. And heartily
had Kerry assailed him, pacing back and forth in the robes (as
he thought) of a finer doctorate, until at last he slammed in a
temper out of Godfrey's door. And it was partly to shame
Godfrey that he had set about finding a new retreat for Pearl
and had stood waiting for her at the gates of Holloway jail.

More than a month they'd lived together in Red Lion Street,
and now, this morning, had arisen this unwanted and rather
repellent idea that it would be a handsome action to go to
Godfrey, largely for Pearl's sake, and, telling him how sharply
his spurning hurt her, suggest that they should all forget the
past and be friends together again.

But the more memory threw up some of the things Godfrey
had said, the more angrily Kerry's mouth set and the more
impossible it seemed to speak amiably and laughingly with him.
Oh, to hell, no! Hadn't he described Kerry's plea for pity and
brotherly help as "mere sloppy sentimentality," and called
Pearl a born sponger? Hadn't the bastard affirmed, "You're
doing it really because you want to feel a rather splendid chap"
—a saying that rankled the more because it held an acid of
truth? Hadn't he striven to make Kerry's attempt at generosity
look weak and even silly because he, Godfrey, wanted to escape
his share of a burden? Oh, to hell.

But the love of goodlooking actions, after recent practice in
the same, had become an enlarging motive in Kerry's heart,
and after a twenty minutes' struggle, he flung "the Old 'Un"
off his back, flung his bowler hat on (as it were instead), and
went out of the room before the old devil could leap into place
again. He went down the stairs like a man with a devil coming
behind him, and out into the street.

Only the old Fleet Valley lay between Kerry and Godfrey
now. Kerry crossed the valley in the neighborhood of Saffron
Hill. By traversing Saffron Hill and Hatton Garden and Leather
Lane he crossed a sloping area that was once as infested with
rogues as a piece of dead meat with flies, and came forthwith
into the world of the lawyers, part of whose occupation was to
deal with—and sometimes for—these gentlemen on the left.
Here and hereabouts were the inns of court and chancery,
those old palaces and halls, those academes and plots, of the
law: Gray's Inn, Lincoln's Inn, Staple Inn. By a dark, mean

passage in High Holborn he came into the walled reservation of Gray's Inn and, halting by the railings of its garden, gazed at the lawns and walks now freckled with the shadows of gently moving leaves.

Not in all its thousand years, he thought, had London been able to drive its roaring tides over this place of virgin earth, now so silent under its trees. The tall plane trees in full leaf darkened the grass beneath them to a deep blue-green; and after the riot of the streets the silence struck like a blow. Only slowly through the silence came the rumor of a distant tide in Theobald's Road.

Being Kerry, who must ever re-create the past and who had had reason to study the long history of these old inns, he saw Francis, Lord Bacon, resplendent in purple satin and velvet, walking under the trees and composing perhaps the sentence "God Almighty first planted a garden." Was it not said that he himself had directed the laying out of this garden? He saw John Evelyn and Goldsmith and Wolsey and Sir Philip Sidney, and others who had been members or guests of the inn, all taking their turn under the trees as if they were contemporaries and history a single now. He certainly saw Pepys walking there with an eye for the ladies, both the fashionable and the frail; for the walks were then a fashionable promenade, like the park in later days. "Hence to Gray's Inn Walks all alone"—i.e., without his wife—"and with great pleasure seeing the fine ladies there." How quiet the walks now—fashion and fine ladies and the ladies of the town having long since deserted them. Only the ghosts pass and promenade under the tall trees for those who can see them.

Moving on to the long, dark barrack called Raymond Buildings, he passed in by one of its six arched entries, his eyes falling as always on the painted names of those firms which occupied chambers or offices on either side of the worn stone stairs. One legend on the arch's side he must always glance at:

1st and 2nd Pairs, Padgett, Liddiard & Co.
Solicitors, Commissioners for Oaths

Removing his bowler hat, for he could pass no lintel with his head covered, he mounted the stairs' hollowed stones and walked through an open door on the second floor.

He was greeted by an enormous young clerk, much too fat for his age and with a voice so high as to make one wonder if

[63]

it had some curious root in the depths of his six feet of fat—
whether the loftier one's head, the higher the pitch of one's
voice. "Yes?" piped this clerk, whom Kerry had never seen
before.

"Could I speak to Mr. Godfrey?"

"You have an appointment?" So high now was the voice that
it suggested an alto singing his descant above the normal me-
lodic air.

"No, I have no appointment, but I have a certain connection
with your Mr. Godfrey. He is my brother."

"Oh?" The young mountain looked so surprised that the
sensitive Kerry wondered if he thought him too small and
insignificant to be Mr. Godfrey's brother. "Believe it or not, it
is so," he said, half facetiously, half irritably.

"Your name, then, sir?"

"Curiously enough, it's the same as his."

"Oh, yes, of course, but I thought perhaps—"

"No, he has only one brother." And ministering to the irritability, he added, *"And* a sister."

"I'll see if he's free."

"I'll wait till he's free," said Kerry defiantly, but then, thinking that the Old 'Un was mounting again, he managed to produce for the clerk a friendly smile.

"If you'll just take a chair in the waiting room, sir . . ."

The window of the waiting room looked out onto the garden, so Kerry did not take a chair but stood gazing down at
those haunted lawns and walks. Nothing moved in them, not
even the mottled shadows under the trees, until, after a time,
Kerry saw some Tudor and Stuart divines strolling across the
shadows. They were in their white lawn rochets and black satin
chimeres—robes which they had scarcely worn when they
walked here in the flesh but which they had donned very properly, now that they were but ghostly shades. Over there by the
old catalpa tree he observed a poet, George Chapman, standing alone with his head down because it was heavy with lines
of splendor that would march alongside the great swinging
hexameters of Homer. There was no reason why he should not
be standing by that old tree if, as all the benchers, barristers,
students, servants, and sitting tenants of the inn liked to believe, it was planted by Bacon or Raleigh, his contemporaries.

Some rooks flew above an elm, and immediately his eyes fell
upon the long gray-black barrack of Verulam Buildings, which
bounded the garden on the far side, and he thought of it as a

rookery for lawyers with black gowns for wings. Beyond this rookery, on the other side of the Gray's Inn Road, were the old rookeries of the thieves . . . not all gone yet, perhaps. . . .

These thoughts filled his mind for a minute or two, only to yield their place to an irritation at being kept waiting like this. The irritation swelled with every second; he beat his fingers on the windowsill and a toe on the floorboard beneath it; his mouth grew squarer; and it could be said that the Old 'Un was nearly aboard again.

In a room along the passage four walls away, Godfrey also stood looking out at the garden. But he was not seeing it, nor any ghosts among the trees, because he was seeing Kerry in the waiting room and Pearl in some other room he knew not where. And since any man dislikes a sense of guilt, he too was beating a distressed and worrying toe.

What could Kerry want? Last time they had parted with angry words, and Kerry had disappeared into a year-long silence, which had suited Godfrey well. And now here he was again, come out of the silence.

Godfrey Betterkin was the youngest of the family, and the only handsome one, rather as if his parents, like some authors, after a series of failures had surprised the critics with a success. He was some inches taller than either Pearl or Kerry; his figure was slight and neat; and his features were handsome enough to have been his undoing, since, if you have a face that everyone admires, you are apt to be unscrupulous in making a career to match it. Unscrupulous in private affairs only, of course— not public; he had built his career on the right side of the Gray's Inn Road and of the law.

His dress matched well this prospering career: black coat, white collar, gray tie, gray striped trousers. And on a hook behind the door hung a bowler hat smoothly shining and an umbrella rolled so tight that it looked like a black staff. Very different clothes from the doublets and hose in the garden— and as temporary.

"Your brother is here and says he will wait," the fat young clerk had said—or sung.

"My brother? Are you sure?"

"He says so, sir."

"Do you know what he wants?"

"He said something about your sister."

"Oh. . . . Very well. I'll let you know when I'm ready."

The clerk gone, he said, "Damn!" and "Damn!" again.

For Godfrey, like Kerry, had a hidden dream which, like Kerry, he would indulge within the walls of his workroom or staring from its window. A dream that would raise him high but demanded that Pearl and Kerry be kept away. He was always a little ashamed of Kerry's odd shape and large head; and as for Pearl, he wanted the cupboard in which she dwelt, the family skeleton, to be as remote as possible.

Just now there was a conflict in him. A desire to impress Kerry with his prosperity was at issue with a desire to say that he had no money to spare; and while he was considering a way of doing both these things, Kerry must wait in that room. He was quite glad to make him wait: it would impress him with his young brother's distinction and importance.

At last he opened the door and called along the passage to the fat clerk, "All right, Edwin. I can see him now."

Kerry heard this and said, "Damn his insolence." The clerk summoned him, "like a jailer summoning a prisoner before the magistrate," and he went through the door indicated. He saw his brother standing behind his desk with a pencil twisting in his fingers. Place and action suggested that he was not expecting, or encouraging, a long visit. "Hallo, Kerry," he said. And "Thank you, Edwin" to the fat clerk.

With a strong effort Kerry had contrived to unhorse the Old 'Un and leave him in the waiting room, so he was able to grin at Godfrey as if there were something comic in this encounter. He looked at Godfrey's black coat and striped trousers. "Ah, the full regalia," he said. "More of a barrister's kit, isn't it? The senior service, what? Do tell me, why do lawyers always wear black, like undertakers? Is it because they're in mourning for the weaknesses of humanity?"

Godfrey did not answer but tossed his head impatiently, so Kerry pursued the jest. "The grave and reverend suitings of the law. You are the fully fledged little solicitor now?"

Godfrey didn't care for the word "little." His success in climbing to his present position was spoken of by other people with serious admiration; why should Kerry treat it with levity? Probably because he was jealous. "I have qualified, yes," he said.

"You passed your finals with some distinction, I heard."

"I did." He would have liked to add "with first-class honors," but felt that this would be too communicative, too chatty. It

would spoil the cold dignity he desired to show. So he said only
—and coldly, "That was months ago. Did you want to ask me
something?"

"Rather, to tell you something. Do visitors sit down in
here?"

"Of course." Godfrey set the example. He dropped to his
chair behind the desk, keeping the pencil in his fingers.

"I am not disturbing any divine afflatus?" asked Kerry before
doing anything so irrevocable as to sit down.

"Any what? . . . Oh, I see. . . ." A joke, presumably. "No."

So Kerry sat himself in the client's chair on the layman's side
of the desk.

"We are busy, of course." Godfrey pulled out some papers
and dropped them, as if to emphasize this. "We are always
busy. And you? You are not at the office this morning?"

"This is my vacation, which I'm spending very pleasantly
walking about the streets of London. Mainly round about the
old Fleet Valley. A wonderful holiday resort, if you've a certain
amount of knowledge and a large amount of imagination. Little
Saffron Hill, Hatton Garden, Vine Street, Turnmill Street—
don't these names make you think of the meadows and the
vines and the saffrons on the hillside, and the water mills that
used to be here instead of all this bricks and muck?" He swept
a hand toward most of Holborn and Clerkenwell.

Godfrey couldn't truthfully say they had done this, so he said
nothing.

"I now live in Clerkenwell, and Pearl lives with me." Ah, that
should be one in the eye for him—but stay! had the Old 'Un
come along the passage to take a part in this interview? Had
he arrived in the room? If so, send him back to the waiting
room. "And, Godfrey, don't you think it'd be ridiculous for us
both to be so close to you and not to see something of you
sometimes?"

So close. Fear lodged in Godfrey's heart. Had these two
come close to his dream to undersap it, to explode a mine
beneath it?

A silence, which Kerry broke. "I'm all for burying the brotherly hatchets, myself."

"You know what I feel about Pearl?"

"Indeed I do." (Or I know what it suits you to pretend you
feel.) "But let's forget that. We can agree to differ."

"Does Pearl want to see me? She doesn't love me, I imagine?"

"I can manage Pearl all right."

"She will never understand that I refused to help her in court because I thought it best for her to take the consequences of her acts and be brought to her senses. Shock treatment, I think it is called. But she'll never believe that I tried to act for her good."

"Probably not." (Nor I.) "But she's had her treatment now."

"Done her any good, do you think?"

"None whatever. Probably made her worse."

"Well, don't be so cheerful about it. It's not pleasant to have a sister who's a criminal."

"Pearl is no criminal."

"Indeed?"

"No, she has some queer mental kink; that is all."

"And are we to say that about every petty thief?"

"Oh, no; not at all. I'm sure plenty of them are very bad lads. But Pearl is not like them."

"I fail to see the difference."

"And to me it's as clear as day. Doesn't the fact that some of the things she's stolen have hardly any use or value show you that the stealing is an irrational act, a tic, a heaven-knows-what? The thing stolen ministers somehow to a sense of deprivation. Pearl is nearly forty and unlovely and without hope of marriage or children. Did you know that one of the things she stole was a child's toy—a doll dressed like a policeman?"

"I thought it was generally clothes she took."

"Sometimes they are. Frilly little garments suitable to someone much younger than herself. Godfrey, she once took a china vase that was exactly like those we had on the mantelpiece when we were children."

"Well, what do you make of that?"

"That it revived for her a time when she was happy."

"Oh, to the deuce with that, Kerry. Who's going to accept *that* as a defense for stealing?"

"No one. But the very fact that it's stealing and against the law is somehow a part of the compensation, I fancy." And to provoke him further, he added, "There's a small defiance in it that's not unheroic."

"Good lord! I should like to hear you tell that to a magistrate. A very convenient defense."

"And perhaps a true one."

"My dear Kerry, the magistrates are sick of this sort of talk. They get all too much of it."

"Possibly because it's often true. Especially in the case of lonely and miserable women. Godfrey, I wish you could have seen our Pearl in court that first time—paralyzed with fright and clutching a testimonial from her Deal Road School as she whispered, 'Guilty.' "

Godfrey looked down upon his blotting pad, not wishing to hear an old story that might require from *him* a plea of "Guilty." And Kerry went on, "Has it ever occurred to you to wonder why these shoplifters are always women?"

"I can't say it has."

His manner as he said this was so superior that Kerry felt eager to prick it with a little sharp indecency. "I should have thought it was obvious. A woman can't release her tensions as a man can by hurrying into bed with a ten-shilling tart."

Godfrey blinked at the word, but said nothing. He just declined to discuss a subject treated in such language. Instead he asked, "Has Pearl any means of livelihood?"

"No. Destitute." Let him have the word in his face.

"And you are keeping her? How do you manage that?"

"By living in an attic among the chimneys."

"And you think that I ought to contribute to her support?"

"Oh, no—not unless you want to. She'll soon have some sewing jobs again. She was always good with her needle, and she had plenty of practice in prison."

Godfrey nodded at the pencil on the blotting pad. "As you know, I've had hardly a penny piece to spare all the time I've been getting qualified. I've had to skimp and borrow, skimp and borrow. Why, I went hungry sometimes."

"So have I. Sometimes."

But Godfrey wished to continue about himself. "Things are better now, I admit. I earn a fair income, but most of it's mortgaged to those good people who advanced me money. And in spite of what everyone thinks, lawyers aren't making much these days. Statutory fees remain fixed while the cost of living goes up and up. If it were not that conveyancing fees were determined by the price paid"—plainly he enjoyed spreading his legal terms before Kerry; was he not now a qualified solicitor?—"and if real property hadn't risen with everything else, we should be in a bad way."

"But I thought I saw that you were acting for the wealthy and notorious Lady Kantz in her divorce case?"

"Lady Kantz is not notorious. She is a very pleasant person."

"I would have called her an old vulgarian, with her mink and her diamonds."

"Nor is she all that old. Forty-two, perhaps."

"In her pictures in the papers she looks an old Jezebel. But, anyhow, I hope you made a lot of money out of her."

"I don't think we went into the case for that purpose."

"Oh, come! You're not going to tell me that the thought of good money was never in your mind. I must say I was surprised at a good Socialist like you acting for a red-hot Tory like the Kantz woman."

"Politics don't enter into it. And in any case Mr. Liddiard is every bit as reactionary a Tory as Lady Kantz. And, for my part, I hope I can respect other people's views. As a person, I quite like Lady Kantz."

"But as a convinced and fervent Socialist you can't approve of all that disgusting wealth and vulgar display?"

"Certainly not. In my private capacity."

"Good. You won the case for her?"

"We got her her decree nisi. Now she's just waiting for the absolute."

"Waiting for the Absolute. . . . Dear me, isn't that what we're all doing?"

"What do you mean? . . . Oh, I see. . . ." A joke.

"And you stung poor old Sir Amiel for buckets of maintenance, I hope."

"He can afford it all."

"Jew against Jew, was it?"

"Lady Kantz isn't Jewish. He is, but she's a Gentile and an ardent Christian."

"Oh, yes, I remember: she's something big in the Anglo-Catholic movement, isn't she?"

"She's a devoted churchwoman, if that's what you mean."

"Well, I suppose it's possible for some sort of Christianity to coalesce with all that luxury and ostentation; but I can never see how, myself."

Perhaps the word "luxury" reminded Godfrey of something he wanted Kerry to know, because he suddenly said, "In addition to most of my income being mortgaged, there are heavy expenses in this profession."

"Such as?"

Godfrey, picking up the pencil, dropped it twice and thrice on the blotting pad, while he tried to assemble some expenses. "One has to keep up appearances. One has to entertain. . . .

Incidentally, for the purposes of entertaining, I'm going to join a club. Boodle's. Mr. Liddiard says he can get me into it, which is really rather remarkable because there's usually a waiting list half a mile long."

"Well, lucky you."

"Yes, but it's an expense. Fifteen guineas subscription." He said this proudly. "And an entrance fee."

"How much is the entrance fee?"

Godfrey was certainly on a tightrope now. How boast of his expensive club without appearing well off and capable of subsidizing the family?

"Thirty guineas; but he has intimated most generously that he'll advance me the money as long as my circumstances are somewhat straitened."

Once again his language was so pompous that Kerry felt the need to tickle the sides of it with a rapier of vulgar slang. "You seem to be this old bugger's fair-haired boy," he said.

Godfrey raised his eyebrows in some discomfort at hearing the senior partner called one of those. "I think I've always stood fairly high in his opinion, if that's what you mean."

"That's exactly what I mean."

"Yes, he . . . do you know what he suggested the other day? He suggested that I might stand for Parliament."

"Parliament? Why not the throne?"

"Now, don't be absurd. Don't be cheap. But I should give him the surprise of his life if I stood for Parliament. He's a keen Tory, and he doesn't realize that if I were a candidate, it would certainly be in the Labour interest."

"Can't you tell him you're a Socialist?"

"Oh dear no! It would shake him a lot and upset quite a few of our best clients. But, between you and me, that's a situation that's not going to last much longer. Very soon it'll be more than respectable to be a Labour candidate; it'll be the thing. Everyone who can really sense the political climate knows that in a few years' time Labour will be the strongest party in the country."

"And then, when it's the thing, you may stand as a Socialist?"

"I might."

"Well, that's interesting. But we were talking about Pearl."

"Oh, yes. Well, I would like to help in a small way. But it can only be small. And only for a limited period. What do you say to—let me see—ten shillings a week until such time as she gets some work?"

"I say that's splendid. It'll keep her for one day a week."

"Rubbish. It'll do more than that. But if it's no use to you, say so. And understand: it's only given on the understanding that Pearl makes no effort to get in touch with me."

"Oh, it's like that, is it?"

"Yes. I am sorry, but I have rather strict standards—I'm not ashamed of them—and I can't appear to countenance petty crime."

"I see. Godfrey, may I ask, are you still an atheist?'

"Of course."

"Why 'of course'?"

"Because I'm at a loss to understand how any man of intelligence can be anything else."

"Then in the name of intelligent atheism, will you tell me where you get your high moral standards from? If there's no God, aren't you free of the old Decalogue and—"

"I can't agree—" Godfrey began.

"But if there's nothing in heaven or earth to believe in, why the hell have any standards but a comfortable, cautious selfishness?"

Godfrey frowned, not seeing an answer immediately before him. "One can arrive at high standards by reason alone."

"Not without belief in *something.*"

"Are you telling me *you* believe in God?"

"Yes, certainly." Kerry told him this mainly because he must needs oppose him. Really he wasn't at all sure that he believed in God.

"Well, it defeats me. You should read Huxley and Spenser. And Tyndall and Karl Marx." Most obviously his tone implied that he could only rate Kerry's intelligence as lower than his own, and that he would like, were it not rude, to dismiss it with a "Sancta Simplicitas!"

This greatly incensed Kerry, who held that Godfrey's intelligence was less than his, and who lived, accordingly, with a sense of injustice that Godfrey should be the successful one. "I dare say I've read quite as much as you on these subjects. And I most certainly believe in God." For a moment this was nearer the truth than it had ever been before. Godfrey's atheism had almost convinced him of the existence of God. If Godfrey didn't believe in Him, it was necessary to create Him.

"And I think Him a medieval superstition," said Godfrey, "only kept alive by a worldwide publicity organization called the Church."

"Well, anyhow, alive or dead or nonexistent, He tells me that I ought to care for a sister who's helpless and unhappy. But I see no reason why you, a good atheist, should think like that, so I feel that Pearl and I had best manage without your filthy ten shillings."

"Oh, if you're going to talk like that—" and Kerry perceived at once that while Godfrey was offended by this spurning of his offer, he was also relieved by it.

"I am certainly going to talk like that. Before I go." Because he had risen from his chair and was holding its back with a trembling hand. It was the Old Self, slipped into the room again and safely on his shoulders, that was making his whole frame tremble. "I'm going to tell you that in my view you're only an atheist because you want to think yourself intellectually superior to other people; only a Socialist because you fancy there's a career there for you; and only a professor of exalted standards because it sounds right in a little lawyer. Your high standards are just as much part of your uniform as that damned silly black coat and that bloody silly rolled umbrella behind the door."

Godfrey rose. "Perhaps, if that's what you think, you'll get out of my office."

"Certainly I will; but not till I've added that you've no real morality except that which advances the career of Godfrey Betterkin; and that, in my humble view, your mind's an incoherent mess."

With that he went out; and in that explosive minute both brothers were relieved: Kerry was shaken and sick but relieved because he'd given issue to surging resentments; and Godfrey was bruised and furious but relieved because a quarrel so violent must surely mean that all links between him and Kerry and Pearl were finally severed.

Kerry stormed out into the Gray's Inn squares, seeing no ghosts anymore, but thinking that one day brother Godfrey would have to look up to him on his seat of greatness with the concentrated envy of all twelve—or was it eleven?—of Joseph's brethren, when they had to come and plead before His All-Powerful Highness in the land of Egypt.

8

Kerry, leaving Clerkenwell Green one evening, crossed the deep railway cutting and came into the pit of Ray Street. All roads, from north and east, south and west, dip down into Ray Street, so that it looks like a basin with a public house in it and a printing works and some tall dwellings built by the city during Victoria's reign. Once a sump of stinking water from the overflow of the Fleet River, it later became a sump of iniquity. In those days it was called Hockley-in-the-Hole (which roughly means slime in a pit) and it rivaled its villainous sister, Turnmill Street, as a reservoir of vice. The streets that dip down into it, Warner Street, Little Saffron Hill, Back Hill, Crawford's Passage, were all streets of ill fame, but none had such a name for depravity as Hockley-in-the-Hole. Apparently the lower the earth level, the greater the pollution.

Ray Street was not like this now. It was quiet, and as respectable as any other tenement area in Holborn or Clerkenwell. And this Saturday evening Kerry's eyes were on the tall block of tenement dwellings called Bethesda Buildings. They rose out of the basin six stories high, row upon row of windows in walls soot-black after years of smoke from factory, foundry, and railway. They presented five railed landings open to the London air; and toward these entrance landings two stone stairways went spiraling up into the bricks, with the twisted route of a corkscrew in a cork. Washing hung from the roofs of these landings, and baby carriages stood pushed against their rails. But Bethesda Buildings, if dingy and grim, were not squalid. You could see by the cheap clean curtains in some windows, and by the window boxes on some sills, with their few disconsolate geraniums, that house pride in plenty bloomed within those soot-imprinted, mold-lichened walls.

Kerry's eyes were on the third landing, watching. Steps sounded up there, and a young woman came around a bend from her tenement door. She leaned over the railings, saw him on the street cobbles, and smiled. Not otherwise, perhaps, did Juliet look down from her balcony upon the young man below, in Capulet's garden. She waved and ran happily to the stone stairs. As she passed, one could see that her figure was no Juliet's; it had none of the richness nursed and nourished in a wealthy home. Her body was meager and slope-shouldered, as if life in that airless block had constricted its sapling growth, but like the windows about her it was cheaply adorned for beauty with a dress of royal blue and a necklace of imitation pearls.

Now she was at the foot of the corkscrew stairs and coming out of the black bricks through one of the arched entries. Odd the contrast between a girl dressed for beauty and the close stale air that came so often from the archway like breath from the mouth of a constipated man.

"How's our Sally Penelope?" asked Kerry, stretching both hands toward her.

"Sally Penelope's fine," she said, and looped his left arm in both her hands.

Her face was no more beautiful than her body. It was narrow, with slightly prominent teeth and what so often goes with them, a slightly indrawn chin. Her only beauties were her dark hair, white skin, and large eyes as blue as her dark-blue dress. The dreaming spirit of the created world found an outlet in those eyes. There the dreams were multitudes.

Kerry, looking first at the blue dress (which she'd put on to please him because he liked her in it) and then at her eyes, grinned and quoted, as he often did, "Sally Penelope, 'girt with dark growths and yet glimmering with one star.' "

"Don't be *silly*," she said, but squeezed his arm gratefully all the same. "Such *stuff*."

"It's not silly at all. It exactly describes our Sally."

"Oh, *stop* it," she begged, delighted. "You're ever so silly sometimes. You are, really."

By none but Kerry was she called Sally. Her real name was Esther Penelope Finch; but in Warner Street, just around the red belly of the pub, there had lived, two hundred years before, a certain music master and songwriter who one day chanced to watch a poor shoemaker's apprentice treating his girl to a real slap-up holiday, with visits to a puppet show and the swings and the Farthing Pye House, where he gave her buns and frumenty and cheesecake and ale. So pleased was he with this London idyl that he went home to Warner Street and wrote a lyric. It began:

> Of all the girls that are so smart,
> There's none like pretty Sally;
> She is the darling of my heart,
> And she lives in our alley.

It was not in Esther Finch to have known this story—indeed, it is doubtful if anyone else in Ray Street, or in all Clerkenwell, knew it—but it was exactly the kind of thing that Kerry would know; and he instructed her in it and thenceforth called her Sally.

Not content with her hands on his arm he removed them and embraced her, and since he enjoyed the embrace it was she who had to disengage herself, but not before she had whispered, "Darling Kerry."

"Exactly," he said. "So why break away?"

"Because it's not quite nice—not in the street."

"On the contrary, it's extremely nice."

"But someone might see." She put her hand near his arm again. "Let's go."

"Where, lady?"

"I don't know," she replied unhelpfully.

"Anywhere take your fancy?"

"No."

"Then it's a case for the royal nose." He took a penny from his pocket, slapped it blindly onto his palm, turned its head upward, and lo! the nose of King George V pointed toward the northeast.

"Okay," he agreed; and, putting her hand back into his arm, led her up the slopes of Warner Street and Bakers Row. Arm in arm, they turned into the Farringdon Road and climbed toward the tossed-up squares of northern Clerkenwell.

The Saturday quiet was in the Farringdon Road. All the factories, works, and shops were shut; the sidewalks seemed empty except for straying lovers like themselves, and a few children at their play; and even the traffic was quieter because it was mainly "through" traffic, passing Clerkenwell on its way. The cars, as if they had caught this weekend mood, seemed to hurry past on muted tires. A bright evening sunlight gave clearness and precision to the house walls and to the refuse and litter of the day; and one could almost imagine that the quiet aided it in bringing all things into focus so clearly.

Since there was no place for courting in the Bethesda tenement or in the attics of Red Lion Street—Mr. Bill Finch sitting in the one, and Pearl in the other—Kerry and Sally Penelope, like most couples in Clerkenwell, had to do their courting in the streets; and today they wandered for mile upon mile, linked together, along Clerkenwell's old residential roads and its long-decayed squares, up there on the hills. At last, coming southward again and down the ramped streets, her arm about his waist, his arm along her meager shoulders, they turned into Clerkenwell Close. This serpentine road with its factories and business houses winds along where once ran the cloisters of St. Mary's nunnery, and these two unbeautiful lovers, the man too small, the girl too thin, strolled along, delighting each in the other's body, where once the nuns of Our Lady paced in their virgin chastity.

As it chanced, both these two were virgins, Kerry because his ardent and nightly creation of a secret dream had drained much desire from him, and Sally Penelope because she lived in Bethesda Buildings and, being ashamed of them, was very proper and genteel.

The Close this evening was almost as quiet as the cloisters it succeeded. Its ancient houses where families could live had been mostly replaced by the premises of blockmakers, glass-workers, engravers, and printers' furnishers; and these workers were gone now to their homes.

Out of the Close they stepped through high railings into St. James's Churchyard, long converted by the borough council into a garden of plane trees, trim grass, and coiling black paths. The displaced gravestones stood propped against the walls around, their white faces peering over privet hedges at people still alive in the upper air. They peered today at three old men smoking in meditative silence, at some children playing on turf and paths, and at Kerry and Sally interlaced on a seat.

Since Kerry and Sally sat with their backs to the privet hedge, a foursome of headstones gazed at the napes of their necks, and at his arm along her shoulders. They saw her press herself against him (since to be proper and genteel is not to lack desire). Later, desire slaked, she began to smoke a cigarette, not very successfully, her middle finger knocking the ash away daintily but far too frequently. It was only lately that she'd consented to smoke in open and public places, and even so she wouldn't do it in the streets. That was not nice, she said. Rather common, she thought. Indelicate. The cigarette ending soon (because she drew at it far too often and too strongly) and desire alive again, she leaned against Kerry and said, "Oh, I wish it were like this always. I want to live with you always and do everything for you."

"So you will. One day."

"No. Never. It's all hopeless. Dad'll never get work again now. He's on the dole for ever. And even the dole isn't much good because he will have his bit on the horses. His bit of hope, he says."

"A pity he and Pearl don't marry. They could look after each other very nicely."

"And live on what?"

"H'm . . . On us, I suppose. We contribute to their upkeep now."

"No. That wouldn't be fair on poor Pearl. Dad's my burden. After all, when he was in work he did pay for me to learn my typing and shorthand instead of sending me out to work. He always said that no lass of his was going to be a factory girl, if he could help it. And Mum was dead then and not bringing in her money. So it's my turn now to look after him. I'm a prisoner just as you are."

"Maybe, maybe, but one day I'm going to build such a prison

as you never saw. Plenty of room in it for you and Pearl—and Dad, if necessary."

She said nothing; as if this intention were easier stated than achieved, and this happy prison but a castle in the far-off clouds.

As she did not speak, he said, "I think he's lucky to have a daughter like you."

"Me? No, I'm not nice. I'm poisonous sometimes. I'm a bag of resentments, and they're always bursting out into irritability. Things that he does aggravate me till I could scream."

"What things?"

"Well . . . there are such a lot of them. . . . One is his habit of taking off his shoes and bending his toes up and down, a hundred times before the fire. He says his feet flatten out after he's walked a mile or so on London streets—"

"They probably do."

"I know—poor lamb—and he says that then they ache and burn like hell. Apparently bending the toes over and over gradually puts out the flames. So every time he comes in he stretches out his legs and bends the toes up and down, down and up, till I want to yell. First one stockinged foot, then the other. They look like two huge gray slugs rearing up on their tails and taking it in turns to bow to the fire. Rather like Chinese mandarins. Sometimes I think, with a quite extraordinary relief, 'Oh, at last it's going to stop, to stop, to stop!' but then the left foot takes over from the right and bows and bows, and I rush from the room. In my room I cry because I'm so stupid and so weak and can't beat these utterly silly aggravations. Poor Dad, why shouldn't he do it if it eases him? Oh, I think I'm *awful*. And usually I'm only a dismal companion for him."

"I don't believe it."

"But it's true, my dear. Most days I'm in the depths of gloom—"

"Like Pearl."

"—and sometimes he breaks out and says he's sick of my everlasting glooms, day after day; he says they're wearisome and driving him potty."

"Oh dear! I've said things like that to Pearl. But why should *you* be gloomy?"

"Because I get into such dreadful states of fear and panic."

"Fear of what?"

"Of being left utterly alone in a few years' time; of never

[79]

escaping from Ray Street and the Farringdon Road; of never being any good to anyone; of life hurrying on and everything passing me by; of turning into a poverty-stricken and unpleasant old woman and taking to drink; of death and going to hell or going mad. Do you know I shall be thirty soon?"

"So shall I."

"Yes, but it's nothing for a man. It's the end for me. Everything is passing me by."

He did not know how to answer this, and while he waited, clouds packed over the sun, the air chilled, and two of the old men knocked out their pipes and went from the garden. The third was asleep with his waistcoat open, and the new cold breath astir in the air played with his flowing tie.

Kerry and Sally Penelope had met and come together before he brought Pearl to Red Lion Street. He had been standing one evening in Ray Street, gazing at the red pub and at the dropping streets, and peopling them with the scoundrels of the past. He had stared at Bethesda Buildings, and after a time, so great his interest, he had climbed the spiraling steps into the heart of those black bricks, much as a bee will visit the heart of a flowerbell in search of honey. The only honey he encountered as he crept guiltily upward was Sally coming around a corner from her third landing. "Oh, I'm sorry . . ." he stammered.

"Did you want anybody? Can I help you?" she asked in the best manner of a draper's assistant.

"No," he said. "No . . ." and swung around and went down the spiraling stairway, three steps in front of her. They emerged onto the street in Indian file and silence.

Realizing that his alarmed about-turn had been ridiculous, he halted on the sidewalk to explain. "I'm just interested in this neighborhood, and especially in your street. You do live here?"

"Oh, yes. Up there."

"And do you know that once upon a time it was one of the wickedest places in London?"

"Wicked? No? Never! How rather thrilling! But it's a quite respectable street now." Clearly she had added this quickly, lest he should think she associated with any but the respectable.

"I know. Its glory has passed."

"Oh, but do tell me more." Standing before him, she put the bright feminine archness into her great eyes. "One never knows anything about the place one lives in."

"Where were you going?"

"Nowhere. I've just had my tea and was going for a walk."

"Well . . ." He hesitated. She looked at him; their eyes met; and there passed between them, instantaneously, a query, a sudden wondering hope, far older than the oldest history of Ray Street. "Would you like me to take you to some of the classic places?"

"Oh yes, do. Show me them all. Especially the wicked ones."

"The wicked ones. Right-ho! Come to Turnmill Street."

So it began, and the query, the hope, which had flashed between their eyes, was fulfilled. He came many times to take her for a walk; she was an enthusiastic listener; and since he was her superior, in knowledge greatly, in social class slightly, he was at ease with her and happy, and his talk flowed fast and sparkled. He began to love her. If she had little beauty, she certainly had no fortune, being but a copy typist at Reid and MacAlpin's, the makers of barometers in Bowling Green Lane; but he, in his most private mind, would tell himself that being small, oddly shaped, and poor, he could expect no better than this pleasant girl. Her private thoughts were similar: she was no beauty and could not expect a lover handsome, rich, and tall. So now each was content with the other. Kerry came regularly to Ray Street and waited for a loving friend who was less than he.

Sally Penelope was a second reason why he had come to live in Red Lion Street across the Farringdon Road.

Both were silent now, she resting within his arm. The clouds packed darker; time seemed to have leaped a couple of hours so that a twilight had dropped upon the June evening two hours too soon; the first raindrops fell. Silently they dabbed asphalt and concrete with disks like farthings; then suddenly the disks were halfpennies and many and noisy, slapping upon the ground. The children, shoulders up to their ears, ran screaming in delighted panic from the garden. The leaves of the plane trees, after shivering, fluttered in the irritated air; their higher branches, complaining, brandished an alarm across the roofs; and Kerry, starting up, said, "Come. Quickly."

"But where to?"

"To cover. Here it comes."

He took her hand and, head down, ran with her across Clerkenwell Green, through the flagged Jerusalem Passage (the rain now chasing them and leaping at their heels), and over St. John's Square. There before them was St. John's Gate, whose twin towers and ragstone walls had withstood the London weather for four hundred years; they rushed gaily, breathlessly, under the wide span of its groined arch and leaned together, laughing, against the sill of the mullioned window within. They looked up at its ribbed vaulting with its keystone carving of the Paschal Lamb. The rain beat north and south of their shelter so that they were enclosed within four walls: two of ancient brickwork and stone, two of rain. Having her here in so private a place, he took his opportunity: he dragged her against him and applied himself to kissing. Let the rain continue as it liked; let it hang its gray curtains for an hour or more on either side of this noble roof; he was well suited here.

Sometimes, lifting his face from hers, he saw that her eyes were closed, as she let him hold her tight against him; and he knew that they were closed upon her dreams. She pressed against him; and he saw that this would-be genteel working girl, no less than Héloïse in the arms of Abélard, was ready to think, if never to say, "Pant on thy lip, and to thy heart be pressed. Give all thou canst, and let me dream the rest."

He gave her all that he might, for a long silent while.

But even champagne can pall; one may weary of the world's sweetest pleasure; and after a time they sighed and took their rest. They leaned back on the Gothic sill, only linking the fingers of the hands they had dropped.

If for years Kerry's one ambition and its creation had thinned the amorous blood in him, the pressure of Sally Penelope's body and lips had lately proved a potent corrective. More, it had become a stimulant that was now an addiction. Nor had it been difficult to feel in her thin, eager body just now the same initiation.

Leaning against the old gatehouse wall, shut into a silence between these two heavy curtains of rain, his body craved the full measure, the emptying of the draft to its lees. And suddenly time itself seemed to appear like a phantom in this rain-walled prison and to threaten him with a sword. As he looked up at the groined roof and the painted heraldry on its intersecting bosses, he felt as if they had rushed into some left-behind and long-forgotten hole in time; they might be standing in a vaulted chantry of Elizabeth's day. Here he was, his body pulsing with desire, and the old cold stones telling him that his only day was now. Now, in the living, throbbing, hurrying world outside this cube of emptiness and silence.

He began, "Sally . . . ?"

"Yes?"

"You said everything was passing you by."

"And how right I was. My dear, I'm just on thirty, and the last ten years have simply rushed by, with nothing to show for them. I don't know about God and his 'thousand years like an evening gone,' but my last ten seem just like that. That wasn't a very naughty thing to say, was it? Not too profane, was it? The next ten years'll probably go even faster, and then I shall be forty, and that's the end."

"It's not."

"Well, the beginning of the end."

"The end of what? Of love, do you mean?"

"Well . . . oh, I don't know . . . the end of everything."

"I wish we could get married. We can't, I suppose?"

"How can we? It's nonsense to think of it."

"Why?"

"We're prisoners."

"Well . . . Sally . . ."

"Yes?"

"Why shouldn't we each . . . ?"

"Why shouldn't we what?"

"Give each other all the happiness we can, without getting married?"

There was a great silence in the arch, between the twin soundproofings of rain. When she spoke, he knew that she understood his meaning and must pretend not to. "But we do, don't we?" she asked.

"No."

"No? But why not?"

"Sally Penelope, will you kindly—in Mrs. Hitchin's phrase—give over?"

"But give over what?"

"Pretending to be too bloody refined to know what I mean."

"Oh, I wish you wouldn't use words like that. I hate them. And I *don't* know what you mean."

"God forgive you for a liar. We're missing the greatest joy in the world and seem likely to go on missing it forever."

"You're not suggesting . . ."

"I am suggesting precisely that." His arm, now about her shoulders, drew her tight against him, as if it must add a beseeching eloquence that his lips could not find; her face was turned from him, its eyes on the ground, its brows coming together, its lips compressed, as if they knew they must suffer no surrender past them. "But that's—that's a terrible sin," she murmured at last.

"Is it? Always? Why should it be a sin for you to give me the greatest joy in life and for me to do the same for you?"

No answer. She only gazed at the ground.

"Why?"

"I've always been brought up to think it the worst sin of all. Dad'd have fifty million fits if he thought I was doing it."

"Well, he can't very well turn you from his door and tell you never to darken it again."

"No, he can't do that, poor sweet. But Kerry, don't joke about it. It frightens me a little. Oh, I wish it'd stop raining."

"It's not the worst sin of all. Cruelty is much worse."

Silence under the arch.

"We're standing here letting life go by."

But that didn't undo the silence.

"Sally . . . if you think this is a case of one of our lewder lads trying to lead a girl astray in a street entry, say so. If you don't believe I'll marry you directly I can, say so."

"I believe you would."

"Sure as hell I would."

She looked down on the path beneath her feet; she looked away at the curtains of rain. "I can't get over the feeling that it's wrong." Her fingers parted from his.

"All right, my dear. Leave it. Leave it."

Her next words, spoken after long thoughts that lowered her face and kept her eyes away, suggested that she had been thinking of this pictured act less as a sin than as a hypothetical possibility, for she said, "It's a shame there's no place but the street where we can be alone."

"Oh, yes, there is. I have an idea. You're a trained typist and I could pretend that you were coming sometimes to help me with my work. No one comes in to disturb me but old George Windsor downstairs—and he's an excuse for keeping the door locked."

"Pearl would suspect things."

"I don't see why."

"Is she there now?"

"She may be. With her sewing. But it's much more likely she's on the flypaper." This was his name for the Windsors' sitting room when Pearl and Evie were there together, each glued to the other's ceaseless gossip. Let Pearl fly down onto Evie's carpet below, and she was stuck to it, buzzing. "If she's on the flypaper, I'll expect her back when I see her: not before. Would you come sometimes?"

"Oh, yes . . . sometimes."

"But not to . . . oh, Sally, you talk of your discontent and of all you miss—so could I—and we could each heal the other. But, instead, here we stand. Here we wait."

The silence after this was the longest of all; and then, abruptly, she put her fingers against his dropped hand and said almost too quietly to be heard, "Come."

He looked into her face; the large eyes were bright with invitation, love, and fear, but nothing else was in them, for these had driven all the daily dreams away; he did not speak; he just raised his eyebrows to ask his question; she nodded, having no courage to answer aloud, and immediately looked away.

The rain was still beating down, but nothing in this creation, neither rain nor wind nor money, has power against an uprisen torrent of desire, and they ran into the thick of the rain—into St. John's Square and down St. John's Passage, that paved alley between the back-garden walls of Red Lion Street. At its end it became an arched tunnel beneath other people's second floors—other people who knew nothing of the excitement and delight rushing like a tide beneath them. For a second Kerry and Sally sheltered there; then ran out again into the lancing rain, he drawing her by her fingers to his door.

More cautiously than a housebreaker he opened the door, and they crept on soft feet, past Mr. Hoss Comfort's landing and the Windsors' landings, to his door beside Pearl's.

He opened Pearl's door. "She's not there," he whispered. "Praise God—or Evie—for the flypaper," and he led Sally into his own room. He felt her hand trembling as she followed, but when he looked at her she smiled.

His door shut soundlessly, and his littered attic staged the last scene of this ballet, the Mutiny of the Virgins.

9

Whether sin or not, it was certainly healing. They had removed from each other some hampering unfulfillment and charged each other with a new self-esteem and new thirsts for life. The elan with which Kerry went to his worktable seemed to be heightened, and a yet larger surge of creative ideas to effervesce within him. Evening after evening he went to his table with this impatient surge in his throat. Always now he locked the door on himself. To Pearl he explained this as a hint to George Windsor that he wanted to work undisturbed, but really it was done that she might not be surprised when he locked it on himself and Sally.

But a locked door was not enough to keep George Windsor out. He was too often empty of occupation and eager for "converse" with a neighbor he now loved. Love laughs at locksmiths. Kerry would come home and declare to Pearl, "The power is upon me. I must write. Bring me grub and bring me wine when you want to, but in the meantime—" and he would go into his room and to his table, where the creative power would pour from him like rich cream. The knights and dames and shaven priests came hurrying into his mind as once through St. John's Gate into the priory—but then a step out-side, a floorboard creak, a movement of his door handle this way and that, and a scattering of the knights, as never they fled before Suleiman the Magnificent. Without doubt the Comer-up; and Kerry would keep quiet, hoping he would go. After a silence beyond the door, like time standing still, his straining ears would hear George Windsor explaining softly to the land-ing (but usually loud enough for the listening Kerry to hear), "Oh, yes. Oh, yes. Of course. I quite understand. The divine afflatus"; and thereupon his feet going down again with consid-erate, deathroom softness.

But one evening, some three weeks after that hour of deci-sion behind the screening rain, George turned the handle three times, and four, and, instead of explaining to the dark landing his perfect grasp of the situation, he knocked with a diffident knuckle. Kerry, never having the heart to discourage him with spoken words, snatched off his spectacles and whipped out his earplugs. If the tongue of the lock couldn't keep this lover out, his own tongue could not do it. "Just coming," he shouted, and rose and opened. "Good evening, Commodore."

"I trust that I don't—"

"No, you don't. Always delighted to see you. I only lock the door to keep old Hitchin out."

"Yes, he's a regular old woman in his fancy for a chat when he's nothing else on hand. He can't understand—as I hope I can—that one can sometimes prefer a job of work to his jabber. He comes up to me and jabbers by the hour, and I could wish he wouldn't call me Dad."

"He comes up here, if you're not there. I call him the Wand-erer."

"I can believe it. When I see that you've locked your door, my heart goes out to you in sympathy, and I tread very gently down the stairs again."

"That is most understanding of you."

"Yes, but any artist, even if old and spent and shoveled out of sight, can understand another." And he sat down on his usual chair against the wall. "I only came up this evening be-cause I thought of something that might be of help to you. Can you hear me?"

"Perfectly. The old earplugs are out."

"Good. People always say that they hear me better than most because I've been taught to enunciate properly. I never needed this modern nonsense of microphones and amplifiers. We knew in my day how to make ourselves heard in the back row of the gallery. Yes, this idea visited me a moment ago, and it came, if I may so put it, like a blast of victorious trumpets. For if I have no further hope for myself, I am replete with hopes for you, dear boy."

"What is the idea?"

"Well, alas, I have little influence in the world now. You are good enough to call me Commodore, but I have no great power at my command—unlike my collaterals at Buckingham Palace. And They have never been of any use to me. No interest has ever been shown by Them in the other George Windsor. I do know, however, one or two actor friends high in the profession—I only thought of them a few moments ago—and they, of course, are members of the Garrick Club. Now the Garrick, I am given to understand—they never elected me to it—is not only somewhat overstocked with judges and lawyers and the princes of my profession; it is also top-heavy with publishers. My dear old friend, Ritchie Dewes—Sir Richard Dewes—with whom I've acted many times, tells me he's familiar there with the heads of many great houses."

"It's kind of you to think of this."

"I only thought of it just now, and I came up at once."

"Thank you, Commodore. Thank you very much. But I'm quite certain no publisher ever published a book out of friendly sentiment, but only because he saw profit or distinction in it."

"But, dear boy, yours will have both. I fully expect it to have a great critical success and a great sale. A *beautiful* book, I am sure. *Most* beautiful."

"But you haven't read a word of it!"

"I have spoken with its author. And I know genius when I see it—"

"And you always say that genius seldom gets any due recognition."

"Genius gets only a few commissions, did you say? How true! And how very nicely phrased! But genius does quite well sometimes: Garrick, Irving. . . . It did with me for a time, but only for a time." He had a real desire to give encouragement to a young and loved friend, but now that the word "genius" had appeared, he found it easier to talk about himself. "In our tragic profession, merit is not enough. There are plenty of actors as good as I was—yes, I am sure there are—but, as with me, they've never really stood on the top. The little extra bit of luck has never really dropped into their scale: the right part, the right play, the right moment, or, best of all, the favor of the collaterals at the palace. Without the luck, you play your parts as well as the best and each part is quickly forgotten, and you grow old and fat, or thin, and are quietly dropped. With me I never had so much as a farewell performance. Just dropped. Dropped. Once or twice the offer of a small part in some old blood-tub south of the Thames—but would I take it? No. Two lines and a spit? No, thank you. But I did consent, after two years without an engagement, and with all my savings spent, to doing a few club turns for a pound or two."

"Club turns? What are they?"

"An engagement to perform at a club dinner or a smoking concert or some such foolery. I would do a comic scene from Congreve or Wilde on a rickety platform—or even on the floor. I've done Falstaff and Malvolio and 'The Arab's Farewell to his Steed.' On a dance floor before a crowd of overfed diners, most of whom were talking all the time. My dear lad, it was little better than entertaining in the street. But there we were: I did it to save my dear comrade, Evie, from starvation. And d'you know, heroic soul that she is, she stopped me doing it. She saw that I did it only with my heart dead inside me. So she said, 'No, George, no; it just dries me up to think of you doing that'; and with the courage of a great soul—women are wonderful—she went forth to her present work. But Evie a dresser! Evie Mac-Neil, that great and lovely artiste! A dresser and junior ward-robe mistress at the Grand. My Evie lacing up the stays of fat, overdeveloped young cows not fit to bend down and touch her shoes. And she's 'Auntie Evie' to them. *Auntie!* Oh, my God! My God! . . . Auntie; and she accepts it gaily and with laughter. I've had one good thing in my life, Kerry"—his eyes filled—"one perfect thing: a truly gallant comrade."

Overcome by these words, he rose and went to the window. To comfort him, Kerry said, "I agree that women can be wonderful," but he did not hear. Kerry said louder that women could be wonderful, but still he did not hear. He gazed over the crowded roofs of London, and all his disappointment with the general human situation was in his eyes. "Since then," he said at last, turning his face back to the room and smiling to cover his temporary breakdown, "I have done nothing—nothing but eat my bread with tears while I await the kind mercy of death. And now, dear boy, I must go. Go. I will not delay you in your career." He sat down again on his chair. "How I envy you: still

[89]

able to pursue your art in happiness. The book comes fast and furious, I hope?"

"Sometimes—and then it's a joy. But now and then it's rather like being on the rack."

"Like Thackeray, did you say? Well, *he* was a great success. Personally, I loved *Esmond.* I once played the part of Dick Steele in an adaptation of that book. Will they be able to make a play out of yours?"

"I sometimes think there's an enormous play in it."

"Then I'll see that someone does it. I really will. And you'll let me speak to dear Ritchie about the great work?"

"Not yet. It's awfully good of you, but I'd like at first to see if it can get accepted without help from outside." Kerry's faith in his story was mounting so high that he had visions of its being accepted by the first publisher he sent it to. But such a dream could not be spoken of by one who wanted to appear modest, and be loved for it. "Perhaps it won't be, and then I shall be most grateful for your help."

"And it'll be a joy to help. Once I could have helped much more. I knew and met everybody. But such as I am, here I am. And now . . . I must go. Yes, I must go. . . ."

This time Kerry did not say, "Don't go, please. Love to have you," because he was straitened and beating a foot and vehement to get on with his work. George waited for this request —waited some sad seconds—but as, alas, it did not come, he rose and, making a virtue of necessity, enjoined with an uplifted monitory finger, "You get on with it, dear boy. God forbid that I should hinder you." And he smiled and went to the door. He smiled there again and went through it slowly and reluctantly, but shutting it very quietly like a considerate man.

The house was quiet as Mr. Hitchin listened from the top of his basement stairs. Mrs. Hitchin was out, and he was standing very still. Not a sound from the second floor; nor from the Windsors' floors; nor—and this was his point of interest—from the attics. And yet that young Mr. Betterkin had just crept up there with his girl. It was the sound of his key and their careful steps and low voices that had shot Mr. Hitchin up from his basement faster than a rush of gas from a pierced main.

Now he tiptoed up the first and second flights even more quietly than they did. And in the dusk of the second landing he stood listening again, his head bent slightly to one side so that one ear might be aimed at the attics. Baloney for that there Betterkin to say he brought the girl back to help him with his work. Heard that one before. Why was he so often bringing her now, and especially when his sister was out? Yeah, and why never no sound of typing? Eh? Listen: only low voices, and a creaking. Typing! First time he'd heard it called that.

Greatly stimulated, he footed it up the attic landing and stood listening at a panel of their door. The front attic door was ajar and the room empty. Then that there Miss Betterkin was out, and no doubt this was why her brother had thought it safe to bring back the girl.

Sly.

Real sly.

A sly young devil, he was. And goings-on like this in his, Mr. Hitchin's, house.

Low.

Another creak.

Gawd! Will you only think of that?

He addressed his ear yet closer to the panel. Kisses—undoubtedly kisses—and soft laughter. They were on that there couch; not a doubt of it. Listen.

Funny. Not the sort of tart he'd have chosen. No bew'y, that girl, with her chin going back for something it had left behind, and her teeth always coming to the front door. Damn it, she wasn't even pru'y.

But now a much louder creak, and Mr. Hitchin slipped down two flights of stairs as fast as water over a weir. At the bottom of the second flight he halted, thinking that perhaps his alarm had been exaggerated. He turned his ear up toward the attic like a microphone seeking the sounds of the nightingale. Hearing nothing, he crept quietly back.

This time he put his eye to the keyhole, but its cover was down inside and he saw only blackness. So he stood there in the dusk, enjoying to the full his reprobation and indignation. He would not have admitted this, but he was delighted with his discovery, first because it might give him a profitable power over this Betterkin, and secondly because there were few entertainments so engrossing and stimulating as spying upon lovers at their game.

He listened to the small sounds for what seemed half an hour, and only when two louder voices suggested that they were rising for a break did he run down the four flights of stairs like a startled rabbit scudding into its hole.

Many times again, when circumstance was kind, did Mr. Hitchin peep from his basement to watch Kerry and Sally Penelope going upstairs, and then, within two seconds of their shutting their door, leap up the stairs after them, like a mountain goat up its Alpine rocks. And stand there at the summit, listening.

After chewing for some weeks on this savory cud which was now his, he decided that it was a pity to let the weeks pass without making some use of it. So one evening, when Kerry had come home alone, Mr. Hitchin, wanting to catch him before he locked his door, bounded with his chamois speed up the first flights but stepped up the last flight with the unhurried ease and the dignified carriage of a gentleman. He knocked. Nervously, leaving his knuckle on the door.

Kerry, hearing this delicate knock, supposed it to be George Windsor and, unable as ever to deny him a visit, called out loudly to show his clever guesswork, "Come in, Commodore."

But instead Mr. Hitchin came around the door, in shirt and suspenders, because his excitement had left him no time to look for his jacket.

"Oh, good evening, Mr. Hitchin." Kerry, seated at his table, pulled off his spectacles with a sigh that he instantly screened with a smile. His fingers beat his pencil top on his manuscript.

"Evenin', Mr. Betterkin. Yes, I—I just wondered if you was in. Bin back long? No?" Mr. Hitchin's smile was geniality itself; it was an ingratiating smile, soft and easy and helpful as lubricating oil.

"No, only just got back."

"Wurl, I'm glad to find you in because I thought—well, what I mean—there's something I'd like to speak to you abaht."

"So? Well, carry on." Kerry did not succeed in making this sound very welcoming.

"Could I kind'a sit down? What I mean—"

"Of course." Why had he no courage—or no heart—to say "Sit down if you like, but please don't stay"? Why instead did he merely smile amicably at this maddening intruder? "You wanted to say something?"

"Yus. I've often wondered if I ought to come up and talk to you abaht it, but I'm not naturally an interferer. Nah, not as a rule. Nah . . . not me meself, personally."

"What is it you want to say?"

"Wurl, Mr. Betterkin, you see . . ." He beamed—if such a word can describe an uncomfortable expression of goodwill.

He turned one all-knowing eye on Kerry, as if one were enough, and he'd leave the other out of it. "You see, I felt I ought to, but I didn't like to till—till this evenin', when I said to meself, 'Here goes, mate!' and here I am. And now I don't know hah to say it. Yus. Comic, ain't it?"

"Sorry, Mr. Hitchin. I'm lost. I don't know what you're getting at."

"Wurl . . . I don't know what's in it, really. Just something that perhaps you ought to know."

"Well, let's have it."

"Yurse."

Kerry offered his cigarette case. "Have a cigarette. Perhaps that'll help."

"Thenk you." He took the cigarette and put it behind his ear. "But I won't smoke it jest nah. Seein' as we—as you might say —know each other well now—"

"Yes?"

"Yurse. . . ."

"I'm more than ready to hear anything you have to say."

"Course, if you'd rather I didn't come aht with it, jest say so, and that's that."

"I'd much rather you did."

"Wurl . . . this . . . er . . . girl."

"Girl?"

"Yep. This young lady you brings home."

"What of her?"

"Wurl . . . I mean to say!"

"Mean to say what?"

"Oh, come! We understand each other, don't we? What I mean to say, I bin young meself."

"I don't understand you at all." But Kerry's heart had begun to beat in guilt and dismay. And with a sudden sadness because now it would be difficult ever to bring Sally Penelope here again. "Miss Finch comes to do some typing for me."

Mr. Hitchin looked straight at him with mischief dancing in the one knowing eye. The eye said "Come off that one, mate," so Kerry swung his glance from it. He spoke grandly. "I take it there's no objection to that?"

"Nah, no objection to typin'—nah, not to typin'."

"Well, what are you hinting at?"

"Gaw-mercy, you make it difficult for me, don't you? I chanced to be passing the other day, and you wasn't typin', was you nah?" He put this question as one reasonable man to another, with the little knowing eye half closing. It was now a slit like a cat's, but much merrier. "You was kissin'. Kissin' good and hard, eh? And I don't blame you. Done it often enough meself."

"What did you pass my door for?"

"To attend to the landin' window. No harm in that, I suppose? It rattles in the wind like my old broken-down truck. I went down again to shape up some wedges for it, and when I come back you was both gawn."

"What of that?"

"Wurl . . . let's come clean. P'raps I'm a bit of a Sherlock Holmes. There's no great harm in that, is there? Jest interest. There was no sound in your room, and I was kind'a surprised. P'raps I was a bit nosy. There, I give you that." He offered it generously. "I give you I was a bit nosy."

"And you opened my door and looked in?" As Kerry asked this his eye went to the door and he saw for the first time that the keyhole cover was gone. Surely there used to be a swinging cover to that keyhole. Had Hitchin unscrewed it? And peered into the room? Horror—and seen him acting the things he was writing about? For Kerry would always act and mime the gestures he wanted to describe, so as to imagine them exactly. He would practise aloud his finer phrases, his angrier dialogue, his more violent curses. Had Hitchin seen him lunging with his sword like a good knight, parrying the thrusts of twenty enemies, kneeling with hands clasped before an imaginary crucifix, pointing to heaven as he preached to the people on Clerkenwell Green, and lying on the floor like a slain infidel beneath the walls of Rhodes?

Kerry was more worried by the thought of Hitchin watching these apparently lunatic performances, this fearful pantomime, than of his seeing Sally and himself on the divan.

"Yes. I admit I peeped in. And your table was as tidy as it was left in the mornin'. No work done there. But it was very different, as you might say, with the divan."

"Mr. Hitchin, will you very kindly understand that none of this is any business of yours?"

"Now don't get your rag out. Don't get shirty. For my part, I'm only teasin' you. Don't matter a damn to me what you do. But it's the old parson."

"Parson?"

"Yep. And that's why I thought it the part of a pal to warn you. I reckon it's my dooty. Father Aylwin owns this house, and if he thought we allowed goings-on . . . What I mean to say is, it's aht-and-aht immorality, ain't it?"

"Don't be absurd. God save us all, if I rent rooms in your house, it's to live my own life in them. Without any interference from you."

"Nah, that's not a nice way to talk. Blimey, I was saying things on your side, so to speak."

"Which I think damned impertinence."

"Oh, do yer? Well, p'raps the Father wouldn't. The Father's the Father, and if he knew that we . . . but of course he needn't know. There's that: he needn't know. I was never one to grass."

"I wish to God you'd get out of this room. I'd have you know I'll do what I like in these rooms."

"Oh, will yer?"

"Yes, and now kindly get out." He rose. "Get *out!*"

"Don't shaht at me! See? Or I might start telling *you* to get aht."

These last words burst like a dumdum bullet in Kerry's heart, expanding after it had entered. Get out? No, he wanted to stay where his inspiration was. Where Sally Penelope was. If he was turned out, where could he go? Where take Pearl? Oh, why was everything suddenly spoiled by this ridiculous old fool? He stood speechless because poised exactly between the impulse to be rude and the impulse to placate.

"Yeah," continued his tormentor, "I suppose it wouldn't interest you to know that we could get twice as much for these rooms. It was only because Mrs. Hitchin kind'a took to you that she let you have them at your figure. I passed the remark at the time it was no proper price at all. And it could be that I could get you aht tomorrow."

"And you really believe that?"

"Course I do. And what I reckon is, if you want to do jest as you like up here you should bloomin' well pay a better price. If Mrs. Hitchin won't take it from you, damn it, I shan't mind havin' it! You can give it me."

"Oh, blackmail, is it? I begin to see."

"Nah, turn it off, mate. It's not blackmail to ask a fair price for a room."

"Oh yes it is, if it's really a demand for silence money."

"And that's what you think, is it?"

"Yes. Exactly. I think it was a very stupid little try-on. And now please go."

Mr. Hitchin waited and then rose, full of thought. "I must

have a word with Mrs. Hitchin about this. Blackmail. I'm not sure that I like havin' that said to me." He carried this uncertainly to the door. "I been accused of many things, but never of puttin' the black on. Not sure it isn't libelous. You wouldn't come out of it so well, if I took you to a court a' law. Nah. . . ."

Muttering, he wandered down the stairs, leaving Kerry to stand in his room, shaking, and fingering a thumb. But when Hitchin was quite out of hearing he went out to the landing, looked through his keyhole, and was comforted because he could see but little. Still, the stamping, the lunging, the shouting, the fiery preaching—Hitchin must have heard these and wondered, standing there, if his tenant were a lapsing madman who had lonely lunatic hours.

10

Toward the foot of the sloping and cobbled Benjamin Street, and opposite the arched footpath into Faulkner's Alley, there is another narrow entry. It leads between house walls into a small, square, cinder-gray garden. They call it St. John's Public Garden because it was once a burial ground for St. John's, and they have furnished it with plane trees and grass plots, but so far as any garden can seem as gray as cinders and coke, this one does. It is gray because the trees have sooted trunks, the graveled paths are dusty and dun, and the whole small square is bounded by the walls of a distillery, a boiler house, and the old houses of Benjamin Street. The few geraniums wear a tired look, and the air is melancholy. One can imagine that the dust on the paths is the dust of the ancient dead. Is it because of the garden's worn and haunted look that you may visit it at any hour of the day and see nobody there, unless perhaps one old man sitting upon a seat, and sending up wreaths of pipe smoke above his memories and dreams?

Nevertheless, at this time, Kerry found a use for it. He might declare that he'd be damned if he'd let that gross old fool, Hitchin, interfere with his life, but the knowledge that at any moment a Peeping Tom might be listening behind the door had almost entirely stopped Sally Penelope from coming to the room. "It's ruined all," she said, "and it's a judgment on us." And so they were thrown again upon the open roads and the garden seats for their times of love; and their love was limited once more. This little garden lay conveniently between Sally's Ray Street and Kerry's Red Lion Street, and so they would often meet here for a while before they went their separate ways, he up the tilt of Benjamin Street, toward his work, she down the hill into Turnmill Street, toward an evening in Bethesda Buildings with her silent and unhappy father.

On an evening in late July they sat here on a bench, their favorite place, beneath the distillery wall. The garden was empty, no faces looked from the windows of the house backs, and they were able to take all they could from their now limited embraces.

"Yes, yes," Kerry said, when he slackened an embrace and desisted from love. "Enjoyment and refreshment, certainly."

This he said because, immediately behind this seat, an inscribed stone in the distillery wall proclaimed to an ever-absent world: "This consecrated graveyard which received for a hundred years the bodies of the Christian dead, here to await the Resurrection, is now for ever dedicated as a garden for the quiet enjoyment and refreshment of the living."

"Yes," he repeated, savoring again the quiet enjoyment just ended. "I sit refreshed."

But Sally, far less happy, was looking down at the gray pathway beneath her shoes and thinking of Hitchin's menacing visit. Kerry had been making fun of it, but to her with her buried guilt the whole story could carry nothing but a sickening flavor, and this evening it seemed to represent a hostility of fate that had dogged all her life.

"That horrible old man! We shall never again have any place where we can be really alone." She was willfully driving the knives of self-pity into her breast. "Never anymore. We may as well give it all up."

"Not at all, dear child," said the cheerful Kerry. "Only wait. Give me time."

"Perhaps God meant him to come in and put a stop to it."

"Not even God's going to put a stop to it for ever."

"But I'm thirty now, Kerry." It was so: she had just passed her thirtieth birthday, and since people marry early in the East End of London, a thirtieth birthday in Clerkenwell was like a fortieth in Kensington. "It's too awful. I've had my best ten years, and I've spent them all in Bethesda Buildings with nothing in sight but factories and an old workhouse and gigantic railway depots and weary, dreary women looking out of tenement windows just like mine. I shall be like them one day, and I shall end up just like the old woman who was sitting under that tree the other evening—just sitting and sitting with her loneliness. You don't think that this place is haunted, do you, and that she was the ghost of me sitting there in the future? Yes, I think she was. Sally's ghost."

"Sally's balderdash. This, my dear child, won't do. This must stop. Forthwith. It is the blues gone mad. Give me a year—or perhaps two—and I shall have made heaps of money."

"Things don't happen like that, my sweet. Or only to one in a million. You are asking to win a lottery."

"It may not be quite as chancy as that." Not even the loyal Sally, he thought, could realize the quality of his book, *Green and Pleasant Clerkenwell.* She, no more than anyone else in the world, knew what was gradually taking shape in his attic.

So little did she realize his thoughts that she went on with her own. "I never approach Bethesda Buildings now, and step on those ghastly stone stairs, without a kind of sick revulsion. Is it wicked to be so discontented, Kerry? It is, of course; I am selfish and horrible. But I can't help it. One craves a *little* beauty in one's life, and I can't help thinking of other girls who live in nice homes with trees about them and have brothers to take them to parties and dances, and fathers who take them occasionally to fascinating places abroad."

"I'll take you one day."

She gave no heed to this, not able to believe it. "I see it's all selfish and beastly, and I hate myself, but can I have the complete grouse? Can I go the whole way and thoroughly enjoy it? It sometimes seems to me that I've got absolutely nothing. I can't even look in the glass without horrid disappointments. The gods—possibly for the good of my soul—have denied me one single beauty—"

"And that's a blasphemous lie."

"Oh no it's not. I can see nothing in me anywhere for anyone to love. I've a face like a goggling hen. Or like a fish."

"Dear lady, you have the most beautiful dark hair and blue eyes, and a skin that most women 'd give their eyes for. And you should always dress in dark blue. Obviously. And bear in mind what the old Frenchman said about love—there's nothing a Frenchman doesn't know about *l'amour*. 'Love,' he said, 'is a matter of skin.' "

But she shook her head, refusing to be comforted for the beauties that were not. To be comforted was to be denied rebellion.

"I must go," said Kerry, and rose. "I must work."

Just now he was revising, improving, polishing, page by page, his roughly completed manuscript, and since this is quite the most delightful part of an author's labor, so that it is less labor than bliss, it was proving a jealous rival to Sally Penelope, allowing him fewer meetings with her and even then luring him away. In her present mood Sally was hurt by this, but hid the hurt; she just kept the irrational resentment to fester quietly within herself. Kerry, she thought, managed to keep gay because he had a drive and a dream to occupy him, but she had no such talent, no such fine fantasy of creation, no such ambition and hope. Her dreams, though many, were limited to a nice home, nice clothes, nice interesting and cultured friends, nice green places to wander in, nice travels abroad, and, at the heart of it all, a lover and children who would adore her.

"All right," she said. "Go and work"; and then immediately tried to smile at him lest this irrational sulkiness had sounded in her voice. "I'll go back to Dad."

"You don't mind my dashing off?" he begged, for of course he had discerned her slight mortification.

"No. Why should I? I want you to work. And I only wish I could go on helping you. But that horrible old man . . ."

"It's largely for you and for our future," he said, picking up her hand and drawing her to her feet.

"I know," she answered, rather as a child might say, "I know," when bidden to take her medicine and told it would do her good. "Let's go. It was getting cold, anyway."

Fingers linked, they walked to the narrow entry between the Benjamin Street houses, and out of that poor Eden.

In Benjamin Street she waved him a sad good-bye as he walked up the tilt, and then herself walked slowly down it. She turned the corner into Turnmill Street—and turned a corner of her life.

Unaware that destiny waited for her ten yards ahead, she came along the once-wicked old street with tears of passionate rebellion in her eyes. The grand evening sun seemed an insult: it shone from a wide and opalescent sky and gave its glamorous benediction to huge hideous warehouses, storage depots, and tenement blocks, and to the deep black gash of the railway cutting, which at this moment was belching steam and stench and din. And she was thinking (her intelligence enlarged of late by her talks with Kerry) that this city of millions had had a thousand years to live and learn, and yet this glaring hideousness was what its centuries of civilization had produced under a splendid sun, and in a sweet evening air. She touched the tears away from her eyes and longed for some counselor wiser than she, wiser than Kerry, who would offer her a meaning to life, a faith by which to live.

Now in those days there was an old junk shop that called itself on its signboard an Antique Dealer's and, fittingly enough, occupied the ground floor of one of the old eighteenth-century houses whose darkened bricks were as genuinely antique as the clutter and clobber in its windows pretended to be—the tarnished silver and plate, the cracked porcelain and pottery, the clocks and bronzes, the dusty golf clubs and musical instruments, the stools and worm-eaten tables. It was probably one of the old sinful houses of Turnmill Street. Narrow, and not tall, with its past memories and present junk, it stood oddly among the elaborate facades of distillery, bindery, factory, and pubs. Its windows had old-time glazing bars and to the sill of one of them was attached a shelf for a few forlorn and slatternly books.

Sally came abreast of this shelf, and because her eyes were now very full and must be turned from the street, she stopped and looked down on the books. One, being a large crown-quarto volume, stood above its smaller companions like a teacher amid a file of children; and because its spine was tooled and gilt around a curious title, she drew it out. Its sides were as prettily tooled as its spine, and its top was gilt—why this garnishing for a book with such a title, *The Shoemaker of Görlitz*? It had a subtitle, "Shoes for the Wandering", and she began to suspect that it was a flowery Victorian volume of spiritual instruction and consolation. "Mid-Victorian uplift," she thought, trying to scoff at it, but she was in no state to scoff long at any hope of uplift. "Shoes for the Wandering": in the good Bunyan's phrase, these were "words to lean a weary soul upon." She leaned upon them, opening the book, while the traffic of road and railway went shuffling by. First a frontispiece: the engraved portrait of a man in Jacobean costume, whose domed forehead and small beard gave him some resemblance to Shakespeare. The man's eyes, gentle, kind, and dreamy, looked straight into Sally's. Beneath the engraving, in decorative capitals, was a name, JAKOB BÖHME.

"Never heard of him," thought Sally, turning a few pages. Someone, perhaps a century ago, had dog-eared a page, and the book, as it were of its own accord, opened at this place. The dog-ear was large (with its maker's thumbmark still visible on it) and it pointed like an arrowhead to a passage marked on the page. Like the volume itself, the print was large and seemed the better able for this to defeat the noises in street and cutting. Sally read:

> I am not a master of literature nor of arts, such as belong to this world, but a foolish and simple-minded man. I have never desired to learn any sciences, but from early youth I strove after the salvation of my soul. Finding in myself a powerful contrarium, namely the desires that belong to the flesh, I began to fight a hard battle against my corrupted nature, and with the aid of God I made up my mind to overcome the inherited will, to break it, and to enter wholly into the love of God. Now while I was wrestling and battling a wonderful light arose within my soul. . . .

Straightaway a hope of light arose within Sally Penelope's soul. She read on rapidly. Her searching eyes dropped to another passage, marked for her by the old dead hand.

> Suddenly my spirit did break through, and there I was embraced with love as a bridegroom embraces his dearly beloved bride [a simile that speeded the beats of Sally's heart] but the greatness of the triumphing that was in the spirit I cannot express either in speaking or writing; neither can it be compared with anything but with that wherein life is generated in the midst of death. It was with me as with a young tree which is planted in the ground and at first is young and tender, but it does not bear fruit; and though it blossoms, they fall off; also many a cold wind, and frost and snow puff upon it. But if thou climbest the ladder on which I climb into the deep of God . . .

There was now a glory of hope in Sally's heart—hope that she was going to climb out of pain. She must know more of this old voice which was speaking so tenderly to her in the once-wicked old street. Turning back to the book's preface, she learned that it was an "easy and popular exposition" of the writings of a German mystic, Jakob Böhme. It began with his life. Born in a straggling village among the hills of Upper Lusatia, he began as a herd boy on the Landskrone Hill, and then, since his little hometown was full of shoemakers, became first a shoemaker's apprentice there, and subsequently a master of his craft in the town of Görlitz. And it was while practicing his craft that he received his first illumination. An ecstasy seized and filled him, and he felt he could "see into the heart of all things." He walked out into the fields, there to see each blade of grass filled like a lamp with the eternal light, "a little emerald set in the City of God." Every spire of seeding grass was on fire with God. For years he told no one of this experience but continued in peace and silence making shoes. In silence he cared for his family and was loved by them, being always lowly in conduct, patient in suffering, and gentlehearted. (Sally, reading, felt a desire to be just like this.) Ten years later, however, a new illumination clothed him in light, and all that he had previously seen only chaotically and in glimpses he now beheld as a coherent whole. And lest these sure revelations should pass through him as a stream and be lost, he wrote his first book, *Aurora, or The Morning Redness in the East.*

Instead of making shoes he began to write.

It was not the story of old Jakob's enlightenment that was tethering Sally to a rusty storefront; all this, though oddly thrilling, was beyond her grasp; she read it quickly and was glad to come to the practical steps that the old shoemaker prescribed for those who would climb out of their dark labyrinths of defeat and loneliness "into the deep of God." They were steps whereby, in his inspired words, a Christ could rise out of the wasted flesh of Adam.

"Into the deep of God"—the words had rushed into her heart like seed into a womb.

Avidly she raked for nourishment of the seed. She read "I sought only for the heart of God, therein to hide myself from the tempestuous storms"; and it was as if the voice of an old shoemaker was telling her how he, three hundred years ago, had suffered all the same disappointments, unrests, and hungers as she, and how he had found the answer and longed like a good brother to give it to her. Here in Turnmill Street he offered it—here between the distillery and the pubs, those purveyors of a different consolation to weary, frustrated, or defeated men.

Der Weg zu Christo. The scholar said to his master, 'How may I come to this supersensual life?' His master said, 'When thou canst throw thyself but for a moment into that where no creature dwelleth.'
   Scholar: Is that near at hand or far off?
   Master: It is in thee, and if thou canst for a while stand still from all thy thinking and willing, thou shalt hear the unspeakable words.
   Scholar: How can I hear when I stand still from thinking and willing?
   Master: When thou standest still from the thinking and willing of self, the eternal hearing, seeing, and speaking will be revealed to thee.

Sally tried to stand as still as this on the sidewalk; but nothing happened.

   Scholar: What hindereth or keepeth me back that I cannot come to this?
   Master: Thy willing stoppeth thy hearing with thine own thinking of natural things, and overshadoweth thee. Loving scholar, if it were that thy will could break off itself from all creatures and throw itself into that where no creature is, it would be ever clothed with the highest splendour of God's glory and it would find in itself the unspeakable words of our Lord concerning his great mercy; it would feel in itself that the cross of our Lord Christ would be very pleasing to it, and it would love that more than the honour and goods of this world."

Der Weg zu Christo. Every word and line, as she read, heightened the exultation within her. Like strong waters to those unused to them, the old shoemaker's liquor, distilled three hundred years before, filled her with an ecstatic hope that she, feeling within herself the unspeakable assurance, was going to be free—that she *was* free. She now had a dream, an ambition, akin to Kerry's, and as potent: a dream of self-conquest, of rejoicing in the hardness and grime and squalor that surrounded her because these things, like the hairshirts of the saints, would train her in selflessness. They would tune the strings of her spirit that it might yield up the true music that

God had hidden in man. In a word, a dream of achieving, since she had no other beauty, a beauty of holiness.

She bought the book for fourpence and came out happily into sunny Turnmill Street.

Until this hour Sally had been driven by no larger ambition than to live like a cultured lady; now in a swift development the desire to be ladylike had become nothing less than a craving for the gentleness and complete unselfishness of a saint. Her desire for a nice home had swelled into a desire for the City of God. Eager for renunciation, she hastened homeward to practice being sweet and patient with her father. She came to Bethesda Buildings and went up those harsh, stone, spiraling stairs in all the glory of old Jakob's rather large but splendid shoes.

11

While Sally Penelope was standing in the street and contemplating sanctity, Kerry was walking up and down his attic, face down, hands behind his back, as he dredged up from the deep of his mind new beauties for his manuscript; and whenever a new pleasing word or sentence came to him, he dashed to the table, sat down, and wrote it in with joy. Sir Nicholas Shelley, that warrior saint among the Knights of St. John, may have been all, or much, that Kerry would have wished to be, but it was proving much easier to create this nobility of character on some feint-ruled foolscap paper than Sally was like to find it, now that she wanted to create it in the fleshly tables of the heart. Sir Nicholas Shelley was a much less exacting taskmaster than old Jakob Böhme. Just now Kerry's task was wholly pleasant. The first rough creating of a book, he would say, could be hell; this revising and reshaping of it, paradise. In the first laboring stage Pearl in the next room might hear him groaning and stamping over a refractory passage and perhaps announcing loud enough for half the house to hear, "*I* can't do it. *I* can't get it right." But in this second happy stage she would hear him laughing and stamping with delight over a comic bit or, if she went in to him with his supper, she might see his delighted tears running with his ink, as he set down real pathos upon his page.

These wholly pleasant activities tonight were disturbed by the sound of his door handle softly turning. Someone had laid a hand on the gate of paradise, late his happy seat. The Comer-up and Dropper-in? Damn. Never had his brain been working better, never the ideas coming faster. Stay still, and perhaps the old Commodore would put about and sail back into harbor, after explaining his repulse to the landing. But no: a knock on the door by an apologetic and understanding knuckle.

"*Come* in," he cried, deliberately putting despair into the "come." And off came the spectacles and out came the earplugs. He turned the key and pulled open the door so suddenly that the Commodore met him with a jump and a blink.

"My dear boy," he said, "not for the world would I disturb you if I hadn't something of outstanding interest here." He held up a folded newspaper. "I wouldn't dream of it. Are you quite sure you can—"

"Quite sure. Come aboard, Commodore. The divine afflatus can wait."

"It is in good form, I trust?"

"Excellent form. Doing its stuff in great style."

"Good. And it can stand still and mark time for one minute?"

"Better than that. It can sit down and get its breath." Kerry sat down at his table.

"I won't detain it for more than a second. It was just that I—"

"Won't you sit down too?"

"No, no; certainly not. I have a conscience. It is just—"

"How are the old earplugs?"

"She's fine, I think. But she nearly always is. She's one of the sanguine type, whereas I—"

"No. I said 'the old earplugs.' "

"Oh, *them.* No, I wouldn't say they were a success. Not really. I can still hear that filthy thrush in the garden."

"Dear, dear! Tut-tut."

"Summer is an awful time, Kerry: children in the street, windows open, women screaming, and radios blaring. I stand at my window and watch the sun come up with dread. It brings out the children and starts the old thrush bellowing on its branch. There's no peace anywhere—neither in my front rooms nor in my back." All this time he had been unfolding his evening paper, and now he pointed with a neat, tapering finger to some paragraphs in its "London Gossip" columns. "I was reading my *Evening Chronicle* when I saw this, and I felt it was my duty to show it to you. I have a heart, and it looks like good fortune for you—"

"For me?" Kerry took the paper eagerly and read: *"Lady Kantz to Marry Young Solicitor.* Some sensation was caused in social and political circles today by the announcement that Lady Kantz, who recently divorced her husband, Sir Amiel Kantz, the Tory M.P., is shortly to marry Mr. Godfrey Betterkin, a young solicitor in the firm which acted for her in her divorce proceedings. . . ."

"Good God above!" This exclamation was designed to express only astonishment. It covered, he hoped, a sharp pain of shock and jealousy. It was *he* who had tried to run the hard, self-sacrificing race, and it was Godfrey who was handed the cup; *he* who had the finer intelligence, and Godfrey who took the prizes. Now he knew that jealousy of a brother could be sharper than all others; and jealousy of a brother who'd injured him the sharpest of all. "Oh, no, no, no!" He hid these unadmirable thoughts behind a mask of laughter. "This is ludicrous."

"Read on, sonny."

Kerry read on with pain. "We understand that Lady Kantz first met her future husband in the offices of Messrs. Padgett, Liddiard and Co., in Raymond Buildings, that long, gray dovecote of legal birds in the beautiful and historic gardens of Gray's Inn. Mr. Betterkin is twenty-eight and Lady Kantz forty-three." Some relief to jealousy here. "Padgett, Liddiard and Co. had not previously acted for Lady Kantz, whose lawyers hitherto had been her husband's; they were recommended to her when she was instituting proceedings against Sir Amiel. Since then Lady Kantz and Mr. Betterkin have seen much of each other, Mr. Betterkin coming often to her splendid mansion in Rutland Gate, either in his professional capacity or to help her in her political work—"

"But, Commodore, this doesn't make sense. My dear brother is a Socialist and an extremely argumentative one. He has an ambition to be a Labour M.P."

"I imagine he has a stronger ambition to be Sir Amiel's successor. And now it would appear that the Lady Victoria Kantz, that old painted galley, has taken him in tow. And if I know anything about her, it's she who'll do the steering." George Windsor, quite pleased to be nicknamed "the Com modore" by Kerry—it was one of the reasons why he loved him so well—would often act up to this role by using nautical terms, of which he had a good stowage in his hold because he had once played Admiral Bolin in *The Quarter Deck,* with his hat on one side. "She's already altered his course hard over to the right. And didn't you say he was a rather cocky and supercilious atheist? Read on."

Kerry read on. "For some time past, Lady Kantz, who never adopted the Jewish faith of her first husband but remained a High Anglican, has been a tower of strength at All Hallows, a member of its parish council, and a munificent subscriber to its funds. It was probably under her influence that Mr. Betterkin was recently elected a councilor and sidesman."

"Well!" Kerry enacted a collapse in his chair, letting his arms fall to his sides, as if he could bear no more. "But this is all fantastic!"

"The lady has proved worth a mass."

"Yes, but this is the speediest conversion since St. Paul's on the road to Damascus."

"The lady is wealthy. One can understand."

"And I can see what's going to happen. Little brother Godfrey is her new lovely horse and she's going to make him into a nice little Tory M.P. Well, that will suit him quite as well."

"But what interests me, dear boy, is that he will surely be able now to give abundant help to dear Pearl and you."

"I'm not eager to take help from him. But one thing I must do: I must go and chip him about this. How am I to do it? I don't know whether or not we are still on speaking terms. I must take him somehow by surprise."

George Windsor, having arrived, did not go; he was only too glad to sit down and discuss these possibilities. After all, Kerry had said, "Don't go."

When he went the attic floor was strewn with the petals of a dozen reputations—those of Sir Amiel and his lady and certain politicians, of certain old actors and young actors (most of whom, apparently, were pansy boys) and, indeed, of some of his collaterals about the throne.

Kerry lifted the telephone receiver from his table in the front office of *The Midland Standard and Star.* His copy of *The Times* lay on the table beside him. There was nothing in its staid columns about Lady Kantz's romance. Presumably it had announced it yesterday among its "Forthcoming Marriages." He rang the Holborn number of Padgett, Liddiard and Co. It would be safe to ask for Mr. Godfrey, who had now joined the ranks of the gentlemen, and would certainly not be at his desk till ten. A high-pitched voice answered: unmistakably the voice of Edwin, the huge fat young clerk.

"Oh, good morning," said Kerry. "My name is Burge. Yes." This lonely, unnecessary, and unconvincing "Yes" so reminded him of Mr. Hitchin that he added, "Mr. Elfred Burge. I represent *The Times.*"

"Pardon?"

"The Times newspaper. We read with great interest the announcement of your Mr. Godfrey's engagement and would so like to tell our readers more about it. I was wondering if Mr. Godfrey could grant me a brief interview this afternoon—say, about half past three."

"Half past three?"

"Yes." Was the young man deaf as well as fat? "We should like it to go into our issue tomorrow."

"Mr. Godfrey isn't here yet. Could we ring you back?"

"Certainly. Fleet 73691." This number, invented for the moment, he spoke far too quickly for the idiot young man to catch and write down. "No, that's no use. Because I shall have to hurry away and cover the . . . the Hitchin Wedding at St. Alban's. Look: I'll take my chance. I'll call round about three-thirty, and if Mr. Godfrey isn't there, well, perhaps it'll be possible to see him some other time. Though, of course, as he will appreciate, an interview is best while the news is still hot. So the sooner the better, *n'est-ce pas?* Ha, ha, ha."

After this geniality, and with a smile into the receiver as if it were the fat face of the clerk, he replaced the instrument. To his colleague at the table opposite who asked, "What the hell are you up to?" he replied, "Never you mind." Godfrey'll be there, he was thinking; he'll never risk missing a piece of publicity in *The Times.* But I wonder if *The Times* reporters really sound like that.

Godfrey, waiting excitedly in his office, looked again at the clock on the mantelpiece. Only three more minutes had passed, and it was only three-sixteen. Still, the fellow might come at any moment now. Before him, open on the desk, beside the piled and sliding papers, were the drafts for a

"Humble Petition for Dissolution of Matrimony" and for the notices to respondent and corespondent to enter appearances. But he could not concentrate on these documents. They could only remind him, sitting there, of Victoria's petition and of this visit by the fellow from *The Times*. Rather wonderful, rather delightful, to be having an article about oneself in *The Times*, the greatest paper in the land. In the world. And rare, surely, for that great journal, to print interviews like this. He saw the article as the best part of a column, not indeed on the principal page, but near at hand. Whatever people might say about the disparity between his age and Victoria's, his stepping into the famous shoes of Sir Amiel was a triumph of a kind. The divorce had been a sensation and now his engagement was another. He was already a public figure. Yesterday the *Evening Chronicle*, tomorrow *The Times*.

His visions of the future, as he sat at his desk, were not less flattering than Kerry's when he sat at his table in his garret. Sir Godfrey Betterkin . . . ?

The clock again. Only three-twenty. How slow Time's footsteps when coming with a gift.

But now the telephone. This would be he. Edwin's voice: "Mr. Kenrick is here, sir, and would like to see you."

Kerry? Damn! Kerry, oh hell! Turning up at this moment after months of silence. Never was his reappearance more unwanted. After the exaggerated picture he, Godfrey, had given to Victoria of his parents and childhood, after the tale he'd provided to account for his severance from a brother and sister —after, to speak plainly, the lies he'd told her—the only thing to do was to keep Kerry out of her sight, permanently, if possible.

So what to do now? Say he was busy and couldn't see him? But he was simply not harsh enough—or not strong enough— to deal him so ugly a blow. He must see him for a few minutes. Why, yes, and then he could let him know that *The Times* was at the door, about to wait on him, his younger brother. This gratifying thought raised something like a kind feeling toward the recipient of such news, and he deliberated whether he wouldn't now, perhaps, offer money again for Pearl's support. He could afford it now. But be careful: this would reestablish friendly relations with Kerry and Pearl and bring them into Victoria's sight. Sometimes circumstances wouldn't allow one to be as kind as one would like to be. No, all things considered, the best thing to do would be to stage a new quarrel with Kerry, and one that would clinch the severance. He rose and stood behind his desk, taking the telephone receiver with him.

"All right, Edwin. Show him in."

Standing there, fingers kettle-drumming on the desktop, he heard Kerry's steps approaching. Like a threat. Edwin threw open the door for him and closed it behind him. Kerry was looking at him with lips compressed in that mischievous and so irritating smile of his. It made him look as though he thought himself clever. And somehow superior to him, Godfrey. Well, if he was thinking this, he had a lesson coming to him. *The Times* didn't wait on Kerry.

"Good afternoon, Kerry."

"Don't worry, I'm not going to keep you. I know we're not loving each other much just now, but we can't let an occasion like this go by. I thought I must pop in and congratulate you."

"About Victoria?"

"What else?"

"Well . . . thank you. . . . How did you manage to get away from your office at this time?"

"I got special permission to slip out and catch you before you went home. The whole office knows about your engagement and they sent me to wish you well."

"Very kind of them, I'm sure."

"Yes. Nice boys. May I sit down for ten seconds?"

This time Godfrey's toe drummed beneath the desk. He did not change his standing posture but waved a hand toward the client's chair on the desk's other side.

"It's quite a sensation, isn't it?" said Kerry, taking the seat.

"Is it?"

"Oh yes. Nothing less. Did you see the *Evening Chronicle* last night?"

"The *Chronicle*?" He lifted his eyebrows to register surprise, ignorance, and inquiry, though he'd read the *Chronicle* paragraphs with a rapid pulse of pleasure. "No, was there something in it?"

"There was a lot. And all very chatty. 'Historic romance in the beautiful gardens of Gray's Inn'—no, 'Beautiful romance in the historic gardens'—that sort of thing. Pithy."

"These papers!" Godfrey picked up the "Humble Petition" and tossed it aside again, as if it were the whole popular press, and contemptible. "Intolerable, this invasion of one's privacy."

But even as he said this, he suspected, from a mischievous light in Kerry's eye, that he was thinking, "Oh, come off it,

Godfrey! You know that you just love having your privacy invaded, if it's the press at the door"; and he felt that strong dislike which anyone entertains for a man whose eye is considering, keenly and not without amusement, a weakness one would hide.

"I take it," said the grinning fool, "that you're going to invite us to the wedding?"

"Naturally. . . . Naturally I shall invite you to the wedding." But how not to; how not to?

"That's fine. I shall look forward to that. Your career is made now, isn't it?"

"How do you mean? I hope I made my career long before I met Victoria."

"But she is a very wealthy girl, I understand?"

"Her wealth is much exaggerated," he said hurriedly, to discourage any exaggerated hopes in Kerry and Pearl. "And, anyhow, it nearly all goes in income tax."

"Oh, no, quite a little must be left. I was hoping she'd help you in your ambition to be a Socialist M.P."

Godfrey saw well enough that Kerry was teasing him with the point of his foil, and he didn't care for the attention. He turned his face, looked out at the quiet and shadowed gardens, and said severely, as it were to them, "You know quite well that Victoria is a strong Conservative."

"Yes, but she must be a sport too. Devil take it, she's marrying a strong Socialist."

Difficult to parry. From his first meeting with Victoria he had concealed his socialism from her, as from his senior partner, and when first he perceived the astounding fact that she seemed ready to put old Sir Amiel's fallen mantle around *his* shoulders, he had decided that the best thing to do with his socialism was to murder it like an inconvenient wife and hide its remains in a trunk. But Kerry had the key of this trunk and might at any time fling it open. All the more reason for getting him out of Victoria's sight. "Look, Kerry," he said, "I'd rather not discuss Victoria's attitude in these matters. It's our private affair."

"Oh, certainly, certainly, old boy. I was only impressed with her broad-mindedness. Which reminds me: I see that you've become a sidesman and a church councilor."

Damnation! Better perhaps if Kerry had never seen that *Evening Chronicle.* "Yes, that is so. I—"

"But I'm delighted. I always knew that the Church of England was broad-minded, but I never knew it welcomed ardent atheists onto its councils. That seems to me the acme of enlightenment. If you believe in toleration and comprehensiveness, go the whole way. I'm deeply impressed."

"Look, Kerry: I really wish you'd keep out of my private affairs. I don't choose to talk about them. And"—he glanced pointedly at the clock—"I don't want to hurry you away but I've a representative of *The Times* coming to interview me."

"*The Times?* Really?"

"Yes. They want to do an . . . an article." This was the first easy moment in an uncomfortable visit. "He's due at"—again the clock—"due now."

"Oh, well, I'll go. What I mean is, he may be here now. The article's about the marriage, I suppose?"

"I gather so."

"And you're letting him in? But I thought you hated these invasions of your privacy?"

"*The Times* is a respectable paper. It is the only one to which I would grant an interview."

"I quite agree. An excellent paper. But I never knew it did chatty paragraphs about people in the news."

"I gather this is to be an interview. Not a chatty paragraph."

"An interview with a newly betrothed? It doesn't sound like *The Times.*"

"I was surprised myself. All I know is that one of their representatives rang up. And he sounded a very nice fellow, Edwin says. And obviously a gentleman."

"I see. Well, I'd better nip out so that he can come in." He rose with a genial smile.

But then Godfrey realized that they must not part on friendly terms like this. He had wanted to effect a final quarrel. How did one effect a catastrophic quarrel with only a minute in hand? Fortunately Kerry in his next words offered a *casus belli.* "Goodbye, Godfrey; but I notice you haven't asked after Pearl."

Godfrey bent and picked up this gauntlet at once. "Pearl's doings do not interest me."

"Oh!" Clearly Kerry was as surprised by this sudden and violent blow as a jeweler would be when an apparently friendly customer hit him for the first time with a hammer. Godfrey, ashamed to see Kerry so palpably stunned, and rather sorry for him, hit him a second time, so as to be done with a distressing situation. "I want nothing to do with her."

"I thought you said you were going to invite us to the wedding."

"I didn't say I would invite Pearl."

"Well, I can promise you: no Pearl, no Kerry."

Excellent. The quarrel was in being; Kerry was affronted; the severance was reestablished and all danger for a time removed. "Sorry"—Godfrey spoke with insolent cheerfulness—"but that's the position."

"All right. Good-bye. If that's the position, it looks as though it'll be a hell of a time before you see me again."

Godfrey shrugged. He smiled sardonically. He felt he could afford to smile. These last words of Kerry's, meant to be unpleasant, were really sweet as a victor's drink.

Well pleased, he watched Kerry going.

But somewhere between the desk and the door the Old 'Un leaped onto Kerry's back, and Kerry paused, wondering whether to say what the old devil was suggesting. He decided that he was not strong enough to resist saying it, so he turned and said, "I shouldn't worry about *The Times*, old chap. That was me who rang up and pretended to be *The Times*. I just wanted to make sure you'd be in at three-thirty. Good-bye. Be happy. I'll now go back to Pearl, my sister."

12

Next evening he met Sally Penelope again at the narrow entrance of St. John's Public Garden in Benjamin Street. Linking
their fingers as usual, they went to their favorite seat beneath
the distillery wall and in front of the inscribed stone. Each had
a story to reveal, but neither spoke until they'd given themselves to a long embrace, for the quiet of the evening invited
this, and the emptiness of the garden allowed it. And after the
embrace Sally suffered him to tell first the story of his visit to
Godfrey. He delighted in telling it and bragged a little, improving the retorts he had made, and sharpening the points he had
scored. She laughed dutifully where the tale demanded it; she
maintained her conviction that "the whole trick had been
rather unkind"—and most of the time her thoughts were
astray.

Then she began on *her* story and, for fear of its sounding too
sanctimonious, tried to tell it with humor. "You remember how
miserable I was when I left here the other day? Well, God must
have been looking down in pity, as well He might, because He
acted very promptly. And rather wonderfully."

"Explain, my dear. At once."

So she spoke quite picturesquely of old Jakob Böhme stopping her in Turnmill Street and of the vision he'd spread before her.

"Good God, these miracles!" Kerry exclaimed. "There's Godfrey seeing a sudden light on the road to his lady's house in Rutland Gate, and now you in Turnmill Street—"

But by now she'd left all joking behind. With stumblings and stutterings she tried to do justice to the vision, and the best thing she said, though somewhat involved, was, "The minute you stop being an instrument for bewailing your own miseries and become one for helping others you begin to be happy. You seem to be alive as you never were before. It's terrific. Kerry, I've never been so happy as in the last few days."

"But I agree!" he protested, not realizing the full quality of her vision, and as if wondering what the fuss was about. "I agree with all you say." Whereupon he took over the talk, to state *his* modicum of religion. Sally was left there as a listener. He spoke much more easily than she, turning toward her on the bench.

He had tried to believe in God, he said, but "belief" was much too big a word for the thoughts he'd come to hold. What could the affirmations of any men anywhere about what God was, what He thought, and how He acted, be but their guesswork, their hopes, their ways of escape from total insignificance and the intolerable bleak emptiness of their universe? All the same, accepting this everlasting doubt, he had still found some religion left to him. It was not much, but it was satisfying because sure. "First," he said, "there is this surge of life in all men, like the zest in a newborn foal galloping around its paddock or a puppy romping with a child; it must draw from Someone or Something, and I am content to call this Source my Unknown God. But that's not all: don't think that this Unknown God hasn't provided any revelation about how we're to behave. I think He has. Because, you see, along with this surge of life there seems to rise a strange unavoidable worship of all kindnesses, charities, and self-sacrifices—of all those things that can be given the one name, Love. So I sum up my creed in four monosyllables, 'Life turned to Love,' which I sometimes change to 'Full Life and Fellow Feeling;' and, my God, by fellow feeling I mean nothing much less than the whole Christian ethic; and, by the Lord, the Christian ethic proves itself to you in practice: you begin to know, with immediate knowledge, that hate and revenge are springs of pain and evil, and that forgiveness is an extremely happy thing. Forgiveness is an end of pain."

"Yes . . ." Sally, hesitating, gazed into the dusty emptiness of that small house-enclosed garden. "Yes . . . But that's not enough."

"Well, what more? What more do you want me to believe in and do?" He didn't yet see what was coming to him.

"One has to change the whole center of one's life. Could you give up your craving for fame and success?"

"Hell, no!" he declared, as his thoughts swung to the manuscript on his attic table. "No. And I don't see why I should. Good heavens, no! It's the driving force of my life, the tap-root. Cut it out, and I should wilt." And so little did he know how serious she was that he began to discourse upon the joy he was having in putting the finishing touches to his book.

"But, Kerry . . ." she interrupted.

"Yes, my heart?"

"Don't you see what it means to me? My thinking and feeling like this?"

"It means you're nicer than ever before."

"No, don't joke. Can't you see that it means we . . ."

"We what?"

"That we can't go on as we've been doing."

"Doing what?"

"Oh, you know, you know."

Now he was face-to-face with it. It certainly stopped all jesting. "No, I'm damned if I can see. Why can't we go on?"

"Because I can't believe it's right. And unless I can justify it, I can't pray or do anything. I feel cast out."

Kerry, seeing the truth of this, fled from its harshness angrily. "No, I can't see it. We're not hurting anybody. All I've said I believe in is not hurting other people. We're doing no harm to anybody."

"To ourselves? . . ." That was all that Sally, so much less articulate than he, could say to express her perception that if she allowed doubt and deceits to come into her life again, corruption must wreck her soul.

"Not to me," he insisted. "I think it's all ridiculous. Everything'd be all right if we were married, I suppose?"

"Oh, yes."

"Well, if life's cheated us out of that, I can't see why we shouldn't give ourselves what happiness we can."

"One must accept that life can be unfair."

"Damned if I'm accepting anything that's unfair. I'm fighting it with all I've got. There's nothing wrong in what we're doing."

"For me it's wrong. I can't help it. You won't ask me to give up the wonderful happiness I've known in the last few days? I've never known anything like it."

As she said this she was staring at the dreary house backs of Benjamin Street, at the sooty trees shadowing the grass, and at the dust-darkened paths, fringed with brown leaves, but she was not seeing any of these things; she was seeing only a paradise garden that she had found.

Kerry saw that there was a new light in her eyes, and he thought it gave her a new beauty. He would not disturb it, so he just murmured, "Oh, well. . . ."

"You won't ask me, will you?" She had turned the eyes on him, and they were now beseeching eyes: the appeal in them stirred his pity. He sighed, shrugged, accepted, and fell back upon humor. "One may still kiss, may one? Or is that wrong too?"

"No, no . . . please . . . I only want us to be just as we were . . . before. . . ."

So they embraced again, but even as he enjoyed her kisses he felt a need to punish her a little by a further show of his wounds.

"I'd better go and work," he said, deliberately sounding a note of despair. "Work on. All alone. Nothing else to do."

Fright chased away the appeal in her eyes. "You're not angry with me?" she begged, and the words drew him back from punishment to pity, from self-love to self-dislike.

"No, I was just feeling sorry for myself and kicking out at you. Like a four-year-old who's been denied his doughnut. But I'll go back and work because this damned book's our only hope for the future. It might, you know, make pots of money. I can't help feeling I'm on a winner. And if by any chance I'm right, we could get married at once, and everything would be in excellent order."

"Oh, how wonderful that would be!"

"Well"—he rose and drew her to her feet—"let me go and set about it."

Fingers linked, they walked back to the narrow entrance in Benjamin Street. There they separated with sad but encouraging smiles. Kerry went up the cobbles, and Sally down them, one mutineer returning to duty.

Sally Penelope now wanted to go to church, and Kerry, in an inappropriate spirit of fun and adventure, declared, "But I'm going with you!" To his surprise Pearl said she'd like to go too and "would they awfully mind?" He said, "Of course you can come too. It'll add to the"—he was going to say "the fun," but decency intervened, and he substituted "the general gaiety," though not quite sure that this was fitting. So he added, "You understand, I hope, that Sally Penelope's business is now complete unselfishness, and I am signed on as her apprentice in this trade." Pearl said, "That goes for me too," and he fell to thinking that Sally and he, preoccupied with themselves, had never given a thought to Pearl's distresses and secret hungers in her front attic room.

To which church? St. James's, Clerkenwell, had never known them; and all three were shy of walking into any temple quite so close and before the eyes of people who might recognize them. But did not the dome of St. Paul's look daily down upon all their streets, upon Ray Street as well as upon Red Lion Street, and when they glanced up at it, say "Come and see. Come and see"? Did not its bells every Sunday morning clash noisily down upon all Clerkenwell as if they were enjoying these plunges and tumbles in a warm summer air? In the great spaces of St. Paul's no eyes would turn in scrutiny and wonder.

So on a Sunday morning the three of them walked along a quiet Farringdon Road, sleeping in the Sabbath, and up the sidewalks of a silent and blinded Snow Hill, emptied of all but one City policeman in a helmet not unlike the cathedral's dome. A luminous and colored mist stood around London's low hill, and hardly a sound came out of its lazy distances except the intermittent and separated bells. In Old Bailey the cathedral of justice slept too, as if Sunday morning were a time for the pities rather than for punishment. Here the bells tumbled onto the very top of their heads, and they quickened their steps lest it was later than they thought.

On Ludgate Hill, the churchgoers ascending toward the majestic temple entrance with its tall flanking towers were many and (to judge from two Stetson hats and one Indian sari) appeared to come from many and divers parts. This further increased their excitement and their speed. But they had no need to fear: the organ was still playing quietly as they passed into the echoing silence of the cathedral, and the congregation seemed to be filling no more than a cloudy dimness far away.

Kerry had placed himself between his two women and during the service rose and knelt with them, though, to be sure, his kneeling was but an inchoate and half-and-half affair, a forward droop shored up by one unkneeling leg and buttressed by the seat behind. He did not, in fact, give much attention to the service. Rather did the rolling organ music and the voices of priests or choir, coming from far away and losing themselves in vault and dome, wake all his dreams from sleep so that he spent this hour with them. Dreams of a world fame when his name would be known to all these people kneeling in front of him, to the canons and dean up there in the chancel, and to the soft-footed verger in the aisle. And to the choirboys. Dreams of a gracious home (instead of an attic), with Sally Penelope in it as a contented wife and proud mother. A home to compare with whatever mansion Godfrey might share with his Lady Kantz—even a home to excite his envy. A home that would discomfit him the more because in one of its wings, in a commodious room, sat Pearl happier than she'd ever been and giving gratitude and admiration to him, Kerry.

Now and then he turned an eye toward Sally and saw that she, unlike him, was giving herself wholly to aspirations that matched with these high pilastered arches, the half-heard chanting of the priest, and the gilded sanctuary beyond. She knelt on her hassock, upright and unbuttressed. Her hands were linked on the chairback before her, and her eyes looked down upon them. Clearly she was rapt and happy in her new creed. He wished he could believe as she did and enjoy the same peace in believing. A new pity came into his affection for her and made of it a better love. But how odd, he thought, the contrast between the woman and the man. Sally would not pit herself against the faith that had raised that mighty temple, whereas he, small though he was, under these towering colonades, dared to lay his ax against it all.

He turned toward Pearl on his other side. She too was kneeling incorruptibly upright but, instead of looking down upon her hands, was gazing at the distant choristers and the robed clergy in their theater of light. He looked at other men and women, kneeling in their hundreds about him, and he thought, seeing their rapt eyes, how every human face was the sacramental expression of a mysterious soul, secretly aspiring, secretly desiring, but ever unknown. Here, if anywhere—here in this muted church the dreams were multitudes. The resonance of far-off voices raised them; this tempered light nursed them.

And there above the altar, for many of these rapt eyes, was the great Shekinah: the glory of the Lord in a cloud above the mercy seat. Kerry with his vague and thin little creed of "life turned to love" felt but a watcher outside the Shekinah's ray, and yet one who would love to be within it.

How different his two women. And were they perhaps more right than he? Were their searching lamps brighter than the dim-lit lantern of a lazy man's soul? When Sally or Pearl buried her face in her hands, what did she pray for? Neither was afraid to talk about herself with the Power that had built the sun and launched a million stars. Sally Penelope, no doubt, was asking for strength to stay in her new road of self-conquest; Pearl, remembering perhaps the miracles of old, the healing of those possessed with devils, prayed for the casting out of that nameless impulse which had laid waste her life and of the dread of madness that went with it, and so for the end of a sadness that carked and tainted every day—oh, how wonderful that would be!

He prayed for it too.

When it was all over and the organ was speeding them on their way, he went toward the doors, somewhat bemused, but a happier man because a slightly more loving. They came out into the City, where finance, like justice, was asleep, and only religion and sightseeing and the bright noon sunlight were abroad.

13

After eight in the evening, and Clerkenwell, beyond the attic window, is silent—its workers gone home, its factories stilled, its children indoors—London stands in silence for the tremendous moment.

Kerry typed a word and then hit the key for the period.

It was the last word of his book, and the click of the period key was a cannon shot for a triumph.

He rose from his Windsor chair, and it was exultation that lifted him to his feet. Besides, one must stand to salute achievement. Not less was his glow of achievement than that of a mountaineer who stands at last upon the summit. The fatigue in his back and arms was joy rather than pain. Now his creation existed in completeness, and since it was made to the exact measure of his taste, it could but seem to him very good. He had believed in it so completely while imagining it and writing it that he could not doubt that its readers must believe in it as fully and be absorbed in it.

Twice he strode across his floor, then stood by the window. The sun had lately set and the wraith of a moon's first quarter hung in a pastel sky above the gently smoking chimneys. He had to stand there while the effervescent joy sank a little and left him more at ease. Of course, as he looked out at the world on the eve of its conquest, he remembered stories of authors whose books, despite years of labor and love, had found no publisher or, if at last they found one, had been quickly ridiculed and slain. Or merely neglected and left to die. But he couldn't believe his book was such as theirs. Indomitable—not subject to reason—rose the thought, "My book is different."

And he would not admit the rejoinder that probably each of them had believed the same.

Now—and in fact it was hardly two minutes since he had impressed that period—he hurried into the front attic where Pearl sat at *her* table, sewing.

"It's finished," he announced.

"What is?"

"Green and Pleasant Clerkenwell."

She leaped up and stood before him. "Oh, my *dear!*" she exclaimed, and the delight and hope in her eyes were hardly less than his.

"Yes, it now exists. Had I been run over in the Farringdon Road yesterday it would still have been an incomplete thing and worth nothing; now—well, I can cheerfully get run over tomorrow and you'll be able to sell it and take the proceeds."

"But, my dear, I didn't know you were so near finishing it."

"No, that's been my little secret."

"Oh, what shall we do? Let's celebrate."

"We shall certainly celebrate. Put all that nonsense away and come out. I doubt if you'll have to do that damn-silly sewing much longer. Come out and get a little drunk."

"Kerry, should we ask the dear old Windsors to come? They'd so love it. And George has always been so interested in it and prophesied such great things."

"No. Just at present I don't want to talk about it to anyone but you. It's too shaking. I'm only at ease with you about it because you've been mixed up with it from the beginning. Funny, but I don't even want to tell Sally Penelope about it yet."

He saw a happiness in her eyes that she should be the only one with whom he could share his secret, and he was glad to have been able to give her ill-provided soul this morsel of pride.

"Come on, woman. Get your hat."

He was glad, also, to be giving her a treat because he was so conscious that he was often unkind to her, and even cruel. Somehow he couldn't arrest this tendency. Her "everlasting glooms," as he called them, fretted and enkindled him; he would try to control the exasperation, but at last her dismal expression, her frequent sniffing as if despair were inflating her and sought this escape, and her protracted silence overthrew all his resistance and he would burst out, "Oh God! A new gloom, is it? Oh, for pity's sake, can't you be jolly once in a blue moon?"

"*You* gloom sometimes," she would say.

"Yes, but not for twenty-five hours on end. Not for day after day. It's so wearisome. It makes me want to rush out to a pub or to some place where somebody's happy. Always gloom and grumble; snuffle and sniff. You sure are the gloomiest creature on God's earth."

Then, aggrieved, she might utter spiteful words or go into a resentful silence, and he would stay silent too because too proud to apologize, though thinking within himself, "I'm a self-centered brute. There's every reason why she should often be in the depths." And he would remember how sometimes, in the night hours, he would hear from her attic a small scream, and in the morning she would admit to having had one of her "Holloway nightmares" when she woke in horror, expecting to find her dark prison cell around her again, and thereafter lay with the bedclothes tight about her, trying to suppress the hysterical dread of madness.

The trouble is I'm fundamentally a lively type, he would think. I can go down into the depths quite often, but I can't *stay* down. What's so abysmally caddish is that when I plunge into gloom I always take her down with me by sharing it all with her, and then, when we're both on the rock bottom, I simply can't stop there. After ten minutes I shoot up again to the sunlight in my own kind of Davis Submarine Escape Apparatus, while she, not having this interesting appliance, stays down there in the depths. Stays there all alone for the rest of that day. And then I get impatient and brag that I've been up for ages. A selfish brute.

"Chuck all that sewing aside. I know you've had no supper, but there are lovely snacks at the Baptist's Head, and you can have everything you want, and as many as you want. Plus wine."

Pearl gathered up her sewing and piled it on one side with a rather ridiculous little skip and dance, too girlish for her bowed figure and large features; and he knew that tonight (to use her own phrase, for she had humor too) she was "determined to be a cheerful soul."

Through Evie's efforts, Pearl had been given work by Harris and Meyer's, the theatrical costumiers in Covent Garden. Scantily paid, since done at home, it consisted mainly in repairing or renewing such period costumes as had suffered after hire by amateur actors, repertory companies, or the guests at a costume ball. Thus Pearl sat much of the day, round-backed, over a motley still-life of velvet or brocaded gowns, beaver hats jewelled and plumed, wire-edged caps bound with seed pearls and colored gems, and perhaps a Tudor stomacher and farthingale. Kerry would feel a pity for her, bowed over her work, a drab figure, spectacles on nose, red fingers scored and pricked, among these multicolored garments gaily begemmed and the tawdry and glittering tinsel.

"Ready, my dear? Then come. Come and be happy."

They hurried out, turning into the tunnel of St. John's Passage under the second floors of neighbors who knew nothing of this explosive excitement passing beneath them. They came into St. John's Square, now all factories and offices emptied for the night, but once the great court of the priory where so much of his story had been staged. And there, spanning St. John's Lane, was the old towered and crenellated gatehouse, its gray walls encrusted with fame, to show it was no lie that great and historic things had happened here.

They passed beneath its painted bosses and its Paschal Lamb into the lane, whence, as with the square, all the glory was departed. But there before them was the Baptist's Head, an old and celebrated tavern, even if now in a dull, modern dress.

"St. John the Baptist is manifestly my patron saint," said Kerry, pushing open the saloon door. "Not only is my first name John but I have written a book about his knights. He will certainly bless and aid the book. He has probably helped me write it."

In the saloon—a new room but presumably on the very site where Dr. Johnson, after working for Cave, the printer, in the Tudor chamber above the gate, would sit and drink with Goldsmith and Savage—here tonight sat another author, quite as hungry for fame and nearly as poor as these.

"I shall have the typescript bound by that little bookbinder in Rosoman Street. In half-morocco. I believe in giving the book every chance with the publishers and their readers."

"Oh, yes, yes!" Pearl agreed, sipping her wine. "And they're bound to like it. They'll be fools if they don't. Do you really think it could make a lot of money?"

"Yes, I do. I do. What I feel—and what I shall point out to every publisher I send it to—is that, apart from the general public and all the thousands who work in Clerkenwell, it should have an appeal for the thousands of members of the Order of St. John and of the St. John Ambulance Association and the St. John Ambulance Brigade and the cadet movement, of which there are—believe it or not—nearly four thousand divisions and some eighty thousand members."

"Oh . . . Kerry! What might it make?"

"Books can make thousands."

"Thousands?"

"Yes, but it'd have to be a flyaway success for that."

"Oh, if only . . ."

And they began discussing what they would do if it flew away. A house in the country, quite large so that Pearl could have two rooms of her own—or perhaps, if she preferred it, a cottage on the estate. Forgiveness for Godfrey, so that he could come and see them in their glory. Frequent visits from the old Windsors. A nice country weekend now and then for poor Nance Hitchin. Travels with Sally, he and Sally and certainly Pearl, to Paris, to Spain, to Baghdad and Samarkand. Dreams. And dreams.

Other drinkers in the saloon watched them sitting and chatting so happily there, and asked of the landlord, were they two lovers rather older than usual? No. Nor husband and wife? No. Just a brother and sister from a house nearby.

Kerry brought back the manuscript, handsomely bound, from Rosoman Street to Red Lion Street, and it grew heavier and heavier under his arm, but its weight was a pressure of joy between elbow and breast.

In the front attic he undid it for Pearl, who exclaimed, "Why, it looks lovely! It looks so important. I'm sure a publisher will be impressed."

"Well, that was the idea," he said. "But of course the printers will tear it to pieces."

"No!"

"Alas, yes: so as to distribute it among different compositors."

"After all you've spent on it?"

[127]

"Even so; but a typescript's of no value. It dies to live as something better—like you and me, we hope. And possibly Godfrey. Dies to become immortal. The manuscript can be of value. I've heard of a manuscript fetching thousands. I'll make a present of the manuscript to you."

He glanced at Pearl's clock. Too late for the post office tonight. So, with the volume in its brown paper under his arm again, he went into his back room and, laying it on his table, sat down before it and typed a letter to Messrs. Harker and Inman's, of Paternoster Court. These publishers had been recommended to him by his friend Hoss Comfort, who lived on the ground floor and had recommended these attics to him— and whom George Windsor held to be "one of those," with a bevy of male mistresses scattered over London. Hoss, a reporter in Fleet Street, had been away from his office for some time—probably, George maintained, living with each of his mistresses in turn—but he was back now, and had told Kerry in a Fleet Street pub, after averring that he knew all about the book trade, that Harker and Inman's had the best distributing system of all the big London houses and though their imprint on general literature was not Murray's or the O.U.P.'s, on a novel it carried weight with booksellers. Every bookseller, said this informative fellow, had to study the fiction list of Harker and Inman.

So Kerry, with a trembling hand, began, "Dear Sirs, I beg to submit for your consideration . . ."

After writing his signature impressively, he put the letter back in the machine and typed it again underneath in the best business style, then packed the volume with geometrical accuracy in its brown paper.

In the morning, ready to go to work, he picked up the neat parcel with a hand that still trembled, said to Pearl, "Pray to St. John for it," and when she had answered, "Oh, I will! I will! Surely he will help," went from the room to the stairs, saying, "Here goes. . . ."

Benjamin Street; Faulkner's Alley—Faulkner's Alley, where the memories of evil hovered and in which he had set perhaps the darkest scene of his book. Even today that long narrow passage, windless and sunless, had pools amid its paving flags and a black sweat on its rickety house walls, and looked evil. Did it not seem to glance approvingly at him as he passed, stressing for him the quality of his book, and blessing it on its way?

The post office in Farringdon Road. Here there was a queue of people waiting to hand their brown-paper parcels through the grating, and soon he was but one in a long file. He waited, thinking, how different his parcel, how different his thoughts, from those of these people before and behind him. How little they knew what his brown paper wrapped. Now at last his turn; and so big was his parcel that he had to lift it over the grating. The clerk took it as if it were an ordinary parcel. He didn't even handle it with any particular care.

"Registered, please," said Kerry.

Saying nothing, not needing to please and ingratiate customers since he was a government servant, the clerk wrote the necessary slip, did the necessary office to the parcel (with an unnecessary violent stamping), and tossed—actually *tossed*—it onto a heap behind him. Kerry took a last protracted look at it resting there; and after thinking, "Well, there it is, my challenge to the world," left it and came away.

14

A record? Had it ever happened before? Yes, once. *Jane Eyre.*
But *Jane* was not a first novel, so perhaps a record after all.
Anyhow, an event so rare as to stand alone. Barely three weeks
had passed and here was a letter from the first publisher to see
the book. "Dear Sir, We have read your book with interest and
Sir Osbert Inman asks me to say that he would be grateful if
you would come and see him as soon as possible to discuss the
question of its publication." As soon as possible! And Sir Osbert himself, the chairman, the boss, the big chief! And 'Iarker
and Inman's, one of the biggest houses in England! Pearl!
Pearl! It has happened. This is it. This means publication for
sure. It could be out in three months. Hoss Comfort says it only
takes three months from delivery of copy to publication. In
three months everything may begin to happen.

Pearl had been putting eggs on the breakfast table as he read
the letter; he flung it down, seized her hands, and danced her
around and around. She begged him to stop, but laughed and
laughed till, breathless, he let her go; whereupon she, breathless too, said, "Oh, it's wonderful. But you deserve it. If anyone
ever did."

Kerry looked at the breakfast table. "Breakfast? I don't want breakfast. Let me write to the excellent Sir Osbert. Just a cup o' tea because my mouth's gone brown. No, I shan't write to him—I can't wait—I'll telephone this morning. I wonder how soon I can see this intelligent man."

"Will you be able to get away from the office?"

"Not a doubt of it. Old Bunderbuss, my boss, has a heart. Everyone has, in Fleet Street. Not many scruples there, but plenty of hearts. Hearts abounding. Pearl, I feel rather sick."

"So do I."

"Yes, and you look pale. Do I? I fear my stomach will lack all constancy till I know just what this means."

"Oh, can I now tell the dear old Windsors? Do let me."

"No, not till it's all fixed and certain. Pearl . . . it can't mean anything but publication, can it?"

"No, surely not. They say 'discuss publication.' "

"Couldn't mean publication at author's expense, could it? If so, there's nothing doing. Oh, my God! . . . But Hoss says none of the great houses do that now. It couldn't possibly be that, could it?"

"No. No."

"No, I don't think so. Oh"—he pressed a hand on his waist-coat—"my heart! That was a bad moment. It *is* good news and nothing else, isn't it?"

"I'm sure of it. Kerry, I've been praying every night for this to happen. And it's happened."

"But it's a miracle!"

"I can't help that. God does miracles on occasion, I suppose. It's your reward. Most obviously."

As she said this, he thought of Godfrey and resolved that somehow or other, whether or not they were on speaking terms, he must encounter Godfrey and inform him of all this. A nobler person would spare him this considerable blow, but he, Kerry, was not good enough for that. This was a triumph which only an extremely austere saint—like Sally Penelope in these days—would forgo. For the next five minutes he roamed the room, unable to do anything but compose sentences in which he would say all that was necessary to Sir Osbert and to Godfrey.

At the office he tried to work properly but found it difficult to do so. How good news, good beyond belief, disabled brain and will! Every minute his hand halted, his brain strayed. He felt he would like to lie down with eyes closed and enjoy a continuing ecstasy of hope. But supposing one woke and found it was all a dream, a mad hallucination? Oh, what a collapse of all joy in living, what a death of the heart.

In the morning he found he was able to live with it. He was used to it. Despite the fact that he was to see Sir Osbert at three that afternoon, he was able to concentrate on the important matter of his dress with a fairly steady hand. He shaved very close, put on best shirt, best suit, applied an oil dressing to his hair, and finally drew on those shoes which, with their deliberately deepened heels, added a half-inch to his height. But once again breakfast had no interest for him; he couldn't keep still; he needed to get out—out into the air—and, after a cup of tea drunk standing, he moved to go. Before he could escape, Pearl rose and kissed him and said, "Good luck."

"By this evening I shall know all," he said; and nervousness tripped up his voice halfway. "Well, here goes again. . . ."

He went out and, since it was so early, walked slowly toward Fleet Street. He stood for a long time outside a bookshop, gazing at other men's books and picturing his own among them.

All the morning he looked over his large spectacles at the office clock whose minute hand, as it seemed, was teasing him by moving with a studied slowness and often, for the fun of it, pretending to stop. Five times must it run—no, limp—creep— around its course before it approached three o'clock . . . four times and a half. . . .

Paternoster Court, before it was laid waste in the Second German War and joined the neighboring deserts, led out of Paternoster Square and, like most of the side streets beneath the great shoulders of St. Paul's, its narrowness made it seem like a deep gash among the tall buildings. In this crevasse the publishing palace of Harker and Inman aped the High Renaissance style as a compliment to the cathedral's baroque towers. With its three long ranks of windows, each window framed in pilasters and pediment, and its deep cornice projecting over the whole wide front, it looked like a younger and imitative, but perhaps less gifted, brother of the Palazzo Farnese in Rome. Only, of course, it was blackened by London's smoke instead of brightened by Italy's suns.

Kerry, coming along the narrow defile, thought, "Saints in heaven! An imposing hospice. My publishers."

The doorway in its midst, set in a massive arch of rusticated stone, had above it a carven head of Sir Philip Sidney, this being the colophon of the house. The heavy rusticated blocks reminded him of the neighboring Old Bailey, not a hundred yards away, and of its gray predecessor, Newgate Jail.

But Kerry's feelings were the very opposite of a prisoner's as he went up the nine gray steps to Messrs. Harker and Inman's handsome door. He felt as one going, not into bondage, but into a new enlargement and freedom.

Within the door was a glazed Inquiries office, and within it sat two girls drinking tea and prattling. The nearer of them, apprehending a face at their window, dropped the prattle but retained her cup and asked, "Can I help you?"

Kerry said proudly, "I have an appointment with Sir Osbert Inman," and hoped she guessed he was an author whom her employers were publishing.

"Your name, please?"

He gave it, but very plainly knowledge of it had not percolated as deep as this. The child merely moved a plug in her switchboard, spoke the name into the heart of the palace, and, on receiving a reply from those depths, said, "Would you come along with me, please?"

He followed her along a wide stone corridor and up wide stone stairs. On the second floor she threw open the door of a back room. "Mr. Betterman, sir." And Kerry entered, saying, "Betterkin." He found himself in a spacious chamber as well carpeted as the passages were bare.

Apart from the red and blue carpet he was at first aware only of a writing desk as large as a Victorian dining table and a man in a chair behind it.

The man rose at once and reached an unforeseen height. But once he'd stopped rising, his breadth and girth gave proportion to the height, so that he ceased to look unusually tall. "Nevertheless, he must be six feet," thought Kerry, and felt more than usually short. He was never comfortable with someone who stood a foot above him. But this man's face under sparse silver hair was fat and friendly, and his welcome hearty.

"Sit down, sir! Sit down, sir!" He indicated a deep leather chair before the desk. "And Jo-jo, dear"—this to the girl from Inquiries—"ask Mr. Armstrong to come along, will you. Say it's *Green and Pleasant Clerkenwell.* Now, sir, a cigarette?"

Kerry, sitting in the fine chair and wishing Godfrey could see him here, took the cigarette. Sir Osbert lit it for him, and sat down—to Kerry's relief, because once he was seated and tilting back in his chair, it canceled the gap between their heights, and they seemed of the same species.

"Perhaps I will; yes." Sir Osbert took one of his own cigarettes. While he lit it, Kerry glanced around the room and saw that the only other furniture was some large mahogany bookcases packed with books still in their colored jackets, some deep chairs like the one he sat in, and a long Caroline daybed, covered with embroidered crewel cushions, on which, no doubt, Sir Osbert sometimes took a nap after luncheon.

The cigarette alight, Sir Osbert began, "Well, now? . . ." with a questioning smile; and Kerry, not knowing the answer, only smiled too.

"*Green and Pleasant Clerkenwell.* A nice title, though it doesn't hole out in one; not until you realize it's a story about the knights of long ago."

"It's an adaptation from Blake's 'Jerusalem,' " said Kerry.

"Oh, I see. . . ."

Good lord, would nobody perceive that at once? Surely it was palpable. Kerry provided the quotation. " 'England's green and pleasant land.' They were knights of Jerusalem, so there really was a bit of Jerusalem in Clerkenwell then, you see."

"Oh, I see."

"Yes," said Kerry, as if confirming an unlikely explanation.

"I see."

And there was silence for a space. While Kerry suffered a little.

"I see; but it doesn't make it clear that the book's a novel. Could be a guide—though Clerkenwell's about the only place in London with nothing green and pleasant in it anywhere."

"It was satirical," said Kerry.

"Oh, I see. . . . And of course it could be a history."

Kerry sat appalled that, with all his high opinion of his gifts as a novelist, he had never perceived these elementary facts. Were there other things he had not yet learned? He couldn't speak.

"Still," said Sir Osbert, "I think we'll keep the title."

Keep it?—then they had really decided to publish? Now he was afraid to speak lest he disturbed this decision.

"You must have done a lot of research into the history of Clerkenwell."

"I live there."

"Oh, *do* you?" Evident that he had never seen Kerry's letter; and disappointing. It must have stayed with some underling. "But forgive me: why on earth should anyone want to live in Clerkenwell?" Evident that his book had made but little impression on this reader.

"I went there, among other things, to write this book."

"You did? Well, that's the way to go about it. I was interested, since Clerkenwell's only around the corner from here, and I even went along to look at some of the places where your things happened: the Gate, Turnmill Street, Faulkner's Alley —though that doesn't look as if it could have been there in Tudor times."

"Poetic licence," suggested Kerry.

"Oh, I see. Yes. We have our connections with Clerkenwell: Wellman and Sons and the Brinsley Press do some of our printing. Good firms. Ah, Mike! Here we are. *Green and Pleasant Clerkenwell.* This is Michael Armstrong, my partner and literary adviser. He's a novelist too. You doubtless know some of his books."

Novelist *too!* Then they already numbered him among that shining company.

"I certainly do," he said politely, to please Mr. Armstrong.

Mr. Armstrong was tall too, but not as tall as Sir Osbert. His slimness, however—for he must have been twenty years younger than his chief—made him seem nearly as tall, and Kerry, rising to shake hands, felt dwarfish again.

"How d'you do?" asked Mr. Armstrong, and without further interest in how he did, said to Sir Osbert, "Sorry if I kept you waiting, O.I. I was on the telephone to—" and he mentioned the name of a very famous novelist.

"Oh, him again? Christ!"

"Yes, and he went on and on. On and on."

"All about the sales of *Auld Tammy Craig,* I suppose?"

"Precisely."

"God. Doesn't he think we've sold enough?"

"No."

"What more does he imagine we can do?"

"Work a miracle."

"Well, we can't do that."

"Precisely."

"You must understand, Mr. Betterkin," said Sir Osbert, laughing, "that authors are the bane of our existence. All publishers are agreed that they'd like to run their businesses without them, but none of us has yet quite seen how that can be done. But that's no way to talk to a new author, is it, Mike? A cigarette, Mike?"

"No." Terse and abrupt, Mr. Armstrong's speech. "Thanks."

"Well, heave up a chair and sit down. Authors are so expensive, Mr. Betterkin; that's another thing. A shocking big addition to costs."

Mr. Armstrong threw an anxious look at his chief as if he feared he was swimming into dangerous and costly waters. He did not heave up a chair, but went straight to bed on the cushions of the daybed. Here he lay full length and fingered his fingers, rather as if he were weary of life and authors and Kerry were a psychiatrist who had come to deal with the traumas they had set up in him. "A curious book of yours," he said from his couch. Kerry's heart pitched at the adjective. "We were interested in its possibilities."

Possibilities only? Oh, had they then come to no decision? The switchbacking heart pitched onto a second, downward slope.

"Was it your first?" asked Sir Osbert.

"Oh, yes."

"Well, I hope it'll be the first of many."

"It's never easy to get a first book started," said Mr. Armstrong.

"No," Sir Osbert allowed.

"It's the devil," said Mr. Armstrong and left it there.

"I suppose so," said Kerry, but thought, That may be true of an ordinary novel, but mine is different.

"Michael thought the world of it," said Sir Osbert.

"Well . . ." Clearly Mr. Armstrong thought this an unwise remark; and Kerry decided he didn't like him as well as Sir Osbert. "I wouldn't go as far as that, O.I. One or two parts needed vigorous work with the blue pencil."

Kerry liked him less and less. "Which were they?" he asked, hiding the behavior of his heart.

Mr. Armstrong, speaking in most unlively tones, mentioned some passages, which immediately became for Kerry some of his best. To one suggestion for a total cutting he wanted to cry out, "Oh *no!*" like a prisoner sentenced to die. But he had to wrap his pain in a silence. He dared not reject these suggestions. To offend these large and powerful men would be to disperse in a dust cloud his great tower of hope; and farewell then to his triumph with Godfrey, with Sally Penelope, with the Windsors. So he said, "I see," and nodded. And, feeling he must say more so as to appear unaggrieved, he added, "I could certainly think over those parts."

Seated there with Sir Osbert leaning back on his tilted chair and Mr. Armstrong apparently composed for meditation on his couch, he felt as helpless and as brittle as Daniel when the lions sat around, considering him. Unless he was to die by a blow from each of their paws, he must feed them with scraps; so he repeated, "Yes, I could look at those parts," and in case this was not a large enough mouthful, threw them another. "At all of them."

"Think it'd be all right to show him the readers' reports, Mike?"

"Quite O.K., O.I."

"Their opinions were roughly the same as yours."

"Sometimes."

Sir Osbert grounded his tilting chair and picked up his telephone. A bell buzzed in the next room, which Kerry guessed was a buffer, a satellite state where a secretary sat like an occupying army to resist all attempts at disrupting her master's peace. "Oh, Di," Sir Osbert began. "Get Editorial to send our readers' reports on *Clerkenwell*. Yes, quickly, please; I've got *Clerkenwell* here. What? . . . Oh, *is* he? What the hell does he want? . . . So? Well, just tell the stinker I'm dead. Far too busy to see anyone. And tell him Mr. Armstrong's dead too. Died at six o'clock this morning. What? . . . *Must* you? Yes, s'pose you must. Yes, perfectly right, my dear. Mustn't offend him. Say I'll return to life sometime next week and be delighted to see him. I'm free—when?—three o'clock Tuesday. Fine. Be reasonably nice to him."

He put back the receiver. "Mike, would you believe it? That was Howard again. Sitting downstairs without any appointment whatever. What more can he want to gas about? His damned book's gone forward. We *have* got other books to attend to, and some of them—though he can't perceive this— are much more important than his."

Kerry, listening, learned anew that in a great publishing house most authors were but a wearisome nuisance. He felt more insignificant than ever.

"Christ," said Mr. Armstrong.

"You know Howard Reece's novels, I expect, Mr. . . . Mr. . . . Mr. . . ."

"Betterkin."

"Betterkin. They're a bit too sweet but they sell like ice cream, so it's important to keep him sweet too. Well, where were we? Oh, yes: *Clerkenwell.* If that's your first, you've certainly got the gift. Agree, Mike?"

"I agree there's promise there."

Promise! A pox on promise. His tale was performance, not promise.

"Yes, we like it a lot. Started on a new one?"

"No." Kerry laughed. "Hardly yet."

"Well, get busy. He's a born storyteller, eh, Mike?"

"Yes, but it's a lifetime's job learning the craft properly." Mr. Armstrong studied his nails, perhaps thinking that the craft was there at least, at these fingers' ends. He put them away and spoke angrily. "I've been twenty years at it, and not a day passes but I learn something more and feel ashamed that I never perceived *that* piece of skill before. And then people come to me and say, 'My God, Armstrong, if I had the time I could write one heck of a novel.' Just as if there were nothing to learn—instead of everything—before you dare ask the suffrages, and the shillings, of the public. I notice they never say, 'My God, I'd play a sonata to the ten thousand music lovers in the Albert Hall.' Oh, no! it's only novel-writing that any mug can do."

Just then a young man with dark, unkempt hair came in and handed two typed quarto sheets to Sir Osbert. "Thanks, Dick," Sir Osbert acknowledged. "I just wanted to show them to the author. Don't wait." And the young man went straight out without one glance at the author. He didn't turn to look at him as one of whom, fifty years hence, he could boast, "I saw him the first time he came to Harker's." He just walked straight out.

"There they are, Betterkin. If you'd like to glance through them."

"Thank you." Apprehensively Kerry took the two sheets, put on his glasses, blinked twice to clear his sight, and read.

"This book has its merits"—damn the man's impudence—"but there is much evidence of a novice's hand." Kerry resisted this, not without pain, and read on. "It needs judicious cutting. Some of the episodes are very well done, but he treats all of them as of equal significance and value, sparing us nothing. In places the story is painfully reminiscent of the early historical romances of Sir Gilbert Barnes, though these, of course, were written with vastly superior skill—"

Damn the woman! Certainly a woman. "Vastly superior," "painfully reminiscent"—a woman's threadbare language. A tramway mind, running along worn-out phrases. And for *her* to lecture him when she couldn't even write. But there! she had to find some faults. That was what she was paid her guinea for.

"But this is not to deny that the book shows talent—"

Talent only.

"—and I would hesitate to advise rejecting it, though it may be difficult to find the right public for it. It might have a strong appeal to boys—"

God!

But none must see his indignation or his wounds. He laid it down and, almost bereft of hope, began to read the second one.

"This book merits serious consideration"—oh, sweet relief. "If it is a first novel, it is certainly remarkable in its promise" —Kerry was content with "promise" now—"and if its author is still young, he should one day do fine work. My most serious criticism of it—apart from some impatience with the excessive detail he gives to relatively minor incidents—would be that from first to last it is out of key with the modern mood, which no longer takes kindly to the heroic, the emotional, and the highly dramatic in its fiction." Ah, I can take that. This is a man writing. "Of its kind it is a very good book, but it is more in tune with the intellectual climate of forty years ago. The author's heart is with the eighties. I would, however, recommend its publication, even though its more heroic and sentimental parts may embarrass and offend the modern mind." A dear man! Worth twenty of that filthy woman.

He laid it back on the desk. "Naturally I like this second one better, but I still can't think the book sentimental."

"I didn't find it sentimental," said Sir Osbert. "But then I'm old-fashioned."

"Sentimental be damned! Emotional, yes—heroic, yes—but sentimental—punk! Sick of the word." This was a sudden, unexpected and startling explosion from Mr. Armstrong's bed. It was such an explosion that it flung him upward and onto his feet, and drove him around the room. "One's perfectly entitled to write a sentimental book if by sentimental one means no more than our terrified critics mean today. One's even right to do it. I say it's one's duty to do it. Because by sentimental what do they usually mean? Merely something that doesn't shiver back in fear from all fully expressed emotion—something that

isn't content to be arid and constipated and partly paralyzed."
Kerry, listening to this sudden spate from an enclosed and
taciturn man, remembered, somewhere in the purling course
of it, that Mr. Armstrong's books were often attacked as sentimental. "In ninety cases out of a hundred the critics have been
wrong in the past, and there are extra-special reasons why the
bastards should be wrong today."

Yes, the critics hurt him properly, Kerry thought. He doesn't
love them at all. If I could have had two words with them before
they reviewed his last book, I'd have told them to avoid the
word "sentimental."

And just as he was thinking this, Mr. Armstrong dashed on
—bullying the subject in front of him. "Criticism is in an appalling state today. Appalling. It thinks it's clever, but in fifty
years' time it'll be seen for the overintellectualized, emotionally timid, utterly destructive thing it is. You see, most critics
just flock like sheep, all afraid to do anything but run with the
time spirit, and it so happens that the time spirit of this present
age is very bad for—indeed, a menace to—great literature.
Why? Why?" He looked at Sir Osbert. He looked at Kerry. He
might have been addressing the boys in a classroom, but neither of these boys offered an answer. "Why? I'll tell you."

He now stood opposite Kerry, looking sad and angry; and
Kerry wondered what was coming. Sir Osbert also stared at the
speaker, but he probably knew well what was coming. It came.
Spreading his hands as if to open a great question, Mr. Armstrong demanded, "In all great literature what is it that's rela-
tive to no particular age, but absolute, eternal, undated? I
sweep the literature of my own country and, so far as I can, the
literature of other lands, and always the answer comes to me
that this absolute thing, this thing which alone endures, is the
fearless, and therefore sufficient, expression of the natural human emotions. And if this is so, then the spirit of our age, and
the pressure of its criticism, are against the creation of the
finest literature."

"Yes," said Sir Osbert, perhaps hoping that prompt agreement would halt the lecture.

It didn't. Mr. Armstrong went on, and in his eyes was a sad
prophet's gleam. "Because, you see, we are frightened of sufficiently expressed emotion. That is the disastrous phobia of our
age. It is, of course, a recoil from the excessive sentimentality
of the Victorians, but it's none the less excessive and unhealthy

itself. And, God save us, just as sentimental, if by that tedious word we mean an emotionally driven recoil from reality. And I ask you—I ask you! How can great literature flourish in an atmosphere so frigid, so withering?"

Since no one answered this, Mr. Armstrong did. "It can't."

"No. There's something in that," Sir Osbert conceded, a man who liked to please all parties. He doused his cigarette and pushed the ashtray toward Kerry.

"That," said Mr. Armstrong, "was why I so liked this book of Mr. . . . Mr. . . ."

"Betterby," Sir Osbert supplied.

"Betterkin," Kerry corrected.

"Betterkin. He wasn't ashamed of his heart." The heart under discussion swelled at these words. "What a would-be clever but imbecile remark that was of Hamish's about the author's heart being with the eighties. It's a favorite crack of all the smart little avant-garde boys and their horrible tough girls. I've had it said of myself. What I'd like 'em to do is to try a little experiment in humility and ask themselves, could it be that when we say of these uninhibited authors like Mr. Betterby"—plain that he really meant "like Mr. Armstrong" —"that their hearts are with the eighties, we are more right than we know, but it's not the 1880s that have their hearts but the 1980s."

Kerry was delighted, if surprised, to think of himself as belonging to a forward movement which would inherit the 1980s —though he suspected that the reading of his heart in Mr. Hamish's report was a better diagnosis than Mr. Armstrong's. But let him forget that suspicion. Perhaps he was destined to lead a new movement. Along with Mr. Armstrong, whom he now liked immensely.

Mr. Armstrong, somewhat out of breath after this exposition, went rather sadly—perhaps in doubt of its wisdom—back to bed. Here on the daybed he crossed his legs like a crusader on a tomb. Sir Osbert said nothing, and Kerry felt he ought to speak. Much encouraged by this promotion of his heart to the 1980s, he decided to put the sovereign but nervous question. "Do I understand, then, that you'd like to publish my book?"

"Oh, yes," said the crusader from his tomb, and great though Kerry's joy was in these two words, it was flawed a little by his sudden perception that one of the reasons for his book being published by this house was that its literary adviser had been called sentimental. And been gravely hurt by such a shock to his dreams.

"You'd like us to be your publishers, wouldn't you?" asked the amiable Sir Osbert.

His publishers! "Oh, rather!" he exclaimed, like a thirsty schoolboy to whom an ice cream has been suggested.

"Well, that's fine. And we'll send the manuscript back to you so that you can glance at those parts Mr. Armstrong mentioned."

"I certainly will," said Kerry, while he thought "Terms?" But he feared to talk about terms lest he should impair these present happy relations. Sir Osbert, however, as if he had trapped Kerry's thought, said, "We'll send our usual agreement along —the usual terms for a first book. Ten percent on the first thousand copies, fifteen on the next four thousand, and twenty thereafter. I quite think the book may reach the thereafter. Twenty-five pounds in advance, on the day of publication. That O.K.?"

"That's fine." And indeed it sounded rather better than what the all-knowing Hoss Comfort had foretold in the Fleet Street pub.

"Well, that's fine." Sir Osbert rose from his chair, and Mr. Armstrong rose from the dead. "Good-bye, Mr. Betterkin. We shall do our best, you can be sure. We'll try to establish you."

"Thank you. When . . . when would the book be out?" Kerry managed to insert this question between his chair and the door.

"Three months' time. Just in time for the Christmas market."

"That's fine," said Kerry, and wished he'd found other words to say; words that were less like a tinny echo of Sir Osbert's.

Mr. Armstrong, with hardly any words at all, escorted him down the stairs to the front entrance.

The narrow defile of Paternoster Court into which Kerry now stepped was gray and greasy and dull beneath a heavy London sky, but to him it was a lane in paradise, and paved with gold, as he walked quickly along it, hurrying home to Pearl.

15

Now to Sally; to Sally with the news tonight. We meet tonight.
. . . Work almost impossible in the office, but must be done.
Can't just sit here with castles in the sky. Force yourself to
work. . . . Godfrey next. Godfrey just as soon as may be. . . .

On returning from the office, unable to eat, for happiness
was a sickness putting an end to appetite, he drank some tea
and then set off, an hour too early, for Ray Street, walking
slowly to wear away time.

In Ray Street he stood under the high dark cliff of her buildings and was more than happy waiting there with hands in
pockets and trying to imagine Ray Street as the villainous
Hockley-in-the-Hole. Sometimes he strolled up the street to
look along the Farringdon Road and watch without interest the
heavy trucks thumping into the City so that they shuddered the
earth beneath his feet, or the endless cavalcade of private cars
purling out of it, homeward. He pitied people who looked from
the tenement windows or passed him by: they had no such
hopes as he; their day was ordinary; and for the most part their
faces were set and tired, the women's with drawn lips and
hardened eyes.

When at last Sally came down her spiraling steps, out of the heart of her black cliff, he greeted her with an ordinary every-day kiss and asked at first about *her* interests, as if he were not standing there with a nimbus of glory around him. Then as they turned to walk, he said, "It may or may not interest you to know, Miss Sally Penelope, that the book is accepted and will be out in three months."

"Kerry! *No!*"

"Three months. In time for the Christmas market." He was proud of this phrase, newly acquired from the book-trade world.

"Oh! Oh, darling!" She flung her arms around him, there on the turn of Ray Street into Farringdon Road, and hugged him, to the scandal of two women passing on the opposite sidewalk. Inaptly, her eyes filled. "Oh, tell me! Tell me all. Quick. Don't stand there grinning."

"Come and I'll tell you."

Fingers coupling, they walked across the Farringdon Road and up the raked roads into the high squares of Clerkenwell. It was now a cold gray night with a north wind adrift in the streets, but though it followed them, and played about them, it could not pierce their warm garments of delight. Around and around the squares they went, because here at least were faded trees and railed gardens, around Granville Square and Lloyd Square and Myddleton Square, while he told her all about his hour with the great men of Harker and Inman's. Or at least all that could sound perfect about that hour: not a word about his suspicion that it was because one of the directors had been called sentimental that his own book had been immediately accepted.

He told her how both readers had "recommended publication" and Sir Osbert had said he'd "got the gift" and "was a born storyteller" and they'd "establish him." (Another good phrase.) In the rush of his narrative he sinned more than once; for instance, he represented Sir Osbert as saying "We'll establish you" instead of "We'll try to establish you"; and he transformed "You'd like us to be your publishers?" into "We'd like to be your publishers. Got any more books?"

Sally did little skips of joy at his side, clinging tight onto his arm with both hands. "Oh, what will it mean? Will it make you an awful lot of money?"

"Well. . . ." He withdrew into modesty. Or into a show of

modesty. He muted the noisy hopes within him. "You can never tell with a book," he said, as though he'd been in the trade for years. "It may sell no more than a few hundreds, or it may run into thousands."

"Oh, I think you'll sell thousands. I'm sure you will. I feel it in my bones," she declared, loyalty being so much nicer than sense.

"No. To do that, a book needs more than merit. Hoss says it needs a heavy drop of luck in the scale."

"But I'll pray—I'll pray that you have it."

"Yes, pray—pray hard. It's with the gods."

But he was veiling the real truth about his hopes. Really they were at that height where they were hardly separable from belief. Encircling Myddleton Square, he went into a silence, and in this silence he was reading the reviews that would appear on the morrow of publication. One said, "We need look no further for the novel of the year." Another: "It seems unbelieveable that this is a first book. Here beyond question is a story that will endure. John Kenrick Betterkin, whoever he is, has arrived." A third: "In the character of Sir Nicholas Shelley, Knight Hospitaller of St. John, Mr. Betterkin has added a new immortal to our literature." He was opening a letter on the morning of publication from Sir Osbert: "You will be glad to know that we can't get *Clerkenwell* out fast enough. The first and second impressions are now exhausted, the third is nearly gone, and we are rushing out a fourth." He was being interviewed by reporters who wanted the story of his life (which he gave). He was reading another review: "Here is pure genius. . . ."

It chanced as they wandered on, Kerry's outward attire of drab modesty hiding an inner flame of expectation, they passed the St. James-at-hill Almshouses in Soane Way. There the houses stood, six little one-storie gabled homes embracing a quadrangle of grass. And he told her how he'd often passed them and thought that, if only he could produce one immortal work—or perhaps two—he would be content to end in these almshouses, a tired old man with a pipe, sitting before his door in the sun or the shade. People would pass, as they two were passing now, and one would say, "Do you know who that old dodderer is? That's John Kenrick Betterkin." And all the others would exclaim, "No!" and stare, and turn their heads to see him again. That was all he wanted, he said.

"But won't I be with you?" demanded Sally. "Or am I dead?"

"Oh, yes, there's that to be considered," he agreed. "Perhaps, alas, it'll be impossible."

All of London's millions, as they trod its hard sidewalks, he said, had their cloud castles in its sky, somewhere above the chimneys and the dome of St. Paul's; and for most they stayed as clouds till the time came for them to dissolve in vapor and float away.

And fervently she agreed, hanging on to his arm and thinking of fantasies of her own. But it would be different for him, she said. She was sure of it.

They sat for a while in the saloon of the London Spa, eating snacks and sipping champagne hopes with their beer; and when it was closing time, went back to Ray Street. There, before breaking from his arms and going up her steps to a lonely bed, she fiddled with his coat lapel and asked, "Do you really think this may mean money and that . . . we could get married?"

"It's on the cards," he said.

"Oh . . . darling!"

"It may be we're on the eve. The eve of something big."

"Oh!" To this hope she responded with a kiss more passionate and deliberately protracted than any she had given him; then sharply put him away, as if afraid of something which had risen within her, and feeling guilty because of it. She touched his cheek with a sudden frightened kiss and ran out of sight up her harsh stone stairs.

To Godfrey now. To an encounter as pungent as this with Sally was sweet.

Though as a rule he hated writing letters, he had found excuses for writing to all his friends, and, late in each letter, as if it were but an afterthought, had told his news. But a letter to Godfrey would make it all too clear that he *wanted* to tell him. What, then, to do? Tell Godfrey he must. Godfrey was the most important recipient of all.

Only one thing to do: he must loiter near the northern gates of Gray's Inn, out of which Godfrey always came, and there in Theobald's Road "accidentally" meet him. So next afternoon he got permission to leave the office early, and since clerks and cashier all knew that he was now "a man with publishers," much banter followed him as he went. "Come and see us again one day," they said. "Come back when you're a millionaire and see how the poor live." "Put us in your next book. People should know something about the world's workers."

By five o'clock he was standing at the mouth of Bedford Row and gazing along Theobald's Road at the gateway of the Inn, so that directly Godfrey appeared he could walk toward him. It was an easily explicable encounter, because Theobald's Road in due course became Clerkenwell Road, and his way home.

From his place of espial he could see the tall gray-stucco gateway just beyond Jockey's Fields, and the high parklike railings guarding the quiet of the Inn, and above them the lofty plane trees heavily filled with their darkening autumn leaves. For a long time no man came out of that silent green oasis into the hustle and rush of Theobald's Road, let Kerry peep and peer as he liked. Shameful, this sly watching while the traffic roared by on its business, and the pedestrians passed, clothed in innocence instead of dawdling with guilt; but was there ever a man who didn't sometimes do things that he'd tell to none? A tedious, tiring wait; possibly a wasted one. Perhaps Godfrey had not been in his office today; perhaps he had left early, or —but no, here he was, at last: Godfrey in his bowler, black jacket and striped trousers, with a crease in the trousers like the fold in foolscap sheets and his rolled umbrella at sway between two fingers—Godfrey, a trim little legal bird issuing from that guarded grove where his species nested and multiplied.

Kerry walked toward him with a close-lipped grin. He grinned because Godfrey would be forced to speak to him; he couldn't do anything so ridiculous as to walk past him with his head in the air. Godfrey did speak. He said, rather unhappily, "Hallo, Kerry?"

"Hallo, Godfrey. This *is* a pleasant surprise; but we pass each other on the road home. You to Holland Park and I to Clerkenwell. And which is better, as Socrates said, God alone knows. Married yet?"

"No. Not yet."

"Soon? When's the wedding?"

"We're not—not certain yet."

"Where will the great occasion be?"

"I haven't the faintest idea."

"But it'll be in your lady's church, surely?"

"Could be. Yes, quite likely."

The lies that were dropping in Theobald's Road, thought Kerry. At this rate they would strew the pavement like the autumn leaves in Vallombrosa.

"You needn't worry," he offered. "I shan't turn up to disgrace you."

"There's no question of *you* disgracing me."

"Glad of that."

Godfrey was compelled to continue, "Come without Pearl, and you'll be very welcome."

Another lie fluttering down to the pavement. Kerry would have liked to retort, "No Pearl, no Kerry," but that would be foolhardy and would put an end to negotiations. So he put a few more questions about Godfrey's activities and progress, receiving favorable answers to all, and then said, in a careless tone, *"I've* had a spot of good news since I saw you last."

"Oh?" Godfrey didn't sound much interested. Nor did Macduff before hearing that his castle was taken and his wife and children slain.

"Yes. You knew I was writing a book?"

"So you told me."

"Well, it's been accepted. As a matter of fact, by the very first publisher I sent it to. Rather rare, that."

Godfrey's face did not move; his brows did not lift or his lips exclaim; but Kerry saw that he had taken a blow of dismay, a shaking blow. So he administered another. "I can't help being pleased because I'm told it's almost unique for it to be accepted by the first publisher that sees it."

"Who's publishing it?"

This was to ask for a third blow, and Kerry provided it. Godfrey was obviously hoping for the name of some small publisher; what he received was "Harker and Inman's, and they're just about the biggest fiction publishers in the country. They really do seem to like it," Kerry said, as if his modesty were surprised. "I had a long talk with Sir Osbert: Sir Osbert Inman, the head of the firm"—vulgar, this brandishing of a title, but pleasant, undeniably pleasant—"and they're going to get it out in time for the Christmas market. I gather they're going to do it in rather a big way."

This was exaggeration, but he was launched now and sliding uncontrolled down the greased slips.

"What will you get for it?" One could hear an anxious jealousy in the words.

"I get an advance of twenty-five pounds and a—"

"Oh, is that all?" One heard the relief; and to hell! a damnable note of pity.

"That's the standard advance for a first novel. And, if you'd let me finish, it's an advance on account of royalties that rise to twenty percent. The book could, if it were a success, make thousands."

"Thousands? No."

"Indeed it could. Twenty percent is one shilling and sixpence a copy, and if it could sell fifty thousand, that'd be quite a packet. Three thousand, seven hundred, and fifty pounds, isn't it?"

"Is it? I suppose it is."

"But of course it'd have to be very successful to do that," Kerry conceded, beginning to feel some pity for a brother who was hearing bad news. "I'm not banking on anything as big as that."

"Well, I do congratulate you. I am delighted to hear this. I hope you sell the fifty thousand."

And those are the two biggest lies yet, thought Kerry: one who likes to think himself the success of the family isn't delighted to hear a brother, whom he's rather despised, padding up behind with a chance of passing him. He felt a need to spare this liar any more pain. "Thanks, old boy. But the whole thing's a lottery."

"Well, I hope you win it." A brave utterance, even if a lie. "I really do. I must hurry along now." Did he want to get away, need to get away? "Good-bye, Kerry."

"Good-bye, chum. I'll send you a copy."

"Yes, do," said Godfrey with a brave smile. "This is most interesting. Thanks."

Watching him walk away, Kerry saw that some of the self-satisfied air had gone from his walk; nor was his umbrella swaying from his fingers as happily as it had been before.

16

While Kerry went to and from his office in Fleet Street with a cloud of ambition and hope enveloping him, Sally went to hers in Bowling Green Lane, and home again, hardly less enwrapped than he. But the longings behind her abstracted eyes were very different from his; they were almost the exact opposite. And, unlike him, she could not speak of them to anyone —not even to Kerry could she tell them in their fullness— because they amounted to a desire—the surely shameful desire —for sanctity. This shameful word she dodged by calling it "selflessness."

Just now she was as happy with this ambition as ever Kerry had been with his self-centered one, and she got a similar joy from her efforts at creating it. These efforts consisted in delightful mortifications every odd minute of the day. No one saw them—no one must know of them—but they took place, one after another, rapidly, in street, in office, in home. Not that all of them, or most of them, were necessary, but that they would develop in time enormous spiritual muscles. For thirty years she had allowed these muscles to slacken almost into apathy, and much ruthless rehabilitation was required. Every triumph over her slack or greedy self carried its joy, with the result that her method now, considered roughly, was to deny herself everything that was pleasant. And sometimes to deny herself this denial, since it could be itself so pleasant. Her whole life now, in street or office or home, was an exercise yard equipped with appliances for unsparing spiritual gymnastics.

But one evening, after Kerry and she had strolled for hours about the squares and were now walking up Benjamin Street toward his home, it began to rain heavily, and he seized her hand and rushed her through a sharp arrowy onslaught to the little arched entry of Eagle Court. This was another brief tunnel under the second stories of two old houses. It backed into a yard, but its mouth gaped at Red Lion Street and at the distant door of his home.

They stood in this flagged channel between street and yard, watching the slanted and plunging rain and its sudden lively travel down the gutters of Benjamin Street as once it must have purled down the same slopes to splash into the old Fleet River. While they watched he talked proudly of his book, whose galleys he had already received and corrected. (He was proud of this professional word, galleys.)

"Yes, I've passed the galleys and now they'll be returned to the printers for makeup."

"Oh, goody, goody!" Sally exclaimed, with a suitably excited rising upon her toes.

"The page proofs are scheduled to arrive in a week or two, and when I've corrected them, there'll be nothing more to do: Editorial will just pass them for press." Page proofs, scheduled, Editorial, pass for press—all good professional words.

"Oh, isn't it all wonderful?" cried Sally, and said nothing of her own progress in her different field.

The rain scampered down, their talk dwindled, and he, remembering how once before they had taken cover beneath the old Tudor arch of St. John's Gate and what that delay behind the screens of rain had led to, snatched her into his arms to take as much from her as she still allowed him. She had been thinking of the same hour, and now his embrace, his kisses, his grasp of her knee between both of his, lit up all that was dry, deprived tinder in her, as well as all that loved him and ached to serve him, so that soon the mass was not so much smoldering as aflame; and when he, taking his mouth from hers, stared up Red Lion Street toward his home and begged, "Come. Come. Pearl is away and no one will know—or they'll think we've run in for shelter. Come . . . *do.* . . ." she was powerless to say no or anything else; her will to self-conquest was burnt up in desire, urgency, and love: the love cried out that love could not be wrong and that it made all things good; and she ran out with him and up the street toward his door. The rain beat angrily upon them both as if it would even yet stay her or, at all events, castigate him for causing her thus to stumble.

When it was over and she was walking home, she did not weep, but she felt like Peter who after he had denied all the faith that was in him went out and wept bitterly.

Nothing, now that the fire was quenched, could persuade her that her surrender was other than sin. And with this one sin the whole happy paradise garden in which she had been living was destroyed around her; it was annihilated and gone. Prayer was no longer possible. She got into her bed that night without a single prayer, and conscience, which had walked home with her chiding her all the way, got into bed with her and went on with its chiding; and when she awoke in the morning, it awoke at the same moment and began its merciless reprobation anew. And all that day any attempt at goodness seemed detached and rudderless and lost. Her whole state was wooden; too dull to be called repentance. A fall so terrible seemed to have plunged her beneath repentance. She worked at her typewriter as if she too were an insentient machine.

In her luncheon hour she did not want to eat. It was a day of St. Luke's summer, with a warm October sun spreading its blessing over trees about to die, and she thought at first of sitting alone in St. James's Churchyard, but she decided not to, since it would remind her of Kerry, and she turned the opposite way. She went up Rosoman Street to a place where they had never been together: Spa Green by the New River Head.

Here in the ornamental gardens laid out on the site of Islington Spa, once a resort of the noble, the royal, and the famous, she went to the only seat on which she could feel apart from all the other luncheon-hour workers taking the sun and the warmed soft air. This was a bench that seemed to retire into an alcove behind a tree, turning its back on Clerkenwell and its face toward the happier Sadler's Wells. She sat herself here with her head drooped and her hands idling on her lap.

She tried to drive her thoughts from Kerry, because when

she thought of him she was angry with him—even bitterly angry—and she must wearily fight this anger because her faith insisted that she must not judge but forgive.

"His dream means all the world to him, but he's absolutely indifferent to mine. He just sets about ruining it. It's ruined now."

This time yesterday she was happy. Serenely happy. How get back again into the exquisite peace that was hers a few hours ago?

"Oh, well . . . oh, well . . . if one falls completely, I suppose there's nothing to do but get up and begin again."

No, nothing; but so far this was only another weary thought and it raised no glow among the clinker and ashes of her self-esteem. It was not until a new set of words, sprung from heaven knew where, stood before her that she straightened her bowed shoulders, turned, laid her arm along the back of the seat and looked toward the great Water Board palace by the New River Head. But she was not seeing this, nor the streaming, shuttling traffic of Roseberry Avenue; she was seeing, as she thought, her road home to the peace of yesterday.

"If thy right eye offend thee, pluck it out. . . ."

Yes . . . yes . . . she considered the words, fell in love with them, and decided, with joy, that the heroic was required of her. Only the heroic act would rebuild her confidence, minister to her remorse, and restore her power to pray.

Yes . . . but it was joy and sorrow both—sorrow because she was determined for a while to see Kerry no more. But there was joy in this sorrow too, since it was mortification, atonement, and proof of power over herself. Pleasure too in the thought that she was going to teach Kerry a lesson; teach him that her ambition was as real as his, that her heart was as set on it as his heart on his, and that she *meant* to achieve it.

She rose from her bench with most of her peace around her again and something like joy in her heart at the prospect of battling for the things she believed in.

The battle was hot and angry on the seat in St. John's Public Garden. Sometimes, in his anger and impatience, Kerry rose and strutted hither and thither, while she sat alone on the seat, with the inscribed stone behind her proclaiming that this was a garden for the enjoyment and refreshment of the living. They could display their impatience with each other because as usual this square pit among the houses had nothing in it except its few worn rugs of grass, its empty seats, and its dying trees.

"It's senseless," said Kerry. "Utterly senseless."

"It is not. I know myself. I know what I've got to do."

"But why in thunder can't we meet and just kiss and be happy, if I promise not to ask anything more?"

"Because I can't trust myself."

"Or me?" He halted before her.

"No. I'm afraid not."

"Thank you for that." And he began walking again.

"How can I trust you after last night?"

"I don't admit that there was anything wrong in it. We love each other and we give each other all the joy we can until we can get married."

"It's wrong for me. And because it seems wrong to me it destroys everything. I can't pray or do anything."

"But it's all antediluvian; it's mid-Victorian; it's worse than that, it's Cromwellian; it's a puritanism that's been dead for—"

"I can't help that. It's me. I don't try to destroy your ambition; why should you want to destroy mine?"

But he wasn't listening to her; he was listening only to himself. "God made us so that we could give each other joy and—"

"The trouble is, you want me to share your ambition, and you don't care anything about mine."

"May I, please, speak? God made us so that we could give each other joy and end each other's deathly loneliness now and then. You're the only person who does this for me, and I'm the only person who does it for you, aren't I?" Looking her way for her answer, he met the irrelevant thought that her great eyes had become even larger since she'd gone hunting after goodness. And that his fury with her was another name for love.

"Oh, yes, yes."

"And yet you say you're not going to see me anymore. Will you tell me where the sense is?"

"I can't make you see it if you can't."

"I can't."

"I can't make you see that it's just because I love you so terribly that I've got to keep away from you."

"No, I'm damned if I can. You may think it's all very high and noble, but I strongly suspect that it's because, like most women, you *want* some relationship in your life that's full of interesting stresses and pains. You'd be miserable without it."

"Oh, it's not that," she protested, but in her eyes was a fear lest there were truth in this idea.

"I'm not so sure. I've only asked you to trust me, but no: you'd rather have a nice dramatic parting."

"Not a parting. It may not be for long."

"Why not?"

"If you make money with your book we could—we could get married."

Kerry, still wrestling with his surprise and anger, had forgotten his book. But now that she'd thrown it back into his memory he saw a new grievance and was pleased to see it. "If ever there was a time when I wanted to share things with you, it's now. Just when the page proofs are scheduled to come. Just when everything's about to happen. And it's this moment that you choose to take yourself off." If Sally was angry with him for not taking her aspiration seriously, he was now angry with her for not feeling all that she ought to feel about his recent triumph. "A nice time to desert me, I must say. It shows wonderful understanding. Wonderful sympathy."

"I shall want you to tell me everything that happens."

"And how, pray?"

"You could write."

"Write? Nonsense! I'm not writing to anyone." Having worked himself into a fever of sulkiness, Kerry allowed his tone to imply "Perhaps I shall no longer want to tell you."

And tentatively, timidly, she asked, "When will you know if the book's going to make money?"

"I shall get some idea, I imagine, directly it's out."

"But when will you know for certain?"

"Three months . . . four months. . . ."

"Well, could we, perhaps—"

"Could we what?"

"Get married soon after that?"

If she had had some notion of punishing him, she had tried to drive it away. She was only "teaching" him. He, on the other hand, not at all disposed for self-conquest just now, had a sullen desire to punish her and did so brutally. "I may have found someone else by then."

Sally rose. Her body may have been meager and her narrow face lack beauty and strength, but she could charge both of them with pride and dignity as well as the haughtiest lady in the court of a king. "I hope you do," she said. "And that she'll make you happy. I'll say good-bye now."

"Sally!" He was too proud to admit he'd said a wrong thing; but too startled also to add his good-bye to hers. "Where are you off to? Where do you think you're going?"

"Good-bye." She walked toward the narrow passage into Benjamin Street, and her head did not turn.

He, standing there full of anger and pride, and watching her go, laughed out loud for her to hear. "Ha, ha! Sally Penelope on her dignity! Do look, everyone!"

She went on with no sign that she had heard or cared, and her head still high. In a moment she would be out of sight, and he must be sure that she'd heard *something* that would hurt. "O.K.," he called after her, "if that's your line, it's mine too. It was you that chose to go. If you want to go, you can stay away—"

But she was gone, and it was useless to shout anymore. He went to the seat where a few minutes ago they had been sitting together, and plumped himself down on it, a sagging sack of anger, self-justification, and self-pity. Not an unpleasant mixture; it was stimulating, and soon there blended with it other thoughts that made of it a mixture rich, pungent, and uplifting: the thoughts that he was punishing her by letting her go; that, however high her head, her love for him could be only temporarily shut away; that if success came to him (as coming it was: his sanguine temperament would not allow this disaster to compete with his huge happy hopes) it must bring with it a reconciliation, and that all reconciliations were sweet.

So before leaving the garden he sat there and built in imagination a fine dramatic scene in which they would come together again. He would leave her to her sorrow and her wonder till such time as it was certain that success had brought him money and a new career. Then he goes, with humor, to find her. He walks to Ray Street to which she must return from work; he sees her coming toward him; he smiles mischievously; slowly she smiles too; he puts out a hand to take hers; she weeps a little; and he says simply, finely, "Come. I have come for you. You've got, if you will, to marry me."

17

"Ah, the day of days!" George Windsor extended both hands. He said, "See the conquering hero comes," but even as he did so, went with courtesy first to Pearl. "We are greatly touched that you should consent to spend it with us, two ancient discards."

Pearl began her usual machine-gun fire of words. "We think it wonderful of you to—a lovely idea—don't we think it kind of them, Kerry—"

"We certainly do, Commodore."

"There's no one, Mr. Windsor, with whom we'd rather—"

But George had not heard. "You sit here, my dear, and have some sherry. The hero here. It's always flattering to the old, and a wonderful surprise, when the young are content with their company."

"There's no one we'd rather—"

"Evie'll be here in a minute. She's just taking a last look at the *rôti.* Or maybe at her face. She's garnishing both in your honor. When she comes in you'll see that she's well trimmed aloft. Evie," he called. "Ee-vee!"

"Just coming." A happy voice from the kitchenette. "Tell the darlings to sit down. Give 'em drinks. Shan't be a minute."

"I do hope we're not putting her to too much trouble," Pearl gushed, in full chase after social ease.

"My dear lady, she's loving it. She's not enjoyed anything so much for a long time. She's been making her preparations all day. I too have played a minor part. But merely as a super. Or maybe not even that: just a stagehand. I laid the table."

"It looks lovely. What beautiful silver you've got. Kerry, look at those candlesticks. And, Mr. Windsor, that bowl!"

"A few treasured relics, dear lady, from the general wreck. As a rule they sleep in the bunk over there but they've come to life for this very great occasion. The Windsor Plate—not, of course, the plate of my cousins at the palace; that is gold, I'm told. But, admittedly, I've never been invited to see it."

Kerry looked at the Sheraton table. It could hardly have been more tastefully dressed, and in this small Clerkenwell room, on a carpet growing threadbare, it looked like an old lady sitting with her fine ancient lace about her in her last shabby lodging. He observed that around a centerpiece of apples and tangerines, with blue grapes draped over them, were four covers with fish, table, and dessert knives, and graceful stemmed glasses for a succession of wines.

"You've taken too much trouble, Commodore," he shouted.

"No, it's but a simple meal. Just a mess of beef and greens in the wardroom. Now, my dear." From the sherry decanter he began to pour out a glass for Pearl.

"Oh . . . only a very little," she pleaded, thereby revealing that she was not used to this sort of entertainment, which was the one thing she didn't want to do.

They sat and talked for a few minutes, and then Evie, in purple and pearls, swam through the door, extending both arms toward them in a rapture. Evie had always the right pantomime for any role she was playing. She went first to Kerry as he rose. "The day of days," she said, unaware that George had already run this fine brave phrase up the mast (doubtless they had used it earlier to each other). Taking both his hands, she drew him toward her and kissed him. "There! I've always wanted to do that. There, Georgy. I told you I would. All my congratulations and all the good wishes in the world. And our Pearl: aren't you proud of him, Pearl dear? A real author. I'm enormously proud to have had him just through my ceiling. I shall tell everybody to my dying day that I used to hear him writing his masterpiece through the ceiling."

"Yes, you can hear that typewriter as though it was in the same room," said George. "The floorboards—"

"Oh, but we do hope it hasn't—" began Pearl, but, as in a waters' meet, Evie's more powerful and natural flow rushed over the lesser stream and carried all before it. "So very nice of you to let us share your triumph. We feel almost as if it were our triumph too, don't we, Georgy? He's been so sweet, dears, sitting at that table all day, cleaning the silver. Nobody cleans silver as he does. Got some sherry, have you? Yes? Well, now just take your places, while I—" An explanatory smile all around, and she was gone.

"What did she say?" asked George.

"I think she wanted us to take our places at the table," Pearl explained hurriedly; and Kerry wondered when Pearl would give *him* a chance to answer someone.

"Ah, yes. She is in command of this vessel. Come. The guest of honor." With a brief, elegant wave of his upturned hand, learned in some old school of the actor's art, he indicated the cover on the hostess's right. "And Pearl by me."

They all sat down, and there was a silence because George seemed to have gone straight into a reverie that Kerry and Pearl did not like to disturb. The silence endured, and the two guests sat there, hands below the table, like well-mannered children at a tea party, till a bang on the door, as with the corner of a tray, lifted George out of his musing with a start. The bang was succeeded by the call "Georgy," to which, rising, he responded with "Ah. Things are afoot. Evie comes," and opened the door for her, unconsciously bowing. She sailed in with plates of cold salmon dressed with cucumber, lettuce, and mayonnaise. "I hope you don't mind it cold, dears. It's so much easier when one has no staff."

"It's really too—" began Kerry.

"I'm sure it's all wonderful," said Pearl.

No use. No chance for Kerry to speak while Pearl was sending her sprays of flattery about the room like jets from a hose.

George now came to each of them with a bottle of golden wine. "I could wish this were a fine Moselle, children, but it's only a Spanish wine; a poor substitute, but still. . . ."

"Don't you believe him," Evie enjoined, sitting down happily to a good meal. "There's nobody like George for choosing wine."

"It looks lovely," said Pearl.

"Ah, well." George was now charging Pearl's glass. *"Je ne*

connais rien de sérieux, ici-bas, que la culture de la vigne. There's truth in that.''

"Yes," said Pearl, and "Yes," murmured Kerry, though neither had a notion of what he had said.

"Voltaire," he explained, as he came to Kerry's glass.·

"Oh, yes," said Pearl, implying there was a time when she had given much attention to Voltaire.

As they ate, Evie asked, "Any news of the book, Kerry?"

"None whatever."

"No nice reviews yet?"

"Not one."

"They will come," George assured him. "Thursday is not a good day for reviews. Any show in the stores?"

"I haven't seen many stores." This was much less than true, because he had rushed from the office that evening to see at least the windows of bookshops in Fleet Street, the Strand, Victoria Street, Piccadilly, Charing Cross Road, and Holborn. And, there being no sign of his book, an ache in his heart had deepened at every window. "The few stores I saw had no copies."

"They've not unpacked the great bales yet."

"Of course, I only saw the shop windows."

"Ah, that's it! That explains everything. They're inside. Piled on the counters."

This was what Kerry wanted to believe—and must believe—because he could not, as yet, begin any dismantling of his castle of hope. If for a moment a sickening doubt tried like a cold hand to close upon his heart, he managed, by taking thought, to escape its clutch.

After the salmon, Evie brought in a round of red beef—in honor of Kerry's Old Tudor England, George explained. He carved it, serving Evie first, because, said he, this was the old English custom: it allowed the guests to see their hostess eat first and so be sure they were not going to be poisoned. All served, he carried around a red wine, apologizing that it was only Australian burgundy.

"I'm sure it looks lovely," said Pearl. "Only a very little, please."

After a charlotte russe, and while they were occupied with their dessert and port, George suddenly coughed once, said, "Well, now . . ." and rose to his feet, glass in hand.

"Well, now . . ." he repeated, fiddling with the stem of his glass. "Silence, all. If you please."

He laid the glass down, put the freed hand in a pocket and displayed the palm of the other to the company in what was plainly the first of many graceful gestures. His eyes stared in front of him; they were rather filmed, for he had drunk well of the wines.

"Our dear Kerry . . . our dear Pearl . . . Evie and I feared it was but a wild idea when I suggested that you might allow us to entertain you on your day of days, and we were touched—touched to the quick, is that not so, Evie?—when you so readily consented to honor us thus. It is, my dear children, one of the happiest things that have ever happened to us. We shall always remember that you were ready to spend with us what I can only call the first day of your fame." His gestures by this time were so graceful and easy that Kerry suspected he had learned these "lines" and practiced the accompanying gestures in his bedroom before a glass, bringing them to a perfect polish as he had done with the silver. "It is a great book which you have given to the world. I have already read some thirty pages of the copy you so generously gave us this morning—and why not more? Because I felt driven, so great my interest, to go and gape at St. John's Gate, and St. John's Square, and Clerkenwell Close —once, as you tell us, a cloister for the dear good nuns, where they would walk in quiet and meditate on their faith. I stood there quietly to meditate on their goodness—though doubtless some were cats—and on the terrible march of time's feet and our tragic destiny beneath them—I was giving myself to these wonderful thoughts, all engendered by your book; I was facing bravely the intolerable truth that the generations rise and pass and mean nothing, when a young lout of a policeman came in sight and quite obviously wondered whether I was loitering there with intent to commit a felony—a practice not uncommon, I understand, in Clerkenwell. This functionary was probably some Irish plowboy dressed up in a blue uniform, and there was nothing under his helmet to tell him how we artists need at times to stand still with very wonderful thoughts. We —I—" At this point he forgot how his lines continued; he "dried up"; but such a situation was not unknown to him, and he was skilled in handling it. He just took a sip from his glass; replaced it on the table; touched his lips with a napkin; and provided a few graceful waves of his upturned palm, while he improvised some patter.

"This foolish young cop was not, alas, one of the charming new women policemen in their natty uniforms and bright lipstick. I'd love to be arrested by one of them. I suppose they're some use, but the crooked boys of Islington seem only to whistle after them. So do our more excitable truck drivers. And I don't wonder. I've felt like doing it myself sometimes, old and decrepit though I be."

"The evil old man!" said Evie and, turning her face toward Pearl, enacted a tut-tut for her.

"Beg pardon, dear?" asked George.

"Come to the point, lovey."

"The point? We're slightly adrift, are we? The whole ship's adrift, is it? I see. Well, what were we talking about? Oh, yes, dear Kerry's book. I left the foolish blue functionary standing there and returned to clean the silver. And all the time as I sat there, making it shine brighter and brighter in your honor, I was meditating on your knightly hero and thinking how exactly he was the man I would have wished to be: heroic, devout, self-sacrificing, and ready to end my life gloriously on the scaffold. I confess that I turned to the end and read about his death and wept immoderately. As for Evie, when she reads about it, she will be but a noisy cataract of tears, and a fearful mess. She has a great heart, has Evie. I too should have liked to go to my death with an air, and a joke on my lips, but since this has been denied me, I can only say that I feel I would have loved to portray your hero on the stage, and I feel I would not altogether have failed the author, so deep my identification with his character—but those days are done. I am as sure as I can be of anything that your book will be a triumphant success—"

Here Evie, who had been staring happily up at him, interposed, "If Georgy says that, Kerry, he is probably right. George is seldom wrong."

"What?" asked George, turning to her. And, seeing her there, he was moved to say, "Is it not strange, Evie, my dear, to think that we have been nursing genius in our midst? Well now, you two dear children, permit Evie and me to drink to the success of your book. You are good enough sometimes to call me 'Commodore'; very good: as shipmates with you two youngsters in this rickety old bottom, we wish your book fair weather and a following wind. I say *your* book, Pearl, because I know you have played no small part in its creation. Where would any of us poor male creatures be, Kerry, without our wives or our sisters to look after us and cherish us and encourage us? How well I know what I owe to my dear comrade here.

She has been my shipmate for nigh on forty years, and many a shocking storm have we weathered together. The best thing I ever did was the day I took her aboard." Now Evie was staring at him with tears in her eyes, and he was not far from tears either. He gulped. "And I know, Pearl, that Kerry would be the first to admit that he owes much to you." Pearl looked down, shaking her head. "Evie dear, is your glass charged? Then drink with me. We toast, sir, the beginning of a great career."

He drank and bowed gracefully.

Kerry, who had foreseen no such speech and had therefore prepared nothing in his attic, could only murmur with head down, "Thank you—thank you, both—I shall never, never forget this."

And Evie, as George sat down, lifting a napkin to touch again his moistened lips, and his eyes, said, "Well done, Georgy! Wasn't that nice? There's nobody like Georgy for speeches like that."

18

Fourteen days. The book had been out for fourteen days, and all that had greeted it was silence—a silence majestic, inviolate; the silence of the night sky, Kerry said; the silence of the sea. Every morning he went down the narrow stairs to the hall-door mat, hoping to find a batch of press clippings there; daily he opened papers in the hope of seeing a review somewhere; daily when people came toward him in the street with greeting in their eyes, he hoped they were about to mention his book; but all that he encountered on all these occasions was the Great Silence. The way people would come toward him with a seeming congratulation in their faces and then speak of something other than the book he likened to a steam hammer, because for a moment he was uplifted only to be dropped with a heavy and total fall. Daily in his lunch hour he hurried to every accessible bookshop, hoping to see the book in window or on counter, and though he did see it once on a crowded table and another time on a shelf well away from the salesman's activities, both pleasant sights proved but symptoms of the silence, because it was plain, on each of his dozen visits, that these two venturesome strays were unmoved, unasked for, unshown.

Nevertheless he went on hoping. A hope that had had a giant's strength could not die in fourteen days.

Then out of the silent deserts came a review. He found it in the Windsors' paper which he'd picked off the hall-door mat.

"Ah!" he gasped. Here at last, perhaps, was the acclaim. He read it by the mat, trembling.

"After reading this book one is left with but one thought: why do publishers waste time, labor, paper, and printer's ink publishing such worthless stuff? From first to last it is palpable that this book is but the wish-fulfilling fantasies of an overimaginative and not very intelligent daydreamer, and, as such, it is of interest to no one but his doctor, who, if he is a practitioner of psychological medicine, might cure the author of his illusion that he has anything of importance to say to the world."

Kerry put the paper back on the mat and walked slowly upstairs to his attic to be alone. There he flung himself into his deep chair for a brief pause, thinking that he could weep if he were not far beyond tears. Not the least of his emotions was bewilderment. Impossible that the book, that labor of love, that labor of years, could warrant so complete a dismissal as this.

The next review came three days later from his press-clipping agency, and again, having torn open the cover with trembling fingers, he read it by the mat in the empty hall. It was not as mercilessly wounding as that first one, but some of its phrases stabbed hardly less.

"This is not a book of any distinction or importance, but it might have some interest for children or for adults with completely uncritical minds. It is really the adventures of a schoolboy's hero, too utterly heroic, selfless, and noble to have any relation to life. Some praise is due to the author for his setting; he has made a brave attempt to re-create from under the towering tenements and huge concrete factories of modern Clerkenwell the green and lively village of Tudor times. But when this has been said, what is the story but the 'halfpenny blood' of our childhood enlarged and dressed up to earn its seven-and-sixpence?"

No distinction? Walking up the stairs to show this to Pearl and get her angry contradiction, he thought of sentences, paragraphs, single epithets even, which had cost him an hour of labor, so resolved upon beauty had he been.

After this, he opened no more papers for fear, but he could not stay his hand from opening the press clippings that came through his door. He had to wait ten days before a couple of them came together, and this time he took them to read in his attic, closing his door on his fear.

The first: "If this book is not a parody of Victorian romances written with the tongue in the cheek, then its author is surely one of the most simple and unsophisticated people to secure the honor of print in the last twenty years. John Kenrick Betterkin is not a name we know; is it possible that it hides the identity of some naïvely idealistic spinster lady who, in her sheltered home, and unacquainted with any literature later than 1890, prefers to indulge the prettiest notions of how people behave?"

Kerry read, breathed out a sigh, and turned without hope to the second. "The pasteboard hero of this 'historical romance,' before dying with extreme nobility on Tower Hill, declares that it is his Christian duty to forgive everybody everything. Influenced by so admirable an example, we content ourselves with saying that, although this book is a singularly pretentious and silly piece of work, reading which we hardly knew whether to blush with discomfort or to laugh out loud, we forgive both it and the author."

Kerry heard himself saying, "Oh, hit me again, do. Hit me again," and "Cheap! Cheap!" Then he took these words into Pearl for her comfort, and for her flaming indignation, which was like a warm stove to sit by.

He would have liked to run with his griefs to Sally Penelope, where the flames of comfort would have been no less high, but his pride would not suffer this yet. He could not yet allow that she had done him no wrong by turning from him, or ask her forgiveness for his hot, cruel words. And this despite the fact that on the morning of publication, after he had gone to work, a small bunch of red roses had been brought to the door. "By a young lady," Mrs. Hitchin said, "who ran away up the street almost before she'd put 'em in my hand."

With the six roses was a card: "All my wishes, Sally Penelope."

A few more reviews came, and the proportion of hostile to favorable was about five to one. None were real praise; some were not unkind; but it was the barbed and poisoned ones that held all his thoughts, hour after hour. Even St. Sebastian, he told himself, was probably more conscious of the arrows that pierced him than of an occasional admiring murmur in the watching crowd.

When eight weeks had passed, and hope lay almost dead, he decided that it would be better to know the worst than to go on living with this sickness. Better one blow and death than this continuing pain. He resolved to call the genial Sir Osbert and ask for the truth.

This he did one dismal wet morning in a telephone booth near the junction of the Strand and Fleet Street. He did not use one of the office telephones on his table, although, Fleet Street being Fleet Street with calls passing to and fro every minute, no one would have minded or listened to what he said; but he wanted to be alone. Alone and shut away, while he took whatever was coming to him. So he shut the booth door on the battering Strand traffic, and on the rain, which, as if it resented this, beat on the glass windows. Now for it, he thought, while the receiver at his ear held only an audible darkness punctuated by the "burr-burr" of a bell far away. I can take it. What will come, will come. He found strength by picturing himself as a man facing the firing squad with his head high. He put on the bravery of his own Sir Nicholas, presenting his breast to the executioners. The traffic and pedestrians of the Strand swept by, unaware of the strong drama in this small red tank, no bigger than a Punch and Judy theater at a street corner. "I can take it. I can take—oh, is that Harker and Inman's? This is John Betterkin speaking." A few weeks ago he had been proud to speak the name of one of their authors, but now was ashamed. "Could you put me through to Sir Osbert."

"Just one moment, sir."

One moment more of hope.

"You're through, sir."

"Oh, hallo, hallo, my dear Betterkin." Sir Osbert's cordial voice. "Nice to hear from you. How are you?"

As though his condition mattered just now! "Quite well, thank you."

"And your sister whom I met. How is she?"

"Quite well too." One was glad that Pearl should be well, but at this moment it wasn't the point. Clearly the progress of the book wasn't occupying Sir Osbert's mind. So Kerry tried to cover anxiety with facetiousness. "I thought that as eight weeks had passed I might ask you how the old book was going."

"What?—oh, yes, *Clerkenwell.*" What else? "Oh, dear, it's very disappointing, but that's so often the way with books. Yes, a disappointment to us all." But how little troubled his pleasant voice. Did he not know that his words were the stab of death? "We'd hoped much better than this. But what can you do with a recalcitrant public?"

One must not reveal that one's heartbeat had become a throbbing sickness; one must speak with a show of ease. "The critics hit it rather, didn't they?"

"Oh, *critics* . . . !" With that single word he pronounced the whole race of critics as beyond understanding and therefore a waste of time to discuss. "Actually I've not seen the reviews. They're rather Publicity's pigeon. But I heard the press was not good."

"Not *good?* It was poisonous."

"Yes . . . well . . . you know what critics are. If a critic wants to feel up in the world he's got to look down, hasn't he? I shouldn't let the critics worry you."

Not worry him! "But they must have damaged the book."

"They may have, but I doubt it. I understand there were only a few notices of the book. Would you like the exact sales figures? I'll have them broken down and sent along."

"Oh, thank you. But the total—what is the total?"

"The total figures to date? Can't tell you that offhand. Wait a mo." His voice turned away. "Fred, ask Minniehaha for the current figures of *Clerkenwell*. Ta, Fred. Glad you're keeping fit, Betterkin. Hard at work on another book, are you? Not yet? Oh, well, I expect you'll be starting soon." (As who should say, "Your child is lying dead? Start on another, old boy.") "You must let us see it when it's ready."

Only, "Let us see it." Not "We shall be eager to publish it." All the ground he had won was lost. The city that he had entered as a victor was his no more. He was but a knocker at the gates again.

"Ah, here they are. Thank you, Fred. Are you there, Betterkin? Sales to date, nine-o-three."

"Nine hundred and three." His heart went down like a lift whose cable had snapped. "Is that home and overseas both?"

"Yes. Both. Home, six-seven-o. O'seas, two-three-three."

"That's not good, is it? You won't so much as break even with a figure like that?"

"Oh, dear me, no; there'll be quite a nice loss. It's a great disappointment, but there's never any accounting for books."

One last desperate attempt to float a little longer. "I suppose it could still pick up and do better? There's still time?"

"Well . . ." Clearly his hesitant word was a ripe fruit from a stout old tree of knowledge. "I doubt if it'll do much more now. Unlikely. After eight weeks one generally knows the fate of a book."

"I see. . . ." Kerry remembered Sir Osbert's exasperation and impatience when Howard Reece had called up about his book, and since he couldn't bear to be unloved at Harker and Inman's—or anywhere else—he hastened to end this call. "Well, thank you for telling me. . . . Good-bye."

But the genial Sir Osbert couldn't bear that anyone should feel abruptly dismissed. "It's very disappointing, I know, my dear chap; but, for your comfort, no fiction's doing well this winter. It's taken a basting. Income tax, depression, inflation —all that. How are you keeping?"

"Fine, thanks."

"Oh, yes, you said you were well. What weather we're having. Winter fairly down upon us now. Hope to see you again some time. 'Bye for now."

Kerry put back the receiver very slowly as if to postpone the end of hope. He walked out into the rain and into the stream of life hurrying by. Suddenly as he hurried along with the alien, heedless pedestrians, he laughed bitterly and aloud, so that a woman in front turned her head as at an idiot loose in the street. She must have been surprised to hear the idiot announce, "Quite clear that what's the center of an author's life is only a point on the circumference of a publisher's." And a minute later, "He could still be merry whereas I felt like dying. And I wish I *were* dead." She hurried on, suffering vicarious shame for him.

That evening he walked homeward through the city streets, touching the bollards as he passed, and the sides of the lamp-posts, and still inclined to speak aloud—to describe his state to himself like the town idiot. "Bitterly sad," he heard his voice saying. "Never more sad." And "I want to be alone." Fortunately this evening there was no one in front of him near enough to hear. "I want to be quite alone and sit in a chair and give myself up to it. . . ." He touched another lamppost. "It's got to be got through. I want an hour with it. An hour alone."

Turning quietly into his home, he went up the stairs, not without the comfort of the banisters, and shut his attic door upon himself.

The Commodore, standing at his wheelhouse window and looking out into Red Lion Street, saw Kerry coming home and idly stroking the lampposts as he passed. He and Evie knew about the book's failure, and he called her to come and see.

"Oh, the poor sweetie!" she cried, for at that minute Kerry had lifted his face toward the house, and she had seen the sadness in it: his brow lined, his mouth tight shut, and his eyes staring less at the windows of his home than at a lost happiness.

"Oh, I can't stand it, Georgy! What can we do for him, poor little man?" she asked, as he turned into his home, looking like a small shrunken vessel of defeat and resignation.

At first in his room Kerry gave himself to a little tidying and cleaning, hoping to work off in action some of his heaviness of heart. But he could settle to no system because his mind bade him always pause and think . . . and think. . . . At one time, lost to all work, he was just standing by the window looking over the roofs of Clerkenwell toward the red and white flag still flying over St. John's Gate. He watched it at play in the wind.

At last he could defeat no more the longing to throw himself into his deep chair. Here he clasped his hands and shut his eyes. How good it would be to sleep awhile with the world shut out. I am tired . . . tired. Sleep. Sleep. But behind the shut eyes the sadness dwelt like a beaver in its hole, burrowing, fidgeting, and gnawing. To know, to be certain, that in many parts, at any rate, the book was good! Oh, yes, yes, I know parts were good. Impossible they could be anything else after all that labor. Sentence after sentence went under the microscope till I got it perfect. Those were good parts. And more of the book was good than bad; I am sure of it. Remember what Sir Osbert said, and Mr. Armstrong, and Pearl. Pearl said it was wonderful. And Sally. Sally said "a *great* book." That lovely poetic part when ten o'clock and darkness came down over the priory and the voices of the knights singing their Compline came through the chapel windows lit with gold—how I thought some of my words there were Shakespearian—and I still do. That comic scene where lean old John de Volles was flung out of the bawdy house in Benjamin Street straight into the arms of his vast waiting mistress—how I laughed aloud and stamped my feet as I conceived it and rushed it down. Falstaffian. Those pictures of the footpads sneaking out of Little Saffron Hill—they were good —I know they were good. That all this goodness should be overlooked or unperceived, and the book derided as if there were no merit in it anywhere. Surely some of it deserved praise. But no: "not a book of any distinction" . . . "pretentious" . . . "a waste of paper."

The futility of effort. Years of effort, and it achieved only sneers. The labor, the self-discipline, the self-denial—all for nothing. Well, I know now that there's no necessary relation between effort and reward. Or between effort and achievement, if the book's as poor as they say. But it isn't, it isn't. And if effort can win nothing, then all confidence is slain. Death . . . death, for if the hope by which one lives is taken from one, then one is ready to die. One's fire is out and one's engine cold —a fine metaphor, that, but what's the good of fine metaphors if no one notices them? I'm quite ready to die. But no, I mustn't do that, while I have Pearl to look after. It would be utterly selfish and the very opposite of "life turned to love"—my only creed, but one I *do* believe in. And it would be like striking Sally to the ground. Sally. Oh, how I'd like to go and tell her all. Tonight—now—but I can't. I can't bring myself to it. I can't beat down my blasted pride. That death scene on Tower Hill. The words leapt for it—it was my great hope, and ha! stillborn! Born dead. It's like losing a child to think it's all lost. It's a death of heart and hope—

The handle of the door. Was it turning? Oh, leave me alone. Leave me in peace . . . please. . . . Yes, it was being turned by a nervous, doubting hand. "Come in. What is it? Come in."

The door opened hesitantly, bringing George Windsor behind it, coupled to its handle. "Forgive me, my dear boy. You know I hate to disturb you—and I never do if I can help it— but I felt you would hardly have started yet. And I'm not coming in—no, I'm not coming in." Nor did he. He just looked around the door, still attached to its handle. "Certainly not."

"You needn't worry, Commodore. I'm not working. And I doubt if I shall, ever again."

"Oh yes, you will, you will. And do great work. But I know how you feel and so does Evie. We both know what rejection and injustice mean."

"Perhaps it isn't unjust. Perhaps I was deluded into thinking the book was good."

"You were not. It was a beautiful book. Beautiful. Evie and I expected great things of it, and my dear wife has taste. She *knows.*"

"Come and sit down. I can hardly see you there."

"No. No. I only wanted to mention Sir Andrew Barton."

What is he talking about? "Sir Andrew . . .?"

"His ballad. You know it, do you?"

"No."

"Well, it used to help me and give me enormous strength when they'd been unjust to me, and I felt like dying. It goes" —and with his fingers still on the handle, as on an anchor against the temptation to come farther, and his body still less than halfway around the door, he recited, his free hand adding some assistance:

> "Fight on, my men, Sir Andrew says,
> A little I'm hurt but not yet slain.
> I'll but lie down and bleed awhile
> And then I'll rise and fight again."

Mr. Windsor saw from Kerry's eyes that this admirable verse had struck home, one pleasing shaft among the throbbing arrows of rejection and ridicule, so, with his sense of the theater, he resolved to make his exit on a good line. "That's all for the moment," he said. "Absolutely all. I'll not disturb you for another second—I wouldn't dream of it—it would be all wrong, all wrong—because I know there's great work to be done."

"Oh, no, don't go," Kerry said, but Mr. Windsor, with a finger up for silence, said not another word. He just moved his hand in a stage farewell, all speech being inconsiderate now, and walked on tiptoe from the room, nodding appreciatively as if he knew that great work was beginning.

19

Godfrey stood in the window bay of the smoking room at Boodle's, his back to its long, cream walls and brown pilasters, its blue and cream carpet, and gold mirrors. He stood looking through the fine bow window into St. James's Street, and anyone glancing in from the pavement would have seen his sleek, black-suited figure framed by gold curtains and a pelmet: a very fair picture of "A Young Man about Town," or of what the papers like to describe, if he is arrested, murdered, or shoots himself, as "a well-known West End clubman." The only thing that spoiled the perfection of this picture was his want of gray hairs. With his dark, oiled hair, smooth and plenty of it, he looked too young and fresh for any London club.

His fingers were linked behind his back as he stood gazing. A six-o'clock whiskey stood on the table beside him, attended by its aide, a miniature bottle of soda. Unlike Kerry, he was not at all unhappy gazing out of this broad window and seeing the dignified facades of the St. James's Street clubs and the long prosperous street that ran so easily—nay, strolled with dignity —toward Piccadilly or Pall Mall. The view always pleased him because it painted a picture of the position he had achieved in the world while still young. And this evening he had another source of pleasure. There was enough of decency in Godfrey to disapprove of the pleasure, but pleasure it was.

"It might make thousands," Kerry had said. But in this fine room at Boodle's one could consult all the newspapers and journals that the country produced, and for weeks he had been turning their pages to see if anywhere there was a review of Kerry's book, and been more satisfied than disappointed when he found none. One that he had chanced upon condemned the book pretty viciously and, on reading its lethal words, he had felt, not without a private shame, a quick prick of pleasure. And just now, before taking his whiskey to the window, he had looked at the Book Page of *Field's Saturday Journal*. No review of Kerry's book there, but after the serious reviews came a few jocular paragraphs under the heading "Novel Comments." And the last but one of these said:

> *Green and Pleasant Clerkenwell.* This highly ingenuous and emotional tale of the noble Knights of St. John is certainly green, but we can hardly recommend it as pleasant. Not that it offends by lubricity or by episodes of sadistic savagery in the modern fashion; on the contrary, it is as pure as a maiden's heart, and as soft and sweet. Perhaps it seems unpleasant only to ourselves who, alas, long ago lost the innocence of childhood and the taste for sweetmeats and ginger beer. For the occupants of the nursery, whether children or nursemaids, we will not speak; for ourselves, with our hardened and cynical minds, it proved so totally unreadable that, doubting our infallibility, as is becoming in those who review, we sounded the publishers to learn how large was the public for a book of this nature. The publishers admitted quite frankly that they were having a difficulty in selling this particular title, and we must allow that we were relieved to hear it. One likes to think that the book-buying public, if not yet wholly adult, is at least adolescent.

If this pithy-paragraph monger was relieved, his relief was small compared with Godfrey's. Godfrey's had a quality of sparkling exultation. He drank up the whiskey because he was now in the mood to hurry home. He wanted to let himself in quietly, walk up to his drawing room overlooking the park, talk of other things to his wife there, and then say casually, "I can't help feeling sorry for that poor brother of mine."

"Why?" she would ask.

"Because that book of his, so far as it's been noticed at all, seems to have been greeted with contempt. And I'm told that it's a total failure. A shame, because he tried so hard, I know.

Extraordinary that the publishers ever agreed to publish it. I can't help suspecting that he paid them to do it. I should like to write and sympathize with him, but I feel, don't you, that it might only pour salt into his wounds, however well meant."

Kerry was shown this pithy notice by a friend in the office, and that evening he hurried home to Pearl for comfort. But, as ever, he found that she was in Evie's room—"on the flypaper" —chattering, chattering; and his keen disappointment became keen irritation. "These women! They—" but no: Pearl had had little chance to talk in prison. Try to be glad that she had now the perfect chattermate in Evie.

He had wondered all along if Godfrey had seen any of these notices, and the thought of his reading them was among the sharpest of his pains. And next morning as he walked to the office, the memory of his bragging to Godfrey in Theobald's Road, and the thought of his reading all this about the children and the nursemaids, so stretched him on the rack that he said aloud, "I wish I were dead," and everyone within ten feet of him turned around to hear more.

Never before had this tendency to speak aloud, as he walked in public places, been so much his master as now.

There was a morning in the Farringdon Road when he announced to the hurrying workers ahead of him, "The battle is lost," and when they turned to hear more about the battle, was so ashamed that he turned also, in the hope they would think this war news had come from far behind. But even this shock of shame did not halt the moonstruck habit. In Fleet Street he heard again a dismal announcement that the battle was lost and observed that others in front had heard it too.

There was an evening when, his despair turning angry, he went defiantly into a Fleet Street pub to minister to it with whiskey. Unluckily he found other Fleet Street friends there and felt it only right that, after standing whiskeys to four of them, he should have his four in return. But his head was untrained for whiskeys, since he could seldom afford them, and by the fifth he knew that he must get out of this place quickly and on to his homeward road. He said good-bye to these friends—so far as he could focus them; he shook hands with two of them once—or one of them twice—and got himself out into the evening air. His walk homeward along the Farringdon Road was rapid, and largely carried on the balls of his feet, because it was a matter of keeping pace with his head, or, rather, of catching up with it. Several times he said aloud, "Oh, dear" and "Oh, lord" and "It's going to be all right" as he nearly pitched forward in his pursuit of that earnest, unhappy, and partly independent head. People turned as usual at the sound of his voice, but he was beyond caring if they thought him mad. Once he said aloud, "I am out . . . out . . . out . . ." and he was not announcing the state of his brain, but his sorrowful conclusion that he'd been hammered on the fiction market. A minute later, thinking of that writer in *Field's Saturday Journal,* he said very loudly: "I wish he'd die." And to those turning around he explained, "Not in agony. Just die."

Another and opposite effect of his daily unhappiness was a drive toward goodness, even holiness. He read books about religion and the benefits of suffering. He read the words of Dr. Arnold on his bed of pain and tried to say them of himself: "I have suffered so little pain in my life, Tom, that I feel this is very good for me." Once, like many others in despair, he opened a Bible at random to see if its words had a message especially for him, and while the first words he met offered no help, he did read on and come upon "It is good for me that I have been afflicted that I might learn thy statutes." Just what the doctor said. Next, after getting from the library in Skinner Street a commentary on the Book of Job, he played with the idea of taking Holy Orders. He could not, however, persuade himself that he believed in the Christian dogmas sufficiently to take orders, so he contented himself with seeking chances of doing good and showing magnanimity. He was, in fact, hard on the heels of Sally—for a little while, at any rate. For instance, he forgave Godfrey everything, and the thought that he was doing this proved a pleasure—if a small one. But far more important than all this striving was his sudden happy perception that, since goodness demanded that he cast out pride, he could—he *must*—go back humbly to Sally. And then all her comfort would be his.

So one evening he stood in the dreary hollow of Ray Street waiting for her return. Why did she not come; why did she not come? Had she not gone to work today, or returned early? No; surely now that he was trying to be good, God would do His part and bring Sally down the street. And here at last—whether or not it was arranged in heaven—here she came, walking down the tilt from Farringdon Road. Her eyebrows rose as she saw him there, and pleasure sprang alight in her eyes. He put out both hands in welcome—just as he had imagined himself doing when he should come to her with his triumph.

She rushed into them. "Oh, my dear, my dear," she said; and he knew by the compassion in her voice that she had seen some of the reviews.

"Please," he began with a grin, to show that he was now humble, "can we be as we were . . . before we . . . I mean, I'll promise to behave myself . . . I mean, nothing'll happen. A few kisses perhaps, and nothing more."

"Oh, yes, yes," she assented. "I've so wanted to come back and say the same myself. I've nearly done so a hundred times, but I wasn't sure if I'd be welcome. I couldn't bear to think of you suffering."

"You have come back now?"

"Oh, yes, yes, *please*. If you hadn't come, I should have come to you."

"Why? Have you seen some of the reviews?"

"One or two, because I'd been looking for them everywhere. Oh, I could have killed them. They were wicked—wicked."

"Oh, I don't know. I begin to think that the book isn't as good as I thought it. I begin to agree now with some of what they said. I didn't at first; I thought they were jealous."

"So they were. Of course they were. And they shouldn't be allowed to write and say things like that. They ought to be put in prison for it."

He shook his head. "No. If you put up a book in the public market, you ask to be a target."

"But why, *why?* They can say they don't like it, of course, and point out what they feel is wrong, but they needn't be so utterly beastly, so brutal, so cruel. And obviously to get a joy from being so."

"Some were fairly kind."

"Yes, but the beastly ones! You aren't allowed to do anybody grievous bodily harm, why should you be allowed to do them grievous mental harm? No; I'd put them all in prison until they learned to behave like decent people instead of horrid little razor-slashers."

"I suppose the book got them on the raw. You see, darling: one's book's made exactly to one's own measure so that it fits one's mind like a skintight garment, but other people's shapes are different, and to them it is only discomfort and friction and pains all over. I've only just perceived this interesting fact."

"It was a lovely book."

"It was not as bad as they made out. But, good or bad, it's the perfect flop."

"I'm not so sure. I've been going around looking for it, and I saw a copy of it on the table of two different stores."

"*Which* stores?" he asked eagerly. And of course she mentioned the two where he'd seen it.

"Yes, I've seen those. Seen them twenty times in the last three months. Unmoving, and unmoved. They are lying around, Face down to the ground, And they can't hear me sounding the Rally."

"The book may pick up yet, mayn't it?"

"No. It is dead. So dead that I doubt if Harker and Inman's will look at any book of mine. I've got to start all over again. If I start at all. Doubt if I will. 'My days are past; my purposes are broken off.' That's Job. The Book of Job. I've been reading it."

"Of course you'll start again. *I'll* see to that. Oh, my precious, have you been awfully unhappy?"

He smiled. "I don't think I've ever suffered so thoroughly in my life."

"You should have come to Sally sooner."

"I know. Sally, do you know what one effect of all the misery was?"

"No."

"It set me thinking of all that you said about there being no real happiness or peace till one begins to think of something other than one's wretched self. I'm much more religious now. Not as good as you, of course . . . but not too bad. I'm coming along. And it's all very funny because I can't feel that God has been nice to me. 'Mine hope hath he plucked up like a tree.' Job again. 'I am now a by-word among the people and an open abhorring.' "

"Oh, my darling, you are so precious and sweet! Look, pet, I'm free tonight. Can't we go off together and talk and talk and talk about everything?"

"You're coming home with me. Just to show that you trust me, and that old Hitchin can think and do what he likes. I find it's the only place where I can be really comfortable and enjoy my misery to the full. And I want to enjoy it with Sally now."

20

Pearl and Kerry were walking in the crowded Clerkenwell Road when the large woman laid a small plump hand on Pearl's arm and cried, "It *is* you! It is. It is. It's Pearl."

Startled, Pearl turned and stopped; Kerry too.

The woman, excited and delighted, let her hand rest on Pearl. "Lor' love you, ducks, I been looking out for you. I remembered you saying your brother'd got you a nice room in our Clerkenwell. And I said, 'Lord love you, but that's where I live.' I took one look at your face just now and I thought, Christ, that's her frontispiece, she's here all right. Where did you say the room was?"

Pearl had no courage to refuse her address. "In Red Lion Street," she provided unwillingly, as one dreading the consequences.

"Gawd, yes! I remember now; and I said, Chrimes, but I used to be a bottler at the distillery around the corner. I remember you told me it was a lovely Queen Anne house. This is your good kind brother, is it? Excuse me taking the liberty of asking."

"Yes, this is Kerry. Kerry, Mrs. Chapman."

"Mrs. Churchman, dear. Don't tell me you've forgotten my name already. Babe Churchman. How jer do, sir?"

"How do you do?" responded Kerry and took her fat hand. She was a big-bosomed, broad-hipped woman with a baby's face: the nose small and boneless, the cheeks round as a peach and ruddy as a maple leaf in autumn. Only her thin gray hair and sagged mouth told you she was sixty. She kept his hand as if it were something picked up in the street and she was estimating what it would fetch. Embarrassed, he longed for her to drop it. But still holding it, she said, "It was you who sent her lovely flowers, wasn't it?"

"Flowers?" He pretended not to understand. But this word had switched on a light so that he saw and understood all. And the alarm began.

"Yes, lovely carnations and roses and all. Dirty shame they only allowed her to keep three blooms each time. And, crikey!" —it was now that she had to drop his hand so as to lay her own, in amusement, on his sleeve—"they used to search the flowers first. Just as though you'd hidden an 'acksaw among them. Why —tell you what, sir—sometimes it was only by the flowers you brought that we remembered whether it was spring outside or summer. Autumn and winter we knew all right—eh, ducks?— knew 'em by the starvin' cold. I tell you, sir, we shivered sometimes for fifteen bloody hours—if you'll pardon my French, sir —from four in the afternoon till about seven in the morning."

Needless now for Pearl to explain, "She's talking of Holloway, Kerry," and she did not. But Mrs. Churchman did, leaving the amused hand on his sleeve. "He's all at sea, isn't he, ducks? We're talking about our time together in the castle. You know all about it. You came on visits often, didn't you, and brought flowers?"

"Yes, I came, sometimes," Kerry agreed; and to himself he said bitterly, "Shades of the prison house begin to close . . ."

"Course you did, and she used to tell me all about it. We saw a lot of each other, being both needleworkers—and she's not 'arf a dab with her needle, is she?—though we'd nothing much to do but to make their bloody dresses (asking your pardon, sir) for the old screws. We always wanted the laundry or a workroom, Pearl and me, because the screws didn't mind you talking there—least, if they minded, they couldn't do nothing about it and they give up trying. Gawd, did we rabbit, she and me!"

"Rabbit." That meant "talk." Kerry could imagine Pearl

talking endlessly to this neighbor in Holloway as to her neighbor, Evie, now—endlessly, loosely and dangerously, with this outcome in Clerkenwell Road many months later. Just now, filling with fear, she was hardly speaking at all, only staring at another chatterer, with the fear reaching her eyes.

And Mrs. Churchman went on, "Upon my soul, I forget what you was birded for. Oh, yes, hoisting, wasn't it?" A look of agony shot across Pearl's face, and she frowned to control it. "I remember when you come in. You looked that miserable and helpless. I see her coming from reception, sir, in that awful blue dress much too big for her and carrying her cloak and her bar of soap, and I thought, 'The liberties they take with you!' Poor *dear.* I thought, 'She never expected to find herself in here, she never. She's not the sort.' And, do you know, sir"— Mrs. Churchman laid her finger against her nose, archly, mischievously—"at first I guessed it might be for a spot of what they pinched me for. Done out of the kindness of her heart. Same as I done. As if there was any harm in it! But when I knew what she done, I said to myself, I said, 'Babe, ducks, you should have thought of that first go. Just the type. Those that can't help theirselves, so who's to blame 'em, really.' You look a lot better now, ducks, than what you did then. Funny, sir, but she lost weight inside, while most of us put it on—though Lord knows what put it on us in that starvation place, unless it was the Quakers or the treacle pudding. Or the good Lord giving us something to keep us warm in those filthy cold cells. Phew! Cold . . . cold!"

"Have you been out long?" asked Pearl, forced to speak lest her staring silence offend Mrs. Churchman.

"Only a week or so, ducks. You been out for months, eh? But I had my three mucking stretch to do."

"Where are you living now?"

"I got quite a nice birch broom at my sister's in Skinner Street."

At any place or time Kerry would have been anxious not to humiliate an ex-jailbird; he would have made it his business to speak in the friendliest way, and as to an equal; but now he had another reason for doing so: he had apprehended Pearl's fear of offending this woman. So he said with a laugh, "Birch broom? I'm really at a loss now."

Instantly her hand came on to his sleeve in amusement at his ignorance. "A nice furnished room, honey," she translated.

"Oh, I see."

"You in good work, lovey?" she asked of Pearl.

"Yes, I've got some work."

"Lucky you! I got no nice brother to help me. What're you doing?"

Pearl told her.

"And quite nice too. Couldn't you get me something similar? Do something for me, there's a love." Her hand was now a pleading hand, on Pearl's sleeve. "You could tell 'em I worked along of you once—though, for Christ's sake, don't say where! And I promise you I'll never tell 'em. We must see more of each other and talk it over, eh? Red Lion Street, yes; but what's the mucking number?"

Again Pearl had neither the courage nor the unkindness to refuse the number. "It's . . . it's 55a," she said. "Yes: 55a."

Mrs. Churchman let loose a scream. "Ow!" and this time placed an amazed hand on Kerry. "What: old Elf Hitchin's? Well now, did you ever? I know Elfy well. He used to work at the distillery as a truckdriver's mate. Fancy you being with old Elf. How's Nance? Gawd, he was lucky when he got her; I bet it's she who pulls in the money nowadays. That old parson thought the world of her, and he fair set her up good and proper in that house. You see, I know all about your Hitchins, Pearl dear. But listen, both of you: watch out with Elf. I like him, but—well"—she winked—"he always said he was fired from the distillery because he was too old at forty—or some such fanny—but we girls down in the bottling hall heard a very different story." She nodded knowingly and laid fingers full of knowledge on Pearl's forearm. "Look: what we heard was that the checker on the loading bank found a nice bottle of gin or two missing, so the foreman told the chargehand to keep quiet and watch out, and, Lor' love you, a month or so later our Elf was gawn. Out on his left ear. Yeah!" She nodded. "Yeah. Gawn for good and the day after."

As her chatter ran on, like an oiled free wheel coursing downhill, Kerry was thinking, Oh, *God*—this must pull down their home about their heads; it must drive them forth into a new exile. A new disaster on top of his book's total failure. The words of Job, so recently read and loved, came rushing into mind, and he likened himself, standing on a greasy London sidewalk, to that great suffering chief of the Bedouin, "the greatest of the children of the East." "He breaketh upon me with breach upon breach . . . He takes me by the neck and dasheth me to pieces . . . His archers compass me round about." So it was that while Mrs. Babe Churchman chattered to Pearl, the Master of the Book of Job, that great Unknown whose voice as of whirlwinds and thunder and angels' trumpets had sounded down twenty-five centuries, now spoke a few of his tremendous lines to Kerry standing on a Clerkenwell sidewalk and being thrust to and fro by a scurry of people passing by.

Lost in these thoughts, he heard no more of Mrs. Churchman's words (much preferring the prose style of Job or of the Almighty) until he saw that she was kissing Pearl good-bye and saying, "It's been a treat to see you again, ducks. It really 'as, dear."

With a merry little wave she was on her way, and Pearl and Kerry stood alone.

"To hell!" said Kerry. "And now *what?*"

"Oh, why ever did we meet her? Come on. Come; don't stand there." She must get out of Mrs. Churchman's sight, out of the road's sight, under cover. "Let's get home."

"Home!" he scoffed, as they walked quickly back.

"Oh, she won't speak to the Hitchins, will she? *No.*"

"If there's one thing certain between this blasted sidewalk and Clerkenwell's blue sky, it is that she'll blow everything over the Hitchins first time she sees them."

"Oh, but she won't see them. Skinner Street is quite a way from us."

"Five hundred yards."

"No, no, she won't tell them. She said something about not telling people."

"My dear, it's no good believing she won't just because you want to." In his present irritation with life he felt impatient with her weak, wish-fulfilling mind. "One must face up to things."

"But what are you saying? Don't just talk like that. This is the end of everything."

"That's exactly what I'm saying; and one must face up to it. Who is the old trout, anyway?"

"She was in for abortion."

"God!"

"She was doing three stretch for it, and she was furious at the sentence."

"*Stretch?*"

"Oh, *you* know. Years. Three years." As in France one begins to think in French, so this talk with Mrs. Babe Churchman had set Pearl thinking in prison terms again. "She'd say over and over again, 'Three stretch for trying to help a poor girl in trouble!' And it was her first conviction for that offense too. But she'd other convictions: one for falsifying entries in her savings book, and the other, I think, for getting marriage allowances she wasn't entitled to; and she was indignant that she only got short sentences for those things that were really crimes and this shocking sentence for something that didn't seem a crime at all. Babe Churchman thought she'd done it out of the goodness of her heart; and I dare say this was true, because she used to tell me that she'd often done it for poor girls without taking a penny."

"Which showed that she'd often done it for money."

"And that she had a heart."

"She has no heart to stop talking. Look how she told us at the first opportunity all about old Hitchin's dismissal. Oh, why in pity's name did you ever mention Clerkenwell to her?"

"Oh, I don't know. One had to talk about something."

As she said this, he saw her sitting in her prison dress, plying her needle at Mrs. Churchman's side, and he forbore to rebuke her anymore. He fell silent until suddenly Pearl stood still, as if stopped by a pistol point.

"Kerry . . . Kerry . . ."

"Yes?"

"She won't put the black on me, will she? No, she has a heart."

"Put the black on?" He had heard something like that before. Where? Where was it?

But before he could remember Pearl explained, "Try blackmailing me. Oh, *no*. She has a heart, but . . . she's inclined to do anything for money. Oh, can't we go from here? The whole neighborhood will know. Can't we go somewhere else? Though what's the good—the good? It always catches up with you in time. Any sentence for someone like me is a life sentence. One's character's gone for ever and one's no use to anyone anymore. I'd best kill myself. I might as well be dead, and I'd at least be out of everyone's way."

Again he felt impatient with her gift for despair and gloom, but he managed to hold himself from hurting her. "Now then, my dear, we'll do something together. We always have. But" —and he tried a joke (from Job)—"we sure are properly delivered over to the ungodly and cast into the hands of the wicked."

"Oh don't, don't!" she pleaded.

Six days later, at three in the afternoon, as he came back into the front office after speaking to the London manager upstairs, Parky (his fellow clerk, Parkinson) announced cheerfully, "One Betterkin. Wanted on the telephone. You come pat on your cue." He handed up the receiver. "Call for you, Betts. Wanted urgently."

"Me?"

"Yes, you. Go on. Take it. I've got work to do."

"But who on earth—who wants to call me here?"

"Your sister, she says. Course, that could mean anything. We've heard that tale before. *I* call 'em cousins. But she's waiting. Seems you're wanted somewhere."

"But . . . where's she phoning from? We've got no telephone."

"Don't ask me. Nobody told me that. Nobody tells me anything. But hurry. The lady sounds anxious."

Excited, a little frightened, and yet feeling a small spice of pleasure in both the excitement and the fear, he put the receiver to his ear. "Yes?"

"Oh, Kerry, can you come? At once? It's Pearl speaking. Please do. They'll let you."

"But what for?"

"It's terribly important that you should come quickly. *Please.*" From whatever distance away, he caught the tears in her voice.

"Where are you? Where are you speaking from?"

"Camden Town."

Camden—that was miles away. "What on earth are you doing there? Where are you?"

"In . . ."

"Yes?"

"In Groves and Simpson's."

The big chain store in Camden High Street. He began to guess. To know. And his heart to sink, and, as it sank, to throb. And nonetheless that small pleasure in excitement still in his heart—that small traitorous spice.

"But what—"

"Oh, do please come and don't ask. They're waiting for you."

They? Yes, this could mean only one thing. Ah, God. . . .

"My dear, of course I'll come."

"Could you . . . could you take a taxi? Just this once? Please do."

"I'll come as quick as I can." That was all he could force himself to say. A taxi was something to which he always grudged money. I'm intolerable; she's suffering, and I simply cannot say at once that I'll take a taxi; even now I'm only thinking that women are always too ready to waste money on taxis. "Where shall I find you?"

"In the manager's office."

Yes. Of course. And pity swept aside these poor dregs of old impatience. "I'll come, my dear. As fast as a taxi can bring me. Don't worry. God bless."

Out in Fleet Street he grappled the first taxi that came by. In the taxi his alarm, his impatience, his pity, his excitement (which still held, shamefully, that small seed of pleasure), and his pride (hardly less shameful) at being summoned to a rescue would not suffer him to lean back in the seat but thrust him forward to look out at the passing streets—when he was not looking at the meter and feeling anxiously for coins in his pocket.

Camden High Street. And—yes, there—Groves and Simpson's wide plate-glass windows brightly dressed from floor to roof. The cab shed him at the door, and he went in. The shop was long as a swimming bath, and he wandered unhappily toward its far end. Between the long counters, laid as it seemed with all the small wares of the world and so making the whole shopping hall more colorful than a Damascus bazaar, the salesgirls stood, or moved, in their red overalls; but they all looked so young that he did not care to surprise them by asking for the manager's office.

Halfway down the aisle he saw an older woman in a blue overall with "Supervisor" on its breast, so he put his request to her, not without a stutter. "Could you show me, please, the manager's office?"

She looked at him, knowledge in her eyes, but her answer was courteous. "Certainly, sir. This way." And she led him through the shuttling shoppers to a door near the back. She tried its handle, but it was locked. *Locked?* She tapped. Within the room a chair slid back and steps approached. The door opened, to show a tall slim man in a dark suit as neat as a specialist's in a consulting room. He seemed young for a manager, for his hair, though silver, was plentiful and his face, clean-shaven, was unpuckered and neatly molded.

"A gentleman to see you, Mr. Westell."

"Is it Mr. Betterkin?" His voice was pleasant.

Kerry nodded.

"Do come in, sir. Thank you, Miss Barker." Kerry walked in, passing him at the door; the supervisor withdrew; and the manager, very quietly, turned the lock home again.

There was Pearl seated on a chair between wall and desk, her face almost as white as the wall's paint. If the manager looked like a young and able consultant, she looked like a patient waiting to hear if she must die. His good height, good clothes, and confident manner made her seem smaller and more insignificant than ever, seated there in a pale terror, her back round and her feet fidgeting on the floor.

"You are this lady's brother, I understand?" His eyes, ash-blue, were not unkind.

"Yes."

"Well, this is an unhappy business, Mr. Betterkin."

"I don't know what it's all about." Said angrily. "I can't imagine. Will you kindly tell me?"

The room was small, its only floor furniture being the desk, three chairs, a filing cabinet, and a bookshelf. On the desk's blotting pad was a sad and guilty little parade of ill-assorted objects: two painted tin toys, two colored juvenile books, and a cheap, glittering dress ornament. On the wall hung a small picture of the king. Also a group photograph of some trade outing, with the manager among friends on a happier day than this.

The manager, now behind his desk, remained standing. So did Kerry. The manager picked up a silver pencil and tapped it on his thumbnail. "Two of our store detectives assert that she took this dress ornament off one counter and slipped it into her basket; also these two children's books from another counter, and these two small toys. She then, they say, went quickly out into the street without any attempt to pay for them. Both detectives went after her and asked her to come back to my office. She says she is absentminded and forgot to pay, but—"

"But can't you believe her? Of course that's what happened." Kerry, his mind beating like an accelerated engine, had decided—what else?—to bluff it out; to stage a scene of high indignation; to threaten actions for false imprisonment . . . wrongful arrest . . . trespass against the person. His very smallness before this tall able man urged him to take this strong line. "It's a thing I can easily imagine myself doing. Indeed, I *have* done it. And my sister's an even dreamier person than I am. Can't you accept what she says? Come, Pearl, what have you got? Of course she'll pay for all she's taken—all she meant to buy."

The manager still tapped with his pencil. "Unfortunately, sir, I can't believe her story. I do *not* accept it."

"Well, I'm sorry, but that's your funeral, not mine. It's led you into something for which she could bring an action against you. I suppose you know that any forceful detaining of a person constitutes an act of false imprisonment. I'm a witness that this door was locked. I know something about the law, and all this is assault and trespass."

"Only in the case of an unfounded charge, I think, sir."

"But that's the whole point. This *is* an unfounded charge. It's—"

"It's no use, Kerry . . ." Pearl began from her chair.

"Keep quiet a minute, Pearl; *do* keep quiet. The whole thing's a bad mistake, and I—"

The manager was shaking his head. "We'd never take this step, sir—we wouldn't dare to—unless we were a hundred-percent certain. My detectives were keeping observation on her from four or five yards away, the woman detective on the far side of the counter—"

"Is that the way you treat your customers?"

"Honest customers have no reason to object."

" 'Honest,' my God. Be careful what you say. There's such a thing as slander." But the manager proceeded, "They know well when an action is inadvertent and when it's deliberate—"

"How? How can they? Preposterous."

"They've been watching long before any stealing's done, and they know every move."

"What moves?"

"Such moves as looking around for the detectives—for the manager—dropping a newspaper over the articles fancied— moving quickly, once it's taken—"

"And if it's their word against my sister's?"

"Unfortunately, sir, the woman detective had recognized her. That was one reason why she was keeping her under observation."

"Recognized her? What do you mean? You've never been in this shop before, have you, Pearl?"

"No."

"No, sir; but this particular detective, like others we employ, was once a prison officer. In Holloway."

All Kerry's guns were silenced, his ship was holed. Pearl was staring up at him with despair in her eyes. Her eyes said, "You see?" Her lips were parted and her breaths coming fast.

And the manager continued, "Miss Stevens recognized her as one who was serving a sentence for shoplifting."

Silence. Two defeated people staring.

"And she knows that it was her second sentence because of some tie or other she wore in prison."

The knockout, thought Kerry. The knockout before the bell's ended the first round. No arguing with two body blows like that. No rising at a count of nine. Unconsciously he expressed the fitness of this metaphor by keeping quiet for some ten seconds more, then sighing and asking, "May I sit down?" So goes a beaten prizefighter to his corner.

"Of course, sir," said the manager courteously, and pointed to a chair beside Pearl's. Kerry took it and pulled at his lower lip, frowning, while he thought.

The manager took his own chair behind the desk and waited, beating the silver pencil on the blotting pad.

Kerry spoke. "My sister has not denied this?"

"In the street she said she was in a hurry and couldn't come back. Why should she say that? She tried to push the detectives away."

Oh, poor Pearl. "But she did come back to you."

"Yes."

"And why, do you suppose?"

"I fear it was because Miss Stevens threatened to call the police."

"And has she admitted all you say about Holloway?"

"Not yet. Miss Betterkin asked to get in touch with you before she said anything."

"And you consented?"

"Certainly."

"Thank you. What have you in mind to do? Send for the police?"

"I have not done so yet."

Kerry sighed again. "I am afraid I was a bit rude to you just now, but I thought the only thing to do was to try to bluff it out."

"I understand, sir. Don't worry about that."

"Mr. Westell—that is your name, is it not?"

The manager responded with a half smile. "That is so."

"Well, look, Mr. Westell. All you say is true. It is best to admit it, Pearl dear. But, Mr. Westell, my sister is not a crimi-

[189]

nal. She isn't really." He glanced toward her. "Does she look a criminal? This thing is just a terrible nervous affliction—some sort of compulsion that is beyond my understanding. And hers. I can give you the name of our doctor and a specialist who would endorse all I say. They have done so in court more than once. But each time we were unlucky in our judge." As he said this, he looked into the eyes of the manager as into those of a judge more understanding or more humane.

The manager looked away. "I don't want to be hard," he said.

Kerry felt that, if he had been knocked out in the previous combat, he was doing better in this return match. By far his strongest motives as he fought for Pearl were love and pity, but, Oh God, God, why this small joy in being the strong and stainless man pleading for a weaker creature who had stumbled? How utterly selfish was the heart of man. Or would, perhaps, a tall man not feel it? Try, try not to feel it. "This hasn't happened for such a long time," he pleaded. "Pearl, my dear, how came it that you did this!"

"Oh, I don't know, I don't know. Babe Churchman came to see me and asked if you could get her work. When I said I didn't see what you could do, she pestered me to help her. I told her I had nothing to spare—and then . . ."

"Yes?"

"And then she went and I heard her talking to the Hitchins."

"Did she tell them?" For a second they had forgotten the manager, Kerry's fear of this outcome being no less than hers. The manager sat watching.

"I don't know, but she will. She will. In the end."

"But what good does this sort of thing do?" He pointed to the toys on the desk.

"Oh, I don't know, I don't know."

"Doesn't the fear of discovery and of imprisonment do anything to help you?"

"Not at the time . . . no. . . ."

He turned to the manager. "You see, sir." Speak courteously, humbly. "The whole thing is quite irrational. She has no need of toys or children's books. We know no children."

The manager could only lift his shoulders as one bewildered.

"Our doctor suggested that the things she takes are symbols of something. Childhood, perhaps, when she was happy."

"I suppose something like that is possible," said the manager.

"He suggested that the dress ornaments reminded her of days when she was young and might hope to marry."

"Then she's taken dress ornaments before?"

Had his hit missed? And left his guard open? "Yes . . . once. . . . That is so. But not for such a long time. May I tell you what I feel has happened? She suffered a nasty mental shock a few days ago—you don't mind if I tell him, Pearl?"

"Oh, no, no. What can it matter now?"

"Naturally my sister has always kept it a secret that she's been in prison; she tries to forget it; but last Saturday a woman who used to work beside her in the prison workroom greeted her in the street, and my sister now thinks that her secret will be known to all—that she'll never escape from it . . . ever. Though why that should drive her to this mad act I don't know."

"I think I can half understand it, sir, but, you see, I have a duty to my employers. Our firm loses thousands of pounds a year through this sort of thing. So many women are given to it."

"Possibly because there are so many unhappy women."

"Maybe, but some are just deliberate thieves. Others succumb all of a sudden—and I can feel sorry for them—but even then it's deliberate."

"But I can give you our doctor's evidence that my sister is different from any of these. I could get in touch with him now."

"A doctor's evidence is for a magistrate to hear."

"Oh, but I do beg you not to prosecute."

"We leave it to the police to prosecute."

"But don't, don't! If they prosecute, it'll be her fourth conviction, and she might get years. Three years. Four, perhaps. Oh, no, *please.* You are our last hope."

The manager sat there silent. Absently he picked up the dress ornament and laid it down. He stayed silent. At least, thought Kerry, he is not saying, "I can't do this for you." But —oh, no! was he now shaking his head as if thinking exactly this? Now Kerry's only thought was "I *must* save her; I must," and, thank God, all pleasant pride in his position of strong rescuer was destroyed by a passion of pity and love, an anguish to save her. And since any passion of love is akin to an onset of genius, it flung up before him, as in a sudden inspiration, a new idea, probably the only idea that could win this desperate game. A last card, but perhaps a good one. "Look, sir. When she was first convicted she was put on probation for three years on condition that she went as a voluntary patient into a mental hospital for six months. If you will spare her now, I promise that we will do this again. Don't you agree, Pearl?"

"Oh, yes, yes. But how can we afford it? I had better go to prison."

"I will manage it somehow. I promise you absolutely, sir, that we will do this. Let her do it and then, if this happens again, it will be proof that she has tried. Look"—he seized a bit of paper and wrote on it passionately—"this is my address so that you can know if we have done as I've promised. Don't send her to prison for years." He turned and looked at Pearl and saw that she was staring at the manager in helpless suspense.

The manager, after considering the address which Kerry had passed to him, asked, "But if I do this for you, will you tell me what I do when next some woman is brought in here with her thefts in her bag? Am I to favor you and not her?"

"That is for you to judge," said Kerry.

No answer coming to this, he pursued, "It's for you to decide if you think we're honest or not." The word "honest" rang like a cracked bell, so he asserted boldly, "Yes, I'm not afraid of the word 'honest.' My sister is an honest woman. And I try to be. But I realize it: we are in your hands."

The manager smiled and, as if he would make the right gesture, walked toward the door. "All right," he said, and opened it. "I'll trust you to do all you have said. But you must do it, you must do it."

"I will."

The manager put out his hand—and to Pearl first. "Well, good-bye and good luck."

Then he shook Kerry's hand and for one moment put a sympathetic and encouraging palm on his shoulder as he went out.

21

"Oh, come, Georgy, come." Evie Windsor in her frothy pink dressing gown stood at her window looking down the street. "There they are. There they go. The little Betterkins. And she didn't even come in to say good-bye."

George came at a leap from the breakfast table and stood at her side in his blue Chinese robe embroidered with mandarins. "She said her good-byes last night," he said. And together they watched Kerry and Pearl walking down the tilt toward Benjamin Street just as once before, at the same hour of the day, they had watched them coming to the house from that corner.

"But that bag's too heavy for the poor little man. George, why don't you do something? Run out and help them."

Kerry was carrying for his sister a large cheap suitcase which, worn now and insecure, was held safely shut by a bright new strap. Overfilled and heavy, it weighed him down sideways toward the curb.

"I offered last night to go with them to the station," said George, "but they refused. They wanted to slip out quietly."

"What did they tell the Hitchins?"

"That she was going to the hospital for an overhaul."

"How long will they keep her there?"

"Six months at least, Kerry says. Depends on the treatment."

"And the poor little man's paying for it?"

"He's paying what he can."

"But it's guineas a week!"

"The almoner arranges what people can afford. And Holloway Sanatorium is heavily endowed. Funny that she should go from one Holloway to another."

"He can't afford anything. I shall never believe in God again."

"I never did. Wanted to all my life, but couldn't quite make it."

"To strike him down like this just when he was in the depths of misery about his book. It's just nonsense, and I'm not going to church anymore. I shall tell the vicar so. And if God says anything to me on the Day of Judgment, I shall explain to Him exactly what I felt about it. The two poor little honeys."

It was never easy for George to resist declaiming Shakespeare, and he did not succeed now; he explained that when sorrows came, they came not in single spies but in battalions. "And, at any rate, Evie love, she isn't going to prison."

"Oh, why in God's name (if there is such a person) didn't they tell us all about her little weakness long ago?"

"I asked them that, but they said they were afraid we'd have nothing to do with them."

"Such rubbish. What absolute nonsense. Why, I'd have had nothing but sympathy."

"Me too. I stole regularly as a boy. Told 'em so last night. Sweets off the shop counter. Picture postcards off the rack. Golf balls off the links. I snaffled a nice little diary once from the Army and Navy Stores. Mercy I didn't know there were detectives dotted about all over the place. I must have been quite a smart kid to get away with it."

"Yes, but you did it wickedly. She can't help it."

"Nor could I."

"Nonsense. You're just a wicked old man. What did you say when they admitted the whole thing last night?"

"Say? Nothing. Went up and kissed her. What do you suppose?"

"My darling Georgy, how right! You're always so right. I did the same when she came in to me. And did she weep on your shoulder?"

"No. It was Little Betts who seemed ready to weep. She seemed stunned."

"If only she'd confessed to me long ago, all this might never have happened. It's not good to keep things bottled up like that. Do you remember them arriving all those months ago, two poor lambs coming up the street, she looking miserable, and he carrying a brown-paper bundle? And wearing his ridiculous bowler hat? I'd never seen two such darlings. And to think that she'd only just come out of prison! An hour before. Why, if we'd known, we'd have made a feast for them. And I'd have been so interested to hear about prison."

"So would I. I'd have had wonderful talks with her about it, and it would have done her all the good in the world."

"Oh, I do hope we've always been nice to them. I think we have."

"Ah, well," interrupted George, turning from the window, "that's that." The two figures had turned into Benjamin Street. "God be good to her."

"There is no such person."

"Well, Holloway Sanatorium be good to her and make her well."

"And the nice Windsors have a lovely meal for him tonight when he comes home. With plenty of drink. George, go out at once and get wine."

It smote him each evening, the emptiness of the attics after Pearl's departure. Empty the front room because Pearl was gone from it. Better her ever-repeated and wearying glooms than this emptiness in the room. Empty the back room because his hope was gone from it. Empty his table because all heart was gone from the happy task it once sustained. Sally was his only comfort now, and what hope was left of marrying Sally?

What was he to do of an evening when he couldn't be with Sally? Read? But to read a novel was to remind him of his own dead child; to read a biography was to set another man's success and fame against his own failure. So, if he read at all, he read books of philosophy or religion that might instill comfort or inject strength. But always their comfort seemed to remain verbal; it did not heal. Often, therefore, he would just sit back in his chair, reading everything of interest in his evening paper, until his heart remembered to be heavy, and he leaned back to let it have its way.

He was seated thus one evening, his only lamp alight, his curtains undrawn, and his window framing the pale fire glow over London. The flag above St. John's Gate was still at its masthead; it caught the London light and flew above the roofs like a wind-torn flame. He was watching it, sadly— when he heard a step on the stairs. A creak; another; and then, strange in its abruptness, silence.

He sat forward to hear better. Those creaks had been close: on the stairs between the Windsors' door and his. It was someone coming to him. He listened for them to begin again. They did not. Then someone must be standing motionless on the treads. George Windsor? George in silent conflict with a temptation to come up for a chat? Let him come. He need worry no more about the divine afflatus, which had gone down into a grave with his book. But—the steps were descending again. Whosoever they were, he must have stood, indecisive, and then thought better of his business. Descending to the third floor— to the second—the first—and out of hearing.

Silence in the house now. A continuing silence. He lay back on the deep waters of his melancholy and floated away down the stream of it, till—yes: steps coming up again. Delicately. Nervously. The visitor must have decided, after all, to come. Downstairs he must have thought better of thinking better of it.

Kerry jumped up and flung open his door. And stood staring down into the face of Hitchin who stood on the third tread down, gaping up at him, as if disabled, paralyzed, by this unexpected opening of the door. An embarrassing confrontation for both.

"Oh, it's you, is it, Mr. Hitchin?"

"That's right." But he stood there, unmoving, until he thought to say, "Good evening, sir."

"Good evening."

Kerry waited. Hitchin waited. Both stood in their places, one at his door, the other on the stair.

"Could I come in?" said Hitchin at last. "And arst you summat?"

While Kerry had been ruminating in his armchair on the top floor, Hitchin had been ruminating on a kitchen chair in the basement. And as he ruminated, his thin-lipped mouth twisted left and right and forward and back. An old familiar money-making hope had returned once more to his breast, and he had been considering it, estimating it, hands on knees, head to one side. In the end this long rumination had sent him up to the top flight and there, after another installment, brought him down again. It had continued in his chair for a third installment until, as Kerry had guessed, it had flung indecision away and propelled him steadily, if slowly, up the stairs again. Only to be stopped, demoralized, by that sudden opening of the door.

Yesterday he and Nance had gone into the Castle pub, at the corner of Cowcross Street, and there seen Mrs. Babe Churchman sitting against the wall. She was ruminating, be-hind clouded eyes, and over a large whiskey, whose stemmed glass she was twisting around and back again. The entry of the Hitchins impinged all of a sudden on her lost eyes, and straightaway she came up from her cloudy deeps, waved her plump little hand at them, hiccuped, and beckoned them to her side. They carried their drinks to her bench. Now Babe Churchman, though so far she had honored—not without difficulty and so not without self-praise—her promise to say nothing to the Hitchins of Pearl's past, always felt a desire to speak to them of this lodger, to ask after her health, to hear about her work, and to repeat how she'd known her ever so well, once upon a time. Today, with one large whiskey down below her belt, and another warming throat and breast, this compulsion rose like a fish from the deeps and eyed the bait. "And how's my little friend upstairs?" she asked. "Little Pearl?"

"Gawn," said Hitchin.

"Gawn!" Mrs. Churchman was amazed. She felt sharply disappointed, cheated, indignant. But almost at once a seed of pleasure dropped into the resentment, and she sent down some whiskey to water it. This treacherous departure absolved her from secrecy. Surely. "Gawn for good?"

"No. To the 'awspital."

"But whatever for?"

"He says it's a nervous breakdown."

"That was quick work, wasn't it?"

Mrs. Hitchin explained. "He says their doctor phoned up the 'awspital and found they could take her."

"Oh, that's what he says, is it?"

"Yes." Mrs. Hitchin, never liking Babe Churchman, and not

at all liking the tone of this question, added, "And if he says so, it's true."

"H'mm. . . ." For Mrs. Churchman was wondering whether the "hospital" wasn't really another castle, not this brightly lit and lively pub, but that old grim fortress yonder, with its battlements and curtain walls, in whose E Hall the remand prisoners waited. "Well . . . maybe. . . ."

Not liking that "Hmm . . ." or that "maybe," Mrs. Hitchin affirmed, "It was a hospital all right. He took her there."

Oh well, thought Mrs. Churchman, it couldn't be the castle: the cops took you there; not your brothers. "What hospital, Nance?"

"Holloway Sanatorium, an ever so nice place near Windsor where they're good with nervous breakdowns."

"Holloway!" Babe Churchman laughed loudly, regurgitated, put her hand over her mouth, and longed to take it away so that she could lay it on Nance's knee and explain the joke. "How long'll she be gawn?"

"For months, he says."

"Months? It don't take months to heal a breakdown."

"Between you and me," said Nance, "I think it's more than that. I always thought her a bit odd."

"I never been so keen on *him,* either," put in Hitchin.

"Oh, he's a dear," Nance declared.

"Dam' dear, if you arst me. Pays for them rooms abaht half what they're worth. And gets up to his games there."

"What games?" asked Babe Churchman eagerly.

Hitchin began to tell, with laughter, but Nance interrupted, "Now then, Elf. Stop it. You've no right to say such things. Why shouldn't he have his young lady to sit with him?"

"As long as they only sit—"

"Now come off it. I won't have a word said against him, nor Miss Pearl either. They're a perfectly respectable couple."

"Ha!" Babe Churchman could contain her knowledge no more. Nor did she feel any obligation to do so now that Pearl had slipped the noose like this and, as like as not, had no intention of coming back. "That's what you think. Well, I'll just tell you something." The hand went onto Nance's knee and she told all. More, she offered a sudden guess at what lay behind this quick and secret departure to a mental hospital. It had happened before. Pearl in prison had talked all too much. "I shouldn't be surprised," hinted Mrs. Babe Churchman, "but what it saved her from another plate of porridge from the magistrate."

Both Hitchins were, as they said, "struck all of a heap." But whereas Mrs. Hitchin, though shocked and shaken, felt compassion because she had grown to like Pearl and love Kerry, Mr. Hitchin felt pleased. Even excitedly pleased because he was indulging indignation and thoughts of punishment, than which there are few more enlarging excitements in our normally disappointing world. That little twerp to come the high-and-mighty over him—to shaht at him to get aht of his room—to call him stoopid, when all the time . . . Gawd's life! *Stoopid*, you know! Not so stoopid as you think. *Oh*, no. We'll see. He 'it me; I 'it 'im; that's only fair.

Kerry said, "Yes, come in."

Mr. Hitchin nodded, came in, shut the door and said, "Yurse."

"You wanted to ask me something?" said Kerry, from the chair to which he'd returned.

"Yurse . . . well . . . I'll sit down too, shell I? Ta." He sat down on a stiff chair that had wandered and stood astray between table and wall. He put his heavy hands with the spatulate, cracked, and dirt-embedded nails on to his knees. "Hah's your sister?"

"Doing pretty well, I think."

"Yes. Nice 'awspital that, a'nt it?"

"Very."

"Yes. . . ." He lifted a hand and scratched a bristled chin. How best to worm one's way sinuously, slipperily, almost pleasantly into the heart of the subject? "It'll be a long do, I suppose?"

"Maybe. They're going to try to build her up."

"Natcher'ly. Bilderup. Yeah. I never thought she'd bin on top of 'erself for some time, I didn't. Nah. . . ."

"Mr. Hitchin, what was it you wanted to ask?"

"Oh, yurse, yurse." He spoke as if grateful for the reminder. But before answering, he touched his chin again. "You know that there Babe Churchman, don't you? Met her last night."

Kerry let nothing show of the fear which this name had shot into his heart. Some of the shot's impact was lessened because for days he had been half-expecting it. "My sister knows her."

He shifted his eyes away. There were now four shifty eyes in that room.

"Oh, she knows her all right. Yes. . . ."

"Well, what about her?" Kerry felt like a man blindfolded against a wall and telling the firing squad he was ready for them to fire.

"She's told Nance and I all abaht—all abaht everything."

"Everything?"

"Thet's right. All about her havin' been in prison. And more'n once. And she has her own idea about this hospital business. But of course you'll know more about that."

"I see." Kerry, heart battering, rose and walked three paces and back again while pondering what to say.

Hitchin sat scratching his prickled chin with the rasp of a grater, and emitting noises like "yep" and "yeah" and "yurse."

Kerry halted in front of him. "It's true. What of it?"

"Wurl, I mean to say—"

"Go on."

"It makes things different, don't it?"

"How?"

"Oh, come. I don't want to be rude, but it's—it's rather as if you'd come here under false pretenses. Wouldn't you say? As you might put it, taken advantage of us. Yup."

"Why?"

"She must'a come here straight from prison."

"She did."

"Good gawd! Gawd aw'mighty!"

"Why shouldn't she come here? She had to come somewhere."

"It was false pretenses, guv, and I'm pretty sure that, if I wanted to—which, mind you, I don't—I could take you to a court a' law for that."

"Court of rubbish!"

"Oh, but yes, I could. Certainly. A court a' law."

"Stuff!"

"You give us to understand she been ill."

Kerry's eyes swung to the window and the night sky where London's amber glow spread high above the roofs and almost quenched the stars. "That's what I *know* it was."

"And you put us in the wrong. That's what you done."

"*You* in the wrong. Why?"

"With the Father."

At first Kerry could not understand whom he meant. "Oh, Father Aylwin, you mean."

"Thet's right. He made it a stipple-ation that we only let rooms to . . ."

"To whom?"

"Well, if you make me say it, guv: to a proper class of people. There're funny sorts in Clerkenwell."

His words released the safety grip from the primed and charged grenade that was Kerry. There would be a few seconds of silence and then the detonation. In these seconds Mr. Hitchin explained uncomfortably, fingering a nail, "Certainly not to no one who's been in prison."

Kerry turned on him so abruptly that he started back in his chair. This was the detonation. "What are you after?"

"After, guv?"

"That's what I said. You want us to go?"

"Oh no—come—I never said that. But I *do* think you—"

"Well then, what the hell's all this about? Why bring it up at all? Why come here and—"

"I do think that perhaps . . ."

"Come to it."

"It's what I always said: if you want us to overlook this, and what you done in the way of false pretenses, you shouldn't expect to have these rooms on the cheap. You should at least pay the price for them. You mightn't be able to get in anywhere else as respectable as this. That's straight. But I'm never one to be down on those that have bin in trouble, and I'll undertake not to tell the Father anything; but fair's fair, and what I suggest—frankly, guv—is that you give us the balance. Nance'll never arst you for it—she's too damned soft—but I'm not so blasted soft—so what I suggest, between ourselves, is that you give it to me, see." A pause. "Eh? Fair's fair, guv."

Kerry, despite his dismays, was staring at him with a look that held the thought, "God, we've had this before from this incredible old fool. Is his brain made of pulse that he's unteachable?" So Hitchin, a little frightened by the stare, added, "Remember I could get you put out of this house any day. Remember that some might reckon it my dewty to."

Kerry spoke. "How much do you want? Let's come straight at it."

"Wurl . . . a quid a week, perhaps. That wouldn't hurt you."

"Fifty pounds a year?"

"I s'pose so."

"Two hundred and fifty, if I stay five years?"

"Wodd'you gettin' at, mate?"

"Five hundred in ten years?"

"Wodd'you gettin' at? Eh?"

"Just wondering how big a blackmail it is."

"Gahn! It's not blackmail, it's jest business."

"You tried it on me once before, you old fool, and I told you to get out of my room. I tell you to go again now. Get out! Get OUT!" He shouted it. In a passion of despair—feeling that this was fate's new staggering shot; that in his fury with fate he'd take sides with his enemies and drive himself from his home; that everything was going wrong for him while everything went right for Godfrey—he was near a child's scream of tears. "Get OUT, I say! And go down and tell your wife you've talked business once too often, and I'll be out of your house just as soon as I can. *Go* on!"

"Don't talk to me like that. This is *my* house."

"This is my room till I go. Get OUT!"

"All right, mate. You've arst for it. You've done for yourself, you have. See if I don't tell the Father everything. And there's a lot I can tell."

"What does it matter to me what you tell him? I'm going, I tell you. Going just as soon as I can. And now get OUT!"

Hitchin gone, Kerry sat back in his chair in the same attitude of utter dejection that Hitchin's step had disturbed.

"His archers compass me round about."

22

But Kerry did not go from that house in Red Lion Street. He did not disappear into the crowded wilderness of London as secretly as he had come out of it. The Windsors saw to this. Only a few minutes after Hitchin had gone, Kerry, craving immediate sympathy and comfort, went down the stairs to the Windsors, told them everything, and declaimed with all the drama of the self-pitying that he was going from the house just as soon as he could.

Evie cried, "No! Oh, no!" and George said, "My dear boy, no, no. No, no. We'll not countenance that, will we, love?" "I should say *not*," declared Evie. "Give him drinks. It's ridiculous. I never heard such nonsense." So they all sat down with healing drinks and went into conference. It was George who brought the conference to a decision. "I know, my dear boy! I know exactly what to do. It's not you or Hitchin who'll speak the last line in this little drama." He leaned forward and rested a hand on Kerry's knee, just as Babe Churchman might have done, only these fingers were long and delicate within their rings instead of brief and plump. "Now listen, dear boy. It'll be like this."

Father Bernard Aylwin sat at Kerry's table in the tall Windsor chair. He was a frail-looking figure, small and tenuous and wan. His hair, cropped like a monk's, but not lately trimmed, made a close silver stubble. His eyes were sunk so deep beneath wiry eyebrows, and his skin so drained of color, that they made him appear eighty and more instead of seventy-six, which was his age.

Kerry sat away from the table on the Father's right; George Windsor yet farther away on the left. George felt he had a right to sit here, since this important meeting, now toward, was all his doing. So sits, presumably, the clerk of the Privy Council by the side of the lord president. Or perhaps one might think of George Windsor as the impresario who, having put on this play, desired to watch its performance from the wings.

Two chairs, pulled in from the front room, faced these three, so it was clear that the attic was waiting for others to appear. The Father, while he waited, tattooing on the table, could well have been an inspector sent by a minister of housing to hear a local dispute.

All glanced up as the Hitchins entered. Mrs. Hitchin came first, looking enraged with someone, but not with the meeting's chairman because she looked at him only sadly and helplessly. Mr. Hitchin came behind her, grinning with an uncomfortable mixture of shamefacedness, cockiness, and defiance.

Before anyone else could speak, Mrs. Hitchin, standing with her husband behind her, addressed the chair. "I know what you want to see us about, Father, and I want to say this straightaway: I want to say that I think he's behaved shameful in this matter, I do." Hereupon she swung round upon Hitchin. "Yes, I told you I'd say it, and for Gawd's sake, don't stand there grinning like a great gowk; it don't improve your looks if you could see yourself; it makes you look proper sawft, *which* is perhaps the kindest thing to think of you."

While she was ejecting these observations before her and behind her, Father Aylwin had risen and come forward with a hand extended. "Good morning, Nance dear," he said.

She stopped her outflow. "Oh, I see. Yes. Good morning." And she took his hand and shook it. He pointed to a chair. "Sit down, my dear."

Then he took a further step, the hand outstretched again. "Good morning, Alfred."

"Er—what?" Hitchin looked at the hand, scratched his bristles twice, and accepted it. "Yus, thank you, sir."

Mrs. Hitchin, now seated and watching, took this opportunity to visit him with further objurgations. *"And* I wonder that you can stand there, ah'ter all you done, with no more shame on your face than a soppy grin."

To which Hitchin retorted in a dropped voice, as the Father returned to his chair, "Oh, shut up, can't yer? 'E understands that I done nothing but what was natural, like, on the whole. Ain't he just shook me 'and?"

"Yes, and proper small you look now. Proper idiotic. Gaw', it's a treat to look at you."

"Aw, stow it! It's you that's unnatural, I reckon. Nothing ever comes of going back on your own flesh and blood. 'E understands."

"We understand this," said Father Aylwin, now back in his chair. "That you came and attacked Mr. Betterkin in a time of very deep sorrow for him."

"No, sir." Mr. Hitchin, seated now on what he held to be a chair of innocence rather than a stool of repentance, deprecated this interpretation. "No. You're exaggeratin', if you'll pardon the liberty. All I done was to talk to 'im as man to man about things that I'd heard. I admit I done that. But I done no more, as Gawd's in 'is heaven."

"You tried to blackmail a suffering man. You threatened to come and tell me all you'd heard."

"Wurl . . ." Hitchin contended sulkily, as if he were the only one talking reason. "Only because I thought you ought to know."

"But not if he paid you your price."

Since an answer to this did not immediately present itself, Hitchin tossed his head as if to say, "I don't see it like that."

"You tried to extort money from him at a time when, as you knew, he needed all he had to help a sick sister. And before this you spied on him and his fiancée."

"No, sir. Not 'spied.' Not as you might say 'spied.' I was interested. And I just wanted to make sure that I was right. And was I? Not half I wasn't. I suppose you know what he was up to. Here in this very room."

"I know everything."

"Wurl . . ." He now spoke as one reasonable man to another. "I had to put a stop to that, hadn't I? I reckoned it was my dewty. I done it in your interest, didn't I?"

"But my interest could go to the devil if he paid you your price."

Again no answer immediately available, so Hitchin put his hands on his knees and stared moodily.

George Windsor, all this time, was watching this antiphonal dialogue with his face swinging from one interlocutor to the other, and his features registering the emotion of each in turn —the sad, tired dignity of the Father, the uncomfortable dudgeon of Hitchin—as if, were he ever asked to play the two chief parts in this drama, he would have learned how to do it.

Weary resignation lined George's brow when the Father spoke; a sulky sneer heaved up nostrils and underlip when Hitchin demurred; his head drooped despairingly to one side when the Father objected again—in all these silent performances his fine old face was as a mirror that reflected (with slight enlargements) the distresses before him.

"My interest indeed!" the Father scoffed. "When will you learn, Hitchin, that we clergy are not the unspeakable fools you think us?"

This question considerably aggrieved Hitchin. He protested, "Nah then, sir. That's exaggeratin'. That really *is.*"

"You're the fool. In all your life you've never been so well off as you've been in this house—"

"We pays our rent." Sullenly.

"Your good wife pays your rent. But, as you told Mr. Betterkin—and how right you were!—I only want decent people in this house. You can go."

"What yer say?"

"You can go."

At this Kerry began to plead, "No, I wouldn't wish that—" but his words were drowned by Mrs. Hitchin's anguished address to her husband: "I told you so! I told you what'd come of it. I said he'd do it. I passed the remark to you, comin' up the stairs. He'll turn us out, I said."

"Nah, sir," Hitchin interposed, as one preparing to come to terms. "I don't want you to do that, jest for *her* sake. What if I admit I acted a bit below meself? What if I say I've learned me lesson? What if I say I'm sorry for what I done? Eh, what then?"

"I shan't believe you. That's what then."

"Well, sir, I don't think that's quite gentlemanly of you, straight I don't. I don't think it's too civil of you."

"It's not; but it's truthful of me."

"You as good as call me an aht-and-aht liar?"

"Yes."

"An aht-and-aht liar?"

"Yes; and a felon."

"Lord!"

"A felon."

"Well . . . well . . . Gawd forgive you for that, as I do."

"Blackmail happens to be a felony."

Hitchin turned his face sulkily aside. "I don't see why I should be the only one blamed. He was using your house for immoral purposes."

"Not so immoral a purpose as blackmail."

"Not . . .? Not so immoral? Gorblimey! Aht-and-aht immorality?" He was about to demur further, but perceived in time the unwisdom of this, so asked instead, "Mean to say you aren't shocked at his goings-on up here?"

"I can understand."

"Oh, well, yurse, I can understand too, but—mean to say you don't mind her having been in prison twice for stealing?"

"No."

"Gawd!" It was confusing. "At least I never been in prison."

"There's time yet. For demanding money with threats you can go to prison for life."

At this awful word Mrs. Hitchin let loose a loud negative that sounded like "Ow, *now! Now!*"

And Hitchin, horror on his brow, said, "Life? *Me?* Why, I only arst him to give a better price for his rooms."

"Yes, the sums involved were not large. Perhaps we could get you off with five years."

"Five—"

"Now listen, Alfred. I'm not going to make a police matter of this because I don't see that you've ever had much chance of being made into a full man and getting much sense or decency."

"No, sir," Hitchin agreed at once, adding, "That's it, sir"; then realized what he was conceding and exclaimed, "*What?*" but decided that perhaps this card was a good one to play, so concluded, "Well, I think there's something in that. What chance? I arst yer!"

"And I'll do this for you, Alfred. I'll keep your wife here as a tenant so long as you never set foot in this house again."

"*What?* . . . Nah, I don't see that . . . Nah . . . a husband's place is by the side of his wife. Every time."

Mrs. Hitchin, like the woodwind after the strings, burst in with the same tune. "No, Father. I don't want you to do that.

I was a fool ever to have landed myself with a man like him, but he's my bed and I must lie on it, as the sayin' is. Gaw'—and the wonderful 'opes and fancies I had, twenty years ago, when I knew I was going to marry him—it makes you laugh! Things don't turn out as you fancied. Ah, well, it's funny: I'm sick of the sight of him sometimes and yet I suppose I should miss him. No, he's done for us, and we'd better get out, as you say. We can go somewhere, and he'll have to do some regular work for a change and p'raps that'll teach him. P'raps, then, he'll get some sense into his great empty head."

"He'll begin to get sense, Nance dear, when he knows he's not worthy of you."

Hitchin, alarmed by this talk of being cast out from his present cosy Eden and driven forth to earn his bread by the sweat of his face, was ready to proffer another card or two from that humility suit, which seemed the one most likely to take tricks with the Father. He pulled in his chin and put a glimmer of repentance in the eye, half-closed, that was nearer the Father. "Well, what if I say I know it? What if I say she's too good for a bloke like me? What then?" Having offered this humility, he leaned back to rest, and the penitent eye, beneath its dropped lid, submitted to the chairman that, though he realized he deserved nothing good, it could at least be said of him that no man in the world more deplored his previous ways than he. Eye and attitude were those of one who, given a chance, would concentrate in future on his nature's finer parts. "Eh, what if I said that?"

"I should say you were speaking the truth without knowing it."

"Well, I dunno. . . . You seem to me a bit 'ard. I—"

But here Kerry tried again to put in a word. "Father Aylwin . . ." and Hitchin, hearing his voice, turned toward him and smiled—a most genial smile that showed the easy unreality of all his recent talk.

"Father Aylwin, I don't want you to turn him out for my sake—"

"Nah," Hitchin agreed, perhaps unaware that he'd expressed aloud his desire to be associated with this sentiment.

"—and not for all the world would I have Mrs. Hitchin leave her home. She's always been kindness itself to my sister and me."

Hitchin nodded his endorsement of this.

Father Aylwin, having listened to this plea in mitigation,

turned, like a magistrate, to the accused. "Alfred, you were in the army, weren't you?"

Hitchin assented enthusiastically. "I joined up—when was it, Nance? In '15, before they started taking us. Before the Derby boys even."

"That's right, Father," said Nance. "He done that."

"Yup."

"And I suppose you were often ordered, Alfred, to do things that were hard to do?"

"You bet your boots I was!—if you'll pardon that expression. There was a time when the captain called me and said—"

"Quite. . . . Exactly. . . . Well, I have my marching orders too, and one is that I forgive my brother until seventy times seven. Sometimes it's heavy going. I count Mr. Betterkin my good friend, and henceforward his sister too. You tried to make money out of their great misfortune. It's heavy going. But if the Captain orders it—"

"You mean Jesus Christ?"

"Who else?"

"Yus. He was the goods, He was. I've always allowed *that*, to Nance here."

"Very well. You can stay here, and it's all forgotten."

"Aw, you don't deserve it, Elfred," cried Nance. "That you don't. You ought to go down on your knees and—"

But her husband wasn't listening. "You mean it, Father?"

"Yes, and I'm not going to say that I'm doing it for your good wife's sake. I'm not. I'm doing it for yours."

"Well . . . well . . . strike me!"

Nance was sobbing into her handkerchief.

"Perhaps she'll explain it to you, Alfred. Perhaps one day it'll break through."

Mrs. Hitchin came out of the handkerchief. "You're too good to us, Father."

"One couldn't be too good to you, my dear. That is all for now. We needn't worry you anymore."

"Gaw' bless you, Father. Come on, Elfred. Come on. Don't sit there gaping."

"Well, nah!" mused Hitchin; but he rose, still musing.

"Come on, I say! The Father's said what he had to say, and they all want you out of their sight, I'll be bound, *which* they're luckier than I am, in not having to see you more than they need."

Hitchin murmured, "Gawd's Christ!" and followed her

through the door. Kerry, watching him go, and hearing him mutter sadly, "Wurl . . . I dunno . . . I don't see . . . Seemed all right to me. . . ." felt suddenly sorry for him. There went another; an old fond fool perhaps, but still: one more whose dream had mocked him.

Father Aylwin remained in his tall chair as a judge might after the prisoner had been taken below. George Windsor remained in his side chair: why was not quite clear to Kerry; unless, possibly, he had arranged, backstage, another act in which the Father was to be his leading man. Kerry stayed in his place because he was in doubt what would happen next.

What happened next was that, when the last of the Hitchins' steps had gone down into a silence, Father Aylwin looked up from the table, turned his eyes to Kerry, and said, "I've read your book."

Kerry could only say "Oh?" not daring to ask, "Did you like it?" He'd had dispraise enough.

"Mr. Windsor told me about it and lent me his copy. The critics heaped plenty of abuse on it, he tells me."

"Perhaps not more than it deserved."

"It deserved praise too. You have a great talent."

A stab of sweetness, this remark: small and quick and unexpected. It embarrassed him so that he could not answer.

"Is it possible, Mr. Betterkin, that none of the critics saw the promise in it? Pull up your chair and tell me."

"One or two said it had promise."

"I'm glad. Glad they were not all blind. May I say what I think?"

"Do . . . please."

"I'm only an old reader who's loved stories all his life and now in his retirement probably reads far more of them then he ought to. I'm a reviewer too."

"You are?"

"Oh, certainly—but one whom no paper has ever invited to contribute his views to it. I have, however, written the review of your book which I should have sent to *The Times*, had they asked me for it. Would you care to read it?"

"Oh, please, yes," said Kerry, and was now sure that George was the impresario behind this new scene.

The Father fiddled in a breast pocket, found a crumpled half sheet of notepaper and passed it along the table to Kerry.

The writing, in an old man's quivering hand, was not easy to read, but Kerry was soon deciphering it. "This young author may not yet have understood the nature of his talents, or got them into order, but he has certainly the makings of a fine novelist. We shall hear more of him. Much more. Every now and then, in the midst of matter that is somewhat strained and stilted, his gifts shine through: a joyous gusto in the writing, a rich sense of fun, an instant perception of human absurdity, and with it all a quiet melancholy that, blending with the comedy, produces a tender poetry. His strongest bent, at present, is for realistic comedy seen through gentle, indulgent eyes, and when he gives this full play, his story is gay, amusing, and moving, his characters alive. It is only when he quits this, his natural field, and tries the grand historical manner—Scott's 'big bow-wow stuff'—that his writing hardens and his people stiffen into marionettes. . . ."

Kerry finished. The Father was watching him with lips compressed in a tight smile. "How would you have liked that as a review?"

"It would have been wonderful. All that I could ask."

"Well, I think it's the truth. But it's not all praise, as you see."

"And where it isn't, it's right, I'm sure."

"Sometimes, in your big set scenes, the characters—if you'll forgive me—are only one part alive and three parts stuffed."

"I know."

"But don't worry about that. It's true, I fancy, of eight historical romances out of ten. The distant past must have been so different from the present that it's almost impossible for an author to imagine it powerfully enough to bring it alive. If he struggles to give his people emotions and language very different from our own today, it irritates his reader and starts him thinking yes, but this is all guesswork; if he gives them the ideas and language of today, they soon begin to look like modern people dressed up for a fancy-dress ball. It is this, I think, which has almost killed the historical novel in our unromantic times."

"Absolutely!" The word came like a shot across their bows from George on the starboard beam. The Father had made an opening through which George desired to come in and talk about himself. "Absolutely. I know the truth of that to my cost. It was the end of me. I could have played realistic parts as well as anyone, but my dear public would never stand for me in anything but a costume play. They had labeled George Windsor as a romantic actor, and when the costume play died,

George died with it. A few posthumous years on the provincial stage, and then the melancholy end. I could only—but with you, dear boy, it is different." He had just reminded himself that Kerry, and not he, was the subject under discussion. "And there's comfort for you in this. It may be a damned good thing —if, in our Elfred's words, you'll pardon that expression, Father—that the critics, always a bloody-minded lot, as I know only too well—though, mind you, I've had my praise from them too—but . . . what were we talking about? . . . oh, yes . . . a thoroughly good thing that the filthy crew killed this first book for you and saved you from the romantic label, which is lethal today, dear boy—lethal. You, unlike me, can start again in a new vein, as the Father's about to say."

Father Aylwin, who had turned his wan face to listen courteously to a new speaker, was now able to return it to Kerry. "What I'd like you to do would be to leave the distant past and direct your gift of gentle comedy and all your gay zest onto things that you really know about because you've experienced them in heart and nerves: in other words, such things as the ordinary man's drudgeries and anxieties and disappointments and heroisms. You want to ride so high, don't you? Well, you could, you could, if, as I may so put it, you would turn your chores into your chariot—forgive me: I'm an old preacher and fall into the tricks of the pulpit. You've tried to be an eagle before you've grown the wings; you've tried to force these wings out of your brain, but I suspect one can only grow them out of one's sufferings."

"Absolutely!" began George. "God, how true! Just what I—" but the Father, feeling himself on a good stretch of road, was anxious to march further. He turned his face to George, let it smile in acknowledgement of a new voice, and quickly restored it to Kerry. "You must turn your fetters into wings. If I'm right, then all that you've suffered of late will be a fine gift to you because it's a dead weight of lead that any true artist can turn into gold. If that's right, then out of the Valley of Shadow you'll bring far more than you lost there."

"Yes, yes." The Father had obviously reached his peroration, so George could say his piece. "You are lucky. All this suffering in the wilderness—fine! Fine! I remember Irving saying to me, when I had my first great success, in *The Pluck of the Shadracks*—I played the lead, and it was a furore—he said, 'Careful, my dear boy. Success is a great test of character. There's only one better, and that's failure. Success can leave you smaller, but you can only rise above failure a taller man.' "

Neither of these two, neither Father Aylwin who'd come into this attic like a magician out of the air nor George who, while wanting to be kind, was apt to talk chiefly about himself, knew that each in his turn had spoken a sentence which, such is the magic in the touch of words, had raised again in Kerry all that appetite for heroism that had created his Knight of St. John. "Turn your chores into your chariot," the Father had said, and apologized for preaching, but before the sermon was at an end, the chariot was at the door and Kerry eager to mount it. "You can only rise above failure a taller man"—perhaps this made its magical appeal to Kerry because he was so short in body and longed to be tall in some other way.

Soon the two of them said good-bye and went, their life-giving business done. George, as the entrepreneur who had staged these two small one-act dramas, escorted his principal player down the stairs and out through the front of the house.

23

In the privacy of his attic or in the noiser privacy of the streets,
Kerry would indulge, as we have told, a habit that helped and
invigorated him better than wine, but could be told to no one
because it was ridiculous. To fortify his self-confidence, to
charge his will with power, he would repeat and repeat to
himself strong affirmations about the indomitable qualities of
his nature. The strange visitation of the Father had roused new
power in him, and he sustained this power by reiterating, as he
walked along the Farringdon Road to his office, or paused in
his work there, or lay in his bed, such statements as "Nothing
defeats me. Ever." "I have resilience. Stupendous resilience."
"They may hurl me down, but I bounce all the higher. Bounc-
ing Betterkin." "I never give in." "I'll but lie down and bleed
awhile, And then I'll rise and fight again."

Not less than Sir Andrew Barton of the ballad, Kerry had
risen and was fighting again. Although at the present he was
but beating the air of the Farringdon Road because he had no
subject for a book, he had bought new pencils, new paper, and
new blotting pads. The tools were ready. He was always helped
to action by new and attractive tools. He wrote better prose,

he said, with a new clean pencil than with an old one. And nightly now, in attics made lonely by the loss of Pearl, he gave himself to planning the mood and method of a new story and searching for it some splendid subject.

Realism. A laughing realism. But not cynical; pitying, rather. No picture of some noble and caparisoned knight doing battle against Suleiman the Magnificent but of some ordinary little Everyman doing battle against harsh circumstance. And not in the picturesque and heroic past but in the unlovely but often heroic present. A hero full of weaknessess like—well, like all of us—but capable of endurance and courage. Lying down to bleed quite often but always rising to fight again. His experiences those one needn't guess about because one had felt them along the strings of one's heart and the sinews of one's brain. Such as . . .?

Such as Pearl . . . Sally . . . Godfrey . . . the good Windsors . . . and, above all, the failure of a big hope.

Of a sudden one night, as he paced his floor or gazed from his window, it all came. He saw the plot; he began to see the characters. Pearl? A character called Megan: not a sister, but a wife; a wife who needed all the hero's help because a sickness —say, a partial paralysis—would attack her intermittently and incapacitate her for work. His help would not be wholly a virtue, because it was in part a vanity. Once this lady had appeared in the pool of ideas, new conceptions for merry chapters when she and the hero gave themselves treats, getting a special fun out of their poverty, plunged like kingfishers from his head into the pool. Megan was soon joined by Jerome, a brother—no, a cousin of hers: a young dressy lawyer, a social climber, a tuft-hunter with a London club, a man of means who always found excuses for not helping her. Query: are cousins ever supposed to help cousins? No; then perhaps not a cousin or a lawyer—a brother in a big way of business. But, whatever he was, he despised the hero in his poverty, and one of the most thrilling and charming things in the book would be the way the hero slowly overtook and passed this conceited young man.

Next appeared, full-grown, the figure of an old actor: one Gabriel Somebody with all the extravagances of manner and largeness of heart that belonged to George Windsor. No need in this case to worry whether George would recognize himself in the character; he would love to. And yes, by heaven, if the book should live (as it would) Kerry would have given George his immortality after all. "So long as man can breathe and eyes can see, So long lives this, and this gives life to Me." Oh yes, it would delight George to see himself heading—and delight Kerry to start him heading—down the corridors of time.

A little difficult to get Sally Penelope into the tale because Megan was the hero's wife, and the plot demanded that he was loyal to her. Where, then, came Sally? Sally should be his sister, a very dear sister, and very religious. Yes, this would inspire him, because his love for Sally had one face not unlike a brother's love for a sister.

The plot; the story-in-chief? Oh yes, he had that: the utter defeat of a dream by which the hero had lived. The failure of a great hope. My God, he could do that! He fails and starts again, and the end of the story is the starting again. God, he could get into the heart of that. The dream must not be the creation of a book and its worldwide success; no, his lost book, lying dead of its wounds, must be transformed into, symbolized by, a business which the hero hoped to build into a firm with customers all over the world. Best of all had been his vision of what this business must be: an "antique shop." This would be a perfect symbol for his book. A shop full of old-fashioned furniture that no one of taste desired anymore.

This last thought would remind him that he'd felt all this confidence about a story before. . . . But forget that. Forget it. Go once again into the old dream's glittering hall, and there forget.

24

So began a sad-happy period for Kerry. Happy because he was creating something again, and everyone down on this earth, whether child or man, knows peace, satisfaction, and joy when he is making something and trying to give it beauty, be it symphony, cathedral, or mud pie. "There's no joy like it," Kerry would say, and he would hurry home from work, cook himself some sausages or bacon, wash them down with a glass of beer, and then take his ideas (which had been burgeoning over the sausages) to his paper and pen. It was lonely without Pearl, but only for an hour: after that he was gone from Red Lion Street and enjoying the company, far away, of the people of his fancy. But the time was sad, too, because always intertwined with the joy ran that thought: "I've done all this before. . . ."

One evening, however, an idea burst upon him between one written sentence and the next, and a new quota was added to the happiness. Father Aylwin had routed Hitchin and sent him away, disarmed, to sulk in his basement tent. Hitchin, for fear of his home, would never again dare to do or say anything that might offend the Father. This meant that Kerry could have

Sally with him in the evenings. They could meal together and stay together. Of course, Kerry would keep his promise and ask no more from her than some kisses (though a fair and proper allowance of these).

Sally was overjoyed. "Oh, can I really come? And can I help with the book? Can I help?" She could help just by being there, he said. And by keeping quiet. Very quiet.

So Sally came. Came and drove him from the stove, where she cooked the meal; then dismissed him imperiously to his writing, while she washed the dishes. This done, she went at a creep to a chair by the wall and sat reading or knitting in a most understanding silence. A silence so resolute, so reverent, such a salute to work, that it was almost as disturbing as trumpets. At times, said Kerry, looking up from his work, it was deafening.

"Not but what I like to see you there," he would say, but when she looked up with pleasure he would add quickly, "so long as you don't talk"; at which she would pretend to pout.

This sacred silence was broken only by himself. When a comic scene was going particularly well, he would laugh and stamp and hit the table with delight, but if Sally looked up, he raised a warning finger to command silence. At other times, when nothing was going well, he groaned and stamped and cried aloud, "*I* can't do it. *I* can't get it right" and, if she ventured sounds of comfort, begged her to keep quiet.

The room was full of Sally's silence one evening, she hardly daring to move in her chair, but he getting up and wandering about whenever he liked; he had sat again to write rapidly a passage that had taken its final shape in his mind—when a creak sounded on the stairs. Hitchin? A spy, a listener? Hitchin coming up like Pluto out of the mouth of hell? Instantly his left hand shot to the distant typewriter, its fingers tapped vigorously on the keys, and his voice dictated sentences aloud. Since the creaker couldn't hear the actual words it mattered not what they were, and he said loudly, "She sat there in what was now universally known as the Great Sally Silence, and though terror leapt into her eyes at these sinister sounds without, she didn't dare to move. Nonetheless, looking at her there, he felt fond of her. Is it Hitchin? I think not."

"No. It was nothing."

"No more creaks?"

"No."

His left hand deserted the typewriter, and his right hand bade her be silent.

The passage when finally written down seemed more than usually fine, so with his fist he hit the table a massive blow that caused her to jump almost out of her chair. She murmured a protest, but he didn't listen because he was preparing to tell her how wonderful it was and that he must read it to her. There was no continuing till he had relieved himself of its presence. "Shall I read it?"

"Of course. That's what I'm here for. Anything you're in doubt about, just try out on me. Try it on the dog."

"But to hell! I'm not in doubt about it! Whether you like it or not I shall still think it terrific, so what's the purpose of reading it to you, I don't know; unless it's to give you the privilege and pleasure of hearing it."

"Why not read it instead of talking quite so much?"

"If you're rude, I just shan't read it at all. You can do without it. Now listen." And he read.

He read with power; with gestures. She said, "Oh, but it *is* wonderful; it *is!*" and he, encouraged, was able to go on writing, his self-confidence now at full steam.

He did not tell her that the magnificent passage came from a part which portrayed the hero's very religious sister. She did not know that she was sitting there as a model. Often he looked toward her and considered that extraordinary phenomenon which is the devotion, on a clouded planet wheeling through space, of one human creature to another. This powerful consideration issued, not only in more poignant affection for her, but in some bright new ideas for the book; and Sally sat there unknowing.

Two hours of work, and he wearied. Then he slapped the pencil down (so that she jumped again) and announced, "Whistle gone. Silence over. Talk please."

She laid her book aside.

He turned his chair toward her. "Talk, woman. The curfew is lifted. Talk."

"What about?"

"I don't know. Religion, if you like."

"All right."

"Well, go on. Start away."

"No, you start. It was your idea."

"I don't know what to say. How's your father?"

"He's peevish to the last degree. About being always left alone. He says I ought to stay with him more."

"Oh, dear! Perhaps he's right."

"No, I don't see that."

"But you believe in self-sacrifice?"

"Yes, but self-sacrifice doesn't mean being someone's door-mat."

"It involves mortification, doesn't it, and what's mortification but doing the exact opposite of what you want to do? In other words, staying with Pop?"

"Oh, I don't see that . . . no, I don't. . . ."

"Because you don't want to." For a minute he wondered whether women took to religion more readily than men because they were more capable of compromise; less spiritually disabled when they were not going "the whole hog."

The whole hog. The *totus porcus*. Perfect selflessness was quite beyond him, but he could see, and none better, that to lose oneself in creating good was the only perfect joy. The surge of life in one converted to love. The supreme bliss of an artist's work, for example, was not won till it was wholly disinterested creation. There was always an alloy in the heart of creation, a slight mixture of dissatisfaction and unrest, till those joyous moments when self was forgotten and you were making the thing for its own sake without thought of praise or profit. Then for a while you entered upon the innermost happiness of creation whose name was less bliss than blessedness.

Filling up with these ideas he shot up from his chair and floated around the room. Even so does a captive balloon rise and drift along the ground as it fills with heated air. But no more than a straining balloon did he speak.

"Well, say something more," begged Sally, following with her eyes this circumambient figure.

This halted him in front of her. "My inability to believe in your Christian dogmas, Sally Penelope, remains total and invincible. Try as I may to overcome it, I can't. The deeper I try to think, the less I can believe in dogmatic Christianity, but— *but* the more I believe with all my soul in applied Christianity."

"Meaning what?"

"Meaning that one should lose one's self in the service of others. Meaning that I've the horrible suspicion God may have tried to destroy my fine castle around me so that my soul might see this. Meaning that it's useless for Him to try, because I'm chained to its walls for ever—and therefore undoubtedly reprobate. Meaning, in a word, that I should be writing this blasted book for its own sake and not for praise and profit."

"Well, yes, that's right. Yes, of course."

"Aye, aye, but don't just say 'of course' like that. It's damn difficult, so don't be so glib. This is as far as I can get—was that a creak?" He went to the door and looked out. "No. Nothing. The Great Hitchin Silence. This is as far as I can get, God forgive me. I say to myself, let me like praise and profit by all means, but let me love the thing I'm creating more, so that if I have to choose between the two, I shall choose the thing itself and not the profit and the praise—"

"Well, that's fine; that's all right."

"Is it? I'm not sure. But please don't interrupt. Let me proceed. This is what I say. If praise and pay be given us, well and good. Let us enjoy them; it's just nonsense to deny that they are delightful gifts. But if they are withheld from us, Sally Penelope, well and good too." And he began to spout with suitable gestures as of an actor's right hand:

"For so the Ark be borne to Zion, who
    Heeds how they perished, or were paid, that bore it?
For so the Shrine abide, what blame, what pride,
    If we, its priests, were crowned, or bound, before it?"

Having recited these fine lines, he went straight back to his chair. "The talk is concluded," he said.

And Sally, shrugging as a woman does when she despairs of a man's sense, picked up her book again.

Not only was there a silence, as of defeat and melancholy in Mr. Hitchen's basement, there was also a quiet, a stillness that seemed deliberate, in the Windsors' flat immediately below. Kerry, "listening" to it one evening outside his door, said to Sally, "Well that's the most articulate silence I've ever heard." On these evenings they saw nothing of Evie or George, and yet both were there beneath the floor. Very occasionally you caught Evie's voice or shrill laugh.

Why this quiet that rose like warm friendly air from the flat below?

Why? At first, after Pearl had gone, Evie, a vessel brim-filled with pity, had wanted Kerry to have supper with them as often as possible. "I can't bear to think of him all alone up there,

cooking his little sausages," she had said to George. And
George had proposed going up to comfort him with a little
companionable talk. More than once he had mounted the stairs
with this comfort.

To both these kindnesses, at first, Kerry had responded
gratefully. He had supped with them a few times. He had put
up a show of welcome to the Commodore's epiphanies. But
after a while he had declined the suppers with perhaps overdeveloped excuses, and he had hinted to George that on his
advice, for which he would ever be grateful, he had now
finished bleeding and was fighting again.

George was flattered but, in spite of this hint, did go up once
again to his young friend, but, peeping in, saw that there was
no doubt about it: the lad was writing hard at his table. The
divine afflatus. So with a finger upraised to signify understanding and the need of silence, he shut the door exceedingly softly.
The click of its tongue in the lock was hardly louder than the
visit of a moth to a flower.

And Evie now could only salve her pity by sometimes "nip-
ping up" before Kerry came home and placing on his table a
delicacy from their own meal. She would garnish it with parsley
and lettuce leaves and one brilliant tomato.

But then one evening they heard voices above. They sat at
their supper table stilled, eyes toward the ceiling, ears directed
that way. Kerry's voice and a woman's: laughter; a sound of
dishes. And this was repeated evening after evening. So one
evening they peeped around their door, as Kerry escorted his
visitor down the stairs, and saw who she was: that Sally Penelope girl. "Ah!" whispered Evie to George, who was peeping
behind her, "go back. At once. And stay back. This is love. Go
on in and shut the door. Leaving yourself about like this!
They're neither of them the least beautiful, and it's so sweet of
them to love each other. Oh, isn't it all attractive? None of your
going up in case he's lonely: you don't know what you might
see . . . and disturb. And none of my pestering him with food:
she's cooking his little sausages for him. This is where we lie
low."

George nodded, appreciating this as wisdom; and not once
thereafter was he allowed to wander upstairs for a brief cau-
serie with a friend, though more than once the mood to do so
descended upon him; and so it came about that the love upstairs was accorded by the flat below the tribute of an enormous neglect.

Pearl gone, the Windsors withdrawn into a silence as of an enclosed monastic order, and the Hitchins buried below, Kerry and Sally were left alone in that high attic, their battle headquarters for their great offensive against the world; while far beneath them in the Clerkenwell Road, unheard by either, the noisy, indifferent world went beating and hurrying by.

The book was going well beneath Kerry's hand. It was going faster than ever his first book went because so little research was needed. Nearly all its matter was stored in the deep closets of his heart and brain; it had but to be taken out and transmuted into new forms; and soon he could but believe that his struggling couple, the hero and his wife—and the very religious sister—were typical of all those who strove daily to better their position against the pitiless odds of the world.

The only research necessary was into the secrets of the antique trade. And here a remarkable thing: he made a friend of the old "antique dealer" in Turnmill Street out of whose junk Sally had dug the wisdom of Jakob Böhme and the seeds of a new life. He would sit for hours with the smelly old man in his tiny back room, which, in its turn, smelt as musty as the heaped and littered shop because, in both, the dust on antique time lay ever unswept. It lay in a like peace, one felt, on the old man's tumbled clothes and in his beard. Kerry was fascinated by all that this ancient delighted to tell him, and thus, oddly enough, he dug up his inspiration from the same ditch as Sally.

Having long discovered the strange fertilizing power of names, he raked and raked for his hero's name; and it would not at once be apparent why "Vincent Garrett" was his choice; only the author would know in his secret heart that "Vincent" means "conquering" and that "Garrett" stirred quickening thoughts of this attic whose very walls were papered with dreams of conquest.

As with the hero's name, so with the book's, the title. He sought among poems and quotations for enkindling words and at last adapted with eager satisfaction some words from Shakespeare: *This Old and Antique Song.* The antique song was the song of ambition in every man's heart, this fool's longing to be applauded widely in life and remembered kindly after death, this irrational dream that was sure of its demolition in life or after, sooner or later—in the end.

Inspired by title and name, and by the hidden symbols of his own sufferings that constituted the plot, he wrote with an excellent speed. A once-beautiful old house in the Pentonville Road was his setting, and here the Vincent Garretts lived, surrounded by beautiful objects which Vincent hoped to sell, his beloved antiques. The hero loved every moment of his work, whether it was his visits to lovely old houses and country manors in search of *objets d'art* that would sell, or his dream, as he praised and sold his wares in his shop, of making his name and his fortune one day. The failure of the great hope was as symbolical as everything else, and the old man in Turnmill Street, loving to talk of his misfortunes, made it wholly convincing: the spurious boom in the first years after the war; the slump; the trade buyers coming no more, and the casual custom in the shop dwindling toward an end.

Much of this Kerry must needs read to Sally (he would be straitened till this was accomplished) but since Sally invariably declared that it was "wonderful" and that she was "absolutely thrilled" by it, her opinion was not of much use except for his encouragement and the general gaiety.

25

The young green spring was now in London, and a tall population of daffodils had come like migrants and invaded even the few public gardens of Holborn and Clerkenwell. They stood in careless clusters on the fresh young grass or in regimental order on old gray, earthy beds. Of all the trees, only the London planes had failed as yet to put forth their first green feathery welcome. Here and there in dusty private gardens the yellow forsythias burst above the walls in splendidly excited sprays to enjoy the new warmth between pavement and sky.

And meanwhile, up in his attic, hardly aware of all these occupation troops in their yellow and green, Kerry, at least as excited as the brimming forsythias, was giving his manuscript the last delicate changes, the last subtle additions, the last verbal pruning and polish. Useless to think, "It seems good to me because it's made as exactly to the measure of my mind as the skin to the apple; other minds are different"—he could but feel an effervescing conviction that this book was good, absolutely, not just relatively. The previous book he could now see had many a technical clumsiness; it seemed prentice work now; and he had imagined it perfect! This discouraging thought could stir the fear "Will I think the same about this book in a year's time?" but his new great hope would not suffer this fear to live. He was hoping just as he had hoped before. And one outcome of this condition caused him some meditation, some scratching of the head. He observed that with this hope in his heart, a hope that swelled often into something like a certainty of success, he was not feeling the need to be religious anymore.

Then one Sunday afternoon, he at the table, Sally in her chair, he flung down his pen, said "Hail, festal day!" and, jumping up, seized her hands, dragged her to her feet, and danced her around with hopping, skipping, and intermittent cries of "Yippee!" This performance he ended with a kiss and the words "It is done. Put by the lute."

She said, "And now I type it?"

For Sally had insisted that she was going to type it. He had typed the previous book, and she had pronounced it "wonderfully done . . . for an amateur, but . . ."

"But what? To hell, what?"

"Well, for example, a professional wouldn't have all the mistakes crossed out with x's. Besides, you'd better let me do it, because I shall do it in half the time."

"You think so?"

"Naturally. I do touch-typing and don't have to turn my face from the manuscript at every fourth word. And, what's more, I use all ten fingers instead of two."

"But when will you do this?"

"When? Why, I'll start the minute it's finished and go on every evening after."

"Where?"

"Mayn't I come here and do it?"

"Oh, my dear, will you? But how about Pop? And how long will it take?"

"Say six foolscap pages an hour—two hours a night—five on Saturdays and Sundays—how many pages is that?"

"I don't know."

"It's a hundred and twenty. Then say three weeks or less."

"But this is wonderful. And awful, because how can I reward you?"

"Don't be silly. As your secretary, it's my job."

"Doubtless. And doubtless the job will be done for its own sake and not for profit and praise. But I feel that some praise and pay must be given it. I must consider what would be a suitable reward. And now come out and celebrate."

Certainly Sally's typescript, taking shape beneath his eyes, with its wide margins, its titles properly centered, its mistakes properly erased and typed over, was to Kerry's uncertain handiwork as a fine lady dressed by a couturier to a woman in homemade garments slightly frayed. As she typed, he could not stop coming to peep over her shoulder; no, not even when she protested, "Go *away*, do!" He had to watch because her neat professional work made his book look better and better, more professional, so that his hopes rose higher behind her head.

Sally finished her task on the eighteenth evening, an evening in May. "There!" she said, and dropped her hands onto her lap beneath the table; then picked them up and rubbed them because they ached. "It's all done."

"Not yet," he said. "Kindly get a clean sheet and take a dictation. Thank you. Center it about four inches down. This sheet will go immediately after the title page. Ready? Then type. In caps. 'To Sally Penelope'—"

"*What?*"

"Continue, please. Do what you're told. Double spacing and then type this, properly indented." He laid a slip of paper before her. On it was written:

To Sally Penelope

To her whose love has spurred
These pages on; then dressed
Them so they please their best,
To her their every word.

"Oh, Kerry! Oh, *no!* And did *you* write *that?*"

"Well, who do you suppose did? Mr. Hitchin?"

"Oh, but it's too wonderful."

"I admit it. It's Horatian in its compression and simplicity."

"Oh, and everyone who knows me will see it! All my friends. How lovely."

"More than that. As I intend to sell thirty thousand copies and at least five people will read each copy, a hundred and fifty thousand people will see it."

"But this is fame! And if the book becomes a classic, as I've a sort of a kind of a feeling it will, everyone will have to know who Sally Penelope was." She sat gazing at the name in its lonely capitals. "That's *me,*" she said.

He put an end to this rapt contemplation. "Here is brown

paper and string. Pack it up. Tomorrow in the lunch hour I will take it up the hill to Harker and Inman's."

"Oh, not to them. They are horrible people. They just let the other book die."

"But they have an option on this one. If they don't take it, and I don't think they will, well, there are other publishers in the land."

"But they're sure to take it. It's a lovely book."

"You forget they've gambled once on John Kenrick Better-kin and lost heavily. I'm not sure that I shall mind much if they refuse it. Then perhaps I can start again with some other house."

The typescript was soon packed and tied up. Very neatly, by Sally's hand. She typed an address label and stuck it on lovingly. And the two stood there and stared at a fair and comely parcel resting on the table. A pregnant silence, and then Kerry said, "Well, there it is. Let it go. I'm trying not to hope. It is best not to hope. Leave it to God."

26

That sharp knock of the postman downstairs. A knock that meant a parcel. That sharp knowledge of what was about to happen, before it happened. It happened: Mrs. Hitchin coming up the stairs; he going to his door; she putting the parcel into his hand.

Back into his room with the parcel in his hand and a weight in his heart. The shape unmistakable, and Harker and Inman's label on the dark-brown paper. Listlessly he opened it and saw a letter on the top. An easy friendly letter from Sir Osbert Inman, thanking him for sending them his new book, stating their opinion that "it had many good parts in his best manner" but concluding that "on the whole, and in view of the sad failure of his previous book and of the present unsatisfactory state of the fiction market" they had decided, with regret, not to exercise their option; and asking after his sister. This amiable letter was signed most amiably, "O.I."

Kerry tossed the letter down onto the opened parcel. "O.K., O.I.," he said.

The great house of Harker and Inman had courteously shown him to their handsome doorway in Paternoster Court.

"Old Sir Osbert Inman, by the nine gods he swore," thought Kerry, "that the great house of Harker's should suffer wrong no more."

And since this seemed a bright remark, he longed to go and say it to someone. But there was no Pearl in the next room; it seemed absurd to go down and break in on the Windsors; so he must wait until the evening when he would have Sally's comfort. Not easy to have heartache for ten hours without telling anyone.

It was eight in the morning, and he trod his chamber around in sadness until he remembered Sir Andrew Barton and resolved that, having bled for these fifteen minutes, he would now resume the battle and send the book to the next publisher on his list. He carried the parcel under his arm for mailing when he set out for the Farringdon Road and his office.

As he had feared, as indeed he seemed to know by despairing precognition, this rejection was but the first of many. One after another came the arrows, shooting into the flesh of St. Sebastian. During the next months, while spring went glorying into summer, and summer went slowly and with blushes into autumn, seven publishers dismissed his typescript back to Red Lion Street. Some returned it with no more than their usual rejection slip; others, kindlier, sent an explanatory, or even an encouraging, note. One firm said that while they thought it showed promise, they felt it to be "unmarketable" because its characters were too commonplace, its setting lacked picturesqueness, and its plot needed stronger action. Another firm wrote that they feared this particular book was "unsalable" for want of a strong story, unusual characters, and an interesting background.

These rejections, repeated through the months, were heartsickness after heartsickness, but he was able to take the blows without the heart breaking because the skin of his heart had hardened. He would, however, think to himself, walking along and recalling parts of the book, "How can they *not* like it?" And then he would remember Evie pointing the difference between herself and Georgy by saying that Georgy was always surprised, even unto a despair of the world, if the critics hadn't loved his performance, whereas she was usually surprised and rejoiced if they had liked hers at all. Not that she didn't think her performance fine, but that she expected little justice in this world.

In the summer he was able to fetch Pearl home and forget himself for a day. It was a happy distraction to prepare her room for her, decorating it with flowers. He was not the only one to think of welcoming her with flowers. Nance Hitchin came up with a few carnations, Sally with roses. Kerry seized this chance to inform Mrs. Hitchin that he wasn't going to tell Pearl that the Hitchins knew the truth of her going; and Nance, delighted to be taken into this confidence, declared, "Trust me. You can trust me, dear, till the cows come home. I'll never say a thing to hurt the poor dear. And, as for Mr. Hitchin, the Father left him too frightened ever to open his big mouth again, the great daft fool."

The Windsors insisted that her homecoming must be cele-brated by a festal repast with them; and Evie spent half the day preparing some dainty confections. George spent it cleaning the Windsor plate, spreading the table, and decanting the wine.

No publisher to whom he sent the book did other than return it. In November the eleventh publisher sent it home. And au-tomatically, without his customary sigh, Kerry packed it up and sent it forth again. "Go your way; behold, I send you forth as a lamb among wolves," he said blasphemously. By this time, though cheerful before others, he walked with sighs when alone, staring sadly ahead of him and widowed of all his hopes. Will-o'-the-wisps were they all. He had a habit now of saying to himself, "If I reach that lamppost before this truck passes me, some publisher will take it." Or in the office: "If nobody speaks before I finish this entry, someone will take it." Or in his room at home: "If Pearl comes in before I've tied this shoe, no one will ever look at it." Always he managed to win the hazard, but never once did he believe in it as an augury.

Sometimes, as once before, despairing, defiant, he would turn into a pub on the way home and medicine his heavy depressions with a pint of beer. So it chanced that one evening he walked into Fleet Street's Old Caxton Tavern.

That fine brown saloon was crowded along its bar by the men of the street: advertising managers, space buyers, London rep-resentatives, political correspondents, cartoonists, critics, reporters, ex-editors, and at least one of the street's rejects, now "on the ribs," who came here regularly knowing that he would receive generous treatment from late warmhearted colleagues. Here and there a woman feature writer, talking and laughing noisily, sat on a high stool with men doing gallantries around her.

Kerry, walking along through the medley of voices to find a gap by the counter, saw of a sudden Hoss Comfort, his plump housemate who when in town occupied the ground floor between the Windsors and the Hitchins. It was long since he had seen Hoss because, as one of the *London Argus*'s reporters, he'd been away "covering the warm situation in the Potteries." (Or so he said. George Windsor suggested that he'd been in warm sexual pursuit of some attractive young cameraman.)

Horace Comfort was large, fat, sleek, and round, with a high-pitched, affected, self-conscious voice. He sat now on his high stool like a slowly deflating balloon—or perhaps, since he wore a shiny black suit, like a big shrinking slug.

"Hoss!" Kerry exclaimed, loudly because of the din.

Hoss swung around on his high stool, saw Kerry, and shrilled, "Hey! The great man! My old pal, Kerry. Come and sit down, Kerry darling, I haven't seen you for ages. I've been hungry for you. When I came home last night and Nance Hitchin told me you were out for the evening, I had a good cry. How perfectly dazzling of you to appear in this extremely forbidding hostelry. What'll you take to drink?"

Kerry had intended to take his usual pint but, knowing that he'd have to stand Hoss a whiskey in return, said, "Oh . . . a small whiskey, perhaps."

"Large whiskey, Eileen," Hoss ordered of an elderly barmaid. "For my little friend here. Isn't he a dream? And Kerry, my sweet, meet Perce. Percy Fells." He indicated his companion on the next high stool: a long, drooping, and apparently depressed young man who sat crumpled and bowed over his tankard. His suit was crumpled too, and his youthful abundance of brown hair dropped a slack forelock toward his right eye so that he often threw it back. Kerry, looking at him, had thoughts of a tall Michaelmas daisy drooping as it went to seed.

"Perce. This is Kerry."

"Oh, yes?"

"He lives in the same house as I do."

"Oh, yes?"

"Not *with* me—don't get me wrong—but somewhere up in the lofts. Up miles and miles of stairs. Be nice to him."

Half lost in a dream but remembering that in his youth one rose if introduced, the young man shot up from his crumpled posture on the stool and stood on the floor. Doing so, he seemed to soar to an uncomfortable height. So in Kerry's childhood sometimes, when he unscrewed a wooden Easter egg, a snake, its compressed springs released, shot up on high and drooped toward him.

" 'Evening," said Percy Fells and, coming fully awake to place and time, went back to his stool.

To Kerry, "Percy" seemed a name too lively, too skittish, for this sad young man, but "Fells" was appropriate enough with its suggestions of desolate moorlands that dwelt in their mists apart.

"Perce is in your racket, Kerry," said Hoss. "Kerry writes very fine books, Perce. But you *are* a meany, Kerry. You never gave me a copy of your last, properly inscribed in ardent terms. How's the latest going?"

"Bloodily. Nobody'll touch it."

"Well, you'd better get Perce to publish it. He calls himself a publisher."

Kerry, giving one glance at Mr. Fells, sitting there like an ill-paid office drudge, dejected and cynical, felt wounded by the suggestion and thought, "God, no! I haven't come to that."

And Mr. Fells expressed this thought aloud for him, without even turning his way, "Good God, no! He hasn't sunk to that yet, I hope."

And immediately Kerry, because he needed to be liked by any stranger he met, demurred, "Oh, I don't know. . . ."

"You've had some published, have you?"

"One."

"With whom?"

"Harker and Inman's." Kerry spoke the name of this great house, not without some dregs of the old pride.

"Oh. . . ." Mr. Fells looked into the depths of his beer as if it were a sea in which the firm of Harker and Inman, in any reasonably ordered world, would be drowned.

"Perce was with Harker and Inman's once," Hoss explained.

"They let me out in the depression," said Perce.

"And they turned down my second effort," said Kerry so as to seem a fellow exile to this stranger and be liked by him.

"What are you doing with it now?" asked Perce.

"It's now at its twelfth publisher, and tomorrow it's due back, I should say."

"Only the twelfth? That's nothing. There are, to be exact, a hundred and seventy-seven publishers in Britain."

"Why not give it to Perce?" asked Hoss; but Kerry thought, "If ever I do, he'll be the hundred and seventy-seventh."

And once again Mr. Fells expressed exactly his thought aloud. "No, he's got a long way to go before he reaches the bottom like that." For which great modesty Kerry began to feel a real liking for him. And he liked him still more when he advised, "Keep going. Work through them all. You may find one with some taste and sense."

But here Hoss, after considering his friend's self-deprecation, and not wanting any associate of his to be undervalued, commented "Bottom my arse!" and he quoted, apparently from some advertisement of Perce's, "A young firm with a small but interesting list of general literature and fiction."

"Which really means," Perce amended, "a few scandalous memoirs that are not quite scandalous enough and a few inferior thrillers."

Thrillers. Kerry felt hurt again at Hoss's suggestion that his book should join a company of thrillers. But he must remain polite so he inquired of Mr. Fells, "What's the name of your house?"

"House! That makes me laugh. I call the outfit Arthur Fells, Ltd. I decided that no one could take Percy seriously, and Arthur is my other name. Not happy about that now. Who can really feel any confidence in an Arthur?"

"Now, now!" Hoss chided. "Don't be naughty, Perce. He's done some quite tolerable books, Kerry. Some of them a bit embarrassing, perhaps, but—"

"Why embarrassing?" Mr. Fells interrupted.

"Well . . ." Hoss shrugged. "That book you showed me by a John Dawsey. A shade too earnest, wouldn't you say? Rather too utterly *démodé*? Yes. Surely. He's done a book about God, Kerry. Think of that."

"Only one. And it was the only one that ever sold."

"Naturally. God sells anywhere. Sin too. But that last John Semple book, Perce dear? Really! Not rather revolting, on the whole?"

"Could be," its publisher agreed.

"Oh, yes. Definitely. A nauseater. Still"—and after a sip of his whiskey he appeared to quote again from one of his friend's advertisements—"an interesting and well-chosen list."

Having emptied his tankard, Mr. Fells laid it down and wiped his mouth with the back of his hand. After drawing in his chin to help an interior adjustment, he said "Gentlemen, excuse me," and walked toward a door in the wall—a quiet, reticent, but responsive door that like a silent and uncomplaining servant submitted to being pushed and shouldered and hurried past, by customer after customer, as their needs overcame them.

Kerry watched him pass through this door and said, "A gloomy guy," when it had swung shut on his temporary abasement.

"*Oh*, no. *Oh*, no. Don't you believe it, my dear." Hoss would have none of this. Having introduced Perce to Kerry, he was determined to be proud of him. "Perce is really a pet. He just dons the melancholy ever and anon because he finds gloom rather more amusing than all this tedious jocosity. As it is, isn't it? Listen to all these tiresome press hearties here. Terrible men. I know them: some are from our office, I'm ashamed to say. None of them have any tastes above sport and smut and shop. They're positively macabre, *n'est-ce pas?* If they're not exchanging smutty stories, they're probably waffling about their murky Fleet Street shop—but it's more likely to be smut." From the men referred to came new uproarious laughter—heads flung back, mouths flung wide. "Yes, horrible shattering guffaws like those can only mean a spot of filth. Actually our Perce is a very live wire. Twice as live as the loudest of those morons. Though I admit I've never seen another live wire that could sometimes look so dead. But he isn't really dead; it's just that he's *thinking* all the time."

"Thinking of what?"

"How to be a success. How to get to the top."

"Oh, well, we all do some of that. I've done quite a little myself, now and then."

"Yes, but Perce seldom stops. He's the champion schemer. He hasn't succeeded yet but, unless I'm much mistaken, all this thinking and conceiving is going to produce something fat one day. He knows a packet about publishing. He was at Harker and Inman's for a year or two, and only laid off because of the slump. Then he was at Moore and Bain's and only left them when his papa obligingly died and left him a pleasing spot of capital, whereupon he rashly decided to start up on his own.

But naturally the money wasn't enough and it was all exhausted in a very little time."

"So how does he manage now?"

"He met a friendly printer in a Clerkenwell pub, and they palled up—"

"Our Clerkenwell! That was the scene of my first book."

"No? Was it really? Go on!"

Then he's never read it, or even looked at it, though we live in the same house. My poor dead book.

"It was called *Green and Pleasant Clerkenwell,*" Kerry felt compelled to remind him.

"Oh, yes, I remember now. So it was. *Green and Pleasant Clerkenwell.*"

Poor wounded name. My bosom as a bed shall lodge thee.

"Have another whiskey, Hoss."

"Well, that's sweet of you, Kerry. Eileen, a large whiskey, please. As you know, Kerry, Clerkenwell's a hotbed of printers and binders, and this printer lad wanted to keep his machines running and his boys and girls employed during the depression, so he gave Perce credit enough to keep him afloat while he found the books."

"Is that how it's done?"

"That's how Perce did it. The really charming thing is that the old depression was a godsend to Perce, a positive godsend, because all those amusing machines were standing idle everywhere, and he just offered to keep them going. It was lugubrious for them, you see. So he came along and gave them a little something to keep their minds off the depression." At this point Hoss raised a hand in salutation to two gentlemen friends who were departing from the pub. He called, "Good-bye, love," and "Ta, ta, my precious," and blew them a finger kiss, then turned again to Kerry. "A promising lad, our Perce. Definitely."

"Where are his offices?"

"*Offices,* did you say?"

"Yes."

"Offices! Perce's offices! My dear, that's a teeny bit ridiculous. But amusing. Definitely amusing. He's got a room in Gooch Street, Holborn. For a pound a week, I think, with the use of a switchboard and a waiting room. Extra for the gas fire —unless, perhaps, he puts a shilling in the slot every morning. When he can afford to."

"Is that all?" Kerry was seeing the palace of Harker and

Inman's, with smart employees, maidens and men, hurrying this way and that along its echoing stone corridors. "But how does he house his staff? What does his staff consist of?"

"Himself and the frippet."

"Come again?"

"Himself and what he calls his frippet. A touching little secretary who's devoted to him."

"But you can't run a publishing business with only yourself and a secretary."

"Perce can."

"How?"

"He has a typewriter and plenty of paper."

Kerry remembered Sir Osbert's fine room and one of his smart lackeys bringing from Editorial the readers' reports on *Clerkenwell*. "Does he himself read all the manuscripts sent to him?"

"Yes, I think so. He may occasionally meet a publisher's reader in a pub and offer him ten shillings to do the job. Or buy him a lunch, if that works out cheaper."

"But I'm still at a loss. What about sales and distribution and trade counter and sales representatives? You're not telling me that he and the frippet do all these."

"They'd do them if they could, but of course it's hardly possible. Perce has a pal who's trade manager of Savery and James, which is a medium-sized house with a trade counter seldom fully occupied—especially nowadays. So Perce got him to handle his books for him as well as their own. He met him in a pub."

"But does he make any money?"

"I don't think so. He may be just about breaking even now. As you see, his overheads are low. Just himself and the girl. But *ssh . . . !*" Hoss touched Kerry's arm and cocked an eye at Mr. Fells coming back into the public domain.

Mr. Fells, returning to his high stool, said, "Thank you, gentlemen." Why they deserved this thanks was not clear, unless it was for their fortitude in doing without him. "I feel younger," he announced; and then, drooping over his tankard and considering its bottom, asked Kerry, "What about this new book of yours? Care to let me see it, if number twelve turns it down?"

"As he will," said Kerry.

"As he probably will. So what about it?"

Kerry, in part because he thought it would do no harm to

have a live wire's opinion but more because he could never hurt anybody by telling the offending truth, answered, "Of course I'll show it to you when it comes back. As it will. Where do I send it?"

"Don't send it. Bring it along. Gooch Street is only a few hundred yards from your Clerkenwell. A mean street in Holborn. Bring it along and meet Mary."

"Mary? Who's Mary?"

"Mary, my frippet."

"Oh . . . I see. . . ."

Some days later Kerry walked into Gooch Street, Holborn, carrying his parcel under his arm. Gooch Street almost overlooked Godfrey and the gardens of Gray's Inn, and No. 10 was a narrow, pepper-black Georgian house—one in a long Georgian terrace. With its flat breast and three stories, it could have been a dark sister of his own house in Red Lion Street, but it was narrower and lacked the ruddy cheerfulness of that red-brick home. Its windows were unbrightened by curtains, preferring the dinginess of wire "office" blinds, and its narrow door, standing with a step onto the sidewalk, was fixed open as a shop's might be. He went in with his parcel. The staircase seemed steeper than his own, and it was certainly gloomier because of the dark brown floorcloth on the treads and the dark brown dado on the walls. He climbed to the second landing and there in the narrow dusk saw a door with some words on its brown-painted wood. In neat capitals he read "Arthur Fells, Ltd., Publishers and Exporters." Below these capitals and in parentheses, as if this were only one of the firm's many rooms, he read "Chairman and Managing Director".

He tapped on the door in the landing's half-light, and through its motionless panels came the voice of Percy Fells. *"Come* in," it invited, but not enthusiastically; indeed gloomily. So, thought Kerry, might one of the dead call to you to join him in the tomb. However, he remembered Hoss's words and hoped that the chairman and managing director was really only thinking.

He went in. A small room with only one window. To the right of the window he saw Mr. Fells before a large desk, and to its left a slim, dark girl before a small desk. Undoubtedly Mary, my frippet. Both desks were bespattered with papers and piled with manuscripts, and each had a typewriter islanded in the mess. The girl's typewriter was a full-sized but old-fashioned model; the managing director's, a small portable, like Kerry's. Apart from a steel file cabinet, the only other piece of furniture in this small brown room was a chair by the managing director's desk.

"Ah! This is Mr. Betterkin, Mary," said Mr. Fells, quite cheerfully. "Writes books. Meet Mary, Mr. Betterkin: my secretary; also my assistant manager in the Editorial, Production, Publicity, and Art departments. The firm should really be called Fells and Mary, Ltd."

Kerry smiled at the girl, who gave back a smile, shy and charming. Thin, dark, twenty-five, unbeautiful, and bowed over a typewriter, she was manifest sister to Sally Penelope in the vast typing pool of London.

"Yes, a capable girl," continued Mr. Fells when he saw that the smiles were complete. "Is that ghastly parcel the great new work?"

"It is. A bit worn and battered, I'm afraid."

"Oh, that doesn't matter," said Mr. Fells, as if most things in his office were worn and battered.

Kerry handed over the parcel, and while Mr. Fells was undoing it, and Mary continued to type, he let his eyes study everything on a publisher's desk. In front of Mr. Fells was a quarto typescript that he'd obviously been casting off and preparing for the printer. Other scripts, quarto or foolscap, stood piled at his side or on the windowsill. An unfinished letter leaned over backward from the typewriter, and this drew his eye to the varied assortment of writing paper in the wide mahogany rack. The firm's paper was in different sizes and with different headings. All had the firm's name at the top, but one had also the words "From the Literary Director"; another "Editorial Department"; and others "Production" or "Art" or "Publicity" departments. Only the one "From the Literary Director" had a table of names on the left-hand side; and Kerry read *"Directors:* P. Arthur Fells (Chairman), D. B. Fells (Deputy Chairman), Emily Fells, Ruth Pettie."

Mr. Fells was now reading the first page of Kerry's manuscript, and he suddenly laughed at some episode in it—perhaps "coughed out a laugh" would better describe the sudden sharp noise. He read on, pleased; then laughed again, this time throwing back his head. He read on, turning pages, and a little later threw back, not only his head, but his whole body, to loose the loud bark. He also murmured, "Well, well."

All this was so gratifying to Kerry that, when Mr. Fells paused in his reading, as if fun itself must rest, he felt empowered to ask a few questions. With a grin, he began, "Excuse me, I like your notepaper but may I ask who D. B. Fells is?"

"My old man. My parent."

"And Emily Fells?"

"My wife."

"And Ruth Pettie?"

"My girl friend."

An answer best left alone. Or pursued later with Hoss.

"Must have some directors," explained Mr. Fells, perceiving that Kerry was silenced.

"Of course. And may I ask: the literary director is you, I suppose?"

"Yes. That's me."

"And the editorial manager?"

"Me too."

"And the literary adviser?"

"Oh, definitely me."

"Production?"

"Mary and me." At the sound of her name Mary looked up and smiled without ceasing to type noisily. The machine was old.

"Publicity?"

"Ditto. Mary and me."

But Mr. Fells's eyes were now on the manuscript again and Kerry didn't like to intervene. Not till he turned a page carelessly did Kerry continue, "And Art? The Art Department?"

"No such place. A myth. Like paradise."

"You don't have illustrations?"

"No. Too damned expensive."

"But book jackets—how do you manage about them?"

"I meet an artist in a pub," explained Mr. Fells, not raising his eyes from a new page, which was interesting him.

"Oh, I see." It seemed easy, put like that.

"Probably he's fresh out of an art school and glad of a job," pursued Mr. Fells, who was now apparently reading at the same time as he talked. "Usually he's quite as good as the expensive boys and ready to do me a dozen roughs to satisfy me."

"I see. Don't let me disturb your reading, but—"

"No, no; please go on. Don't apologize. Or be grateful. All part of the Arthur Fells service."

"Warehouse? Concerning a warehouse?"

"Savery and James's trade counter has bags of room these days. And my printer is a pal with an ample warehouse and a thirst."

"And the packing and distributing are done from the trade counter?"

"Certainly. Bill Guthrie has plenty of packers and I help him keep them employed. Good stuff, this, Mary. You'll enjoy this."

Feeling a stab of pleasure at this praise of his book, Kerry went at once into silence, to enable Mr. Fells to read on and enjoy more. Mr. Fells did read on, resting his elbow on the desk and his cheek in his hand. Mary tapped away on her machine, sometimes smiling at the visitor as she shared with him an amusement at her boss. The traffic banged and clattered in Gooch Street down below; and Kerry sat there with fingers interlaced, thumbs at play, and legs changing position, while Mr. Fells read on. At last Mr. Fells stopped reading straight on, and turned several pages quickly; and Kerry felt free to speak again.

"Forgive me," he said, "but I have a sense of completeness and can never leave any threads in the air. About a cashier and the accounts and all that?"

"Bill's trade department takes care of the accounts."

"But then there are salesmen, aren't there? A book has to be sold."

"Arthur Fells's books go out with S. and J.'s representatives. At a charge, of course. Anything else?"

"I see that you call yourselves exporters."

"Indeed we do. And why not? Overseas sales—that's to say, Australia, New Zealand, Canada, and general export amount to at least thirty percent of any publisher's business."

"But where do you export from?"

"From S. and J.'s trade counter."

"And—I hope I'm not being a nuisance—"

"Not at all. All part of the service."

"You do some advertising, I suppose?"

"Oh, but yes! To be sure. I know all the advertising managers. Meet them in the Fleet Street pubs."

"But advertising's very expensive, isn't it?"

"Not always. Any decent bloke tells me when he's got a two-inch or four-inch space going cheap. I buy it. And a beer for him. Or even a whiskey. Mary, this is a good book. The hero's just like me. Struggling to make a success of his shop. All my dreams and hopes are here. But he's never beaten. He fights back. He's got our guts, Mary. I believe we could do something with this book. It's all nonsense to say that people only want to read about violent action in romantic places; I believe they're far more likely to be fascinated by reading about experiences just like their own; about how to make ends meet and pay the rent and educate the kids; yes, and about the tremendous dreams of their youth that haven't come to life yet and probably never will because the years are passing and it's getting late—too late. Just what *I'm* always feeling. Forty in a few years, and none of my castles built; only this mucky room. Gosh, it's salable, Mary. You must take it home and read it all night, and then give me your expert opinion."

Kerry was so pleased with this outburst that he was able to stomach the untasty mouthful of having his book submitted to a frippet for an opinion. Evidently Mr. Fells couldn't conceive that a request for Mary's opinion could hurt anybody, for he continued, "If Mary likes it, I suppose you wouldn't let us have a shot at publishing it? We'd go all out for it; we'd really let our hair down and go to town with it."

That a publisher, even so small a one as Arthur Fells, Ltd., should approach him as a suppliant was an experience pleasant enough to countervail those chafing words, "If Mary likes it." But he didn't know what to answer. He was beginning to like Mr. Fells with his mummery of gloom hiding all the fervor of youth, and to love Mary with her shy smile, but he didn't take kindly to having a beloved book published by a young man from a mucky room.

"I should be the thirteenth," said Mr. Fells, to encourage him. "And that should be lucky."

The thirteenth. The word reminded Kerry of all that dreary, weary, searing business of receiving the manuscript back, reading a rejection slip, and mailing it off again, without hope. Better to settle for something, even if disappointingly small.

"It's often better to trust your book to a small man," pursued Mr. Fells, as if reading his thought. "Because if he believes in it, he looks after it personally. In your big houses it's just one of a long list and unless it quickly shows signs of selling, they generally leave it to perish. They have other and bigger stewpots on the stove. They give it perhaps three weeks of their time and then, if it hasn't begun to sell briskly, they leave it to die of inanition, quietly. But with your small publisher it's one of his only hopes and he'll nurse it—nurse it and rear it into a winner, if there's half a chance. If both Mary and I like it, well, just you wait and see what we get up to."

"I would be honored if you would publish it," said Kerry.

27

Anything more different than Kerry's experiences with Arthur Fells, Ltd., and those with Harker and Inman's he could not have imagined.

At Harker and Inman's, after that first interview with Sir Osbert and Mr. Armstrong, he heard not a word from the great house until the galley proofs appeared with a letter in an unknown hand. As for Sir Osbert and Mr. Armstrong, he never saw either of them again. There was that genial conversation over the telephone about the book's failure, and there an end. Kerry had felt all the time like a peddler who had entered their palace, sold them a fairing, and was now back in the street again.

Not so with Arthur Fells, Ltd. So far from being a peddler at the door of that house, the house came to him. And came upstairs. A dozen times, and more. That is to say Mr. Fells, the chairman, Mr. Fells, the editor-in-chief, Mr. Fells, the production manager, Mr. Fells, the publicity man, was—or is the verb "were"?—forever coming around to the attic in Red Lion Street to discuss an inspired amendment, the costs of production, the typeface to be used, the paper, the binding, the jacket, the opportunities for publicity. Kerry called him "the Comer-round." He came around on a weekday evening or a Sunday morning—whenever he felt sure Kerry would be at home. Sally as secretary would probably be in the attic because Kerry was now busy on a new book ("in case," as Mr. Fells said, "the antique song echoes around the world"); Pearl would be there because Kerry didn't want her to be lonely; and to all three, Percy Fells, sipping the tea, or cocoa, which Pearl had made—and not noticing it—would descant upon, say, the type area on the page. "It's sad, sad, children, Kerry and I have taste, Miss Pearl has taste, Sally Penelope has taste, and we would all like wide margins at head, outside margin, and tail, but there it is: when you sell fifty thousand, I'll give you these. At present I must print the book as cheaply as possible, which means setting the page solid, with only narrow margins and no leading. I'm thinking of setting it in eleven point Perpetua because that's the font with the narrowest face so that one can get a shocking mass on a page. Your readers, Kerry, will have to get their esthetic joys out of your writing, not out of my printing, but that's probably all right, because no one in England knows or cares anything about typography."

Harker and Inman had known nothing of Sally and little of Pearl, but Arthur Fells, Ltd., was on Christian-name terms with all.

He appeared one evening with a specimen page and a sample of the paper. "I could wish," he said, "that it was a sweeter paper, but we have to use this blown-out stuff so that the book bulks an inch or more, because the British public wants bulk for its money. But what they're really demanding is wind in the paper. That's what they pay for, wind. Good Lord, pat some of Carson's books on the back and they'd belch like babies."

The chief editor, in person, brought the proofs around on a Sunday morning, and at midday insisted on taking the "whole family" out to a pub to "wet" their arrival. He had already taken them out to wet the paper, the binding, the lettering on the spine, and the design for the jacket. "It's a publisher's business to dine and wine his authors," he said, "but I can't afford that—yet. I can beer you all up, however." And when Kerry said, "But it's no part of a publisher's business to dine an author's secretary and his sister," he replied, "No, thank God. But I'm not beering them up for your sake but because I love them." He knew the Clerkenwell pubs well, having done business in most of them with printers and binders, and on these wetting occasions he led the family, generally one step ahead of them, to the Baptist's Head in St. John's Lane or to the Castle in Cowcross Street or perhaps, for mischief's sake, to the Coach and Horses over against Sally's buildings in Hockley-in-the-Hole.

All this was friendly and informative and amusing, but a source of doubt in Kerry's mind, even of dismay. He was now fond of Perce as a friend but a little ashamed of him as a publisher. After that distinguished old gentleman, Sir Osbert, he found it difficult to believe in a publisher whom he called Perce. How could such a publisher's imprint have any value with booksellers or critics? Perce by this time seemed less a publisher than an accomplice. These assemblings of two men and two women in a Red Lion Street attic savored of a plot. Kerry likened them to the Cato Street Conspiracy when a dozen desperados met in a raftered loft to plan the assassination of the government. He didn't like to tell anyone, not even the Windsors downstairs, that this long droopy young man with the hatless head and the slack garments (and a polo sweater if it was Sunday) and his hair falling over his temple was the publisher of his new book. He had no desire, when asked, "How big a house is Arthur Fells?" to reply, "Well, there's a man and a frippet." He didn't, in fact, tell anyone that he was publishing a new book. After his fiasco with Harker and Inman, his was the silence of a man who had known a public shame. He must hope and hope, of course, in spite of the polo sweater and the tumbling forelock, but it was difficult to have faith anymore.

Published in three weeks' time now—two weeks—one week. Try not to hope. Remember last time. Never mind if there are no prepublication puffs in any paper anywhere, but just silence. Silence.

"The advance sales are only ordinary," Perce had said one evening when he came around to report on the prepublication sales. "The few idiot booksellers who've glanced through it say the story and its people are too commonplace. Such nonsense! If the people are properly commonplace, then the readers can really identify themselves with them and live through their defeats and their triumphs as if they were their own. I am right. I know it."

"What do 'ordinary advance sales' mean?" Kerry began nervously.

Perce dropped his eyes. Obviously he was going to evade an exact number. "Somewhere about a thousand firm sales . . . so far. . . ."

"I see." Show no disappointment. Say nothing of that ten-thousand dream. You expected nothing, only hoped. And, anyhow, is it not strange that there are enough persons in the world to order a thousand copies?

"Your last book hasn't helped the sales," Perce explained. "Some of the chaps had copies lying about which they regard as dead stock, and that's made 'em cautious."

"Yes, that poor dead book. It's been dead for months and, like Lazarus, by this time he stinketh. And now I've sent another to join him."

"I don't believe it. Not yet," Perce rallied him. "Can't judge by the advance sales. A few good reviews, and the repeat orders will come in."

"If there *are* any reviews," corrected an author resolved upon despair.

The book was published on a Thursday in February and the next day, a Friday and a good day for book pages, Kerry hurried after work to the Finsbury Central Library and there scanned every newspaper available, morning and evening, in the hope of some notice somewhere. There was none. But he was not too disappointed as he came down the steps of the library, for he had climbed them dreading such whipping as he'd been given before, and it was almost a relief to come out into the street with his skin unbroken.

Perce had promised to come around with any reviews that reached him, and every evening Kerry listened for his steps on the stairs. They did not come.

The first week of the book's life, and the second, passed away, and still nothing—not a sound from near or far. The Clerkenwell streets, as he walked to work, the Farringdon Road, Fleet Street—all were loud with voices and beating engines and rush of wheels, but Kerry, insulated in his cloud of despair, heard only the silence of the dead. Once, when he felt sure that this book had joined its elder brother in a limbo of the stillborn, he said aloud to the silence, "I wish I were dead," and people in front turned about to see who it was who thus addressed them. Realizing that he'd made a public fool of himself, and this being almost the least bearable thought in life, he heard himself a little later announcing loudly, to the street outside his office, that he wished he was dead. Yet another week passed, and one Friday morning brought a shameful moment in the Farringdon Road when he heard his voice proclaiming to all—with dignity—"I write no more."

But then one evening Perce arrived with a few notices from provincial papers. Kerry snatched at them, trembling in fear of a lash's sting—in fear also of a happiness too sharp. All but one occupied little more than an inch of space and were patently nothing but an abstract of the blurb. One was good—even very good—and happiness drove like a spear into his being. It was strange and sweet to feel a pat on his back instead of a scourge. "Well, someone's liked it," he said. "I can always remember that. Look, Pearl. Our Perce has flown around like a dove with one olive leaf in his beak. Could it be, Perce, that the waters are abating?"

"Could be," said Perce.

"And we may yet beach our ark on dry land?"

"Certainly: on a land flowing with milk and honey," said Perce whose knowledge of the Bible was somewhat fogged. "It's a good book, but unfortunately, as we've always said, merit is not enough. Merit's got to be there, of course, or nothing on earth'll make the book sell, but it needs a spot of luck in the scales as well. There are too many meritorious books about."

"What sort of luck?" asked Kerry, hungry for hope.

"Well—the mood of the moment just in time for the book —or the prime minister mentioning it in an after-dinner speech —or the Bishop of London recommending it for Lenten reading—or, better still, some critic attacking it as filthy. Could be anything, but we need it."

Far away, two miles away across a boundless reticulation of London streets, some deep as chasms and full of the noonday noise, others shallow and silent, a figure came out of a great club building into the wintry sunlight of Pall Mall. The great building of blackened stucco and stone, with its three wide ranges of pedimented windows and its crowning cornice presented the Italian Renaissance, in blacks and grays, to the pedestrians and motorists of Pall Mall. Thus it was of the same handsome family as the palace of Harker and Inman in Paternoster Court, though very much larger. There were those among the experts who called it the finest club house in London; others, less reverent, surveying those three wide stories and that cornice, said it reminded them of an ebony chest of drawers turned upside down. The centered doorway and steps certainly seemed rather small and lost under the pedimented windows of the *piano nobile,* but the figures that came out of that door, like bees out of a hive, were palpably men of distinction, their attire in keeping with that dark and dignified front.

This figure today, however, while as expensively dressed as any, had an appearance and an air slightly different from those of his fellow members, and you felt that he was a man who thought a touch of difference desirable in such as he. His hat was no neat bowler but a black felt with a broad brim. His bow tie had the wide wings of a spotted butterfly. His blue, waisted overcoat hung open to allow his fawn-vested paunch to emerge and the gold chain and seals at his fob to enjoy the air. His slow walk along the street was that of a man well content to move on top of the world, but his face did not register this content today. A slack mustache drooping over his upper lip, together with his pouted cheeks, gave him just now a look both bored and misanthropic.

And he *was* bored, just now, and empty of love for the world. His meat dish at lunch had been unsatisfactory—a tough cut and an inadequate portion—so much so that he had complained to the head waiter, and such complaints always left him soured. Then his companion at the table had been a huge Tory general of maddeningly illiberal views. Here in this most famous Liberal club the old fool, as he ate an expensive dish and sipped a choice wine, had declared of some strikers in the north that he'd *make* the bastards work or imprison them. Listening to this blind nonsense, the man with the drooping mustache had wished that he'd lunched at his other famous club in Theaterland, for, having sprung from the people, he felt nearly always, no matter how unloving his look, on the side of the workers against their masters. Two glasses of port after this unsatisfactory meal had not lessened the sourness; they had only added to it a certain somnolence, a heavy disinclination to go home and work.

That damned Book Page of his in the *Evening Express.* Its accursed reputation was like a ton load placed once a week on his back. Eight hundred or a thousand words of brilliance must he go home and write for it now. The weekly effort of sustaining that reputation! The strain of making it somehow different from all other book pages; of giving it variety and surprise; of keeping it charged with the enormous sale-boosting power that the book world was now attributing to it! They declared—everyone declared—that it could "make" an author's book overnight; that it could lift a sale of one thousand to twenty or even fifty thousand; and that never before had one critic possessed such power. Pleasant, but oh, the strain of keeping out of the common rut, and of ever and again discovering someone new among all these capable young authors who came crowding into the market with their commonplace wares at the rate of fifty a week. Someone who was worthy to be one of "Antony Standen's Discoveries." Someone who was worth buying so that the booksellers' faith in "Antony Standen's Choice" took no fall. Strictly one should wade through fifty books to find one. Good God! Fifty! Sometimes he hated books.

It was nonsense the power his word enjoyed. By desire and training he was a creator, not a critic; but just because his novels had a readership of hundreds of thousands, people supposed that his recommendation of a book was the last word in literary wisdom. Faddle! He hoped he had intelligence enough to know that, just because he was a market rival among his contemporaries, his judgment of them, no matter how he strove to be dispassionate, was all too likely to be impaired by biases, conscious or unconscious. His criticism was no more than one intelligent man's biased response; and sometimes, though he always wrote with pungency as one full of confidence, he had secret fears lest his recommendations might become hereafter subjects for derisive laughter.

Fifteen minutes later he stepped from a taxi and entered a palatial block of mansions in Baker Street. The lift carried him to his large flat on the fifth floor. Here he entered his study: a fine room that he had splendidly equipped for work and for rest. Around the walls were seven thousand books in fitted steel shelves. On the hand-woven carpet fitted to the walls the most conspicuous piece of furniture was his great desk. Elsewhere on that expanse were some beautiful old chairs, armchairs, and tables: antiques. On mantel and shelf tops were many fine pieces of old English porcelain: Worcester vases and Chelsea, Bow, or Derby figures. But the one thing he really saw as he came in, because it was the thing on his mind, was the monstrous stack of books defiling the honeyed surface of his satinwood console table.

He bent over them. Most were new books by standard authors—all of them competent, no doubt, but what could you do with merely competent stuff? Two books near the top carried unknown names. One was called *This Old and Antique Song*, by a John Kenrick Betterkin. The imprint? Fells. Never heard of them. One of these new mushroom publishers, no doubt. Still, that might make his discovery all the more striking. He picked the book up and read the blurb. About an antique dealer. And, partly because the story did not look too long and wearisome; partly because this pile of books was so damnably irritating; partly because powerful persons, peers or publishers, *would* write asking him to review their son's, or their friend's, books and this didn't seem fair to the weak and unfriended; partly because he always liked to help a small man, having been once poor and small himself; but mainly because he loved antiques, he carried the book to his wing chair (Queen Anne), flung his legs on to a cushioned Directoire stool, and began to read.

He read a little way and knew the book was good—or, at any rate, good enough. And he was glad of this because he didn't want to have to read any others. Good—yes, certainly—but perhaps not quite as good as he wanted to say. Still . . . he felt the phrases coming.

28

This time it was to the office, not to the attic, that Perce came around. He came hurrying; even scampering; even, it might be said, stampeding. Disturbing the stream of pedestrians on the Fleet Street sidewalks as a speedboat parts the water on a tideway, and running aground in the front office. At three in the afternoon. When the clerks were at work.

At the window of the front office he asked if he could speak to Mr. Betterkin at once. The clerk at a counter behind the window, not hearing him because he was entering something in a ledger, completed the entry and, looking up, asked, "Can I help you?"

"Good God, yes!" Perce drooped over the clerk and his counter. "I must speak to Mr. Betterkin at once. Explain that it's important. Apologies and all that, but terribly important."

The clerk showed no readiness to be impressed by the importance. "May I have your name?"

"Name?" repeated Mr. Fells. In his excitement he had forgotten it—or it would be truer to say that, not having expected or wanted this question, he experienced some resistance to any immediate answer. Tossing his forelock off his brow, he said,

"Oh . . . Fells . . . yes, Perce Fells. . . . But just say Fells. That'll fetch him. Believe you me."

The clerk went into the hidden heart of the office, and Perce was proved right: the name Fells brought Kerry to the window at once.

He came, not quickly, but with excitement behind a mask of calm, because nowadays he lived each hour with the hope of news. And Perce at the door must be news. And more likely good news than bad. He said only, "Here! What are you up to? You can't come around, interrupting me like this. You'll be getting me fired." Which was nonsense, because that office was the atrium of a Fleet Street Liberty Hall with the clerks coming and going much as they pleased.

"Aw, nuts to getting fired! What does that matter? You needn't worry about the people here. You're *made*, my dear boy, *Made*. So'm I. So's your publisher."

"What do you mean?" That a sudden expectation of joy could hurt like a violent blow on the breast. That good news could be like a footpad with a knife. That joy could come full circle and take on the character of pain! "What is it? Come away. Come into the passage. We can't talk here."

Perce followed him into the passage just by the open street door. "Have you seen this?" He held up a folded newspaper.

"No. What is it?"

"Only a personal gift to you from the gods. Only a minor miracle specially worked on your behalf." He began opening the paper. "Only that the pillars of your firmament have fallen. The incredible has happened."

With a quivering hand Kerry took the paper. He saw a thick headline: "A Book to Enchant," and his heart ached as he read on. "Rare is it to be able to recommend a book in the confident belief that no one will contest your counsel. Usually one is hamstrung by the knowledge that a book will suit one class of readers and offend another. But here at last is a book that will enchant all. It is a book for all lovers of London, but they are not the whole world; what is more to the point is this, that it is a book for all those who are still poor but struggling upward with dreams for company; for all those who are rich now but remember the days when it seemed that success would never come; and perhaps most of all, because of its gay courage, for those who hardly expect success anymore. . . ."

And so it went on, to the length of a thousand words.

Kerry, when he had finished, lifted a face as pale as the

passage wall. "But, Perce, how did this happen?"

"Don't ask me. Probably because he's interested in antiques."

"Or could it be that the book is really good?"

"Could be, I suppose."

"But supposing he hadn't liked antiques?"

"Then the book would have probably lain quite still and gradually died. Instead of that, you're booked for fame."

Kerry remembered his horrid idea that Harker's had accepted his first book because one of their directors had been called sentimental. "But, Perce, supposing one wrote book after book and never had a single spot of luck like this?"

"Then you'd probably have death after death. Chancy business, literary fame."

"God, I wonder how any writer ever knows how good his book is, or how bad. It always seems good to him, but—"

"To hell with whether it's good or bad. All that matters just now is the effect of this."

"What'll the effect be?"

"Merely that every bookseller when he reads this will say, 'Betterkin? Betterkin? Who the hell's Betterkin?' and rush to the phone and order fifty copies. They've started already: this bird is the lawgiver to the bookselling world. I've just rung up S. and J. and they say that some repeat orders have come in already, including one from Short's Libraries for five hundred copies. The snowball's rolling. And am I going to kick it hard? I've just seen Harry Bentwich and bought a four-inch two-column space for Sunday, and now I'm going to ring up Joe Pannet and buy space from him."

Strange this family likeness between good news and bad. That it should trouble the heart so, and disorder the mind, and empty the body—an emptiness that was like the vacuum before sickness!

"What do you reckon it will sell now?"

"Twenty thousand, and maybe fifty."

"Nonsense! Don't be an ass."

"I'll be very surprised if it doesn't. Generally speaking, it's all or nothing with books. In ninety-nine cases out of a hundred, it's nothing—or very damned little. In the hundredth, it's thousands. And that's you. The first big seller I've had."

"What'll I make out of it?"

"Two or three thousand, maybe. And there's America. What this fellow boosts America buys. But none of that's the point."

"Well, what is the point."

"That you're safe for the next ten years. Just turn out a book a year and you may not make a pile but you'll certainly make a living."

"But supposing the next book's a flop?"

"Won't be. For ten years. You can't shake the British public off in less than ten. And only then by letting them down badly. If you'll just produce them decent books, they'll be loyal to you for twenty, thirty, forty years. Got a book ready for next year?"

"I've started."

"Well, push on with it." He waved a hand at the stairs. "Get shut of all this. Run upstairs and give 'em all notice at once. You must devote your time to writing for me. Look: can't stop now; got to go round and work the publicity boys. There's one hell of a story for them here. It's always a story: sudden success; fame overnight; Byron; *Jane Eyre;* book written in a London attic. . . . If you don't mind, we'll make the attic a bit humble. Call it a garret. Yes, garret's better. Young struggling clerk with an invalid sister to keep—"

"No, no; you can have the garret, but you're not having the sister."

"O.K. As you like. Plenty of copy without her. And you've another spot of luck, my son: you're a Fleet Street boy. And the street stands by its own. They'll do you well. You'll be having the reporters around at any moment. I'll see them in the pubs tonight and sink a few pints down them. So be ready with your life story. Put away anything that looks prosperous in the garret and let 'em see that wilderness of roofs out of the window. *Sous les toits de Londres.* Oh, yes, and tell 'em how the book was turned down as unsalable—by how many publishers?"

"Twelve."

"Make it fourteen. I must go now."

Kerry swayed a little as he went back to his table in the office. An uncomfortable lightness in the head, like a softening of the brain, seemed to have damaged his controls. "I am there. I am there. It has happened. It has happened." Twelve minutes past three. Over two hours to run before he could go home and show the paper to Pearl . . . to the Windsors . . . to Sally Penelope. This article—and that headline—seen by a million at least. Men reading it in the train as they went home. Sir Osbert! Seeing it and beginning to wonder. Perhaps lifting his house telephone and asking who was the fool who rejected this book. And all those other publishers. Mildly cursing themselves. The paper lying about in pubs. In clubs. In *Boodle's*! Godfrey turning its pages and seeing "A Book to Enchant. By John Kenrick Betterkin."

Never before had he walked up the tilt of Benjamin Street with such a burden of joy. So often he'd come down this narrow cobbled gulch, quietly grieving, and today!—today its ascent was the more wonderful for the memory of those despairs. Past the entry to St. John's Public Garden, where he'd quarreled with Sally, whom soon, by heaven, he'd take and marry; past the arched entry into Faulkner's Alley, whose sinister passage had filled him with ideas for a book that had failed; past the tunnelled entry of Eagle Court, where he'd tempted Sally for a second time and so lost her for a while; and here before him his own Red Lion Street. Yonder the restless and hammering Clerkenwell Road. These places were no different this evening —and yet they were all changed. It was early evening; the tall street lamps had not sprung or shimmered into light; no window of house or store had become a sudden oblong of amber-gold; no glamour fell from a cold and cloud-heavy sky upon the gray and varied scene; but the light in his mind flung a glow upon it all. All this was London, its ugly streets and paved alleys, and he was of the company of Whittington and the other apprentices who had come poor to its streets and found in their stony ore the veins of gold.

Never before had he opened his front door and gone up these stairs with such a vesture of joy around him. The paper under his arm created this vapor around him. Past the Windsors' door—what news for them! They little knew. And here the door with Pearl behind it. One must rest a moment before taking this burden in.

He went in. And there was Pearl at the table with her spectacles and needle, and her round back bent over a particolored doublet which she was braiding. By its side lay a Tudor head-dress that she had been beading with pearls. Pearl laboring there, unbeautiful, ungifted, and a little unhappy because of things she remembered. He looked at her, and in this, his hour, his love swelled.

He arranged his face to reveal nothing and said only, "Hello, Pearl."

"Hello," she answered formally and pushed back the spectacles on her nose.

"What are you doing?" Not a bright question in view of those bright garments, but his brain was aloft in some rarefied ether high above intelligence.

"Sewing."

He tossed the folded paper, like a thing of small interest, on to the table. "Cold, isn't it?"

"Yes."

"But nice and warm in here."

"Yes."

"Only a few weeks more and it'll be spring. There's Antony Standen's weekly article in that paper. Don't I wish he'd praise my book to the skies as he does other people's? Perce says it turns a book into a seller at once. He says the greatest people in the land, if they've got a nephew publishing a book, pester him to review it."

"But that doesn't seem fair."

"No, it doesn't. What chance does it leave poor little people like us?" He sat down to cast off his shoes. "A pity, because Perce says it could make all the difference between a book making enough to keep one in matches and earning thousands. Where are those slippers?"

"Thousands?"

"Oh, yes. Certainly. If it sells. And what's more important, it establishes your earning power for ten years at least—and for life, if only you do your stuff properly. What's for supper?"

"I got you some ham and lettuce."

"Good. I'm fond of ham. And lettuce. Yes, he says the booksellers buy in hundreds all over the country. Wonderful if we ever had a success like that. Let's dream. Let's dream that Antony did an article on us. We'd have a flat in London, a cottage in the country, and a car. Only a little car—but a car. Sally and I'd get married, but you'd be with us; we've always said that. Can't do without Pearl. And we'd have nice little dinner parties for really interesting people, and plenty of drinks in the house for our friends. No more pinching and scraping. No more worrying over every penny. Anything interesting happened while I've been away?"

"No."

"No letter from anyone saying how greatly they enjoyed your brother's book?"

"No."

"Anyone come up to you in the street and say they'd read it with acute delight?"

"No, my dear."

"Nor that it was a book to enchant?"

"To what?"

"Enchant."

"No. I'll just finish this and get supper."

"Anyone stop you even to say, 'I see your brother's published a book'?"

"Afraid not."

"Oh, well . . . I suppose not. The reviews have been so few. And none in the London papers." Slippers on, he rose and stood near her. "Surely you've done enough sewing for today. You'll tire your eyes. Rest a bit and read a paper." He slid the folded paper toward her.

She glanced at the news headlines, read a few sentences, and returned to her sewing.

Hell! he thought and, drawing back the paper, opened it at the Book Page with its thick headline, "A Book to Enchant." After pretending to read something, he carelessly shot the paper so that it fell beside her.

And waited.

"There, that's done," said Pearl at last and threw down the gay Tudor doublet. "Now I'll get supper."

"No, no. Don't want supper yet. Rest a bit. You look tired." Why would women always rather do something else than read a paper? "I'm not hungry yet."

"Oh, well. . . ." Idly she picked up the paper, and her eyes fell on the headline. She read the first sentence. And the next. And the next. Then *"Kerry!"*

"Yes?" he inquired as if he couldn't conceive what this cry was about.

"Oh, Kerry! . . . *Oh!*"

"Anything wrong? Can I get you something? Some sal volatile?"

"But, *Kerry,* what does this mean? Why didn't you tell me at once—"

"Sal volatile's excellent for faintness."

"Oh, don't be absurd. Let me read . . . read."

"It's good for the gripes, if that's troubling—"

"Kerry, what'll this *mean?* Isn't it something rather marvelous?"

"According to Perce, if everything runs true to form it'll mean all that I said just now. Probably we shan't make any fortunes, but we'll have everything that poor little people like us can want."

She was staring up at him from her seat at the table. "Oh, Kerry, oh, my dear, I don't know what to think. I want to cry."

"Do. I've felt rather like that ever since I saw it. Let's all cry."

"But it's unbelievable." She got up and put an arm along his shoulder. "That's *you* in the paper. What does it feel like to be suddenly rather famous?"

"It could feel worse. It—but listen." People coming up the stairs; voices; George Windsor's voice. "It's the Comer-up and Dropper-in. And for once in a way he's completely welcome. We'll tell them."

A knock on the door, and George peeping around it; then, on sight of them there, walking in without permission, without any reference to the divine afflatus, but with the *Express* in his hand and Evie hard behind. And he, like Kerry, acting a part, since all men are clowns. "There's a little something here that may or may not interest you. But don't read it if you don't want to. I thought I'd just bring it up."

Evie, being a woman, had no wish to clown, only to rejoice. "Oh, Kerry! Oh, Pearl! Have you *seen* it?"

"What is it, pray?" asked Kerry of George.

"Oh, stop your buffoonery, Kerry," said Pearl. "He's shown it to me, Evie."

"Oh, my dears. I've never been so happy in my life. I'm a little sick. George says it means certain success. Isn't that so, Georgy? Tell them all you say. He knows about this sort of thing."

"I should say it means a sale of ten thousand."

"There now!" said Evie. "Ten thousand."

Hearing this moderate figure, Kerry couldn't hold himself back from immediately correcting it. "Perce talked about twenty thousand, and maybe fifty, but I expect he was exaggerating. He's an excitable fellow." But lest they should think Perce was exaggerating, he told them about the repeat orders and Short's five hundred copies. He also mentioned America.

"Fifty thousand!" George gaped. "What's that mean in filthy lucre?"

"Perce spoke of two or three thousand pounds."

"Oh! . . . *oh!* . . ." Evie just breathed. "You two dears!"

"Do we not celebrate?" George demanded. "Is it not a case for the Baptist's Head? Come, children, we invite you as our guests."

"No, Commodore, no," Kerry begged. "Thanks awfully, but I'd rather wait and be sure first. Pearl and I celebrated too soon once before, and the gods humbled us for our hubris."

"Again, please. Your *what?*"

"Our insolent pride. It's Greek. For waxing fat with arrogant dreams and hoping to conquer the world."

"My dear, he's been celebrating before he came in. I used to get scholarly like that after a drink too many. Hubris. Will you only listen?"

"I can't be sure that all Perce says will really happen."

"But the book's on the move, he says?"

"And books can stop as suddenly as they start."

"You mean to say you're going to work as usual on a night like this?"

"Probably."

George touched Evie on the shoulder. "Come. Then we must go, my dear."

"But I don't want to go," objected Evie. "I'm so happy. He can't possibly work tonight. Is your adorable little Sally coming?"

"No. Not tonight."

"But she'll come racing around when she sees the paper."

"She won't see it. What girl ever buys an evening paper? Sally's probably deep in *Woman and Beauty* just now."

"Then, my dear"—George laid fingers on Evie's elbow: a new thought had descended upon him in power—"what are we thinking of? Have we no sense? He must be aching to go to his little lady with his news. He's wishing us in hell, my dear. I fully suspect he's charging us under his breath, 'Oh, go, go, *go.*' I always do this when I want some old bore away—or two old bores. I say, 'Go, go, go, go,' and, do you know, after a time they feel the influence. They go. Naturally he wants to get to his beloved. My first great success in *The Troubadour*—it was a riot, children—wasn't it, Evie?—the audience simply ate it—and didn't I rush with all the papers to you and talk about getting married? Well, come. Have some sense. Surely we know our exit line when we hear it."

But his words had put a lovely idea into Evie's head and, as she was being dragged to the door, she turned and asked, "Kerry . . . Kerry, my darling . . . will you marry her now?"

"That's rather my idea."

"Oh, when will it be? Don't *drag* me, George. I hate being dragged. Will it be soon?" George had almost got her through the door, and this was her last desperate throw. *"When?"*

"The minute I know that Perce wasn't exaggerating and the future is fairly secure."

George turned his head at this. "Publishers never exaggerate. At least not to their authors. Only in their advertisements."

"Perce is unlike anyone else. He is himself alone. He's *sui generis.*"

"My dear, he certainly *has* celebrated before he came home. He's back on his Greek again."

But now it was she who was pushing him toward the stairs. "Go on; get yourself out of the way. He's going round to ask her to marry him. Fancy standing there in his way. Oh, I've never been so pleased about anything in my life."

With a wave of her hand and a blown kiss, she got George and herself out of the way, so as to let the bridegroom pass by.

No sooner were they gone from sight than Kerry seized the paper from the table and his hat from a chair. "Bye-bye, Pearl."

"But aren't you having any supper?"

"I could no more eat than fly. Good-bye."

He raced down the stairs and out of the house into the streets of a London still invested with a sorcerer's light. Clerkenwell Road, Farringdon Road, Ray Street—nothing much uglier in all the gray unsightly masses of industrial London; nothing more harshly oppressive in their apparent indifference to all but heavy labor for enlarging gain; nothing noisier than the wide soot-mossed railway canyon and the long traffic-hammered highway between warehouses, offices, depots, and tenements that was the Farringdon Road; nothing drearier than the aspect of these streets when the dusk had not yet drained from them and the tall lamps seemed prematurely and anxiously alight—and yet he loved them all for an hour and would not have been anywhere else in the world. He ran through these grim city places as if they were the green pastures of Arcadia. This sudden bright hope of worldly success, as it had swelled his loyalty to Pearl into a love, so it had ripened his love for Sally from a day-to-day affection into a certainty that she meant the world to him—and there is nothing like that for throwing its light on every place you hasten by.

Now he stood in the pit of Ray Street between the two cliffs of the old Clerkenwell Workhouse and the high Bethesda Buildings that held Sally. From the middle of the pavement between the tilted sidewalks he looked up at the railed landing of her tenement. There was a light in one of her rooms, and since the curtains were not drawn, it poured out upon the dankly white garments hanging there to dry. How draw her down? The window was shut, so a soft call would be useless. A play of shadows showed that someone was moving in the room and as the movements were brisk, it could only be Sally. Yes, she came to the window, flung it up, and shook the dust from a duster onto the balcony floor.

"Sally. Sally."

She paused, listened, and came out onto the balcony among the drying garments. She leaned over the railing and saw him there on the crown of the cobbled roadway. "Kerry!"

"Come down. Come into the garden, Sally."

She came spiraling down her stone stairway and out of the entry onto the sidewalk. "What is it?"

"It's will you marry me?"

"Of course. I shall be delighted to. But when?"

"Just as soon as you like . . . I *think.*"

"What are you talking about? Are you mad—just a little?"

"Today is not as yesterday."

"No, that is true. I grant that."

"Something has happened. The world has changed. Since about noon today."

"I do wish you'd talk some sense. What *are* you trying to say?"

"Have you seen this?"

He led her to the lamppost under her buildings and beneath its fall of cream light showed her the headline. But as she was about to read on, he snatched the paper away and said "No"; for first he must tell her all that Perce had said about the effects of an Antony Standen review. He did so, and her great eyes stared at him with their multitude of dreams transfigured into a single amazement. Then he allowed her to drop the eyes on to the paper and read.

"Oh, Kerry!" she cried when she had finished; and after one second of thought she added an idea that had not so far occurred to him. "This is all the result of my prayers."

"Beg your pardon?"

"I have prayed so hard. Every night for at least six months.

And every morning too. And at great length in church. But I don't think I ever believed my prayers would be answered like this. After all, God must have so many other things to think about. Did Perce really mean all he said or was he exaggerating?"

"Well, it has happened many times before; all that he said. And it looks as though it's starting to happen again."

"Oh, I'll pray and pray that it may happen again."

"If it does, Sally, then . . . then my seven long years are up and I shall marry Sally."

"Oh, *Kerry!* But . . . what'll I do with Dad?"

"There'll be plenty of money to park him somewhere. We'll be kind to him."

"Oh, Kerry, I can't believe it. *Me* married! *Me!*" She stood there in Ray Street, under the lamp—in Hockley-in-the-Hole, that is, and in heaven—or in as much of heaven as ever descends upon a harsh metropolitan street.

29

It happened again. The miracle that is likely to happen only to inventor or artist whereby his state is changed in a moment, as at the touch of a magic wand, from indigence to affluence. Not to wealth, perhaps, but to a prosperity beyond the belief of one who has long been poor. The first touch of the wand had been the Standen review; then the press seized the wand and waved it around for a few days till the miracle arose like a conjurer's fire beneath it. The sudden descent of success and celebrity upon a Clerkenwell garret made, as Perce had foretold, a pithy tale for the paragraph writers, and not only in the cheap papers: it even found a place in serious columns on Sunday. Many writers now reviewed the book, and some who likely enough would have praised it if Antony Standen hadn't done so now set about assaulting it; but this only swelled the general talk.

Most of the gossip writers, liking their story to be really remarkable, overrated the triumph; and this, such is the power of publicity, only drew the truth nearer to their fantastic estimates. They allowed their imaginations an area of free play and declared, dramatically, that the telephone had hardly stopped ringing at 55a Red Lion Street, so many were the inquiries from agents, reporters, foreign publishers, and celebrity-hunting hostesses. There was no telephone at 55a Red Lion Street. The only seed of truth in this happy statement was a certain number of calls on Mr. Fells's switchboard, which he shared with other tenants in Gooch Street.

Perce, of course, with the enthusiastic help of Mary, my frippet, had fed the pressmen with stories just as long as their appetite lasted, which was just as long as this news was warm. He told them about inquiries for American rights, film rights, and translation rights, and although these were still only inquiries the warmhearted pressmen wrote of them as "offers" so that they could assess their local boy's profits as ten, twenty, and even thirty thousand pounds. One of them, a human type, and possibly a father himself, recorded as a human touch: "This young clerk hasn't dared as yet to leave his humble desk in Fleet Street lest the whole affair should prove a flash in the pan, but his publisher assures us that a career of successful and money-spinning authorship lies before him."

Mr. Fells was getting, and enjoying, his publicity too.

Not one but many of these paragraphs did Godfrey see. All too many. He met them—or, rather, they encountered him each time with a blow upon the heart—as he lifted the daily papers in the smoking room at Boodle's or turned the pages of his evening paper in the bus going home. Each was a blow of dismay. In his better moments he could wish it were not dismay, but dismay it was. Kerry, who was so much smaller than he; whom he'd thought so inferior to himself in ability; whom he'd avoided because of his poverty and working-class home; Kerry, who'd taken (to speak truth) that gratifying fall with his first book—Kerry had now passed him at a bound and might leave him far behind. Was Kerry going to be wealthier than he?

In his office one evening, having just seen Perce's four-inch, double-column advertisement in the office copy of *The Times*, he left his desk, went to the window, and looked at the green walks of his Gray's Inn Gardens. They were empty, and very silent and shadowed, under the tall bared trees. Yes, empty: it was not in Godfrey to see the old ghosts crossing the stretched shadows in their gay Tudor or Stuart costumes. Indeed, he hardly saw the grass, so green after winter rains, or the long skeleton shadows thrown the whole breadth of the lawns. He was seeing Kerry in that garret which, to his dismay, was now "news."

How was he to act now? He couldn't pretend that he'd read nothing about the book in the papers: Kerry would know this for a lie and interpret it as jealousy. *He* jealous of Kerry! Oh no; not that. Better to appear generous. Better to seem magnanimously pleased and full of congratulation. Besides—a new idea came and stood with him by the window—if Kerry was going to be a man of position in the world, he could be of use to his brother. This sudden thought that there might be something for him in this hitherto disturbing news proved a small compensation. And another thought joined it: he'd quite like to see that garret.

These new ideas were potent enough to decide him, not to write, but to walk round with his congratulations that very evening to Kerry's home. A graceful way, surely, to show his lack of all jealousy. This Red Lion Street was only half a mile from Gray's Inn, and the early March evening was invitingly cold and fresh, under the sun. But—Pearl? Strange how he'd forgotten her, how one's mind hid from sight what one preferred to forget. But this new idea of visiting Red Lion Street was now so much in power that he could not abandon it, and he told himself that if he was to be friends with Kerry, he must sooner or later make friends with Pearl.

So at five o'clock he shut his books and, taking his bowler hat and rolled umbrella, left his silent gardens and walked eastward along the Clerkenwell Road. It was almost like turning out of the still and voiceless past into the clamor and hubbub of today. He passed Back Hill and Saffron Hill, those narrow alleys that dipped down into Ray Street, and he wondered how anyone could live in such dingy parts. The whole neighborhood smelt strongest of sweet tobacco because of the great factory across the road. He went down into the old Fleet Valley, crossed with distaste the deep, steam-clouding, smoke-smelling tank of the railway, and walked the gentle incline to the corner of Red Lion Street. What a street! How different from his own Rutland Gate. Children playing around the listing bollards; shop awnings, and only an odd dwelling house here and there; trucks standing at workroom doors; litter in the gutters and horse dung on the camber.

No. 55a. So this was Kerry's home, and Pearl's. A working woman, plump and pleasant-faced, opened to him. No, Mr.

Betterkin was not home from work yet. Was he a reporter?

Godfrey didn't much like being taken for a reporter. He instantly became conscious of his hat and his perfect umbrella. "No. I'm his brother."

"His brother! Go on!" He saw her eyes sweep over his clothes and up to his face again. Not an approving look; and he wondered guiltily if Kerry or Pearl had said ugly things of their brother to her. Pearl was an invincible talker and would say nothing good. . . . "There's no one up there at the moment, I'm afraid."

A heavy-jowled unshaven face and the open front of a collar-less shirt appeared above the basement stairs. And there stopped. So might a triton show only his head and breast above the waters, all below his waist being a dolphin's tail. It was some comfort to Godfrey in his still-unconquered jealousy to see what a rough class of man was Kerry's landlord. The eyes in the face peeped at him around the woman's back, and the jowl spoke. "Nah, there's no one there. Miss Pearl's aht."

Astonishing the relief: one could postpone the task of mak-ing peace with Pearl.

"Would you care to leave a message?" asked the woman. "Or would you like to step in and go up? He's usually back about six. But of course now, with this here book—"

"Yep, he's usually back about six," interrupted the jowl, and its owner thereupon brought up the rest of his body into the passage, for a further discussion of Mr. Betterkin's undoubted absence and likely return.

"Yes, I'll go up, if I may. Top floor, isn't it?"

"Thet's right." The man was now at the woman's side. "Like me to come up with you, mate?" Godfrey wasn't pleased to be called "mate" by shirt sleeves and braces. Nevertheless, he grinned and said, "Oh, no, don't trouble. I can find my way."

"Yeah. No difficulty. Jest go on and on. Up and up. Never sideways."

"I see."

"Then you'll get there. Top door of all. Can't go any farther, or you'd go through the roof."

Godfrey had no wit to give in exchange for this humor. He just grinned uncomfortably. "Well, thank you, I'll go up and wait."

"You'll find a nice chair there," the woman promised him.

So Godfrey went up the stairs, and his guilt made him a little ashamed of, or perturbed by, the loud sound of his feet on the uncarpeted treads. When he was within three steps of the third landing a door opened and another face, peering around, considered him. No rough workman's face, this; on the contrary, an aristocratic, fine-boned face beneath volutes of white hair. It stared at him, and in due course asked, "Were you seeking someone, sir?"

Godfrey, unprepared for another confrontation with a face, stuttered, "Yes . . . Mr. Betterkin. . . ."

"About the book?"

"Well, yes. He's my brother."

"Oh, but I'm only too pleased to bother." Apparently the man was deaf. "If it's about the book, come in and talk. I tell him he can't have too much publicity. I know. I've had it myself. Never can have too much. Anything you like to ask *me* about him, I'll willingly tell you. For his sake. I've had my days, but he has all his to come, bless him."

Kerry raised his voice. "I'm his brother."

"You Kerry's brother? You Godfrey? Good God! Evie, my love, this is Kerry's brother. This is Godfrey. But, my dear boy, he's not there. Neither of them are there. Come in and wait here where there's a bit of fire. He'll be back soon. This way. Yes, he's talked often about you." And said what? "So has our dear Pearl. Evie, meet Kerry's brother."

"How do you do?" asked a large woman in a chair from which she did not rise. One would have imagined that a big blond woman like this would have had a warm heart in that capacious breast, but no: that stove was cold. She's heard no good of me, he thought, and she's less forgiving—or less forgetful—than her old man. Desiring, no whit less then Kerry, to be approved of by all, he strove to ingratiate himself with them by saying, "I came to congratulate him."

"Yes, wonderful, isn't it? Sit down, dear boy." Her husband thrust forward a chair, rather as if he hoped it would occupy the enormous lacuna of his wife's silence. "We're so pleased, Evie and I. If anyone ever deserved a success, it's our Kerry. We love Kerry, don't we, my dear?"

"Yes. And Pearl too," said the woman significantly.

"Pearl too. Of course. Dear Pearl."

"He's always been so good to her," said the woman, looking at the window instead of at the visitor.

They know a great deal, thought Godfrey, and an unhappy "Yes . . ." was all he could offer in reply.

"If anyone ever gave up everything to support a sister, it's

he. He'd have starved himself for her." She might not be looking at him, but he felt her feminine eyes scan his clothes and
guess their cost. "I'm sure it's been a lesson to us all to watch
him with her. One doesn't see enough of that sort of thing
these days."

"No," Godfrey agreed; and he dared not add, "I offered to
help once," because this would reveal that he perceived her
innuendos and had a sense of guilt.

"Yes, and she's never been really well," said the husband
from a chair by the table, on which he was now seated with a
forearm at graceful rest on the table.

"She was in hospital for months," said the woman, "and he
was so good to her there, visiting her often and taking her
flowers." (*You* never went near her.)

"But listen, all of you," interrupted the man. "Listen, my
dear boy." He looked at Godfrey for a brief spell; then, like his
wife, turned his eyes away. His fingers beat upon the table.
"One day all that he's done for Pearl is going to be repaid to
him a hundredfold. He has cast his bread upon the waters and
he'll find it after many days. Yes, yes, I see what's going to
happen."

"What do you mean?" asked Godfrey nervously.

"I'll tell you. My dear wife and I are old actors, as you may
have guessed from these few photographs about the room. We
are quite forgotten now, but if I may say so, we had our day.
George Windsor was my name—"

Godfrey could pretend to no recognition of the name; and
the old man, disappointed, went on, "But there! You wouldn't
know it. Naturally, like all artists we would have liked a lasting
fame, but that's not an award given to actors—or only to those
whose names become legends: Roscius, Garrick, Irving, Sid-
dons. All the old actors of the past knew with sorrow that
unless a Charles Lamb came along and wrote about them, their
names must die. 'In vain they schemed, in vain they bled, They
had no poet and are dead.' "

"What's this got to do with anything?" demanded the
woman, in no good temper.

"You'll see, my love. I'm not being as foolish as you think.
Patience. Patience. It is not like this with an author. His art can
be enjoyed after he's dead. And *if*—*if* our Kerry can write but
one book that becomes a classic—or even that endures for a
long time—then someone will write his life story. This present
book may not be the classic, though I do think it is excellent

. . . excellent . . . it's making him thousands—"

"You really think so?" Godfrey intervened.

"Oh, yes . . . yes . . . thousands . . . thousands. . . ." The old actor sustained this affirmation with an expansive flourish of a ringed hand, and Godfrey, seeing the fine gesture, took comfort in the thought that all this talk was probably but the eloquent rant of an actor. "And it's only his second book. Sooner or later he'll write the one that'll endure. And now"—he lifted an instructor's finger—"now"—he addressed the finger to his wife after pointing it toward Godfrey—"now comes my point—"

"Well, I'm glad of that," said his wife sulkily.

"My point. Of all the books that endure after their authors' deaths, the ones that have the greatest chance of traveling down the ages to posterity are the ones that have a legend around them. Consider the dear Brontës. Good books, no doubt, but those girls had an advantage over all their competitors because of the fascinating legend around them: the lonely parsonage on a Yorkshire moor; the tombs besieging the garden wall; the drunken brother. Yes, think of brother Branwell. How that poor tipsy boy has repaid his sisters a thousand times by the fame his drunkenness brought them. Poor Branwell gave them their legend . . . and died."

Godfrey began to see, with a sick dropping of the heart, what this old devil was after. Disposed at first to be friendly, he had been reminded by his wife's coldness that Godfrey had left Kerry and Pearl to fight their battle alone. And now, with the grace of an actor, and the mischief of an old devil, he was wielding the whip.

"Or consider Chatterton. Who would read his poems if there were not that legend of the 'Marvellous Boy' who wrote and starved and at last killed himself, while still only seventeen, in an attic just over against your Gray's Inn? I think Kerry said that Gray's Inn was where you work, Mr. Betterkin?"

"Yes . . . it is. . . ."

"Well, we know there's a plaque on the site of the house where Chatterton died. Perhaps, dear friend, there'll be a plaque on this house one day. Because when they write Kerry's life story—as they will, I'm sure, I'm sure—they'll dig up all his past and, don't you see, sir?—don't you see, Evie?—a wonderful legend will be built up about his slaving in a Clerkenwell garret to support an ailing sister. We shall all be in the story, Evie and I and that nice Fells boy. It will be pleasant, my dear, to have our little place on the outskirts of his legend, as his friends in the days of adversity." He played again with his fingers on the table, sadly. "Posthumous fame as an artist will never be mine now, but perhaps I shall have it, after all, as a friend."

Could it be that the old devil was speaking the truth or might one hope that this was only the easy flamboyance of an actor? If the truth—good God! All my neglect of Pearl will be uncovered and published to the world. Am I to go down to history as the bad brother? Is this what my self-centered pursuit of my own career has won for me? Oh, no: the old fool is exaggerating. Kerry will write nothing that could justify researches into his past. But . . . one can never be certain. Must I live the rest of my life with the fear that my selfishness may be written about in books? Oh, Lord and heaven . . . if this old devil has really wanted to castigate me, he has plied his whip well.

"I shall not live to see it," the old tormentor was saying, "but I have a strong suspicion that that's what'll happen. I do firmly believe that great fame is coming to your good brother, my dear sir. I am so happy to tell you this."

"Yes, and Georgy—my husband—knows what he is talking about," said the wife, who was probably now *au fait* with what her horrible old husband was up to. "He's read books all his life."

"Well, I don't pretend to be among the greatest critics, but I think I know good work when I see it, work that has a very fair chance in the posterity stakes. I think—nay, I *know*—you will have reason to be proud of Kerry. Ah, but here the great man comes. Those are his steps upon the stair. None but Kerry and your sister, Pearl, pass our door." Having whipped his guest, he rose to escort him courteously from the punishment chamber. "We mustn't keep you from him, dear friend."

Godfrey went out, dazed by a sense of overthrow.

Not without courage he greeted his brother on the stairs, "I've read all about the great book, Kerry, and I thought the only thing to do was to come round and congratulate you in person."

Kerry was so happy these days that he was ready to be reconciled to anyone. "Thank you, old man," he said with a special heartiness, as if there were no quarrel anywhere that needed mending. Guessing at Godfrey's dismay in these past days, for he was not without fraternal jealousy himself, he perceived this effort at decency now, and took his hand and wrung it. "It's fun, isn't it?"

"It's absolutely splendid," Godfrey declared, continuing in good works.

"Yes . . . not too bad. . . ."

"Gosh, Dad and Mum would have been proud."

A fine effort, thought Kerry, and he felt anew for this brother, not love perhaps, but much of the kinship which had been theirs when they were children and played in the streets together.

"I think they could have been a little proud of both of us, Godfrey."

"Think so? I don't know. . . . The old gentleman in there says you are making thousands."

"What? Old George? Oh, you mustn't take him too seriously. He's an actor, and they speak only in superlatives."

"He thinks the book might become a classic."

"Oh, come! That's just absurd," Kerry protested. "That's utter rubbish"; and Godfrey was glad.

Gladness set more magnanimity free. "It's had some fine reviews. I've read them."

"And some dirty ones too. But come up; it's cold on the landing. Come and see how the poor live."

"Pearl is not in, is she?"

Kerry perceived the anxiety behind this question and hastened to allay it. "No, and she won't be back for some time. But I'll tell her you came to congratulate us. She'll be pleased."

They mounted together to Kerry's back room, and Kerry produced gin and vermouths, sweet and dry, not displeased to exhibit before Godfrey these habits of the prosperous. He drank to Godfrey; Godfrey drank to the book; and Kerry, in thanking him, announced, "You can also, if you like, congratulate me on being engaged."

"Why, that's wonderful!" said Godfrey; and could say it without effort, since it did not imply a biography hereafter.

"Yes . . . not too bad. . . ."

"But to whom is it?"

"To one Sally Penelope."

"Tell me all about her. What's she like?"

"I'm quite pleased with her."

"Is she beautiful?"

"Nothing to write home about."

"And is she . . . has she any—"

"Not a bean. She's just a humble little soul—like me. Just a typist. But religious. Very religious. Wants to be a saint."

"Oh, lord," said Godfrey, somewhat deploring; for this was a vision that had so far absented itself from him.

"Yes, but it may be useful. She may need some sanctity when she's married to me. You must see her. I'll parade her for you and your wife one day."

"We shall be most happy to judge."

So they sat and talked as friends, and sometimes laughed: Kerry at his table, Godfrey in the chair so often occupied by George. Both were enjoying that rather gaseous pleasure that sparkles in any wine of reconciliation. They passed the loving cup from each to other. Godfrey could really enjoy his quaffing of it, now that he knew the book would not be a classic.

Though what of future books . . . what of them? Would he ever be really happy again?

They were engaged in mutual information when abruptly Kerry stopped listening and turned an ear toward the door. Downstairs a familiar voice—a loud voice; a merry one; coming nearer. "Don't you disturb yourself, my dear. Back to your kitchen and your old man. Good blazes, I know my way up by this time. What d'you say? Someone with him? Can't help that."

"Lord preserve us," said Kerry. "It's the Comer-round."

"The who?"

"My publisher." A pleasing phrase to brandish before a brother, even after forgiving him. "He's liable to come round at any hour of the day. No, don't worry; don't move. It's only that he's been seized by a new idea. He reminds me of the Pool of Bethesda. Every now and then an idea descends upon him like an angel and troubles the water. Don't be surprised at anything."

A new idea—no word could have found the target more certainly. Mr. Fells exploded through the door. "Kerry, I've an idea. It came upon me at 2:15 P.M., but I didn't come round till I guessed you'd be home. Oh, I'm sorry. I beg your pardon." He had seen Godfrey in his chair.

"This is my brother. Godfrey."

"How do you do, sir? I didn't know you had a brother. Pearl, yes. But no mention of brothers. I should think you're proud of Kerry, aren't you, sir?"

"Of course. Naturally," said Godfrey. "It's splendid."

"Splendid? It's more than that, sir. I don't know about Kerry, but as for me: it's such a fulfillment of all that I ever hoped and wanted, my dear sir, that it almost ceases to make sense. Can you understand that?"

"I think I can. Yes. And I'm pleased for you too."

Quickly, to protect him from further strains on his generosity, Kerry asked, "What's the new idea, Perce?"

"You've got to marry Sally Penelope at once." He gave this answer, standing before Kerry with his plume of hair adrift over a temple.

"Delighted to, but why?"

"Because I'm giving a cocktail party."

"Oh, I see."

"Yes, but it's not just a case of 'Oh, I see'—"

"Not at all; it's an excellent reason for marrying."

"It certainly is. This is going to be a reception to celebrate the success of your book, and you'll be the guest of honor. I'm inviting all the boys who write the paragraphs, and all the girls too, and most of the buyers. See? It'll cost me a packet, but it'll probably pay for itself five times over." In his excitement he began to tramp the room, to port and starboard, like an anxious captain on the bridge of a record-seeking ship. "The boys'll do their stuff. First, because they all love me—Christ, I've stood 'em drinks enough—and second, because you're a Fleet Street boy. But that isn't all. That, my dear boy, isn't all."

"Well, what else?"

"Just this. The party'll be not only a discreet celebration in honor of an author who's hit the headlines but a gathering of the clans to celebrate a betrothal—if you see what I mean. I'll spring this surprise on them about halfway through. It'll be a story for them, if ever there was one. Human. A success story's good, but not so good as a *ro*-mance. It's certain copy. Sally'll be there, and so will the photographers. She won't mind being offered up on a plate if it's to help me—I mean *you*. She'll be invaluable in helping us both to make money; and if I'm a pimp, I'm a pimp. Leave the telling of the story to me. I'll do it." And indeed he proceeded to tell it with all the art of gesture that Mr. George Windsor, down below, would have given to it. "Loved each other for years; no money to marry; just quiet devotion; she typing all your books for you, evening after evening, night after night. In an attic. And now you're going to marry and live in luxury—no?—well, don't interrupt—in comfort. My dear chap, it's a perfect story. Isn't it, sir?" He had turned to Godfrey.

"It sounds like it. Sounds like a fairy tale."

"Precisely. Human. They'll leap on it and it'll put another ten thousand on our sales. Good horrors!"—tramping back and forth, he had come opposite the mantel mirror—"I begin to look my age." A pause for study. "God, I'm a ruin."

"Where's this great party to be?" asked Godfrey, so as to show a brother's happy interest.

"I've thought that one out." Mr. Fells came away from the mirror. "Not the Connaught Rooms or the Holborn, Kerry, or any places like that. Their rooms are too big. We've got to be crowded. You don't get the full sense of success unless you've no room to move. The more you're barged about, back, front, and sides, the bigger your feeling that something important is afoot. The King of Moravia, in Long Acre, has a fine reception room upstairs with a lot of gold about, and the boys'll be happier in a pub. Feel at home. The Tivoli Room, it's called; and look: I can do a deal with Ted Wallis, the landlord. These damned caterers ruin you. Ted'll play fair, and just charge me for the cost of the drinks and the snacks. Damn it, it'll be publicity for him. Besides, I'll tip him the wink, and he'll make the drinks weaker and weaker as the evening goes on. After the first hour, nobody knows or cares what he's drinking. Now, who do you want to be there? For my part, I only want the parents, and Emily, my wife, and Ruth Pettie, my girl friend. You'll come too, won't you, sir?"

"More than pleased to," said Godfrey.

"Who for you, Kerry?"

"The Windsors. The old Windsors, please."

"Of course. As long as George doesn't want to entertain the crowd with a few speeches from Hamlet."

"And Nance Hitchin. She's always been a mother to me."

"But that'll mean her frightful old man. Still, if *you* don't mind—"

"No, let him come. He's behaved properly for nine whole months together. And Nance'll dress him up in his best."

"Okay. I don't mind. Let 'em all come. But, heck, there's one person we've forgotten—one person more important than anyone else. *Yes,* sir!"

"Who's that?" asked Godfrey, still striving to play a brother's happy and interested part.

Mr. Fells turned to him and explained. "Mary, my frippet."

Godfrey stared, defeated; and Kerry translated.

30

"Ladies and gentlemen, *if* you please!"

Mr. Fells stood on the square dais in the Tivoli Room and hammered with his gavel on the table. He had provided himself with this gavel because, as he said, he knew what crowded cocktail parties could engender in the way of vocal din and, anyhow, a gavel was a joyous instrument in the hands of an artist. Behind him a grand piano, more usually played upon this dais, had been pushed toward the walls and now served as a display counter for three pyramids of *This Old and Antique Song*. Two other pyramids stood on the table, and one of them collapsed like a house of cards as a result of his artistry with the gavel.

Behind table and piano, against the blue wall, a tall setpiece of ferns and spring flowers reached almost to the gilded cornice. More daffodils, narcissus, and ferns, flanked by palms, stood along the brink of the dais, so that Perce seemed to stand knee-deep and happy in the spring, while palms bowed toward him. His enthusiasm for this celebration had risen in excited company with the sales of the book, even perhaps soaring a little ahead of them, and he had resolved upon this expensive floral decoration, not without some anxiety, but allaying it with the hope that the magnificent and happy display would so impress the company that the hearts of the booksellers, dancing with the daffodils, would blossom themselves into handsome repeat orders, and the hearts of the pressmen, no less fertilized, flower into blooms of picturesque writing.

His work with the gavel was necessary, since the lively uproar of a hundred voices in the room was hardly less in volume, if less shrill, than the uproar of a school during recess in the playground.

"Ladies and gentlemen, *if* you please!"

The talkers nearest to his clamor with the gavel stopped and turned toward him. Not so those farther afield. So he hammered again longer and louder, and a well-ginned bookseller of ample belly turned toward the company and bellowed, "*Shut up!*" This silenced a few more groups but had no effect on those around the buffet at the far end of the room; so this helpful, or bossy, bookseller amended his public cry to "Shurr'up, I tell you!" which advanced the frontier of silence a few yards farther. The expanding area of silence enabled Perce's next impassioned hammering to break through the last sound barrier, so that all the laggards around the buffet turned their faces toward their host and their backs to the white-coated waiter, perhaps unwillingly. All in the room held their cocktail glasses breast-high, and some of their eyes seemed as washed with liquor, and as bright, as the glasses above which they gazed.

In front of the now silent—or fairly silent—audience stood Kerry and Sally Penelope. Sally was in a new royal-blue cocktail dress that Kerry had chosen and bought her for the occasion. Her large sapphire-blue eyes were as bright as anyone else's and her narrow face was flushed, but this brightness and full color were as much the gift of unaccustomed excitement as of unaccustomed gins. But more wonderful wear than the blue frock was the sapphire and diamond engagement ring on her finger: she was feeling it and fiddling with it every few minutes, and would go on doing so for many days yet.

Beyond her, Pearl and Godfrey and Godfrey's wife stood side by side, and this was a small miracle; this was a conversion; it represented a triumph for Kerry. "If Godfrey's going to be there," Pearl had said, "I'm staying away." "Oh no you're not, woman," was Kerry's reply. "Sally, teach her some of your

Christianity." "Well, if I come and he's there," said Pearl, "I'm not speaking to him." "Oh yes you are," Kerry persisted. "I'm not the perfect Christian that Sally is, but one day I shall manage to teach you what I've learned a hundred times over, that all hate and vindictiveness are sources of pain, and that forgiveness is happiness." Perhaps it was this last argument more than anything else that had converted Pearl; for she was tired of pain.

The old Windsors sat against the wall and George had talked often and pleasantly to the Godfrey Betterkins because he had decided that he had a heart and that this organ urged him to demonstrate some kindliness to Godfrey after Evie had been so shockingly cold to him, and he himself a trifle sharp with his whip.

Only one person in the room had no glass in her hand, and this was Mary, the rest of the firm of Arthur Fells. Appropriately she stood at the feet of her managing director, under the platform. In her hands were some typed foolscap sheets, and her attention to them at this important minute seemed studious to the point of strain.

Mr. and Mrs. Hitchin were at the back. Certainly Nance had dressed Alfred in his best, and herself too, but Mr. Hitchin preferred to stay at the back because, though he would never have admitted to any shyness in a crowd of gentry, he was, in fact, subject to this weakness, and he preferred to limit his communications to the buffet and to one of its white-coated servers. With this tall lad he had established a chatty friendship, to excellent purpose. "Same again, mate," had left his lips many times, even before they were wiped on the back of his hand. And it must be allowed that Mrs. Hitchin had not refused any of the refills that this new friendship had won for her.

"Ladies and gentlemen . . ."

"Hear, hear," encouraged the ample bookseller, and since a few of the weaker ones had now backslid into chatter, he shouted it louder. *Hear*, HEAR!" and "Shut *UP!*"

This produced the final silence; an ultimate silence, as if the world, in a moment of shock, had ceased to roll and all its wheels were stilled.

Amid the multitude of voices before this abrupt silence George Windsor's had been one, at a moment when he and

Evie were sitting by the wall and Kerry had tried to weave his way past their knees. George had put out a hand to stay him, and Kerry had stayed.

"We are so happy for you, my Evie and I," he said. "I've been sitting here thinking that you, at least, have created your dream. There are not many who do that."

"Created *some* of it," Kerry corrected. "You wouldn't believe what I've sometimes imagined myself doing."

"Oh, I can, I can." He mused, remembering times when he'd imagined very great things. "There were times when Evie and I thought we'd created the whole of our dreams, but"—he shrugged—"it faded slowly away."

"That may come to me."

"No, dear boy, it need never. Because *you* can always hope. Your books go on, and you can always hope that some day, even after death, someone may find the best of them and acclaim it to the world. It's only old pros like us who know they can hope no more."

"Oh, Georgy, do be cheerful on his great day," Evie protested.

"I am being cheerful. I am telling him he can hope everything for ever."

"Oh, I don't know," Kerry demurred; but the demur was insincere. He knew that to the end of his life he would go on doing just this: hoping all things for ever.

Turning to move away, he bumped into the violent sortie of a large-breasted and well-decorated woman who had come to him with a supercharge of gush. "Oh, Mr. Betterkin. I am Elinor Wilde"—a name that meant nothing to him, though he smiled as if delighted to recognize it, and said, "Oh, yes?" "Yes," she agreed, "and I do want to congratulate you. And what a title! What a quite lovely title!"

"You think so?"

"Oh, yes, yes. It was an absolute inspiration; it was really. *This Old and Antique Cup.*"

"*Song,*" he corrected.

"I beg your pardon?"

"Song. Not *Cup.*"

"Not *Cup?*"

He shook his head.

"Oh, well, it was a quite lovely title anyway. It was the title that sold the book."

He wanted to suggest that perhaps the story that followed the title had played some part in the success, but there was no chance to speak till she had turned off her standpipe gush; and just then Mr. Fells, shouldering a path through the multitude, saw Kerry and, hardly stopping, said, "Gee, I forgot to tell you: your old Sir Osbert Inman called me today and asked whether my advertisements in the Sundays were all lies. I said, 'Certainly not, sir,' and he said, 'Bloody hell.' Just like that. I said, 'I can quite understand your feelings, sir,' and he said, 'Well, anyhow, young man, I can see about getting out a new edition of *Clerkenwell* at once.' "

"Oh!" This was a gasp of joy from Kerry.

"I offered to take the book over from him, and he said 'Not on your life, young man. That book's ours.' A genial old bastard."

"Gosh, am I pleased!" said Kerry. The Knights to live after all! Sir Nicholas and his Knights of St. John. The book to which he'd given such labor and love to rise again and walk the world. His joy was not unlike that of the prodigal's father whose son had been dead and was now alive again. For the rest of the evening he felt for and dwelt upon this happy memory much as Sally Penelope was feeling for and fingering her ring.

"Yes. Fine," said Perce. "But I can't stop. Got to make a filthy speech and I'm as nervous as ten cats. I'm all of a dither inside. The strangest things are going on inside me."

"Then," said George, "you'll do well. Every sensitive artiste suffers these nerves before getting his entrance cue and going on the stage. Irving—Forbes-Robertson—they've all assured me that they invariably had the needle and the butterflies before going on. And dear Ellen Terry too. In fact, the greater the artiste, the more miserable the torments. God forbid that I should tell you of the upheavals and gusts and eddies that went on in my stomach when I stood in the wings, waiting my entry. Sometimes they were audible above the dialogue—or so it seemed to me in my grievous state. But I never failed. Nor will you, my boy. All nerves stop with the first words spoken."

"Well, thank you, sir, and I wish I could believe you. But anyhow, if the worst comes to the worst, I've got Mary there with it all written down. She'll see me through." He gave them the sketch of a farewell wave and continued threading his way to the platform.

"Ladies and gentlemen." One last touch of the gavel on the table. A gratuitous touch since now there was not a sound in the room. "Thank you. As you are aware—"

Kerry in an onset of shyness fled to a window. Knowing that he was about to be publicly praised, he was in that state which both longs to hear the praise and dreads the embarrassment of it. With his shoulder toward the platform, he turned an edge of the blind and looked down at Long Acre. The broad thoroughfare was dark beneath its lamp and wet after a shower. The only vehicles on its glistening pavement were the cars and buses returning from the opera doors and the intermittent trucks coming from beyond the City. On its greased sidewalks there were but few pedestrians to wonder what was astir behind the blinds of this brightly lit room. It could be that they heard for a moment a loud voice speaking praise as they came by, but they passed on, symbols of the hurrying world that heeded little or soon forgot.

"As you are aware, the purpose of this gathering is to enable you to meet Mr. John Kenrick Betterkin. It is not designed to secure publicity."

"Oh, no," derided the wags, loudly.

"Certainly not." Mr. Fells agreed with them. "I am not a man much interested in publicity—"

"No, nor in sales either."

"In sales I will admit to some interest, but they are no part of my purpose tonight. I simply feel that you will want to drink to the prosperity of our guest and to congratulate him on having already sold twenty thousand of his delightful book, and being now in the process of selling it at the rate of a thousand a week—"

Applause; and a voice near Kerry: "Divide that by four."

"Accordingly I feel that, however little it may be to my liking, I must say a few words about him."

Murmurs of encouragement; and there followed one of the most remarkable speeches Kerry was ever to hear. Remarkable, not for its relevance, which was seldom in sight, nor for any information it vouchsafed, but for the ingenuity with which it contrived to connect into an orderly and seemingly proper sequence a series of anecdotes and gags, not one of which had any natural connection with its predecessor. One could have likened the speech to a daisy chain if every flower in the garland had not been different, and all of them had not belonged to different seasons of the year. Anything so skillful must have been carefully prepared and then conned by heart, so it was easy to see why it had been necessary to have Mary beneath the speaker's feet with the script of this vaudeville act in her hand. Any break in the chain, and she was there to murmur the cue for the next joke. Since Perce was waving the gavel about as he spoke, she somewhat resembled an auctioneer's clerk with the catalogue of antiques before him.

But not once did the speaker lean on this staff. He delivered the speech with ease, and not only because, as George foretold, all nerves had stopped directly he started, but also because, like his guests, he had drunk well, and the strings of his tongue were loosed.

"I'm not saying I disdain publicity. When I see before me a whole heap of pressmen like this I feel about them as the old rustic felt about parsons. He said they were like muck because, while they were little use in a heap, they did a power of good when spread about."

Much laughter, since the pressmen were delighted to be called muck.

"Therefore, gentlemen, nothing that I shall now say need be considered as copyright; it is free copy for anyone who cares to use it. You will all know of the success of Mr. Betterkin's book, so you may be surprised to hear that no less than twelve publishers turned it down as unsalable. I do not envy them their feelings now. They make me think of what the Scots minister said about Dives when he was suffering suitable torments for having spurned Lazarus from his door. 'The dearr Lorrd,' said the minister, 'declined to let Lazarus go doon and comfort Dives. He said, "Nay, Dives, he shall no come doon, because ye have sinned, Dives." And Dives agreed, saying, "Aye, Lorrd, but I didna ken." And the dearr Lord, looking doon in his infinite compassion and mercy, answered, "Weel, Dives, ye ken noo." ' "

A splendid roar of laughter, since many of the company were Scots.

"And so that all these misguided publishers may ken noo, I hope you'll publish abroad that I expect a sale of fifty thousand. Also, if you like, that the book's author and its publisher are receiving a big fan mail: letters from England, letters from Wales, letters from Ireland, and postcards from Scotland."

Scots in joyous acclamation again.

[283]

"Another thing that pleases me as the book's publisher is that none of its success is due to obscenity. I'm not a man who cares for obscenity."

"*Oh*, no!"

"And from cover to cover there is nothing even suggestive in Mr. Betterkin's charming book. But, d'you know, in these days of library censorship, that is not enough: one has to be careful even about the title. Censors who have neither the time nor the inclination to read a book submitted to them can be misled by a title. I could tell you of a book of children's prayers that was instantly banned on sight of its title." Effective pause. "The title was, *Before We Sleep and When We Wake.*"

The loudest of the ha-has that greeted this came from Alfred Hitchin: it was the first joke he'd really heard and seen. And Perce, well pleased, went on. His next joke missed fire, but any sag in the audience's appreciation was stopped by the gale of laughter that greeted the one after it. "I will weary you with but one more instance. Recently an admirable study of soil erosion was banned because of its title, *Rape around our Coasts.*"

Came an enormous ha-ha from Mr. Hitchin, who was now giving as much delighted attention to the speaker as to his white-coated and well-provided friend behind the buffet.

"Yes, one must be careful with titles for the sake not only of censors but of booksellers and librarians. I know of a man who asked a lady librarian if she'd got *The Plague,* and she replied, 'No, I'm always spotty like this.' "

So he ran on with his vaudeville patter, and so entertaining was it that no one wanted him to stop. All had forgotten what the speech was about. But he was artist enough to stop before he jaded their appetites.

"Ladies and gentlemen, by the purest accident I am able to close these informative remarks with the most pleasing and up-to-date news of all. You will be able to congratulate Mr. Betterkin not only on his book but on his immediate marriage—"

Sensation. Prolonged applause. Pencils drawn to write in notebooks.

"Now I'm sure you will not mind if I say a few words about the lady. She is here tonight."

Much applause for Sally.

"She is a Miss Sally Penelope Finch, God bless her." And he told the company their story, much as he had rehearsed it to Kerry in Red Lion Street; then extended a long arm down to

Sally beneath the dais and the flowers. "Come, Sally Penelope. Come and show yourself to the world."

"Oh, no!" pleaded Sally. Her fingers flew from the engagement ring, and she stepped back, colliding with the portly bookseller behind. "Oh, pardon," she said, to which he replied, "Not at all; I loved it." And his wife, apparently used to such infidelities, urged Sally, "Yes, you do what the gentleman asks, dearie."

"Oh, no, *please.*"

Mr. Fells's long arm found her hand. "Oh, yes, my pet. Everybody wants to see you and drink to your happiness. Mr. Wilberforce there, push her up and I'll pull."

"Oh no, Perce, please."

"Now, darling, don't be silly. They want to photograph you with Kerry. Look at 'em all coming up with their flashbulbs. Must have a photograph."

" 'Ear, 'ear," from Mr. Hitchin at the back. He was now drunk.

"Well, they can do it down here," Sally insisted.

"There's no room down there. Besides, we want all these books as a background." He dropped his voice to a deeply charged whisper. "Come on, ducky, for all our sakes."

So Sally clambered up between the daffodils, on to the dais with the proper parade of unwillingness. Applause followed her up, and Kerry, as if he were little more than driftwood washed up by the wave of applause, followed too. "Sally Penelope," Mr. Fells proudly announced; while Sally shot her face away from the public gaze.

The photographers thereupon leaped onto the platform from all corners as if it were a boxing ring and Sally and Kerry the two flyweights who were about to fight. And Mr. Fells their beaming referee. Not but what Mr. Fells stepped aside, declaring, though with no overwhelming sincerity, "You don't want me, I'm sure." When, however, some shots had been taken of Sally and Kerry and one of the photographers said, "Now, let's have one with you, sir," he assented speedily, "Oh well, if you really want it. All right: the happy man with fiancée and publisher. Pose me drinking his health. Like this—what? . . . That's fine. Thank you. Now a picture with one or two more in it. You, sir, Mr. Windsor. You'll lend distinction to any picture. Photogenic. And Pearl darling, you, of course. Mr. Betterkin's sister, gentlemen. And Mr. Godfrey? Yes, come along, sir. Famous lawyer."

In this group the two who posed most skillfully and gracefully were George Windsor and Mr. Fells. And Mr. Fells with his glass uplifted to the happy pair and his smile downthrown upon them, provided a performance at least as good as the veteran actor's.

With so many pictures to be taken, the audience lost their interest and fell to loud chattering again in dissociated groups. In other words Sally's moment in the public eye was over in a few flashes, and time and the multitudes had left her again and passed on. So quickly turns the single page, and some new fresh story waits.

But the reporters had not yet done with her. When the photographers had finished, the reporters, pencils poised over notebooks, surrounded her as if it was now her hour rather than Kerry's. "Oh, dear," she protested in the center of this siege, but with laughter; and they opened their bombardment. Where would the wedding be? At St. James's, Clerkenwell, she said, but only a quiet wedding.

"Yes, only quiet," said Mr. Fells from the sidelines. Standing there behind the reporters, taller than any, drooping over them, he might have been the producer, directing the scene. Or perhaps a proud father beaming upon a triumph of his children.

And where were they going for their honeymoon?

"Italy," said Sally. But that wasn't good enough for Mr. Fells. He gave it precision. "Rome and Naples," he said. "And they'll almost certainly go to Capri. All authors do."

"Yes, isn't it all wonderful?" said Sally, gaining ease and venturing for the first time an unsolicited comment.

"Put that down," said Mr. Fells.

They wrote it down, as he added, "That's good human stuff."

And where were they going to live when they came back?

They hadn't found a home yet, Sally said, but fortunately Mrs. Hitchin would soon be able to give them another room in her house, and they'd still keep Mr. Betterkin's rooms on the top floor.

" 'Ear, 'ear." An enthusiastic endorsement from Mr. Hitchin at the back, surprising, perhaps, in view of his past exchanges with Kerry, but just now he was filled with a joyous goodwill, real enough for the moment, but fragile as a bright evening haze, and destined for the dark.

"The old attics," Mr. Fells reminded the reporters. "Where Mr. Betterkin wrote the masterpiece."

"Yes, we've grown fond of them," said Sally.

" 'Ear, 'ear."

"Tell them about the cottage in the country," recommended Mr. Fells, who believed in keeping the copy picturesque.

Sally said they had seen a cottage in Buckinghamshire and were "ever so taken" with it. It had a lovely garden, and—

But Mr. Fells improved upon this. "It's their dream cottage," he said. And as he offered this interpretation he saw suddenly how to develop it further, to Kerry's profit and his own. "It's almost every Londoner's dream and aspiration, isn't it: a cottage in the country far beyond the sidewalks' ends. An old and antique song . . ." but this pretty shaft flew too high to impinge on any of the reporters, though some looked up to watch it pass. And Mr. Fells, ready to welcome success or failure with equal friendliness, continued to smile upon the hero and heroine of his little production.

Sally was explaining that their idea was to keep the top floor at Red Lion Street as a kind of little flat in London—" 'Ear, 'ear"—because Mr. Betterkin so loved London and Clerkenwell.

And would she continue at her old office work?

"No, only as my husband's secretary," she said proudly.

"Her husband's secretary," Mr. Fells repeated, lest they hadn't all got that. It was rather human.

And what did it feel like to have a husband who was suddenly famous?

"It's ever so wonderful. I never expected anything like this to happen."

"What did you say?" asked one, for she had looked away in her shyness.

"She never expected anything like this to happen," Mr. Fells repeated, almost at dictation speed.

"And you are very happy, I'm sure?"

"You bet!" said Sally, carried away at last and looking at them joyfully. "I'm the happiest person in the world. To think of everyone reading the book that *I* typed! Everyone everywhere! And it's dedicated to me! I can't help wondering if the king's read it . . . and seen my name."

"Don't put down 'You bet,' " Mr. Fells advised. "Nor that

about the king. Better not. Any case, I doubt if it's got round to him yet. Just 'I'm the happiest person in the world.' "

They put these words down and went from her with smiles. They were good words on which to close their books and go.